Falling Too Late

Dae Graves

FALLING TOO LATE

DAE GRAVES

Warning

For those of you who wish to read a trigger warning, please continue to the next page for a complete list. Those of you who want to go in blind, continue to the prologue.

Please keep in mind that this is a dark romance and contains dark subject matter. I do not condone any actions done by the characters of this book.

If while you are reading this book, the subject matter becomes too much, don't continue. Your mental health matters and you should do everything you need to, to keep your peace.

Trigger Warning

- Level 2 rape of a child. Level 2 means that it's insinuated through metaphors on page. This is in Chapter One.
- Rape of an adult Level 3, blatantly graphic on page. This is in Chapter Twenty-Five.
- Death of a family member
- Blood
- Murder
- All the abuse (mental, physical, emotional and sexual)
- Talk of suicide
- Drug abuse (overdose)
- Discussion of abortion
- Discussion of sterilization

CONTENTS

*To the voices in my head.
We fucking did it.*

*To my husband, for your unwavering support.
I couldn't have done this without you J.*

PROLOGUE
WREN

Even after everything they did to me, I never wanted to die.

I never wished for death. I only wanted the pain to stop.

But I knew they would never stop; she would never love me again.

I was no longer her daughter, and she wasn't my mother.

We were too far gone.

But even though I never wanted to die, even though it was never my idea, I tried anyway.

Unfortunately, drowning was not an option. I couldn't just allow myself to sink to the bottom.

I always knew how to swim.

CHAPTER 1
WREN, 11 YEARS OLD

"It's all your fault. It's all your fault!"

Mom flipped the coffee table and its glass top shattered everywhere. I was on the floor hiding between the side of the couch and the wall. I wasn't really hiding; she knew I was there. That's why she chose the living room to destroy.

She ripped photo frames off the wall and tossed them into the pile of broken glass. Then she pulled a picture out of the last remaining frame and ripped it into tiny pieces.

It was the last picture we had of dad. She'd destroyed the rest.

It's my fault he's dead.

"Get out here. Right. *Now.*" Mom's voice was quieter now.

Slowly, I crawled out of my spot and stood, keeping my head down. She didn't like it when I looked at her. She said I had Daddy's eyes, and I didn't deserve them because I'm the one who killed him. So I kept my eyes to the floor, willing myself to shrink into nothing.

"You are pathetic. You are worthless." She said the words slowly. Quietly. "Everything wrong in this world is your fault. You are the reason we live like this. You are the reason he's dead."

I heard the slap before I felt it. It was slow to hurt. I bit my lip, trying to get it to stop shaking. I balled my hands in my shirt to keep from touching my cheek, to soothe the pain.

"Mrs. Jacobson, open up!" Three loud bangs hit the front door, causing us both to jump.

"Shit."

She jerked me by my hand, pulling me to the door with her. Suddenly, she was mom again. Her voice was high-pitched. She opened the door.

"Hello, Mr. Lloyd," she said in a sickly sweet tone.

"Mrs. Jacobson, I'm getting complaints about you again."

Mr. Lloyd looked to be my dad's age, with greasy dark hair and a round belly. He had a newspaper rolled up in his hand, and he was using it to point at my mom. I could tell she didn't like it because her nails bit into the skin of my hand. He craned his neck to see around her inside the apartment.

"Lynn, your downstairs neighbor said they heard a loud crashing sound. What's going on in here?" He wiped a hand across his sweaty forehead.

"Oh yes, I'm so sorry. You see, my daughter was running around like a crazy kid." She dropped her voice into a harsh whisper. "She got into some sugar, and you know kids and sugar these days." She waved a hand absently. "Anyway, she tripped and fell onto our glass coffee table and broke the glass top. Lucky for her, it's that tempered glass, so she didn't get all cut up," she explained, as if that was the silver lining.

I covered my eyes with my free hand, trying to stop the tears. She always had some lie ready on the tip of her tongue.

"I'm so sorry about that. It scared me and I yelled. Once we are done cleaning up here, I will have her go down there and apologize to him."

Mr. Lloyd shook his head, looking at me. Mom bumped me with her hip to get me to look at him. "Apologize for the trouble you caused Mr. Lloyd."

"I–I'm s–so sorry." I couldn't stop crying now, taking the opportunity to bury my head in her dress and hug her legs. "I'm sorry, Momma."

For a moment, she was my mom again. She ran her hand over my back in soothing circles and hushed me.

Then there was a rough finger brushing down my cheek. "You know, they can put kids on medicine now to help with that behavioral shit. Maybe you should look at having her evaluated." His voice was closer in my ear. "Pretty little thing," he murmured. I buried my head farther in my mom's side.

"Oh, you are so right, Mr. Lloyd. I will have her checked out at her next doctor's appointment."

He pulled his hand away and called as he headed to the stairs, "Keep the noise down."

As soon as the door shut, she locked it and pushed me to the side. I fell onto my butt.

"Clean this mess up and then go make nice with the downstairs neighbors before you get us kicked out of here."

She left me there and slammed her bedroom door shut. I sat feeling sorry for myself for a second. I found the broom and pan, cleaned the mess up the best I could, only getting cut by a few glass shards. One in my hand and one in my foot. I vacuumed the glass shards that I couldn't see up and took the bag out and threw it away.

I didn't like our downstairs neighbor. He smelled like cigarettes and alcohol; it always burned my nose when they were outside smoking. Mom would go outside and smoke with him when she wasn't working.

I headed to the bathroom and was able to get the glass shards out with a pair of tweezers, only to realize I was going to be late for school. Quickly, I changed out of my pajamas, throwing on my cleanest shirt and looking for pants, when she walked in.

"What do you think you are doing?" my mom asked, standing in my bedroom door. I jumped, startled.

"I'm . . . uhm, getting ready for school?" I looked toward her over my shoulder, avoiding her eyes. Instead of looking directly at her, I found a divot on the wall to stare at. Looking directly at her made her mad.

"I told you to go downstairs and make nice with the neighbor. You know what? I'll just go get the neighbor. You sit right there." She pointed to the bed before she left.

Quickly, I grabbed the closest pair to me and pulled them on before taking my seat on the bed. My hands fidgeted in my lap as I waited for her to come back. I was so late now that I would probably get a detention slip. School was the calm part of my day, aside from sleep. My mom was like a hurricane. She would scream and yell day in and day out while I was home, and it would take everything to keep my head above water.

The door opened and closed again, and heavy footsteps grew louder. I kept my head down, eyes cast to the floor. Pointed brown boots came into my vision. They were old and had a tear in the side that showed a little bit of white sock poking through.

"So this is the noisemaker, huh?" His voice was gruff, like he needed to clear his throat.

"That's her. I asked you up here so she could apologize." I could see my mom's painted pink toes standing next to the boots.

"Well, she can't do much apologizing if she keeps looking down." the man spoke.

"Look up here, Wren," Mom said.

"Wren? That's an ugly name," the man said. My shoulders fell. My daddy always loved my name. He had called me his *birdy*.

"Oh yeah? You don't like her name?" Mom huffed. "Her father named her."

"And where is dear old dad?"

"Dead."

"What a shame." The boots walked closer to me. "No one to raise you right. No one to protect you." Something felt wrong about him. I wanted to scoot back under my covers and hide from him, but I knew better.

As they talked back and forth, I still didn't look up. A sinking feeling started in my stomach. A dirty hand appeared in my sight. He put one finger under my chin, forcing me to look up at him.

I did.

Staring down at me were ice-cold blue eyes in a withered face.

"Pretty little thing." His cigarette breath brushed my skin, making my nose crinkle.

That was the second time that day I'd heard those words, and I was beginning to think they weren't good things.

"How do you plan on apologizing to me?" He gripped my chin harder so I couldn't turn away. I craned my eyes to my mother as he held my face in place.

I pleaded to her with my eyes.

I saw no love for me in her. Only hate. She blamed me for Dad's death, and she was never going to look at me the same. "What do you want her to do to apologize?"

Want me to do? What, is she going to send me downstairs to clean up his house too?

He turned his head to look at mom, and something passed between them that I didn't understand. "If I let you do this, I get more than just you not complaining to Lloyd anymore." She crossed her arms over her chest, hip popping out.

"Sure, but this never ends."

"Deal." My mom turns to the dresser right next to her, opens it up and pulls out a pair of my socks.

"Hold her down."

One second, I am facing them, the next I'm flipped over onto my stomach across the corner of my bed.

"Mom sto—!"

She crammed the socks into my mouth. Then her hand was clasped over them. My pants and underwear were pulled down around my ankle, one leg freed. Panic choked me as I tried to breathe through the socks in my mouth. I pushed and tried to lift my head off the pink sheets, but I couldn't. Her hand was holding my head down.

I heard the sound of his belt jingling. The slow pull of a zipper. The shift of clothes moving.

Then white hot pain entered my body. I felt like I was being split in two, all the air leaving my lungs in a clogged gasp. A loud ringing started in my ears, but it wasn't loud enough to block out the grunts, the whimpers, the hot air on the back of my neck.

I was in so much pain I couldn't breathe, I couldn't scream.

I wanted to disappear. I wanted my daddy to come back.

But he's never coming back. He's dead. And it's all my fault.

I squeezed my eyes shut, but behind my lids, all I could see were ice-blue eyes. Opening my own eyes, I looked at the floor. I could see my mom's toes and his brown boot with the tear in the side standing on the dingy brown-stained carpet. Her pink, chipped polish. The white sock poked out the tear.

I focused on them until I felt his weight lifted off and my mom's hands let go of me. They said something, then once it felt like they had left the room and the door clicked shut, I curled into a ball on my pink bedsheets, my hand shaking as I reached up and pulled the sock out of my mouth. The contents of my stomach went with it. I gasped and heaved through the pain, spitting out the bile, and cried.

CHAPTER 2
WREN, 13 YEARS OLD

I wondered if dandelions could kill someone. In the world in my head, I picked lots of dandelions and sprinkled them in Mom's food. I put them in a little metal ball and steeped them like tea. They were poisonous, and the more she drank, the sicker she got.

I slowly walked home from school, picking the dandelions that grew in the cracks of the sidewalk and between the concrete and fences. Ahead, there was a break in the fence that let the canal run through. I watched the water rush under the road for a minute before plucking the heads off the flowers one by one and tossing them in.

I thought about death a lot. I wondered what dying would be like. Was there heaven and hell? Was Daddy at peace now that he was dead? Had all his pain stopped?

I didn't really want to die.

Well, sometimes I did. But when creepy Kevin, Mom and Lloyd weren't around, when I was alone, I didn't want to die.

CHAPTER 3
ALEX, 17 YEARS OLD

"ALEXANDER JA—!"

My mother's voice was cut off by my slamming the door in her face. I hiked my backpack up higher on my shoulder and headed down the stairs of the fourplex I'd lived in my entire life. I followed the sidewalk till I got to the back of the property and cut through the fence and over the train tracks to school. This was the fastest route to get there, even though my mom had yelled at me numerous times to not take the shortcut. She didn't want me walking through this part of the neighborhood. It wasn't uncommon to hear gunshots at night or see police lights over here or hear about the break-ins.

Poverty Flats, as we called it.

I didn't know what it was with her and controlling everything I did when she was never home in the first place. I was seventeen now and had been taking care of myself since Dad died.

To cover the bills, she started working doubles at a diner. The tips were better at night, so she preferred to work then. She left for work when I get off school and came home while I was eating breakfast.

As soon as she got home this morning, she started harping on me about my grades. She got my report card in the mail and wasn't impressed with the D average I had been maintaining all year.

I didn't care enough to try. I hated school. I hated the teachers who didn't care enough to help me when I had asked for it. All's they cared about were the students who were in sports or cheerleading. They didn't care about the rest of us.

The outcasts. We were a menace to them. You could see it in the way they looked down their noses at us. I didn't have the nicest clothes. I didn't always have a clean and fresh haircut. My hair stayed longer than the others, and without fail, some teacher had to make some comment about it.

It's time to get a haircut, Alex.

You should talk to your mom about getting a haircut.

A haircut cost about fifteen dollars plus tip.

Fifteen dollars that could've gone to the power bill or be our laundry money.

I cut through an alleyway and found myself on the sidewalk about a half mile from school. I rushed out so fast that I was going to be a half hour early. I slowed my pace as the wooden fence ended and opened to the irrigation canal that ran through the city. Soon, it would dry up when the city turned off the water.

Right as the fence ended, somebody turned the corner and ran into me.

"Hey!" I stumbled backward, catching myself last second, but the person who ran into me didn't, a plume of dust forming.

They were on the ground on their knees scrambling to the edge of the canal. "Shit! My book!" they said, and I heard the distinct *KERPLUNK* sound of something falling into water. I looked down at them to see a plastic bag torn open and their things on the ground.

They rose up onto their knees, head tilted down, shoulders shaking.

"You okay?" I reached down, offering my hand to help, but the person—a girl with long black hair—stared at my hand, leaning away from it. She pushed herself up and walked to the edge of the canal where the bank sloped down and all we could see was the water rushing under the road.

I waited for her to yell, to scream to tell me it was my fault, but it never came.

"That was my biology book," she stated, still staring down at the canal as if she could pull it back if she looked long enough.

I looked on for another minute before I pulled my backpack off my shoulders and took out my biology book. "Was it this one?" She nodded. "Here," I shoved the book in her direction, "take it."

Her face screwed up in confusion. "But don't you need it?"

I shook my head as I handed it over. "Nah. I don't really care either way." I zipped my backpack up before picking up all her things. "You know, if you check the lost 'n' found, there's always a couple backpacks in there that you can claim."

"But they aren't mine." She reached for her things, and I passed them to her, shrugging my shoulders.

"Someone lost them and then you found them. It becomes yours." My eyes fell to the plastic bag on the ground, understanding passing between us.

We came from the same situation. Lack of money. I could see it all over her. It looked like she was wearing men's clothes, probably her dad's or her brother's. Everything she was wearing was too big for her. Other kids our age were getting their licenses and driving to school. We were footin' it.

"You'll get into trouble if you don't return your book."

"Don't worry about it." I brushed the comment off. We started heading to school. She followed a few steps behind me. I didn't know her name or recognize her from any of my classes. It wasn't not a big deal though, our school was so big, with kids jam packed into every class, that it only made sense to not know every face. We hit the school grounds, and I didn't miss her breaking away and heading in the opposite direction.

"Alex!" I redirected to my name being shouted across the parking lot. Jonathan, my best friend since grade school, was standing by his white Audi, talking to Chance, who drove a fucking BMW to school. Their dads worked together, so those two made sense as to why they were friends. "Hey, do you want to hit Teddy's party this Friday?"

"Yeah. Sounds like a plan." The one benefit from my mom constantly taking night shifts was that she was never around to keep me from going out. I could go out, get drunk, come home, shower, and sleep the hangover off, and she never knew.

If she had known, it would have broken her heart.

"I'll pick you up." I didn't miss the way Chance snickered at that comment.

"No," I said quickly. "I'll just leave school with you. You don't have to pick me up."

"Cool," Jon said, shoving Chance and giving him a look.

We headed into the building's commons area. I glanced at the lost and found bins, one blue and one pink for girls and guys, that sat next to the trophy case, which displayed years of awards the sports teams had won.

The girl was there, shoving her things into a backpack.

I smiled to myself, glad she'd found one. Nothing worse than displaying *I am poor* to the rest of the school by using a plastic bag.

From where I was standing, it looked like a few new things had showed up that I would have to look at when I could.

School ended but I didn't leave. I paced around the building, buying time till I started to head home. I was waiting Ma out. She had to leave no later than four to make it to work on time for her shift. If I left now, she would probably catch me and lay into me for this morning.

It wasn't one of my finer moments; I knew better than to do that to her. My dad would have had my ass, but he was dead and there was no point in yelling.

What did she think getting good grades were going to do? It wasn't going to open any doors for me. As soon as I hit eighteen, I was going to get a job so I could start paying some of the bills. Ma hadn't had a day off in years. She was overworked and still, we barely made ends meet.

I had tried getting a job before, but no one wanted to hire a kid, so I was waiting it out.

I looked through the lost and found bins, finding a hoodie that looked like it would fit okay.

I made my way out of the school when the janitor came out, picking up trash from the hallways. I crossed the yard and decided to head home the back way again. There was no way my mom could miss work, so I wasn't worried about her staying home.

I kept walking and saw, up ahead, a familiar figure standing by the canal. I shoved my hands in my pockets as I approached her.

"Hey." I stopped in front of her. She was holding the biology book to her chest. "Nice backpack." I nodded to it. It was a dark blue one with black Sharpie stains on it. I had seen it in there for a while.

"Thanks." A small smile formed at the corner of her mouth. "Here." She tried handing me the book.

"No, seriously, keep it."

"You need it to get today's homework done."

I shrugged my shoulders. "I'm not doing the homework." Her brow furrowed, but she opened the book up and pulled some papers out of it, handing it to me. I took it. "What's this?"

"The homework," she stated. I looked down at it and it had her handwriting on it. The top of it where we were supposed to write our name on it was blank. "I'll keep the book, but I'll give you the answers."

"I'm not trying to cheat off of you." I tried handing it back to her.

"I know, but I'm already doing the homework. It doesn't bother me to write the answers down twice." She shucked her backpack off and put the book inside it.

"I'm Alex," I said finally.

"Wren."

She put her backpack on, and we stood there for a minute. She dipped her head, scuffing her worn shoes in the dirt, like she was waiting for permission to leave. The canal rushed under the road, drowning out all the other sounds around us.

"Well, I better start heading home," I said, starting to walk along the sidewalk, turning to look backwards as she still stood there.

She peeked up at me through her lashes as I walked away from her, then turned to take the path along the canal bank.

I TOSSED MY NEW-TO-ME BACKPACK OVER THE FENCE and squeezed myself through the gap where the fence went from wood slats to chain link. Dusting it off, I put it on, following the path I made for myself to get to and from school.

Living in Poverty Flats meant having weirdos on every corner. Not everyone was like that, but I had found out I could slip through the fence and walk along the canal to avoid most people. There was never anyone back there. The city combed through this part consistently enough to keep the homeless from setting up camp here. We were already an embarrassment to the town of Ashwood. It didn't bother me much; I got to walk the canal and be left alone. No one whistled or hollered at me.

Today was a good day.

My mood started to plummet as the apartment came into view. There were four apartment buildings that bordered the parking lot. All the same ugly brown color. The paint was peeling, trim was popping, hard water built up on the first-floor windows from when they used to water the grass. If the stairs to the second story had been wood, they would have been rotting through. Thankfully, they were steel.

I crossed the tracks and got through the thicket of trees the town was named after. Passed the maintenance shed, the playground, and then scanned the parking lot for his truck. I didn't see it, which was a plus, but mom's old white Honda was parked in its usual spot, so she was home.

I wasn't sure which was worse these days.

I trudged up the stairs that led to the second floor and stared at our apartment, number 4A. The door was unlocked like it always was, inviting fuck all into this place. Opening the door, I was hit with an unpleasant smell.

Mom was sick again.

I could hear her heaving the contents of her stomach up in the bathroom. Setting my backpack down, I filled a McDonalds to-go cup up with water from the tap and headed down the hall. Her head was hung and a hand covered her face. She was pale, with red-rimmed eyes and severely cracked lips. Her hair was graying, and she looked older than her thirty years.

"Don't look at me like that," she hissed before snatching the cup out of my hands, the water sloshing everywhere.

I didn't take offense to her words anymore. She was in a constant state of hatred toward me nowadays, and I was numb to it.

Since dad died, I was only a pest to her. A responsibility she didn't want.

She used to be beautiful. Both my parents had black hair. I got my curls and my green eyes from my dad. I didn't know what I got from her. I didn't really think we looked alike. She had brown eyes and her hair was thin and flat.

That was why she didn't like to look at me though. I think the older I got the more she could see Dad in me. Maybe she'd started to see me as a real human and not her meal ticket.

"Need anything?" I asked, keeping my distance as she clung to the wall to get to her bed.

Blankets were hung over her windows, casting a red hue into the room. Her light bulbs had burned out months ago, but she'd never bothered changing them. Trash accumulated on her dresser and bedside table. I grabbed a sack from the floor and started to pick up what I could of the trash, tucking the half-empty water bottles under my arm.

I could just leave it, but then one of them would use the mess as an excuse to call me in to clean it in front of them. So, I tried to stay ahead of them, picking up their trash, cleaning the kitchen, bathroom, and living room the best that I could without cleaning products.

They didn't like to spend their money on what they deemed unnecessary. Just cigarettes, booze, drugs for Kevin, and the occasional takeout.

Mom crawled into bed, groaning about her headache and the nausea that she was plagued with. I told her she should go to the doctor, but she refused.

Nothing good comes from doctors.

So instead, she would suffer with no solution in sight.

Whatever, I didn't care. If she died my life would be better off. If she died, there would be no one to claim me. I could go off and be forgotten.

I'd tried leaving this hellhole before but was dragged back kicking and screaming every time. I was deemed a runaway. Anytime I had tried to leave, they had my face and name on a list and would just bring me back. No law enforcement took me seriously, and it wasn't because of what I did.

It was because I lived in Poverty Flats.

"Get out," she moaned from her bed as I went round to the other side. I glanced to the floor, where the blanket I had pinned with clothespins had fallen onto the baseboard heater.

I set down the makeshift garbage bag and went about re-pinning the blanket.

The last thing we needed was this place to go up in flames.

I left her room, closing the door behind me.

I cleaned up their mess in the kitchen the best I could with what I had: hot water and an old sponge. I dried and stacked what dishes we did have, refilled the water bottles with tap water and arranged them in the fridge, noting the Sharpie dots I had put on some.

I took my backpack to my room, leaving my door open. If I closed it, they would take it off the hinges, so it stayed open. I tucked my new backpack under my bed. If they found it, it would be another thing for her to destroy. I pulled my pajamas out from under my pillow and laid them on my chair. In my closet, I moved an old box to the side and pulled out the tiny shampoo bottles I had stolen from the high school girls locker room, placing the bottles on my pajamas.

I wasn't allowed to use her shampoo or bodywash.

Crawling onto my bed, I opened the curtains and stared outside. Clouds were rolling in, and I hoped it would rain.

I loved falling asleep to the rain. It was cleansing.

It washed away everything: the dirt that accumulated up on the sidewalk from the walking traffic, chalk from the kid's recess. It was the reason the dandelions grew and the canal was full.

The front door opened then closed.

Kevin was back.

The jingle of keys dropping on the counter.

Boots walked the short distance to my room.

"Hey, baby."

Then the door shut, and my nightmare started.

His weight lifted from the bed as he retreated from my room. I faintly heard his belt clink as the roaring in my ears lessened. My mother's bedroom door opened, and the TV droned for a minute before the door was shut again.

He was in a foul mood today.

On shaky arms, I lifted myself from the bed. Even after all these years, it still hurt every time. I would never understand why people willingly had sex. Every time Kevin left my room, I was raw and sore.

I clutched my pajamas to my chest and went to the bathroom, pushing the button lock as soon as I closed the door. The pipes rattled and hissed before the water sputtered out of the shower-head in all different directions due to the hard water build up.

I place the shampoo and bodywash on the edge of the dingy tub before climbing in, closing the mildew-covered shower curtain. I let the water pelt my body. It felt like I was standing in a hot hailstorm. It hurt my skin, but it displaced the pain away from between my legs. I reached forward, bracing myself against the shower wall and, with my free hand, reached between my legs and washed the sliminess away. Attempting to wash away the feel of him inside me.

I couldn't ever enjoy a long shower because one of them ends up pounding on the door, so I quickly washed my hair and body, drying off with my threadbare towel before tying my hair up and slipping into my clothes.

I brushed my teeth and then cupped in my hands under the faucet and drank greedily before returning to my room. Tucked under my covers, my hair still wrapped in the towel, I lay in bed staring out the window, the only light coming from the streetlights.

I think of the boy I met today, Alex, and his warm brown eyes. He didn't hesitate to help me even though he didn't need to, and I wonder if there are other people like him out in the world.

CHAPTER 5
ALEX

EVERY OTHER DAY, I MET WREN AT THE CANAL, AND she'd give me a copy of the finished biology homework. I really didn't care to take the biology homework, I didn't want to use it to get a good grade, but it was my excuse to see her. I could tell she was smart. Every time I got the homework handed back to me, it was an A. I liked to stare at her handwriting. It was a mix of print and cursive. Neat in some areas and then it would get kind of messy. Like her hand couldn't keep up with what she was thinking.

I started to try and mimic her handwriting. Writing my name repeatedly until it matched her writing. The way her *l*'s had big loops along with her *h*'s. Sometimes her *m*'s would have extra humps in them when she wrote too fast and got a little sloppy.

We never stuck around very long after she handed me the homework, but I did learn that her dad had also died.

We had an understanding then. We were similar in more ways than I had realized.

We were both members of the Dead Dad's Club. As morbid as it was, it made me feel something.

I'd started to look forward to seeing her every other day, but on my way home that day, I didn't see her. I thought maybe I got here before her. Like maybe I was so excited that I rushed to see her. So, I waited.

And waited.

And waited.

I waited until the sun dipped below the horizon. When she didn't show, I finally went home. The next morning, I woke early, rushed out the door, and got to our spot. I hoped she would pass this way on her way to school. I waited until I couldn't wait any longer, or else I would be tardy for class. Too many tardies would get me a write-up that I would have to get signed by my mom, and I wasn't good at faking her signature.

Her absence consumed my thoughts. I walked through the halls between classes and tried to catch a glimpse of her. I looked for her long, wavy jet-black hair and that blue backpack with the Sharpie stains on it, but not once did I see her.

"Hey, do you know a girl named Wren?" I caved and asked Jonathan on the second consecutive week of her absence. I didn't want to ask him. I didn't need his or Chance's shit, which they were bound to give me. Especially about me looking for a girl.

Chance was a nuisance I had to deal with whenever I was with Jon anymore. He'd transferred into our school at the beginning of this year and, because their dads knew each other, he was always around.

"Who the fuck is Wren?" Jon looked at me and then Chance. Chance shrugged and kept texting on his phone.

"Probably some chick he's trying to bone."

"No one," I muttered, looking out across the parking lot, still hoping to see her face.

The two of them started to talk about another party they wanted to go to, but I tuned it out. Hanging out with the two of them had become a habit. We lived totally different lives and really didn't have much in common, but Jon always made me feel welcome. He knew my mom worked a lot and was always inviting me to different things his family did together. I almost always declined. I didn't want my mom feeling like she wasn't doing enough. It never failed that there were some kind of clothing requirements for whatever thing they had going on.

I recognized something familiar in Wren that I didn't see much at school. I wasn't self-centered enough to think I was the only kid in school who didn't come from money. There were lots of kids whose families struggled, but I could easily see it with Wren. And something about that was comforting. It made me feel like I wasn't alone. I wondered if maybe her mom worked all the time, too, and if she spent time alone as much as I did.

Instead of following the sidewalk home like I normally did, I decided to walk Wren's route along the canal. I walked for a while, wondering if maybe there would be a gate somewhere in the fence, figuring that her home butted up against the canal, so that was why it was easier to take this route than the sidewalk.

I had jumped a lot of fences before, but a wooden slat fence like this that was probably six feet high was hard to jump unless you got a running start. And there were only about fifteen or twenty feet between the edge of the canal and the fence. Even I would have a hard time jumping it, let alone Wren. I watched the water rushing in the opposite direction of me. The edge of the bank was steep and littered with rocks. I moved closer to the fence.

The canal curved hard to the left, and as I rounded the corner, I spotted a small figure with her hood up walking ahead of me. I immediately noticed the white sneakers with blood stains on the back.

"Wren?" I said once and then again, louder.

She jumped and turned around quickly. Wide green eyes were on me. I shoved my hands in my pockets and tried to walk slowly to her. Embarrassed at how excited I was to finally see her.

"Hey, where have you been?" I tilted my head down to look at her. She didn't look good. Paler than normal, and her eyes had dark half-moons under them.

"Uhm, I'm sorry, I don't have the homework," she said hesitatingly, and averted her eyes.

"I don't care about that. Have you been sick?" She looked down, digging the toe of her shoe in the dirt.

"Yeah. I've had the. . .flu."

"That sucks. Glad you are feeling better though. Did you go to school today?"

"No." We fell into step next to each other, continuing to walk down the bank. "I just came out for a walk while I could."

As we walked, I noticed the path became narrower. I went to reach for her without thinking, to put her on the side with the fence, but when she saw I was reaching for her, she jumped, rushing away from me.

"Wren, sto—" But it was too late. She had stepped too close to the edge of the bank and started sliding down. A shrill scream ripped from her throat.

Without a second thought, I dove for her as she was falling, grabbing her and pulling her to my chest while sitting down on the ground. We slid down the bank, but my foot caught on a rock only inches from the rushing water, stopping us.

I had one arm banded around her, keeping her back tight to me. "Wren, crawl up me and get to the top." I rushed the words out. I could feel her heart racing in her chest and her nails biting into my forearm. I gritted my teeth, the rock I had almost my whole weight on starting to slip out from between the other rocks. "Hurry! Go!" If we fell in, the current would pull both of us under.

But she didn't move. It was like she was frozen to me. With my free hand, I gripped a rock close by, trying to transfer some of my weight to it so the rock under my foot would stop moving. "Wren, come on, I got you, but you need to move."

Something in her clicked finally, and she slowly turned in my arms, crawling up me and using my back to push herself up the rest of the way.

With her safely at the top, I managed to adjust my footing to a different rock and turn, climbing my way out. With every lift of my foot, rocks tumbled into the canal, splashing back up. Wren took my hand, helping me the rest of the way.

We stared at each other, dragging in heavy breaths, when Wren turned around and heaved next to the fence. I got up and gathered her hair in my hands, rubbing her back like my mom did to me when I was little. My brows furrowed in confusion. I could tell she was wearing layers under the hoodie, the thick fabric obvious under my touch, but I could also feel her spine down the middle, ridged under my hand. It protruded more than what I thought was normal, even as she's bent over.

She heaved up nothing but bile for another minute before she straightened.

"Sorry," she mumbled, wiping her mouth with the back of her sleeve. We were both covered in dust and mud.

"Don't worry about it." I brushed at the dust on my jeans. "You okay?" I looked her over.

She nodded, her arms wrapping around her middle. "Just still a little sick."

"Want me to walk you home?" I glanced up at the sky. The sun streaming overhead cast an orange hue to everything.

"No." The word was instant, rushed, and made me feel like I did something wrong. But she continued, "My, uh, mom's boyfriend is kind of an asshole. I won't hear the end of it if he sees you."

"Ohh." I couldn't imagine my mom dating anyone. My dad had been dead for seven years, and I didn't think she'd even looked at another man the same way. "Well, can I walk you as far as you will let me?" She looked up at me with hesitation. "Or not. I promise I'm not trying to be weird or anything."

I wasn't ready to walk away from her yet. She seemed spooked from the fall, and I wanted to make sure she got home okay. I wanted to make sure *she* was okay.

I could see she was debating it. "Okay. Just until the tracks though."

We walked together in silence for a while. I kept her walking next to the fence line. She ran her fingers over the panels absently.

"Have you always gone to this school?" I had wondered if maybe she'd transferred into it, and that was why I had never noticed her before.

"Yeah. Why?"

"I've just never noticed you before," I said aloud.

"I'm not very noticeable."

"Why do you say that?"

"I've been out of school for two weeks and the school hasn't called my house and asked where I am."

"Does the school really do that?" I had no idea.

"Yeah. If you don't give the school notice as to why you are gone or bring in a doctor's note, they call your parents to make sure you aren't ditching."

I wondered then how many times the school had called my mom with no answer. She disconnected the phone during the day so the phone wouldn't wake her up.

"Huh. I didn't know that," I mused.

"I guess you have never been sick before." She looked up at me with those forest-green eyes.

"No, not really. I have ditched before though," I admitted.

"Me too." Her face fell a bit.

"Where did you go when you ditched?"

"I went to see my aunt."

"Why would you ditch to go see her?" I couldn't imagine ditching just to be around an adult. I had ditched to go on adventures with Jon, though. We would do dumb shit like drive around and get drunk somewhere. Go bowling and sneak fifths in, but I didn't want to tell Wren about that.

"I just. . .hadn't seen her in a long time." She shrugged, and for some reason I felt like she wasn't telling the whole truth. We got to an area of the fence where it changed, meeting with a chain link fence, and I could barely see beyond it.

"This is me." She stopped.

I looked over the fence, and something seemed familiar about it, the tree line beyond and everything.

"Wait, do you live in a house?" I looked back where we had come from at the roof peaks that we could see over the fence. The line of small houses where I thought one of them could be hers.

"No. We live in an apartment building." She nodded in the direction of the trees.

I turn and look down at her, "I live in the Cherry Woods complex."

Her eyebrows shot up. "Really?" She showed me how she slipped through the small gap between the woods and the chain link fence. I had to jump the fence, the gap being too small for me.

"Yeah, I've lived here my whole life."

"My mom and dad moved in when I was about ten."

"That's so weird. Why haven't I seen you around?" We crossed the train tracks, and I pointed out the gap where I cut through. "I cut through down there and go up the alleyway."

"Oh, I won't go through the alley. There are some creeps that way."

I nodded, and we walked over the tracks till we got to the tree line. She's hesitating again so I spoke up. "I'll wait here till you get inside."

"Thank you." She looked relieved.

"Can I meet you here in the morning and walk with you to school?" I hedged the question before she could walk off, feeling a little nervous.

"I'd like that." A small smile played on her lips before it disappeared. She brought her thumb up and chewed on her nail, something I had seen her do a lot over the last few weeks. "I have to go."

I watched as she cut through the yard and rounded the corner between two of the apartments. I waited a while longer before I did the same, heading inside. There were four buildings that lined up around the cul-de-sac. I found myself wishing I would have asked which one she lived in.

CHAPTER 6

WREN

Alex and I had been walking to and from school everyday since the canal incident. We talked about a lot of nothing. The best thing about walking with him was that he brought breakfast bars and shared them with me.

It took a lot of self-control to not inhale the bars in one bite. My stomach constantly felt like it was eating itself. I had been doing my best to stash things under my bed and save them for as long as possible.

Quietly, I turned the knob to my battered bedroom door and pushed it open, carrying my shoes and stepping out as quietly as possible.

Kevin slept over last night, and I was trying to get out of the house this morning without him waking. It was something I knew I was going to regret tonight, but I didn't want to deal with him this morning.

I didn't want to think about him sliding out of me and pooling into my underwear as I walked to school with Alex.

I didn't want to feel the ache at the back of my head from when he pulled my hair while he hammered into me.

I didn't want his voice to be the thing that I heard this morning. Not this morning.

Today was the last day of school, then it was Christmas vacation. Being the end of December, I was at their mercy for two whole weeks for winter break. My stomach dropped at what I knew would happen.

I wasn't scared. I had resigned myself into acceptance and decided to just enjoy what little freedom I had left. I was tired of fighting. Tired of plotting my way out of the hell I was put in. I just wanted to keep doing my homework and pass. When I graduated and turned eighteen, I was leaving this place and never looking back.

Kevin's interests had changed in the last few weeks. He started questioning me and asking why I wasn't getting home at my usual time. I hadn't been waiting for him like normal.

Why are you taking so long to get home?

What are you out doing?

Are you whoring yourself out to other men?

I used to only dawdle a little on the way home, easily telling them that the teacher held me after class for a bit to talk about the homework I'd turned in. I hated the suspense of what would happen when I got home. The buildup of what mood they were in, if they were fighting, if he was going to take pleasure in hurting me. If I just headed straight home, he would get it over with and then he and my mom would either go down to his apartment or he would just go to her room, and they would smoke weed and pass out together. He never spent any extra time with me besides that.

Now, he would be waiting for me at the front door.

I'd been taking longer to get home, not wanting to leave the little slice of peace I had gotten with Alex. Alex was warm and only a little rough around the edges; he chased away that growing anxiety that would build up while I walked home. He was caring and didn't make me feel like used garbage. He didn't touch me, except the one time we fell.

Tonight, when I got home, Kevin would be here, and he was going to lock us in my room. He had become clingy. He didn't immediately leave after he was finished. He would stay, try to have a conversation. He even bought me a new shirt last week. He wanted to talk about his day at work, telling me about his coworkers and other odds and ends. I didn't know how to respond to him, but I acted like I cared the best that I could. If I ignored him, I'd end up with more bruises.

Mr. Lloyd didn't come around much anymore since Kevin had been staying the night at our place more and more. I would see him every so often, walking to and from school when he was talking to someone else that lived in the buildings. He didn't say anything to me, didn't try to talk to me.

A sick part of me would rather deal with Lloyd than Kevin. If I had a choice between them, it would be Lloyd.

I made it out the front door, walking barefoot on the cold ground until I got down the stairs. Once I was down, I slid my shoes on and bolted for the tracks, not stopping until I got on the other side of the tree line.

"Hey there." Alex was on the other side of the fence, leaned up against it, looking over his shoulder at me.

"Hey," I panted, trying to catch my breath. The exhaustion had already hit me from that short run.

They kept me underfed so I wouldn't have the strength to fight him.

Alex chuckled. "Why did you run?" He straightened and reached over the fence. I shrugged off my backpack and handed it to him, the simple routine comforting.

"Was trying to get out before my mom and her boyfriend woke up." I slid myself between the two fences and took my bag, putting it back on.

"Oh, I get you." And then, "Is it weird with her dating?"

I was quiet for a minute, a snarky response on the tip of my tongue, but I bit it back. Alex asked a lot of questions, but I thought he did it because he was lonely, not nosy.

I never kept friends long. They always started to ask questions that I couldn't answer.

"They got together a few months after my dad died. Her boyfriend used to live in the apartments below us but moved in."

"I see."

We started along our path home. He handed me a breakfast bar. He had been doing this more and more lately, bringing me food. I restrained myself by putting it in my pocket. I wanted to devour it right now. "Do you and your mom go anywhere for Christmas?"

He shook his head. "No. We don't have any other family. Dad is dead. My mom's sister is dead. So it's just her and me."

"No grandparents?" I always wondered what it was like to have grandparents.

"Nope. Never had any. I think they died when I was little. You?"

"My mom and her parents don't talk, and she rarely talks to her sister."

"So, no Christmas plans?"

"Nope," I confirmed as we turned onto the sidewalk.

We walked along in silence. Today felt melancholy. I thought we were both thinking about how we wouldn't see each other for the next two weeks. It's a different kind of pain than what I was used to.

I'm going to miss this.

I'm going to miss him.

"Since you aren't going anywhere, maybe we can hang out? I can give you my apartment number and you can come over and watch a movie or something. Or we can go for a walk." His words came out in a rush.

I felt my heart lift at the thought of spending more time with him, doing something other than just walking to and from school, then broke, knowing it wasn't possible.

I'll kill you and anyone you tell.

"I'd love to. . ."

"Yeah? Ah, that's great. I have a deck of cards and I can teach you how to play. . ." He finally looked over at my face, stopping. "What's wrong?"

I was fighting back the tears. There was a part of me that wanted to tell him everything. I wanted to confess to him all the things that were happening in that fucking apartment. I thought he would listen and believe me. I thought he would do something to help me, but Kevin's words slash through me.

Go ahead and tell someone, but I'll kill you before they can ever get you out of here.

I didn't have a doubt in my mind that Kevin would kill me, and my mom would let him. She wouldn't even bat an eye, but I couldn't let anything happen to Alex.

I didn't want to die. There had always been a small sliver of hope that this wouldn't be my whole story. That there was more to my life than the beginning.

"My mom is taking me to work with her every day," I lied. "She works for this cleaning company and cleans people's houses and company buildings at night. So, she's going to have me pretty busy the entire break." I watched his face fall and it honestly was one of the saddest things I had ever experienced. I could tell Alex was lonely. His mom was never home, but he never talked badly about her. When he did talk about her, he only spoke highly of her. I could tell that he missed her.

Watching movies at his place sounded like a dream. The only movies I had seen recently were whatever the teachers played in the classroom. Last one was on cell division for biology.

"Oh," was all he said, his face dropping. "Well, if you ever have a day off, just let me know."

We had made it to the school grounds now, and I nodded at him. "I will."

CHAPTER 7

ALEX

I could hear the neighbor yelling again. It was a strange mix of garbling that I couldn't quite make out. She'd been yelling a lot more recently. There would be days where I wouldn't hear anything, and then she would go on for hours. It became mostly white noise.

I'd lived in these apartments my whole life. The walls were paper-thin, with chipped yellowing paint. The neighbors below us smoked, and it seeped up through the floor. The landlord never took care of anything that was broken. If you bothered him too many times, he was known to send eviction warnings based on lies just to get you to shut up about the issues. I'd watched people come and go. The kids I used to play with moved away with their parents. Adults with no kids started to fill this place up, and eventually it felt like I was the only kid here.

Other than Wren, but I didn't even know what building she was in.

I didn't think Ma had noticed just how bad the yelling got. By the time I came home from school she was ready to leave for the night shift at the diner. We lived in the same place but had completely opposite schedules. Plus, Ma was so dead tired by the time she got home, I was sure nothing could wake her.

Even while I was on break, I still rarely saw her. The diner was open on Christmas Day, and I had gone down and read a book in the corner booth while she worked. Ma would sit with me and chat for as long as she could before she had to go check on tables.

"There's food in the oven. It's still warm, so use a mitt to pull it out. Do your homework and read for an hour before you sit in front of that television," Ma said. She kissed my cheek roughly before she headed out the door. Even over the break, the teachers had handed out a bunch of homework.

I was trying to read, but there was a lot of thumping and yelling. I couldn't tell if the woman was fighting with her boyfriend or what. I hadn't seen her out of the apartment in over a year. Sighing, I realized I couldn't focus on my book. I closed it and shoved on my shoes and coat, deciding to walk out to the playground just to get away from the noise. I took the book with me, knowing that Ma would be quizzing me on this chapter this weekend. She said reading was good for the soul, and one day if I couldn't afford to have a TV or the newest games out there, books would be an escape good for all ages. I read because it made her happy. I hadn't seen her happy since my dad died.

I made sure to lock the door behind me, putting my key in the safety of my pocket.

I headed out to the playground behind our apartment. It was the Friday of the first week in January. On Monday, I would finally see Wren again.

I aimed straight for the swings, brushing off the snow before taking a seat. There were a few streetlights out here keeping it lit, just enough that I could read. It was too quiet now. I started reading aloud.

I wasn't sure how long I was reading out loud before I heard the scream. I looked up from my book to see someone running out from around the apartment directly toward me. They slipped on the ice, falling hard and sliding before they scrambled back up and headed for the jungle gym, running up one of the smaller slides before climbing into the big slide.

Wren?

I was about to get up and go to her, but behind her, someone else was running out of the apartment. It was a man and a woman. The man, who was walking weirdly, was behind the woman I recognized as my neighbor.

Oh shit.

"Where'd she go!?" It took me a moment to realize the woman was talking to me.

"Who?" I forced myself to not look toward the slide. I wasn't sure what was going on, but I wasn't going to rat her out.

"The kid who ran out before me!" she yelled louder, rushing toward me.

"Oh." I looked out past the parking lot toward the main road. "I saw someone run that way a second ago." I nodded my head in the direction.

"Shit, Kevin, if she—"

"Shut up, Lynn!" he bit out. I recognized the man as the guy who lived down below us. The smoker.

Holy fuck.

They rushed toward the parking lot, the man slowing them down before getting into a car and driving off. I shut my book and ran over to the slide, looking up from the bottom of it.

"Hey, they're gone." She didn't say anything, and I wasn't really sure if she'd even heard me. "Wren, you can come down now." Still, she said nothing, but it sounded like she slipped, the familiar screeching sound of skin on the slide. I reached up, tugging gently at her leg. I must have pulled too hard, because we ended up on the frozen ground with her lying on top of me.

"What the he—" I started before I opened my eyes to look up into wide emerald-green eyes. She stared down at me, her hands braced on my chest, holding herself up. I could feel her shaking.

I finally found my tongue after a minute of silence. "Wren, what's wrong? Are you okay?" She scrambled off me and climbed up on the lip of the slide, her eyes wild, scared.

I got myself up off the ground and brushed the loose bark off my clothes. Hoping I didn't dirty anything up too bad. It would be a few more days till we had enough change to go to the laundromat. I looked back at her. The first thing I noticed was her small red feet. She was barefoot and it was freezing out here.

I looked back to the apartment, expecting to see the red truck pulling back in, but the parking lot was quiet. "Was that your mom and her boyfriend?" Still, she said nothing. I looked her over and noticed that blood was seeping through her pink sweatpants.

"You're bleeding." I pointed to her knee. She finally looked away from the parking lot and at her knee. Then it was like she remembered she'd fallen, and she looked at her bloodied hands too. I could see the black specks of gravel in her hands. I could already hear the lecture my mom would be giving me right now if she saw me out here with no shoes in the dead of winter. She wasn't even wearing a coat. I looked her over some more. Something was wrong.

When she still didn't say anything, I picked my book up off the ground, looking it over to make sure I hadn't damaged it. It was from the library, and I didn't want to lose my library card because I messed up a book.

"Wren." I tucked the book in my inside jacket pocket. "Come on, get on my back, and I will take you into my apartment."

"Alex. . . I. . ."

"Come on, let me get you inside before they come back."

At that, her head whipped back to where they'd driven off. I sat on the edge of the slide, bending forward so she could get on.

"I can walk."

"Just get on. My mom would have both our asses if she found out you were out here with no shoes." I wasn't going to let her walk through the snow and ice.

"I'm not your mom's problem." This was the most she had said.

"My mom mothers everyone. Just hurry up." It took her a minute. She placed one hand on my shoulder gently, a few times, like it was going to bite her, before she wrapped her legs around my waist, her arms around my neck. I lifted her with ease; she didn't feel like she weighed anything. Once we got up the stairs, she wiggled until I put her down. We got to my door, and I unlocked it and looked over my shoulder. She was staring at my neighbor's door, and a slight tremor started in her body.

"You live next door?"

She nodded. "I'm sorry."

"For what?" I looked up at her, confused, while she was still standing by the front door.

"The yelling and screaming from my mom." I wanted to ask her more, but before I could, her stomach spoke for her: a loud gurgling noise that shattered through the night and seemed to echo on and on. Something in me softened, my concern moving from her mom and the boyfriend to her hunger. After my dad had died, Ma and I went hungry a lot.

Her, more so than me.

"Uhm, are you hungry?" I asked, softening my tone. Wren looked rough, her posture like the stray cat that lived somewhere around here. Like she would hiss and growl while she ate the food you gave her. Something was wrong, something was different with her, but I didn't know what.

"No," she immediately answered, defensive. Her voice was rough.

I couldn't help but laugh, but it died off when I wondered if maybe her mom didn't have food at home. It was a normal thing around these parts, choosing between food or keeping the lights on.

"Your stomach says otherwise." I watched her and sighed. "Come on, my mom left some food in the oven. I haven't eaten yet either." I was already in the kitchen, putting on a mitt for the oven. I pulled the meatloaf and mashed potatoes out of the oven, dividing up the food onto plates. I placed the food on the kitchen table before walking back and grabbing two cups, filling each with tap water. She stood by the door still, staring at it. I could see the blood soaking through her sweats, and she held her palms out gingerly, blood and gravel still on the surface.

"Here." I set a cup down for her and one for me. "Come back to the bathroom; let's clean your hands up." She didn't immediately follow me, but I headed back to the bathroom and started the warm water, just like Ma did for me whenever I cut up my hands as a kid. I found a washcloth and wet it. When she still didn't show up, I headed out into the hall. She was still standing at the entrance, just looking into the apartment. "Do you. . .want to come in here by yourself?"

She brought her thumb up to her mouth and started chewing on her nail.

Confused, I set out the washcloth, alcohol swabs, and Band-Aids on the counter.

"I left everything out on the counter in the bathroom." I walked out and headed to the kitchen. When I passed her, I couldn't help but notice the way she flinched, turning so her back wasn't to me.

I sat at the counter and waited for her to come back. It took a while, but eventually she did.

"Uhm," she started, holding her hands out to me, "I keep messing it up." I looked into her hand at the big Band-Aid that had folded in on itself, sticky touching sticky.

"Oh, here." I turned in my seat and reached to help her. Again, she flinched. I paused, looking up at her. Her eyes were squeezed shut and she pulled back like I had just hit her.

Slowly, she opened one eye and stared at me. She took a deep breath.

I smiled at her. "Okay. I'm going to reach toward you and fix your Band-Aid. Is that okay?"

Wren stared at me for a minute. Eyes guarded, before she finally nodded slightly.

"Okay." Slowly, I reached for her hands, looking up at her face to gauge her reaction as I did. I could see the way she leaned back, away, but not far back enough to take her hand out of my reach.

Carefully, I pinched the Band-Aid in both hands and pulled the sticky sides apart before gently laying it back across her palm.

I pulled my hands back. "There."

Once she was situated, she took a seat across from me, not hesitating to pick up her fork and start eating.

"Why were you reading outside? It's cold. Were you reading outside 'cause of the noise?" She fired off the questions in a whisper.

"Yeah."

I hadn't eaten much of my food. I had a bad feeling that something had happened to her, but I didn't know how to ask. I wished my mom didn't work the night shift. I wished she would be coming home any minute now to deal with whatever this was. This girl needed help.

"When is your birthday?" I asked, just trying to find something to talk about.

"I'll be seventeen in April," she answered. Slowly, she started to relax at the table. I watched her set the fork down. She had inhaled the entire plate of food.

"Wren?"

"What?"

"What happened?"

She brought that thumb up to her mouth and started chewing on her nail again. She looked at me then, her green eyes shining with what I think were tears. "This is really embarrassing, and you can tell me no." She fidgeted some more before she finally spoke, "I know we just met a few months ago, and this is asking a lot, coming from a stranger. My mom. . .won't let me take a shower. She gets mad at me and does this sometimes. Do you think. . .do you think I could take a quick shower? I promise I won't be too long. Just five minutes. I promise I'll be quick."

"Take as long as you need." The words were out of me without a second thought, my mind whirling with what kind of parent kept their kid from showering.

"Really?" Her green eyes shone up at me.

"Yeah, here, the shower is back here." Numbly, I took her. "Use whatever you need."

"Thank you." Her voice was quiet, small. It sounded like she was going to cry.

"Yeah. I'll get you a towel." I closed the door behind me and immediately heard the shower turn on. I went to my room and grabbed a clean towel that I hadn't folded or put away yet. Without thinking, I just opened the door.

Wren's back was to me, her hair pulled over her shoulder, her shirt already off. I could see her spine, all ridged and defined. Her shoulders were knobby, small. She looked sick. And then I saw it, a large yellow and greenish bruise that traveled over her ribs and around, almost reaching her spine.

She froze, her shirt clutched to her chest.

"What happened to you?" I was reaching out, but she flinched away. I dropped my hand.

Things started to make sense now, but I didn't want to assume. I didn't want to say it out loud. The yelling, the crying. When things sounded like they were rearranging themselves.

She was hesitating again, and it was like I knew what was about to come next.

"Don't lie to me." I sounded different, mad, even to my own ears. I didn't know what she'd been going through, but whatever it was, wasn't good. It wasn't right.

"I. . . My mom. . . " I saw her eyes moving back and forth, like she was looking for the answer somewhere on the peeling painted walls. Looking for a lie to tell. An excuse.

Standing in the small bathroom, I could smell her now, but I didn't react, I didn't make a face. "Wren, let me help you." I went back to my room and found a T-shirt and a pair of sweats. "Here." I handed them to her. "You can change into these. Use whatever you need."

"Thank you." Her voice was small.

While she showered, I cleaned up my room. It wasn't dirty by any means, Ma wouldn't have that, but I picked up anything that was out of place. My mind reeled with the thoughts of what her mom had been doing to her. What that man had been doing to her.

When she was done showering, I showed her my room. She wouldn't look me in the eyes. She looked even smaller in my shirt and sweatpants. She smelled like my bodywash. "Do you want to stay here?" I couldn't imagine sending her back to them. The look the woman had had in her eyes. . . Wren wasn't safe with them.

Her eyes widened. "You would let me stay here? What about your mom?"

I moved away from her and sat at my desk chair, turning it to face her. "I don't know what's going on, but I hear your mom yell a lot. And I think I hear your dad too." The word just slipped out without even thinking.

"He's not my dad!" The anger in her voice startled me, and I couldn't mask the look on my face. "My dad would never do what Kevin does. . ." She started shaking, her hands gripped into fists.

I was quiet for a moment. "What does Kevin do?"

She stared down for a minute before her eyes glazed over. It was like she was lost in thought, remembering something.

"I'll protect you, Wren. Whatever it is, I won't let it happen to you ever again." I didn't know where these words came from. I didn't know what had been happening to her, but I could see the fear written all over her face. I saw the evidence on her body. Things started to click into place. How she was always so jumpy, why she didn't want them to see her with anyone.

"What about your mom? Won't she send me back there?" The anger was gone, and her voice was small again, defeated.

"I'll worry about her," I said dismissively. My mom wouldn't let her go back there either.

I think Wren fell asleep as soon as her head hit the pillow. She curled herself up in a little ball and was out. I shut the door quietly, went into the bathroom, and threw up everything in my stomach. I retched until it was only bile coming up. My mind reeled with what I was going to tell Ma.

I had an Aunt Ginny once. My mom's sister. She stayed with us for a few months after her husband had beat the crap out of her. It was only a year after Dad had died. I remember watching the bruises on her face heal from a dark color to a yellow-green. Ma tried to get her to stay with us, but Aunt Ginny went back to her husband because of marital promises.

We were at her funeral a few months later, and Uncle Todd was in jail.

It was five in the morning when I heard Ma's key slide into the lock. I sat up straight, having dozed off on the couch sometime in the early morning.

My mom's eyes were on me as soon as she walked through the door. "Alexander James Harper, what in the world—"

"Ma'am, I need to talk to you about something."

She stood there, her coat half off, almost frozen. Whenever I had to talk to her about something important, I always started off by calling her *ma'am*. It was almost like our warning words. She would call me *son*, and I would call her *ma'am*.

Ma and I had been at odds lately. I had slacked off with my chores, my grades were terrible, and I had been causing her more heartache than what she deserved.

But I would do anything she asked me to do if it meant she would help Wren.

"Alright," she said, caution in her voice. "Get me a glass of water and let's sit at the counter."

I got her a glass but stood next to my usual place. I tried not to fidget, but I was nervous. I didn't know how she would react. Ma was looking older these days. Working nights was getting to her. I wish it wasn't this way. I missed her. I missed spending time with her in the daylight. Her dark brown hair was pulled up in a pony-tail. Her work shirt was rumpled, and I could see holes in her jacket. She needed a new one, but she never spent money on herself.

I told her everything. I told her about the neighbor who was always loud, yelling all the time. I told her about the crying that I'd always thought I heard but hadn't been sure. I told her about meeting Wren down at the playground. About the people who chased after her. How she had no shoes, how her mom wouldn't let her shower. I told her everything I knew, even about the bruise and the way Wren looked like she hadn't eaten in months. Ma didn't touch her glass of water, and she even looked a little green.

Since Dad had died, we went through tough times, having to decide what bill was the most important to pay that month and having something else be turned off. Ma knew struggle. Ma sympathized with struggle. But even at the worst times, she never laid a hand on me.

Abuse was something Ma wouldn't tolerate.

She sat there for a minute. "You slept out on the couch so she could have the bed?"

"Yes, Ma'am." I took a deep breath. "Ma, I haven't asked you for a single thing, and I know I have been a royal pain in your ass lately, but please, help Wren. I'll get my grades up, I'll do my chores, I'll read twice as many books, I'll do anything." I was desperate, and I think she understood.

"Honey, you know I'll do what I can." She nodded to the hall. "Alright then. Go wash up; I'll start breakfast and then I want you to wake her."

I did what I was told, washing up and then waking Wren.

"Hey." I patted her shoulder gently. The light from the hall giving just enough to see her face. She startled awake before remembering where she was. "My mom is home and wants us up for breakfast. I don't have an extra toothbrush, but you can use mine."

Wren nodded and was waiting for me in the hallway, her hands wringing the shirt I'd lent her.

"It's going to be okay."

Wren followed me out into the kitchen. Ma was at the stove, her back turned to us, but her sixth sense tuned in. "Take a seat, the both of you."

I pointed to the chair and took a seat for myself.

Ma turned around and spoke while loading up both of our plates with pancakes. "My name is Gloria. You can call me that or Ma. I have rules in this house, and they will be obeyed for as long as you stay here. . ."

CHAPTER 8
ALEX

I was trying to remember learning what rape was. It wasn't something I could pin down in my memories, and it wasn't something that was taught to me. My mother woken up one day and said, "Alex, today I am going to teach you the definition of 'rape.'"

I was raised by the golden rule. The one that was painted down the halls of the elementary school I went to.

Treat others how you would want to be treated.

I can remember one day on the playground, back when there were tons of other kids living in the apartments. I was sitting with Ma when a fight broke out between two other kids. We were all around the age of six at the time. I can't remember what the fight was, but I do remember Ma telling me that quote. Then once I could read, I saw the quote everywhere.

I would've never dreamed of forcing someone to do something. It wasn't in my nature.

Wren sat curled on the couch. She was still wearing my shirt and sweats. I leaned against the edge of the couch on the farthest end from her. Ma stayed home from work today, even though we couldn't afford it. She was pacing across the living room floor. She still hadn't changed out of her work uniform.

Back and forth.

Back and forth.

"Do you have any other family?" Ma stopped, turning to look at her. Her hand had run through her hair so many times now that it kept frizzing, catching snags on her fingertips.

"I have my aunt Katie." She looked down at her hands. "But I went to her when it first started happening. She brought me back to them."

Ma's hand clasped over her mouth. She had to spend a few minutes in her room alone. When she came back, she had been crying. Wren hadn't told us everything. I could tell that much, but she'd said enough to show the gravity of the situation.

My mom lets her boyfriend fuck me. It started when I was ten.
Wren, it's called rape.
I know.

"Wren, we need to go to the police." My mom had been begging her to go to the police for the last few hours, but the immediate fear in Wren had her pausing.

Even I was worried Wren would up and run out the door, and how could we help her if she did?

Wren's eyes welled up. "They don't believe me."

She hiccupped and wiped her nose with the back of her hand. "I'm in the system as a runaway. Every time I try to leave, they pick me up and send me back to them."

I watched them. Wren was terrified, and she had already reached out to someone she thought would help her, who just put her back in the same situation. Ma wanted to help, but we had experienced the police before. We lived in Poverty Flats. The police seemed like they were in this area constantly. A robbery, shooting, drug bust, prostitution on the corner, you name it. We were a bother to them. A pain in their ass, and they didn't want to deal with us, oftentimes ignoring pleas for help all together.

A slam sounded from next door; Wren jumped. We all grew silent, listening.

"Where the fuck is she?!" It was the man's voice; they were back from looking for her.

"I don't know! She's probably dead on the side of the road somewhere," her mom yelled back.

"She hasn't been in the news and no police have shown up here, Lynn. And when they do, you are going to fucking jail!"

"Oh, give me a break, they bring her back every time. Stop your fucking whining!"

He said something but I couldn't make it out.

"We just have to fucking wait! If she ain't dead, she's running back to my sister's house. Kate has a perfect life and doesn't want some brat fucking that up. She will call, and we will bring her back here. Then we will deal with it from there. I'm going to bed." A door slammed.

My eyes blurred and then focused again. Wren had her hands clasped over her ears, and she was curled into herself.

This was the first time I bothered to pay attention to the yelling. Listening to the words rather than just turning the TV or radio up louder, or just leaving till it stopped. Before I didn't care. I'd had no reason to care; I was always just annoyed with it. It was just another day with another fight.

I should have paid more attention. I could have done something. If I had only known, maybe I could have saved her.

Now, I had a reason to care.

"Okay, this is what we are going to do." Ma's voice was soft, quiet. As if they would hear that we had her. Ma walked over to the couch and sat down next to Wren. Her palm came up, but Wren flinched away, so Ma placed them in her lap, clutching them tight. "Wren, I would like to take you to the hospital."

"But—"

"Listen, I have a friend, and she's a nurse." Ma reached out for Wren's hand and waited. Wren stared; slowly, Ma took it and grasped it tightly in both her hands. "You can have a rape kit done. You will lie down on a table, and they are going to examine you. They have to swab your insides, to collect his DNA. They will take pictures of you. Showing the bruise, the scrapes," Ma shook her head, tears freely falling again, "everything. They will do a report, account for everything you tell them. And then they will save it."

"Save it?"

"Yes, sweetheart. They will save it until you are ready to do something about it. You can wait a month. You can wait a year or even five years. You can wait as long as you want until you are ready."

You could see the wheels turning in her head.

"But I'm only sixteen."

Ma's voice cracked and shook with emotion. "I know. I know, sweetheart. I don't know what happens with your age, but my friend will know. We can figure it out, but please, let me take you to the hospital. Let us help you."

Wren started crying with Ma. They were sitting on the couch and hugging each other. I just stood there, guilt eating at me. I should have done something sooner. I should have said something —if I had, then maybe it wouldn't have lasted this long.

The two of them left for the hospital. I stayed behind. Plotting.

I wasn't going to let Wren end up back with them. The cops weren't going to take her.

No one would.

CHAPTER 9
WREN

I'D BEEN AT THE HARPER HOUSE FOR TWO WEEKS. I'D run away before; this wasn't something new to me. One day when I was twelve, I went to the office and asked to see my second emergency contact in my file, faking it like my aunt had moved and I needed to update her address. The secretary rattled off her address to me, and I repeated it in my head over and over again until I could write it down. I walked fifteen miles across town to her house. I told my aunt Kate what Mom was doing, and to my horror, Aunt Kate put me in her car and took me back to Mom.

Mom locked me in my room, and I listened to her and Kate yell at each other for several hours. Kate had just gotten engaged and didn't need her sister's bullshit fucking up her chance at happiness.

Mom hadn't let me out of my room for three days.

But Kevin could come and go as he pleased.

Kevin and Mr. Lloyd.

I didn't know of any other family. Mom had said something about hating her parents, so I never knew them. I didn't even know if they were alive.

I could hear her talking to herself through the walls of Alex's room. She was louder than I thought, her voice warbled like she was possessed. I could make the words out that she said if I really tried.

"That slutty bitch."

"She's fucking useless."

"Out fucking the whole town."

She sold me to Kevin and Lloyd. At first, I was just Kevin's. He would give her cash and she would pay the bills with it, but eventually, Mom realized the way Lloyd looked at me. I had noticed it first, having firsthand experience with the way creepy older men looked at me. Lloyd started to come around every so often. He wasn't as consistent as Kevin, but nonetheless, he didn't charge Mom rent anymore. She only had to pay utilities.

Kevin fucked me, thinking he was paying for rent, but really Mom had quit her job and was using the money to live off of.

Alex walked me home, and I always hid while he unlocked the door. Mom would hear his keys jingle, and she would rush out, question him, put on the facade of a concerned mother. Her daughter was missing. She was good, too, she could start the waterworks and everything. The only reason she wanted me back was to take her anger out on me. I was just her punching bag.

Alex just told her he didn't know what she was talking about. Hadn't seen me.

Mom would pace the hallway, look over the railing while I hid behind the apartment dumpsters, waiting for her to go back inside. Alex would give me the all clear, and I would run up the stairs and into the apartment.

I was wearing some sweatpants of Alex's and one of his T-shirts. Gloria went down to the shelter and brought some girl clothes back. She also brought home some clothes from her work. She promised she didn't tell anyone my situation, just that she needed some girl's clothes. I picked anything that didn't have white or pink on it.

Especially the socks. I didn't want white or pink socks.

Gloria was a sweet woman. She opened her home to me without a second thought. The Harpers were just overall kind people. I had never met a family so welcoming. Especially someone my own age.

I was used to the sneers from the other kids. I would show up to school wearing the same thing several times a week. I would bring an extra shirt to school and try washing it with hand soap in the sinks at school. The apartments didn't have a laundry room on site and Mom wouldn't take my clothes to the laundromat. Some girls walked in on me trying to wash blood out of my underwear one day. They teased me about bleeding through and getting my period. I couldn't tell them that I hadn't gotten my period yet.

I heard whispers about it for the rest of the week.

I was slicing potatoes while Alex was grating cheese. We were making some kind of cheesy potato casserole. I popped a piece of cubed potato in my mouth, the crunch sounding like an apple.

"Stop eating raw potatoes," Alex chastised me again. I duck my head down a little lower, embarrassed.

I couldn't help it. It was weird having food in the house. Food available. Being allowed to eat. Cooking things rather than just eating everything raw. I was used to hiding food under my bed and saving it before it rotted, trying to make it last long enough that I could steal my next meal. Mom would make me sit at the counter and eat in front of me. I thought once you have starved, the empty, cramping feeling you get in your stomach never goes away.

"Here." Alex nudged me, holding out a small triangle of cheese.

I took it, popping it into my mouth, humming my delight.

It was Friday night. Alex's mom had taken a double shift at the diner and left us cooking instructions. I didn't know how to cook. When I'd told his mom, she said it was time for both of us to learn. Every day for the last few days we'd had instructions on how to cook whatever meal she had the ingredients for. After dinner, we would divide the chores up and get them done, and afterwards we would finish our homework and read for an hour every night.

There was this strange peace in the routine of the Harper home. Wake up, wash up, eat breakfast, go to school, eat the brown-bagged lunch with Alex, finish school, walk home with Alex, who would talk about his class or whatever funny thing had happened that day. Alex talked a lot. I think he did it to distract me. I liked Alex. I liked to listen to him talk about anything and everything. I think he was lonely, with his mom working all the time. Spending every evening by himself.

I always wanted to be alone. If I was alone then *they* weren't hurting me.

He wasn't touching me.

"Better than the potato, right?"

I nodded at him, my cheeks reddening. I felt the shame start to creep in, the embarrassment of doing things wrong, not under-standing.

"Don't worry. I've got you." He placed a hand on my head, and I did my best not to flinch away. Alex had said this to me so many times over the last two weeks. Alex was affectionate in every way. I would crawl into his bed, and he would move my hair from my face or throw another blanket on me when he thought I was cold. He would grab my hand and pull me through the halls of school, bump his shoulder against me while we were walking together. He reached for me like he had been reaching for me his whole life.

I had a lot of nightmares. Every night, I would toss and turn and wake up in a cold sweat. The first night was the worst.

Alex clasped his hand over my mouth because I had started screaming in my sleep.

"I'm sorry. I'm sorry." I could hear his voice break. "Wren it's me, you have to stop screaming or they will hear you." Once I finally calmed down, Alex would be there with an ice pack wrapped in a towel. He would hold it at the back of my neck, and I would let him. He would whisper apologies to me all night. Then say sorry again in the morning.

I wasn't alone anymore. Even at school. Since the night at the slide, Alex could find me anywhere. Someone who I had never noticed before, I now had a radar for. Sometimes he'd catch me in the hall. Now, he knew my schedule, where I sat in each class, and sometimes I would find little ziplock bags of pretzels or nuts in my desk. It was like he knew I was in a constant state of starvation. Or at least my stomach sounded like it was.

I looked like I had been starving.

I had been starving.

I was all sharp edges, no longer having that layer of baby fat. One day it had just vanished. I'd watched my body change the last two years. I grew taller, thinner. My face looked hollow, with dark circles around my eyes. I bruised easily, and the bruises lasted for months.

I felt like I was disappearing.

We combined the ingredients into a pan, wrapped the top in foil, and it went into the oven. Alex twisted the timer and set it on the counter. Letting it click away.

"These places are so small, there's not a lot of room to store things," Alex said, staring at the oven. "Where does your mom keep all the pots and pans?"

I looked at him, confused. "Same place you guys keep yours." I pointed at the oven. "In the oven. Obviously when she's not using it. . ." I shook my head. "But she mostly just uses the microwave. Not the oven." We had lived off of boxed mac and cheese and ramen most of the time. Sometimes, dinner would just be a box of rice I would make.

"Well, that's done. Wanna watch a movie?" It was freezing outside. We could hear the wind howling through the alcove of the apartment. When Mom got bad, Alex would take me outside. We'd walk along the train track that ran behind the playground beyond the trees just so he could get me out of the house long enough to not have to listen to her anymore.

"Sure." Alex disappeared down the hall, and a few minutes later, he came back with some VHS tapes.

"We don't have a DVD player." He held up the tapes to me. "Pick one." I read all the titles, the covers all looking worn. One was worse than the others, even having been taped back together.

"Which one is your favorite?"

Just like I suspected, the one with the most worn cover was what he pointed to. *The Outsiders.*

"Then let's watch that one." While he crouched by the TV and put the tape in, I asked, "Can I grab a blanket from your room?"

"It's our room, and you don't have to ask, Wren. Take whatever you need."

I opened the door and flipped the lights on. The room was tiny, a mirror of my own. A twin bed shoved into the corner on the right-hand side and a small desk on the left side. It had a window that had foil blocking out all the light, with plastic taped over it to help keep the room warm. In between everything, on the floor were extra blankets and pillows. Alex had made himself a makeshift bed on the floor and given me his bed. We shared the room. All the apartments were the exact same. It was a two-bedroom, one-bath with a small living room and kitchen.

I grabbed the fleece blanket from the bed and headed out into the living room. We crowded ourselves on the small couch. Alex was tall, with broad shoulders and long legs, so he took up most of it. He wore a hoodie with sweatpants. His brown hair was messy and a little long. I curled up in my corner, tucking my legs under me and laying the blanket over my lap, pulling it up to my chin. The apartment was never quite warm. We were always layering up. Alex shoved his bare feet under the blanket, too, his cold toes touching my calf. I jumped at the shock of it; he just leaned back into the couch and grinned at me. I tucked the blanket better around his feet. He relaxed back into the couch while the opening scene started.

I liked to watch movies with Alex. I didn't feel like I had to whisper. He would turn the volume up and we could laugh and talk without worrying someone would hear us.

I was wrapped up in the movie when Alex handed me a bowl of cheesy potatoes. I held it in my hands, letting the warmth seep into them.

"Your food's going to get cold if you don't eat," Alex said. I realized I had just been holding it for the last ten minutes. I polished off the bowl quickly. Not long after, Alex handed me his own bowl, his food barely touched. I look at him.

"I'm full," he stated, and I didn't argue. I ate it all and hoped he wouldn't give me another serving. I'd eat it, but I was sure I would be sick afterwards. I wasn't used to having food every day.

Once the movie was over, I wiped the tears from my eyes and looked at Alex. He was grinning at me like a loon.

"Good movie, huh?"

"That was freaking sad." My voice warbled but I eventually dried my eyes.

"Yeah, but it's still good."

Alex got up and hit rewind on the VCR, kneeling in front of it. The machine whirled loudly. With the absence of his heat, a chill ran over me. He had sun-kissed skin, even in the winter.

I felt my cheeks redden at the thought. I never looked at boys. Mom would call me ugly names when I had never even kissed a boy. Anytime I told her that, she called me a liar.

"Do you play any sports?" I asked him, trying to stop my mind from going to the dark place. Alex looked over his shoulder at me, his brow in a V shape. When he still didn't answer, I started to feel self-conscious. "What?"

"Nothing, just a random question, and you just haven't asked me anything about me before."

I thought about that then. I had been living with him for two weeks, and he was right. I really hadn't.

"I'm sorry."

"Don't be, and no, I don't play any sports."

"Why not?"

He looked at me again, then down at the VHS case in his hand. "Ma can't afford to pay for it. You have to pay for things like the right kind of shoes or equipment. Baseball bat, helmets, jerseys." He shook his head. "And I guess I never really asked. I hate asking her for things." The VCR clicked and stopped; Alex ejected the tape.

"Oh." I felt awkward. Like I shouldn't have asked. I had noticed pictures of a man who looked a lot like Alex, but I was nervous to ask. Taking a deep breath, I finally said, "Who's the man in all the pictures? Is he your dad?"

Alex nodded. "My dad died when I was nine. Had an accident at work. He was working in a factory; some equipment malfunctioned, and it crushed him. They got him to the hospital in an ambulance, did a whole bunch of surgeries on him. It all looked well, I guess, like he could recover, and then he had a stroke. Blood clot to the brain." Alex tipped his head back, staring at the ceiling. "Ma kept him on life support for a week before she finally had him taken off."

He reached below his shirt, pulling out a necklace. It was a corded necklace with a gold band looped through it so it lay flat on his chest. "This was his wedding band. Ma gave it to me like this after his funeral." I watched as he slipped the ring onto his finger, it was too big and just slipped right back off.

I moved off the couch as he spoke, knelt next to him and listened.

"He was my hero." Alex's voice broke. "He would bring Ma home flowers, and they would dance in the kitchen to some old music that I think they got married to." He shrugged his shoulders, and a smile was at the corner of his lips. "I would try to squeeze between them, I wanted to join in all the fun. Dad would pick me up and sit me down on the counter and say, 'Give your ol' man a minute with the love of his life.' And they would dance and dance. My dad loved my mom more than anything else in the world." Alex spoke with wonder in his voice, and I could hear the love he held for his parents.

My hand was on his arm, and I felt tears streaming down my face.

"I miss him, so much, but what I think I miss the most is watching them together. Watching him love her and her be loved by him." He looked at me now, and I could now see the tears rolling down his face. "She still cries for him sometimes. After he died, she started working doubles at the diner. Their savings dried up paying for the bills. I just kind of watched her wither away for a while. Me wanting to play sports didn't seem like a good enough reason for her to work more."

The guilt ate at me with every word he spoke. "I shouldn't be here." I covered my hands with my face, shame filling me. I was taking away from what Alex could have. I was a burden to them.

In the first five minutes of meeting him, I went from terrified to hopeful. I froze when he pulled me from the slide, and I fell on him. He was so warm that I wanted to stay there. Then I sat at that table across from him and took a chance on asking for more than I deserved. And then his mom told me I could stay here as long as I followed the rules.

"Wren, you are the first thing I have ever asked Ma for." He gently tugged my hands away from my face. I could barely see him through the tears. "And I'm so happy I did."

"Tell me a secret." Wren walked along the fallen tree trunk, her arms outstretched to keep her balance. I walked along with her, watching her carefully, afraid she was going to fall off the thing. We had snuck out early this morning and run to the thicket of ash trees that surrounded the area. It wasn't very big, and eventually you would find the train tracks, but we were happy to wander around in the area for hours on end. Wren liked to look at plants and lie on large fallen tree limbs. The air was cold and crisp still, but we didn't mind. Wren borrowed clothes from me and layered up.

"A secret?" I thought about it for a minute. I didn't really have secrets. I hadn't had anyone to keep anything from. "I don't have any secrets."

Wren blew a raspberry at me. "Come on, you have to have a secret. Something you think or have done that you wouldn't want anyone to know."

I tried to think of something, but I couldn't. I just shrugged, and she rolled her eyes. Wren had been relaxing more these days. She wasn't quite so jumpy anymore. Every day more of her personality started to shine through. I liked to watch her. We would watch movies that I had seen so many times I could recite them word for word, but Wren was watching them for the first time. I liked observing her reactions. The surprise and wonder on her face. I heard her laugh for the first time. Truly laugh to the point that she had a tear running down her face.

She loved to listen to the radio. I had found one in a dumpster on the way home from school one day and brought it home to find out it would still work if you wrapped tinfoil around the antenna and pointed it in a certain way. She started to learn some of the songs and sing along quietly.

"Why?" I asked, curious.

She reached the end of the trunk, jumping off of it and landing on her feet. "Because I have a secret that I want to tell you."

With her safely on the ground, I shoved my hands in my pockets, warming them. "Okay, so tell me."

She brought her thumb up to her mouth, chewing on it, and I fought the urge to grab her hand to stop her. She would chew the skin around her thumb until it bled.

"You'll think I'm a bad person."

I screwed my face up at her, confused. "You're not a bad person."

"If you knew my secret you would hate me."

At that, I walked over to her, grasping her shoulders gently and stooping so she couldn't avoid my eyes.

"I would never hate you. There is nothing you could ever do that would make me hate you."

We stared at each other for a beat before I stood, giving her more space. She fell into step beside me.

"I wish they were dead." Out of my peripheral, I watched her tilt her head back and look up to the tree branches. "I wish they would get into a car accident or fall asleep and never wake up." She shook her head. "I think about it all day, every day. I wish they were dead."

I didn't have to ask who she meant.

"I wish they were dead too," I said the words and meant them. What kind of mother did that to a kid? Her own daughter.

We took a few more steps before I felt her hand slip into mine. My heart kicked up a notch and I tried not to react. I didn't want to make her feel weird or regret it. So, I gently held her hand and walked with her to the edge of the grove.

"I got you, Wren."

I promise.

CHAPTER 11
WREN

"Momma, please?" I tried to keep my voice from trembling. I tried not to cry. It had been three days since she let me out of my room. I smelled of urine. The sour smell made my nose hurt. The insides of my legs hurt. They were red and raw. It hurts to pee now too. I was peeing blood.

Everything hurt.

Kevin was the only one who came into my room anymore. He visited me twice a day. The roll of duct tape sat on my bedside table, half-gone and haunting me. Mom didn't hold me down anymore. He handed me a pair of socks to put in my mouth and then made me put duct tape on.

Lately, I had it done before he even came into my room.

Anything to make him less mean. Anything to make it go faster.

"Momma, I'm bleeding," I said through the closed door. On the other side, I heard something drop and then footsteps. I moved away from the door quickly, crouching next to my bed.

"What do you mean you're bleeding?" There was no concern in her voice. Venom was the only thing there. She covered her nose, the smell not so easy to ignore when you were standing in here.

"When I pee. There's blood." I pointed to the towel I had been using to clean up with. It was stained a light pink color.

"Well, fuck." She turned around and headed across the hall to the bathroom, opening the medicine cabinet and coming back with an orange bottle. "Take one of these." It was a big white oval-shaped pill.

"Wh—what is it?" The question slipped out, and I prepared myself for the slap, but it didn't come. I was always cautious about taking pills from her. She would make me take some, and it never failed that I would wake up a few hours later groggy and sore everywhere.

"Antibiotics. You just have a bladder infection. It will go away in a few days." She stepped out of the room, her face scrunched. "Fuck, this room reeks."

I dry swallowed the pill. If it made the pain go away, then I would take anything.

"Clean this room up before Lloyd gets here. I don't need his concerned, pathetic bullshit." She walked away from the door. Leaving me by myself again.

I gathered up the dirty clothes and towels, taking them to the bathroom where the laundry basket was. I turned the sink on and drank from the faucet greedily. Once the thirst was better, I wet a washcloth and wiped off the inside of my legs, rinsing it out and washing myself again. Afterwards, I headed to the kitchen and got the cleaning supplies from under the sink, grabbing some more plastic grocery bags too.

I did my best to clean the room and cracked the window to help with the smell. With Mom still in her room, I grabbed the two plastic containers I had been using to store water in and stashed them back under my bed. I placed the mop bucket in the sink and started filling it.

Maybe if I cleaned the kitchen up, Mom would let me eat tonight.

I opened the cupboards and snagged two Pop-Tarts out, stashing them under the bed with the water.

The mop bucket was still filling up, steam lifted from it. I glanced at the door. The chain wasn't in place. I could try to leave again. This time I would just find someplace to hide at the school. Eat lunch and go to class. Hope the janitor didn't notice me sleeping in the locker room. I could do that until I graduated, grow up and get a job. Leave this place and never have to see them again.

The sound of splashing pulled me out of my daydream. Quickly, I shut the water off and started to lift the bucket out of the sink.

"Wren!"

I turned around to mom, slipping on the water, but she caught me. Her eyes no longer blue but brown.

"WREN, WAKE UP!"

Startled, I opened my eyes to Alex shaking me.

"Fire!"

"W-what?" I asked, sleep clogging my voice.

"Come on!"

I could smell the smoke now, but I couldn't see the flames.

"Here, put this on." Alex shoved a hoodie on me, and I quickly pulled on some shoes.

I could hear screaming now. "Alex, what's happening?!"

"Do you trust me?" His eyes bounced between mine.

"Yes."

He gripped my hand tight and pulled me down the stairs. It was still dark outside; I couldn't tell the time. I could hear the sirens coming. Alex pulled me through the parking lot and to a shed behind the playground. The shed door didn't face the playground. It was behind it and normally it was locked, but this time it was opened.

"Get in here, hide behind all that stuff back here, and don't you come out until I tell you."

"What are you going to do?" Panic crawled up my throat. I didn't want him going back there.

"Wren, just trust me. Stay here." He closed the door, and I was drowning in darkness except for what I could see between the boards. I had an almost perfect view of the apartment. Then, I could finally see it.

The flames burst out of my mom's bedroom window. I covered my mouth, horror engulfing me.

Were they dead?

Police cars and fire trucks swarmed the area. Hooking up to a hydrant and they got to work, spraying the flames through my mom's window. Black smoke billowed above the apartments.

I could see Alex standing off to the side on the sidewalk behind the yellow caution tape. His hands were in his pockets. More people came out from the other apartment buildings and gathered on the sidewalk. Lloyd, his hands in his hair, was waving his arms around crazily next to two police officers.

Two ambulances showed up, taking one person away in it.

Gloria ran up to Alex, grabbing him by his shoulders and shaking him. She looked around, but Alex hugged her tightly.

I wondered what she was thinking. A sinking feeling fell in my stomach. Their home was up in flames. All the memories of Alex's dad gone with it.

Hours passed, the sun rising and granting more light through the slats of the shed. I had to adjust my positioning, standing for a while before sitting back down, moving around a lawn mower and other yard tools in the rundown shed.

Finally, Alex started walking my way. I stood, moving to the door. As soon as he opened it, I wrapped my arms around his neck, and he held me tight.

"Everything's okay." He didn't let me go, giving me the time I needed to just hug him.

"Thank you," I whispered in his ear.

"I got you." He squeezed me tight. "Come on, Ma wants to lay her eyes on you for herself."

He took me along the back of the property, coming up behind one of the other apartment buildings. The farthest one from ours. He opened a door on the bottom floor and pulled me in, quickly closing it behind me.

I was enveloped in arms immediately. The sweet smell of maple syrup and Gloria's floral bodywash engulfed me.

"Oh my god, I was so worried about you." Her voice was laced with tears, and she held me tight to her chest. After a minute, she held me at arm's length, looking me over. "Oh, you are alright," she said, as if reassuring herself.

"Told you, Ma." Alex spoke from behind me, a grin in his tone.

"I know you did, sweetheart, but sometimes a mother needs to see for herself to reassure her poor old heart." Gloria brushed her tears away.

I felt awkward. I wasn't used to being doted over, but that didn't stop the warm feeling spreading through me.

"What are we doing in here?" I looked around at the barren room. Void of all furniture and pictures on the wall. It smelled like fresh paint and musk.

"The firemen closed off our apartment building and required Lloyd to put us in a different apartment. Thankfully, he had this one empty still," Gloria answered.

I tried not to react to his name. I hadn't seen him since I had gotten out, and I didn't want to see him. I didn't know if he would tell my mom where I was at.

"Who got taken away in the ambulance?" I had been too far away; I hadn't been able to see if it was Mom.

Alex and Gloria looked at each other. I couldn't tell if I was worried about my mom or not.

Or if I was hopeful.

Did I really care if she was hurt?

Yes, I did. Because I wanted her dead.

I didn't voice it out loud. If I didn't say it, it wouldn't be true. I wouldn't be a bad person for wishing them dead.

"It was Kevin," Gloria finally said. I could feel Alex's eyes boring into me.

I wanted to ask but held back. Gloria must have seen the question on my face.

"He wasn't dead when they took him, but," Gloria hesitated, "from my understanding, he was burned pretty badly."

I watched Alex's face. He didn't show any emotion.

"What about my mom?"

Alex finally spoke, "Your mom's arm was bandaged up, and she had smoke in her lungs or something like that." He walked closer to me, watching me. "She was asked if anyone else was in the house, and she told them no. That you had been staying at your aunt Katie's."

I looked away from him, nodding. Of course, Mom would say that to save her own ass.

"How did the fire start?"

"We don't know yet, baby." Gloria rubbed my arm. "But we are allowed to get some things out of the apartment. The firemen are going to help before they seal it up for investigation."

My eyes bore into Alex, but he didn't give me anything.

Could he have done it?

I tried to banish the thought. Alex was too kind to have done something like risk two people's lives to start a fire. He couldn't be capable of it.

Maybe he was trying to kill them for you.

The thought hit me hard and made me hopeful.

Alex spent the next few hours bringing things from the other apartment. He would bring them into the living room, and I took a wet cloth and wiped them all down, trying to get rid of the smell of smoke.

Gloria left and headed back to work. She wanted to stay home, but we knew how tight money was. She couldn't even miss a half-day on account of an emergency.

Alex and I worked separately, trying to get the place put together. We didn't want his mom coming home and fussing with anything.

In the bathroom, I was putting things away under the sink when I heard it.

"NO!" I screamed and clambered into the bathtub, crouching down and covering my face with my hands.

"Wren?!" I heard him shout, but I didn't respond. My heart thundered in my chest and I tried to stay as quiet as possible. *He won't find me. He can't do this to me.*

"Please I won't scream, I promise!" The words flew out of my mouth and I begged repeatedly: "Please! Nononono!"

"Wren, what's wrong?" Hands were on my shoulders, and I screamed louder.

I'm sorry. I'm sorry. I didn't mean to hurt Daddy, I swear!

My hands were pulled away from my face.

"Look at me!"

Alex's panicked eyes were on me. "It's just me, Wren, I wouldn't hurt you, you know that."

Time seemed to slow as I stared at him.

What had I heard?

I couldn't even register what it was, past the fear that it instilled in me.

"Wha-what was that?" I tried looking around him. He leaned over the edge of the yellowed, fiberglass bathtub.

"What was what?"

"That noise?"

"Noise?" He turned, looking behind him. "Hold on." He got up, leaving the bathroom and coming back with a silver roll.

Seeing it already had me shrinking farther into the bathtub.

A roll of duct tape.

"Was it this?"

I nodded.

"Did. . .did they hurt you with this?"

Hesitantly, I nodded.

". . .How?"

I couldn't find the words, so I pushed up my sleeves and showed him. Halfway up my forearms, there was a discoloration in my skin from where they repeatedly put the tape and ripped it off. They started to tape my arms behind my back after I had scratched them too many times.

Alex stared down at it in his hand. "I was putting it on the cracks in the window seals."

My heart was still trying to escape my chest. Seeing the tape made me feel like it was tugging at my skin again. The way it felt when they ripped it off me.

Alex tossed it out of the room and reached his hand out to me. I took it and he helped me out of the tub.

He wrapped a hand around the back of my neck and pulled me to him.

Safe. I am safe with him.

CHAPTER 12
ALEX

Fives months later

I open the door to Wren lying on the bed with a few pillows behind her head, propped up with a blanket draped over her lap. She was wearing a pair of my gray sweatpants and one of my hoodies with the hood pulled up, reading one of the books we'd picked up from the library.

I smirked at the scene before me.

"What?" She was looking at me over the top of the book. Wren had relaxed since the fire. She wasn't as jumpy and had started to smile more. I knew I had done the right thing.

I would do anything to make her feel safe. Even if that meant killing anyone who hurt her.

"Nothing." I crawled onto the twin bed next to her. Like we were in sync, she lifted her head, and I put my arm behind her. She moved her head so it was in the crook of my shoulder, and she brought the book up, continuing to read. The bed was too small for the both of us to sit without touching. I liked sitting on the bed with her. Liked that she let me put my arm behind her. Liked how her legs would tangle with mine.

With Kevin still in the hospital's burn unit (information given to Ma by her nurse friend), Wren had been able to relax. The nurse said it didn't look like he was leaving anytime soon. Still heavily sedated and getting skin grafts. After the fire, the landlord had to move everyone out of that fourplex. We think he got the insurance money and rather than fixing it up, he just kept it. There was a shiny brand-new vehicle in the parking lot the other day, and it couldn't have been anyone who actually lived in this dump.

Mentally, I was making plans on how to finish the job. I'd failed to kill him in the fire, but at least I hurt him enough to keep him hospitalized for a while. Kevin being gone had been everything for Wren.

It took her a while to get used to being here. Took her a while to stop jumping every time I said something or brushed up against her. She was easily spooked. Always waiting for the other shoe to drop. Waiting for my gentle touches to turn into hits.

This made me want to touch her more. Wanted to show her that I was the last person on this earth to lay hands on her. She was like a low-burning fire, and I just wanted to feel her warmth.

I held back though. It wasn't until she started reaching for me that I started reaching for her too.

We had finished with the chores and cleaning up after dinner. I finished my homework out in the kitchen and came to find her.

I read the book over her head. She had been reading a lot about plants. She would pick up two or three books and write things down in a notebook she kept. On the page was a meadow with tiny flowers all over it. They hung upside down, like little bells.

"Why all the plant books?" I leaned to the side a bit to see her face.

The book relaxed in her hand. "Don't make fun of me."

"I won't." Now she really had my attention.

She sighed, "When everything was happening with them, I used to pick flowers. Well, weeds really. Dandelions, and imagined that they were poisonous." A small laugh escaped her. "I imagined poisoning them. I wanted them dead." She picked the book back up, looking over the pages. "I guess I still like plants." She tipped her head back to look at me.

"Have you ever done it?"

She was quiet before asking, "Done what?"

"Did you ever try to poison them with plants?"

She was silent, and I felt the weight of it.

"Would you think I was a bad person if I did?" She hedged the question.

Would she think I was a bad person if she knew I was the one who set the fire?

"No. They deserve to die." The silence grew between us. I thought of telling her what I did, but instead I changed the topic.

"What's wrong with you?" I asked her.

"What do you mean?" She put a torn piece of paper between the pages as her bookmark.

"You barely ate any dinner." Wren typically ate everything in sight. Tonight, she took about four bites of her food before calling it quits and holing up in our room.

"I'm just not feeling well." Her head tipped farther back against my shoulder. I brought my hand up to her forehead like Ma had done to me to see if I was actually sick or faking it.

"You don't feel warm."

"It's my stomach. It just hurts." She sighed heavily, adjusting her position slightly. "And my back has been killing me all day." She handed me the book and I leaned down, setting it on the other pile of books by the bed.

"It's this shitty bed." I'd had this bed my whole life. Wren rolled off my shoulder, moved down the bed, and hugged the wall. "Are you taking a nap?" We were supposed to go to the laundromat.

"I'm just so tired today." She sighed again, her voice groggy.

I stared at her, moved myself down the bed, and laid down next to her. I threw my arm over her waist and pulled her closer to me, nudging my leg between hers. She moved and adjusted until she got comfortable. Soon, her breathing leveled out.

I did my best not to move much. I wasn't tired but tried to convince my body to rest next to her.

I thought about her birthday last week and how happy she looked when Ma surprised us with small pieces of cake in the morning. We sang *happy birthday* to her, not worrying about anyone hearing us. Ma even brought her home an almost brand-new pair of shoes. You could see the tears in Wren's eyes when Ma hugged her. Ma cried too.

I had grinned at both of them like a fool. Ma was happy, Wren was getting happy. Gaining weight and getting closer to looking like a sixteen-year-old girl rather than the shell of a person she was when she came to us.

What would have happened to her if we hadn't met that day? Would I still be oblivious to her existence? The thought made me angry and choked me up. Wren meant so much to me in the span of the last five months.

I wasn't sure how long I had dozed off, my arm still slung over Wren. My leg was still trapped between her legs. I rolled away from her carefully and stretched. I got off the bed and headed to the bathroom. As I was walking, I felt something cold and wet on my leg. I looked down at my black sweats. In the dim light of the hall, I couldn't see anything. Once I was in the bathroom, I flipped the light on. Something shown on my pants. I touched the spot, and brought it up to my face it to see better. It shone red.

Blood.

"What the. . .?" I hurried back to our room. Wren was still sleeping, but that's when I saw it.

Wren's period.

I didn't know what to do.

Wren hadn't mentioned anything about it to Ma, unless it was in private. I hadn't pulled anything out of the bags when I was unloading things from the grocery store.

I closed the bedroom door quietly and went to the phone and dialed the diner's number.

"This is Tony's, Candy speaking."

"Hey Candy, it's Alex. Can I talk to my mom?" The words came out in a rush, and I tapped my foot impatiently.

"Oh hey, doll, yeah, let me get her for you."

"Alex?" My mom's voice sounded on the line.

"Ma," I started.

She must have heard the urgency in my tone. "Alex? Is everything okay?" The worry was thick in her voice; I never called her at work.

"Yeah, Ma, everything's fine." Then I paused. "Well, I don't know."

"What's going on?"

"Wren and I took a nap and when I woke up, I saw that she bled through. . ." The words felt weird coming out of my mouth.

"Bled through?"

"Yeah. . .through the sweatpants. . ." I knew what it was, learned about it in health class a few years ago. The halls erupted with jokes about women bleeding and how it was gross. I went home and Ma explained it to me better than the school ever did.

"Oh. . . OH. Oh dear." The meaning of my words finally clicked for her.

"Do you have anything for it here? I can't find anything." I'm whispering into the phone, not wanting to wake Wren up.

"No, baby, I don't have anything there. I haven't needed anything in a long time." The phone muffled for a minute, and I could hear her asking someone behind her a question.

"She's still asleep. I don't know what to do."

"Take the money for the laundromat and go get her some tampons and pads from the corner market. It's closer than the diner is and she shouldn't sleep like that."

"Do I wake her up?" I glanced back down the hall.

I could hear Ma hesitate on the phone.

"I don't want her waking up like this alone, but I also don't want to wake her up and then leave," I explained.

"Just let her sleep and run fast."

Without another word, I ran for the door, only to be jerked by the phone cord that I had managed to wrap around my chest while pacing. Untangling myself, I went into Ma's room, getting the coin purse where she kept quarters for the laundry days. I left the apartment, making sure to lock it behind me, and ran the eight blocks to the corner market. Once inside, I found the aisle.

This wasn't going to be as easy as I thought it would be. I stared blankly at the rows of different boxes, not understanding what I was looking at.

"Can I help you?" I jumped. A lady, who looked to be about my mom's age, watched me.

"Uhm, yeah." I gestured at the wall of products, too in a hurry to have the time to be embarrassed. "I don't know what to buy."

She laughed. "There are a lot of options. Did she tell you what she normally uses?"

"Uh, no." Awkwardly I said, "It's her first time."

"Oh, well. . ." She picked out a few things, telling me that Wren would need to read the directions, and if she didn't like one, to use the other.

"Is she cramping?"

"I don't know. She just hasn't felt good all day."

The lady took me to another aisle and handed me something called Midol. "This will help with her pain."

She took me to the front of the store, ringing everything up. "That will be $15.08." She looked at me, and I pulled out the coin purse, counting out the change.

I was short. I only had $11.75. I didn't have enough. I looked at the things, trying to figure out what to put back.

"Here, just take it." She bagged everything up. "Oh, take this too." She bent over the counter, and I stepped back, giving her room. She grabbed two chocolate bars. "This always makes girls feel better." She winked at me.

"I promise I will pay you back."

She waved me off. "I'm sure you will, sweetheart."

I stumbled into the apartment, sweat trickling down my back, with the plastic bag in hand. I was relieved to see that Wren was still asleep. I put everything in the bathroom, setting it on the kitchen sink before I went to Wren. I took a breath, trying to stop panting before I went inside.

I gently woke her up. Slowly she opened her eyes, rubbing them.

"Hey, how long did we sleep?" she asked sleepily.

"A while." I took a deep breath, trying to keep my face neutral. "I think. . ." I paused. "You started your period."

Her brow crinkled, confusion written all over her face. The moment she understood what I was saying, I grabbed her hand, gently tugging her out of bed. "Come on, let's get you to the shower."

After I got her another pair of sweats to wear, I went back to the bedroom and changed my own sweats. I shoved them into the hamper at the bottom. She came into the bedroom a short time later. Her hair was towel-dried, her head down. I felt like I'd made the right decision, not waking her up before I left. She would have just felt like crap the entire time, and there was no need for that.

"Hey." I waved her over to me, pulling her down gently to sit next to me. "How're you feeling?" She made a little noise. I chuckled. "It's okay. Don't worry about it."

"I ruined your sweats."

"Wren, don't you ever feel awkward about your body around me. There is no reason for that. Things like this happen and it's normal." We resumed our lying back on the bed together. She was quiet and I didn't like that she felt awkward.

I would do anything for her.

"Hey, Wren?"

"Hmm?"

"What happened to your dad?"

She was quiet for a bit, and I thought she might have fallen back asleep, but then she rolled over in my arms, staring up at the ceiling. I rose up on my elbow and watched her.

"We had just moved into the apartment and my mom had the flu or something." She laughed. "I remember my dad teasing her about it. 'Who the hell gets the flu in the middle of summer?' So, mom was sleeping inside, and dad took me outside and had me sit in the car while he was working on it. He promised me we would go get ice cream when he was done. So, I'm sitting in the passenger seat with all the doors open, singing along to the radio. I swear we were out there for what seemed like hours, and then I heard him say, 'Alright birdy, I'm done.' I had laid the passenger seat down, and when I went to get up, I grabbed something, and the car started to move and then you just hear my Dad scream. I had pulled the gear shift into neutral, and dad didn't have the parking brake on. It rolled over his hips and broke them."

She took a deep breath and continued.

"He was hospitalized for a few months. Had lots of surgeries and then physical therapy. Mom had to pick up more shifts at the cleaning agency she worked for. She worked lots of nights, so Dad and I would just lay in his bed and watch movies. He got better for a while, went back to work, but he was always in pain. Eventually the hospital stopped filling his prescription. It got really bad when he went on disability. He stopped going to therapy and just stayed home all the time. I don't know when it started, but he got his hands on street drugs. The day he died, I was sitting on the floor of his room behind some laundry baskets."

Wren's eyes glazed over as she spoke, like she was remembering it as she told me.

"I didn't understand what they were talking about then, but I do now. The guy that dad normally got his pills from had been picked up and was in jail. Dad was in a lot of pain and told Mom to go down to 32nd Street and just buy something from whoever would sell it to her. Mom argued with him, but he yelled at her.

Dad used to never yell. So, Mom got her coat from the laundry basket and saw me sitting there, and she said, 'This is all your fault.' I knew she blamed me. She wouldn't look at me anymore. After she left, I crawled into Dad's bed, and he said, 'Don't listen to her, birdy. Things have been rough for her too. But it will get better.' At some point I fell asleep tucked up next to him. I woke up to the smell of vomit. I sat up and tried to wake him, but he was already gone. He had thrown up on my head." She tilted her head back to look at me. "I don't know if he died of an overdose or drowned in his vomit."

I brushed her hair out of her face, giving my hands something to do. "It wasn't your fault."

She shrugged her shoulders. "It was, though. I pulled the stupid gear shift into neutral."

"You were just a kid, and from the sounds of it, I don't think your dad would want you to blame yourself." My heart ached for her and the little girl she used to be.

"No, he wouldn't. He never blamed me. Not once. When I was little, I tried to wait it out. Wait for her to forgive me, but she never did."

"What was she like before he died?"

"She wasn't the greatest mom. Dad and I annoyed her a lot. She always told me to be quieter or wanted me to go outside. She hated the rain because Dad never wanted me to be outside in it. Her and Dad would be cuddling on the couch, and I would sneak out after my bedtime. Dad would laugh and let me cuddle with them for a bit, but it always made her upset." She shook her head. "I don't think she ever wanted me."

This was something I couldn't relate to. I never felt unwanted by my parents. Even after Dad died, Mom never made me feel like she didn't want me.

"Do you miss her?"

"No," she said without hesitation. "There's nothing to miss. She was barely a mom to me. I don't miss her at all."

There's a loud knock on the door first thing in the morning. It startled Wren so badly that she launched out of my arms and curled herself into the corner of the bed, pressing herself against the wall.

"Wren, it's okay," I said calmly, trying to force the sleep out of my voice. "Kevin is in the hospital, your mom isn't around anymore," I reminded her.

Her green eyes shot around the dimly lit room, looking for the threat. Eventually, she peeled herself off the wall, her hand going to her chest and taking a deep breath.

"Sorry," she said sheepishly.

The knock sounded again and I got out of bed, shoving jeans on over the shorts I'd slipped into last night before going to sleep.

"Who the hell is that?" I asked, knowing she couldn't answer the question.

Wren pulled on the first pair of sweats she could reach and a hoodie. I watched her tie her hair into a quick bun on top of her head.

We both walked to the front door. Wren stood off to the side a bit, and I unlocked the door, opening it slightly.

"Good morning, sleepyhead," the feminine voice spoke, causing my stomach to drop.

Shit!

Amanda, Jon's younger sister, stood on the other side of the door, dressed in a skintight blouse, a bra that pushed her cleavage almost to her neck, and skinny jeans.

"Aren't you going to let me in?" She took a step closer to the cracked open door. I brought my arm up, bracing it against the adjacent wall, and rested my forehead against it.

What the hell was I going to do?

I could feel Wren's eyes boring into my back. I had been avoiding Amanda for the last few months. Today was the worst day possible for this. Not when Wren and I had plans to deal with her mother today.

"Hold on." I closed the door and turned to face Wren.

Wren's bottom lip was pushed out slightly, concern on her face. "What's up?"

I ran a hand through my hair, feeling like a two-timing piece of shit even though I wasn't in an actual relationship. I hadn't told Wren about Amanda because there was no reason to. We weren't in a relationship. We hooked up a few times at parties and she started coming around my place every so often.

Jon never cared so it wasn't an issue in our friendship.

Why the hell was she here so early?

Because you have been avoiding her at school, dumbass. Of course she would show up when she knew your fucking mom could be home any minute.

"That's Amanda. I. . .used to date her. . . Sort of." I didn't want to outright say I used to have sex with her. I didn't want to bring up any unpleasant memories. "I've been avoiding her at school, and it looks like I can't avoid her any longer. Do you mind if I talk to her real quick. . .alone?" I felt like shit. I was asking Wren to leave her own home, the home I'd drilled into her head that it was just as much hers as it was mine.

I watched a dozen different emotions cross her green eyes. Surprise, confusion, understanding. . .

"What about our plans?" she asked. Remnants of last night's conversation filtered through my head.

I couldn't forget.

"I promise I will be right next to the window. I won't let you do this alone."

She bit the inside of her cheek, before turning back to the bedroom, grabbing the book with some papers sticking out the sides of it. She stood in front of the door, opening it.

Amanda stood a few inches taller than her. The blonde didn't seem surprised that Wren was here, a smug smile on her face. I knew rumors spread quickly at school but had been ignoring them.

Wren brushed past me and Amanda. Amanda moved next to me, her arms crossing over her chest before she spoke. "Bye-bye."

"Knock it off, Amanda," I barked out, causing the blonde to jump. I never yelled. Never raised my voice to anyone, but I could tell she got the point.

Wren paused in her stride, glancing over her shoulder at Amanda, and I swear I could see a smirk on her lips.

CHAPTER 13
WREN

"WHERE THE FUCK HAVE YOU BEEN?!"

I looked up from the book I had been reading out in the playground. My mom stood there. She seemed older, her hair was visibly thin and greasy looking. I could still see the gauze wrapping her probably burned arm. She was wearing some ratty clothes; all her belongings had burned in the fire.

I wished the building wasn't standing anymore.

The only window in apartment 4A that hadn't been broken was my room's. Sitting out here on the playground, I had stared at it for a long while. Sometimes, I thought I could hear my own muffled screams coming from it. Staring at it made me remember the taste of them in my mouth. It's like a gag reflex, something I just couldn't seem to get rid of. The nightmares had gotten better. Less intense. I woke up in the morning, and I knew I'd had a dream, I just couldn't remember exactly what it was.

Sometimes I ran to the bathroom to throw up.

Alex said I needed therapy. I couldn't tell if he was serious or if it was a joke. I just laughed and told him I'd get some when we won the lottery. It's going to be Alex and I until the very end. That was the one thing in this entire fucked up existence I had, that I did know.

I had been preparing myself to see her again. She had been

sniffing around here a lot lately. Lloyd didn't have any vacancies from my understanding.

I glanced back toward the apartment, waiting for Alex to show up. Amanda had really thrown a wrench in our plan this morning. I tried to stay focused on the woman in front of me and not the one at Alex's home.

Our home.

The words rattled me for a second. Home. I had a place I considered home now. Somehow, just that thought comforted me. Added salve to the odd burn I felt about this stranger showing up. Gave me more strength to face her alone.

I turned my attention back to my mother. She didn't look as scary as I remembered. She looked small, frail. Kevin's money wasn't padding her pocket anymore to help her look like upgraded trailer trash. Even from this distance, she reeked of cigarette smoke and alcohol.

Now maybe she knew what it felt like to starve.

"What do you want?" I asked, pushing a bored tone. Trying to mask the slight tremor of fear that came from being this close to her.

"Excuse me?" Her voice was rough.

I almost laughed at her bewildered tone. I wasn't ten years old anymore. I talked back.

I leveled her with my gaze.

"What. Do. You. Want."

"You little fucking bitch." She took three steps toward me, and I stood, dropping the book to the ground. I was prepared to fight this time. I would hit back. I wouldn't ever let her lay a hand on me again.

"HEY!"

Alex's voice shot out like a bullet across the yard. He was in a full sprint heading our way in jeans, barefoot and without a shirt. Once he was close enough, I shook my head, and he stopped only a few feet away from her.

Alex never left me alone for very long, but this time I asked him to. I made sure to sit on the swing set closest to the new apartment. I wanted to lure her out. I wanted this to be over.

I actually needed something from her this time.

She wasn't going to live in my nightmares anymore.

"You fucking lay a hand on her and I'll—"

"Do nothing." I shook my head. "He won't do anything." I picked up my book, brushing off the bark. I took a few steps over to her, and like I knew she would, she held her ground. She had no reason to fear me. The only reason I was sure she did fear me was because I could tell someone about what she did to me. "But I," I lowered my voice, "will make sure you don't survive the next fire."

I watched as her eyes went wide, and it sent a thrill through me.

She was finally scared of *me* for once.

She didn't know if I was bluffing or not, and honestly, I wanted her to think I was the one to start the fire. I wanted her to think that I was capable of killing her.

Because honestly, I thought I could.

The results from the fire inspection seemed to point to the curtains hanging too close to the baseboard heater. The ones Mom had pinned up when we first moved in. Before Dad died.

I could barely remember who she used to be before he passed. I don't remember her being overly loving or caring. She made sure I ate, had clothes, and got me to school on time. She hadn't been a bad mom, but she hadn't been a great one either. Dad had always been the one to play with me and bring treats out. When he got home from a long day at work, he always made sure to read to me and teach me things. He let me hang out with him and included me whenever he could. Mom would be there, too, telling him to be careful with me, or to not let my dress get dirty.

"So, mother dearest," I made a circle around her, "you have two options: Go to the cops, tell them I started that fire. Or," I opened the book and pulled out the documents I had gotten from the courthouse, "you can sign these papers, relinquishing parental rights over me."

I was tired of worrying about every single time a cop passed us on the road. I was tired of wondering when we would get found out and they would take me back to my mother or put me in some group home. Letting her or someone else figure out a way to sell me to the next person. I did all the research I could into granting guardianship over to Gloria. I just needed my mom to sign these, and then Gloria to sign them. They technically made me a ward of the state, but Gloria would get a stipend to help take care of me, taken out of whatever social security my mom may or may not have.

"I'm not signing shit." She spat at me. Alex's face darkened, hands fisted at his side, and I wiped the spittle off my face, looking at my hand, seeing it glisten.

And then I slapped her.

My hand stung, and it felt good to finally hit back. Her hand went to her cheek, eyebrows raised in shock.

"Oh, you will sign this, because if you don't. I will go to the hospital; I will ask them to pull my rape kit out, pull out all the photos they took of my body and the report. I will tell them I want it run. You will be put away for sex trafficking, I will figure out what prison you are in, and I will find a way to make sure someone kills you in there. That's what they do to people like you. They will rape you with every object they can get their hands on and shove it up your cunt and your ass, just like you let Kevin and Lloyd do to me." I let all the hate and venom I had for her spill out. "Do you remember that last beating you dealt me?" Kevin had shoved his pencil dick in my mouth. We were in the living room and the door wasn't latched at the top. I just needed to get him down long enough to get out.

So, I bit down as hard as I could.

What I hadn't realized was that she was walking out of her bedroom directly behind me just as I did. She'd kicked me in my ribs with her boots three times before I was able to reach the lamp that had fallen over in the mess and hit her with it.

Alex moved directly behind her, startling her with his height. "Sign it," he hissed in a tone that I was grateful wasn't directed at me.

I put the papers over the book and handed her the pen I had been holding onto for this moment.

"Dude, where the fuck have you been?"

I tensed at Jonathan's voice. I had managed to avoid him since Wren moved in with us, only chatting with him between classes and not meeting him at our usual spots. Every time he invited me out, I declined. Trading time with him for more time with her.

I had been so consumed with making sure Wren was okay that I honestly hadn't thought much about Jon.

And after dealing with her mom over the weekend and Amanda's curiosity, I had no desire to deal with my best friend.

I turned to him and brought my hand up. He clasped it and slapped my back in our usual greeting. "Hey, man. Nothing, just been busy."

Jon's face fell. "Did I do something to piss you off?"

The guilt hit me then. Jonathan had been my best friend for years. He had always been there for me, and whenever I needed something, he handled it. There were times when he bought me shoes because mine didn't fit anymore. Or if he caught me grabbing something out of the lost and found, the next day he would have bought me some new hoodies or jeans.

It was embarrassing, but I appreciated it. I knew he did it because he cared, and he didn't try to make me feel bad about my situation.

I just didn't know how to tell him about Wren, or if I should. "No man, just have had some things happen, that's all." I closed my locker.

"Who's this girl you have been hanging out with, then? Did you get a girlfriend and just drop me or what?"

"No." I sighed, running a hand through my hair. Wren and I didn't have any classes together, and if I wanted to see her at school, I had to go out of my way. All her classes were in opposite halls from mine. "Dude, some shit's happened and it's complicated." I didn't want to tell him about Wren. I wasn't ready to share her with him yet.

"Well, you know I've always been there for you." He shoved his hands in his pockets. "I don't know why you wouldn't just talk to me about whatever it is that you have going on."

In reality, Jonathan and Chance had been hanging out a lot more lately, and I didn't want Wren around Chance. He could be a douchebag and was pretty shitty when it came to girls. Normally, I wouldn't care. I could easily ignore his shit, but I didn't want Wren around him. "It's not you," I admitted. "It's Chance." I glanced around for prying ears. "I just don't want him around her."

"I don't get it. What did Chance do?"

"Nothing." I sighed, feeling awkward and frustrated. "Everything. Look, Chance can be a dick sometimes. You have been around him at parties and shit, would you want your sister around him?"

Jon thought about it for a minute before he said, "Okay, I get it. So, this girl, she's like a sister to you or something?"

"What? No. She's not like a sister to me. She's. . ." I tried to find the words. What did Wren mean to me? "Meet me after last period at my locker. I'll. . .introduce you to her." I felt like an ass. Jon had never done anything to deserve me being cagey about her.

I just wanted to protect her. Or maybe I wanted to keep her to myself, but I wasn't going to stand here and analyze my feelings surrounding her right here in the middle of the hallway.

Wren

Everyone knew about me and my crazy mother the next day at school, thanks to Amanda. I should have stayed home like Gloria said. She was worried about the stress from seeing my mother again, but I just wanted to move on from it. Alex had told her about the incident the other day.

There were whispers in the hall, other kids stared at me while I was getting books out of my locker. It had been an awkward morning.

I tried to not think about Amanda and. . .whatever her and Alex used to do together. Or still did. I didn't want to think about it.

Alex and I didn't talk about sex.

I didn't want to talk about it. Sex was the worst thing to ever happen to me, and I didn't think I ever wanted to experience it again.

Not even if I loved someone.

It was lunchtime and I was sitting in the commons, waiting for Alex to get here. I needed to borrow the biology book. We had an open-book test today, and it was all luck that Alex and I had the class at opposite times of the day.

I would get a replacement soon. It was kind of a blessing; I hadn't been able to bring any of my books to school those weeks before the fire. After the fire, I was able to tell the teachers about the fire, bring in the newspaper clippings of it, and soon I would get new ones.

I also wouldn't have to pay for them.

Since I'd moved in with him, Alex made a point to find me at school, figure out my schedule, and sit with me at lunch. He was the only person who knew my situation.

"Finally, it's halfway through the day." Juniper sat down next to me, her dyed teal-colored hair a nod to her name. The bright color had gotten on a few of the teachers' lists, but she was so free-spirited and inherently good at academics that she never stayed on the lists long. "So, what's all this crap about your mom being crazy?"

That was another thing about Juniper; she didn't know when to not ask a question.

"I don't want to talk about it, Juni." I kept my voice low, avoiding the stares of the other kids.

Juni was sort of my friend. I helped her with homework and listened to her talk. I got all the school gossip that I really didn't care about through her. Juni talked a lot, and I think that annoyed others, but I liked not having to be the one doing the talking.

After Mom had signed the paperwork, it was like she blew a gasket. She just started screaming at the top of her lungs. Amanda had seen the entire thing. We hadn't noticed her watching us through the window from clear across the park.

We also didn't explain to her why I was walking into the house afterwards.

Alex just told her it was time for her to leave, and we left it at that.

"You may not, but everyone else is," she said in a sing-song voice. "Hey, how did Amanda of all people get involved?"

"She was at Alex's place when my mom lost it. Watched the whole thing, called the cops. It was a mess." I sighed. The cops took my mom away on a mental breakdown. Stress from the fire, the burns on her arms, her boyfriend still in the hospital. We spun a story the best we could.

I ran the paperwork to the courthouse to get it recorded first thing this morning.

"Amanda's dad works with a lot of police officers, so it makes sense she would jump to call them," Juniper said.

Juni didn't know much about my situation, and I never volunteered the information. As it was, I had always felt like an outcast, worried people would smell me when my mom wouldn't let me shower or notice my torn clothing.

"How do you know Amanda?" I had been curious about Amanda since I saw her. Alex had never mentioned he had a girlfriend, and I'd never asked. It hadn't crossed my mind that he was dating anyone.

"We have math together." Juniper laid her head on her arms and looked up at me. "What I want to know is when did you and Alex get so close?"

I hadn't told Juniper that I had been living with Alex the last few months. I didn't know how to tell her or want the implications that the situation would cause.

"He lives in the apartment next to mine," was all I said.

"Well, rumor says you guys hold hands on the way to school."

I look at her, confused. "Yes. We hold hands. Why is that such a big deal?"

Juni looked at me like I was an idiot. "Wren, only couples hold hands. People who are dating." She raised her brows as if that would explain everything.

"Well, Alex and I aren't dating; we are just friends, and friends can hold hands."

Just then, Alex dropped his bag on the table across from us.

"Hey there, Alexander." Juniper's head sprung up from the table. "I heard you had a wild first period." A Cheshire cat grin spread across her face. I looked between the two, confused. I didn't have any classes with Alex. Juniper and I only had biology together.

Alex dug into his backpack and pulled out his biology book. He picked up my replacement backpack and put it into it. "Juniper, mind your business," Alex said quietly, without annoyance in his tone.

"Huh? What do you mean?" I asked the two of them, and then it was there. Alex's knuckles were busted open, blood dried on them, a deep purple blooming across them.

"Alex!" I reached out and grabbed his hand. "What the hell?"

He pulled his hand away. "Don't worry about it." He brushed away my concern. "Hey, I want to introduce you to my best friend after school. Are you up for that?"

I could feel my brow furrow. Best friend?

"Yeah?"

"Okay. Meet me by the gate after school."

I rolled my eyes, shaking my head. I couldn't fight the smile. I tried to direct him back to the topic at hand, but Alex just brushed me off.

"You two are so cute together." Juni had her elbows on the table, her grinning face cradled in her hands. I rolled my eyes at her, trying to pull myself out of the memory.

"Juni. . . " I warned but could tell she wasn't listening.

"So, Alexander, why don't you tell me when you started dating my little Wren bird over here?"

"Juni!" My voice rose the angrier I got. "Alex and I are not dating! I am not going to date him! I am never going to date anyone!"

"Jeez, Wren." Juni lifted her hands, gesturing for me to calm down. "You don't gotta get your panties in a twist."

The day went on, and I found out through Juniper that Alex and some kid named Jacob had gotten into a fight. Juniper said Jacob had said something about me and my mom, and Alex took it into his own hands. I was glad it was Friday. Hopefully I wouldn't be the topic of gossip by Monday. I rubbed my face in embarrassment at my words during lunch. I could tell it was no skin off Juni's back. She really didn't care and was used to pushing people's buttons until they blew up at her. Alex, on the other hand, looked like I had slapped him, excusing himself from the table shortly after to head to class.

I was waiting by the school's front gate for Alex. Planning on apologizing to him. The look on his face stayed in my mind all day, and I felt horrible.

Juni had embarrassed me at lunch. Dating someone meant

having sex, and having sex with someone felt like I was saying what Kevin did to me wasn't okay.

It wasn't okay.

"Wren!"

I turned around and there was Alex, with his megawatt smile, as if this afternoon had never happened. I felt my own smile grow.

Behind him was a boy I didn't recognize. He had blond hair and bright, icy blue eyes. I looked down, away from his eyes. My stomach dropped.

It's not him. It's not him.

I fought to look up at him, school my face into an emotionless one. He was about Alex's height, maybe an inch shorter. He didn't look anything like creepy Kevin, but those eyes. . .

"Wren, this is Jonathan."

CHAPTER 15

ALEX

I DRIBBLED THE BALL BACK AND FORTH, MY MIND NOT really in the one-on-one game I was playing with Jonathan.

It was Sunday, and Jonathan's parents were on a weekend getaway. Wren and Ma were at the senior center helping with lunch today. I was supposed to go with them, but Jonathan called the house and asked to hang out, just the two of us today.

"Alex." Jon's tone was irritated. My mind hadn't been in the game this entire time. I may have been with him, but my mind was on Wren.

"I'm sorry, man." I passed the ball to him and he ran up the court, making a basket.

We were at his house, in his family's personal court. I looked down at my shoes that he had bought just for whenever I was here, because they didn't use outside shoes here. Something about not wanting to mess up the floor.

"It's fine. Your mind is on her, right?" He bounced the ball through his legs and passed it to me. I mimicked his moves before trying one of my own, passing it back to him.

"Yeah." I had talked to Ma about getting a part-time job for awhile. I wanted to make some money and buy Wren some things. Everything she had, as little as it may have been, had been burned up in the fire. Ma wouldn't have it though. I had pulled my head out of my ass right at the end of school, managing, with Wren's help, to raise all my grades to Bs and Cs. We were coming up on our senior year, and she wanted us to enjoy the summer before.

"How's she doing?" Jon asked, breaking away from the court to the side where he had a water cooler.

"Good. Her and Ma are working down at the senior center today."

Jon's face screwed up. "You know, I noticed that she wears a lot of your hoodies to school."

"Yeah." I caught the ball at my chest, dribbling toward the basket and taking a shot. "Most of her clothes burned in the fire so she doesn't have much. Her and Ma will look at the shelter's community closet to see if there is anything that will fit her."

I didn't miss the way Jon's nose scrunched in disgust. He knew my situation. He knew that we weren't rolling in cash like his family was. Even now, taking Wren in had taken its toll on my Ma, but she hadn't said anything.

I watched as Jon schooled his face and continued on like he wasn't revolted at the knowledge that we got our clothes used.

I tried to not be offended or upset by his reaction.

"You should bring her to my birthday party," he said then, and I paused. I had completely forgotten about his birthday, if I was being honest. He'd had a party every year since we'd met. It was always a big deal that he invited a ton of people from our school.

"I don't know if that's something she would be up for." I hesitated to jump on the offer. Wren was getting better, yes, but I didn't want to push her too fast out of her comfort zone. She set the pace and I followed.

"Well, the invite is open for her to come if that means you will go. You are allowed to have other friends, just don't forget about the rest of us." He slung his arm over my shoulder, and I grinned.

"I won't."

CHAPTER 16

WREN

"Are we going the right way?" I hoisted the tote bag up higher onto my shoulder. The hot July sun beat down on us, and even standing in the shade didn't help.

"Yeah, it's a few more blocks this way." Alex held his hand out to me, and I passed him the tote, trading for the towels. Jonathan had invited us to his house. We rode the bus as close as we could, but now we were on foot.

The incline got steeper the farther we got into the subdivision.

"Do you know who else is going to be there?" I asked. Jonathan had gotten pretty popular in the few short months before summer break. He was kind and very friendly to everyone.

"Not sure. All I heard was pool, and food. Plus, this is going to be better than hanging out at the city pool."

I didn't mention that I hadn't been to the city pool in years.

I got lost in thought and only focused on the ground to keep walking. The school year had ended, Alex and I had spent most of the summer at his place watching movies, reading books, going for walks. It had honestly been a dream.

Lost in my thoughts, I ran into Alex's back. "Sorry."

"We're here."

I looked up. We were at a gate with a pin pad. We couldn't even see the house through the stone fence and thicket of trees on the other side. I didn't even know there were places like this in the city. I was used to our little old apartment next to the train tracks.

"Is this really his house?"

Alex smirked down at me. "Yeah."

"Have you been here before?"

"All the time."

I didn't know anything like this could even exist. Alex hit the button, and a voice on the other side of the speaker spoke.

"Can I help you?"

"Hey, Burt, it's Alex. Can you come down to the gate to grab us?"

"We will send a cart to get you," the voice on the other end said.

The gates slowly opened, and we moved to the other side.

"Well, Toto, I have a feeling we're not in Kansas anymore," I muttered to him. He elbowed me gently.

"It will be fun. Trust me."

A few moments later we were in the back of a golf cart and whizzing up the path. The wind on my face felt nice for the short duration. It was a freaking stone mansion, with a circular drive and a fountain in the middle.

"Follow the path around back and you will see the party," the man, in what seemed to be some kind of golf getup, said, pointing to the side of the house.

We got out of the cart, and it zipped away.

"Party?" I said to him, and soon we could hear it. The music and voices grew louder.

Doing as the guy said, we followed the path and soon saw a big white tent with people all over the place. I stood with Alex, frozen. There were probably hundreds of people here, all wearing fancy clothes and chatting in groups.

"Hey!" Jonathan came bounding out from between some people. "You guys made it!"

"Happy birthday, man." Alex grinned.

"Thanks. Yeah. I told my parents I didn't want them to use my birthday as a social event, but they never listen." He was dressed in a button-down that had a few buttons open at his chest and swimming trunks underneath.

"Wait." I frowned, confused. "It's your birthday?"

"Yup!" Jon beamed, his blue eyes bright.

Alex hadn't told me it was his birthday, and a part of me felt bad that we didn't bring anything for him. I wasn't sure what we could have gotten him. From the looks of it, Jonathan could have anything he ever wanted.

Jonathan went to put his arm over mine and Alex's shoulders, but I ducked out of the way. He gave me a confused look but recovered quickly. "You guys came, that's all I wanted. Come on, there's another pool our friends are swimming in over by the gardens."

Jonathan said *our friends* like it was a no-brainer. I recognized a lot of people from classes; even Juniper was here. There were lawn chairs, and we claimed two of them, laying out our towels and setting the tote bag to the side. The property was surrounded by tall trees that provided a good amount of shade.

"Come on, Alex, the drinks are over here." Jonathan slung an arm over Alex's shoulders and tried to pull him along. It looked awkward. Alex had gotten taller in the last few months and stood a few inches taller than Jon.

Alex didn't budge. He looked at me. "What do you want to drink?"

I shrugged my shoulders, overwhelmed by the crowd, the music. Drink options? We always just had water. Alex just nodded at me and then followed Jon to some coolers on the other side of the pool. I scanned the crowd and caught Juniper's eyes, waving at her. She came around the pool and plopped down next to me.

"Hey!" She stretched her long tanned legs out in front of her. I was relieved to see someone else I knew here. "I was wondering if you guys were going to make it. Did you know that Jon was rich?" Juniper's hair was tied in a smooth bun on top of her head, and I wondered vaguely what would happen if she dunked her hair in the chlorine pool. Would it dye the pool the same green color?

"No. I had no idea. I didn't even know it was his birthday. He just gave us an address and said we would be swimming." I didn't mention that we hadn't even known that it was going to be more than just the three of us.

After Jon and I's initial meeting, Alex had walked us home and cautiously asked if I was okay with meeting him and how I felt about going to Jon's for a swim day.

I quickly realized that Jon was one of the more popular kids at school. It was something I had never paid any attention to. He was nice, funny, and seemed to be okay with including everyone in whatever they were talking about. He talked about the private school his parents wanted to send him to, but he hadn't wanted to transfer out of our school.

I looked across the pool and tried to remember some people's names. I watched as a girl pulled out a white bottle from her bag, which reminded me.

"Hey, do you have sunscreen we could borrow?"

"Yeah, it's in my bag. I'll be right back." Juniper ran off.

I had searched under the bathroom cabinet before we had left but couldn't find any. I was prone to burning and didn't want to start the summer off by being miserable. They didn't have central AC at the apartment, and once I burned, there wasn't much to do to cool off except take a cold shower.

"Here." A few seconds later, Alex startled me by placing a cold can of soda on my bare arm. "Thanks." I cracked the can open and took a long drink. It was cold and sweet. A nice treat that we rarely got.

Jon shot off and started talking about some guy named Chance from school who wasn't going to be here, but I didn't recognize the name and started to tune them out. Juniper walked back over and handed me the sunscreen before we both heard someone call her name from the other side of the pool. She shrugged her shoulders and headed over to them.

I turned my back to Jon and Alex. I had worn a pair of Alex's basketball shorts and had rolled the waistband down to accommodate our height differences. I wore one of his shirts that I tied back with a rubber band. I tugged the shirt off and used the rubber band to tame my unruly curls up in a manageable bun. Kicked off the shorts and put them on the lounge chair.

Underneath I wore a bikini that Ma had brought home for me one day. She found it at the shelter lost-and-found a few days ago. She volunteered there in her spare time; she got first pick when it was time to go through the bins. It was a black top with blue bottoms. They were a little big, and we had to safety pin them to fit me right, but it was a swimsuit. Something that Gloria didn't have to do for me, but at the mention of us going to the pool to stave off the hot summer days, she found a way.

The bruises finally were completely healed, only a slight discoloration here and there on my body, but it wasn't as bad. My hands shook as I squeezed out some sunscreen and worked it into my arms, stomach, and shoulders. I felt naked, but kept looking around at the other girls who were wearing bikinis.

This is what normal high school girls are wearing. This is okay.

But it felt wrong. I felt exposed.

I turned to offer Alex the sunscreen, nudging his arm. He and Jon looked my way. The sunscreen was plucked from my hand, and Alex was squeezing a dollop into his. I went to take it back from him, hold it while he was putting it on himself, but he stopped me, had me turn around, then worked it into my back.

"Your hair."

Automatically, I reached back and swept the loose strands at the base of my neck up. Alex's hands were warm and felt good while he was working the sunscreen in.

It fell quiet all of a sudden. I glanced over my shoulder again and realized that Jon had stopped talking. His eyes bounced between Alex's hands and me.

"So," Jon started, "how have things been, living with my guy?"

I glanced over my shoulder at Alex, who was still working in the sunscreen. He didn't look at me. The way Jon said *my guy* sounded weird. Like he was subtly claiming Alex as *his* friend.

"Good." I didn't know how much Jon knew about my situation, so I kept it short. Alex had told me that they had been best friends for a long time and I had decided then that, if Alex trusted him, I could trust him too.

I kept my mouth shut most of the time Jon was around. I was better at listening than I was at talking. Alex had always been the more approachable one. People had been asking us how we became so close. Alex always intercepted their questions easily.

We both lived in the same apartment. We both took the same route to school. These answers appeased just about everyone asking. I never knew what to say or how to answer them. There was never a label good enough for what we were. Alex seemed to always say the right thing.

Jon shifted on his feet, eyes on me. I could see he wanted more of an explanation from us. I tried to muster up something to give him. Some answer that would satisfy his curiosity. I looked from him to Alex. Alex and Jon had been friends for so long, and I didn't want to put a wedge between them.

"Th-they were really great about taking me in after the fire."

"So how is your mom doing?"

"Her mom is still in the hospital." Alex threw an arm over my shoulder, tucking me into his side. "Wren lived close by, so we would hang out together a lot. Now she's living with us. She's my girl." Alex shrugged nonchalantly. Before Jon could ask more questions, Alex directed his attention to me. "You ready?" He grinned, a mischievous glint in his eye.

His girl?!

The words shocked me. I wasn't sure how to feel about them. Like he was claiming me, and I wasn't sure how I felt about it.

"Ready for what?" I asked, puzzled, the thoughts still running wild in my head.

I squealed when I realized what he was doing. He ducked down, throwing me over his shoulder, and launched us into the pool together.

The chill of the water washed away the awkward encounter. We both came up for air. Alex's arms were around me, holding me with ease above the water. Jon stared at us from the edge of the pool, an odd look on his face.

Was he...mad?

"You okay?" Alex's brown eye were on me, our heads ducked close together. "Sorry for the 'my girl' thing. I know you don't want to date anyone, so I just said it so maybe some of the guys will leave you alone."

I felt my cheeks heat. "Oh. It's okay. I just don't know how much you want people to know about the situation." It wasn't a new revelation that I felt like I was imposing on them. I watched as water dripped from his hair and onto his shoulders. The beads ran down and caught on his necklace. I reached up, tracing the cord, surprised he was wearing it in the pool.

"Wren, you aren't a situation." He moved me into one of his arms, the other treading water to keep us afloat. "You can tell anyone whatever you want. It's your life. I'm not ashamed of having you with us, and neither is Ma."

The day went by fast. We played games in the pool like chicken and volleyball, ate hot dogs and hamburgers until we couldn't move, and had soda and juice.

It was just an overall good day. A day to relax and enjoy the summer.

Alex was still in the pool playing water volleyball with a few other guys. They had brought in a net and put it across the pool. I laid out on the lounge chair under a big umbrella, a soda in my hand.

"You look like you are enjoying yourself." Jon sat down on Alex's lounge chair next to mine. He was just in his navy-blue swimming trunks, the water beads falling off him.

"Do I?"

He laughed, shaking the water out of his blond hair. "Yeah. You do." We both turned our heads looking at Alex.

I found myself enjoying watching Alex. He was competitive, his jaw set, a determined look on his face as he moved through the water to get to the ball.

"You and Alex got close fast." His eyes were back on me. "Do you like him?"

I was taken off guard by his question. "Of course I like him," I stated, confused.

He laughed again. "I mean, do you want to date him?"

Date him? I hadn't thought about it. I liked looking at him. I liked living with him and Gloria.

"The only reason I ask is because my sister *likes* him," Jon explained.

"I didn't know you had a sister." I tore my eyes away from Alex to look at Jon. He nodded at me.

"Yeah. She's a year younger than us. Has always had a crush on him." He looked back to Alex. "I thought they were going to start going out last year. Alex liked her, too, but then he disappeared for a while, and now he's with you." His eyes were on me again. "So that's why I was asking if you liked him. If you do, that's great. I want my best friend to be happy, but you know, as her older brother, I want to protect my sister from heartbreak."

No, I didn't know. I didn't know what it was like to have a sibling who you wanted to take care of. I barely could take care of myself. I did the best I could with what I had, but my sense of self preservation wasn't strong.

I had almost curled up and just died.

I had wanted to, but I kept getting back up.

I swallowed hard. "Alex and I are just friends. He doesn't see me like that." I was grateful for what Alex said to me earlier, but it felt muddled, like even though he was giving me something to hide behind, I was holding him back from what could be.

"Jon!"

He straightened and looked over his shoulder.

"Hey, Amanda."

I tensed at seeing her again. She had a bikini on and a white cover tied over her hips. She was tall and slender. Seeing them stand side by side, it was obvious that they were related. They both had the same warm blonde hair and icy blue eyes. Everything was clicking into place now.

Amanda was Jon's sister.

Amanda and Alex had had something going on between them before I came into his life, and since me, Alex hadn't been seeing her anymore.

What did that mean?

"I got that stuff for you." She handed him something. I thought I heard the jingle of keys. "Where's Alex?" She looked around, her eyes giving me the once over before Jon pointed to the pool where Alex was jumping to spike the ball over the net. Her face lit up, and she untied her skirt.

"Alex!"

Alex turned just in time for her to jump in, splashing him.

I watched the way he laughed, and they both started chatting animatedly.

I hadn't seen this side of him with her back at the house.

It doesn't matter. He can see whoever he wants.

"I guess he might still like her," Jon said. I felt his eyes on me as I watched them. There was a knot in my chest, and I didn't know what to make of it. Did I disrupt Alex's life with my problems?

"I heard you lost all your things in the fire." Jon stood. His movements made me sit up, feeling uncomfortable with the way he towered over me.

"Uh, yeah," I said as I swung my legs over the side of the lounge chair. "Nothing was salvageable."

"I got you some things."

"You what?" I tilted my head up to look at him.

He held his hand out to me. "Come on, I'll show you."

I stared at his hand, looking back to Alex, who had hoisted Amanda onto his shoulders, and they were playing chicken with some other people. Taking a deep breath, I took Jon's hand and let him guide me through the crowd of people and into his home.

The house was like a mansion. All white marble and expensive-looking decorations. Our footsteps echoed as he guided me to the front of the house and off to a room on the side. There were several bags of things. I pulled my hand from his. It felt odd to hold someone else's hand.

"You got all this for me?"

"Yeah. I took a guess that you were about my sister's size. You are shorter than her, though." He shoved his hands in his pockets, shrugging like this was no big deal. I couldn't remember the last time I had gotten brand-new clothes.

I stared at everything, feeling overwhelmed.

"Look." He moved to a bag, opening it up and pulling out a floral dress. "My sister has pretty good taste I think, so she picked everything out." He held the dress up to me. I took it, marveling over the soft fabric.

"Do you like it?" He tilted his head to catch my gaze. "Look, Alex had mentioned my sister was a bit of a brat towards the end of the semester and I talked to her about it. Picking out these clothes is her way of apologizing." He shrugged a little. "Amanda doesn't know how to verbally apologize for things. She takes after our dad in that regard."

"Jon, this is. . . It's beautiful. . ." I didn't know what else to say or how to react to this. I didn't feel like I deserved them. "I just don't understand why you two would do this?"

Yes, Amanda had been kind of rude that day, and then talking at school about what she witnessed had sucked, but I hadn't thought much of it.

"Well, honestly, I noticed you wear Alex's shirts a lot, and he told me you lost all your stuff in the fire, so I just wanted to do something nice. You have been through a lot and deserve it."

"Jon, this is too much."

"No, it's not." He laughed, coming to stand in front of me. "Wren, I don't know if you haven't noticed yet, but my parents have more money than they know what to do with. This is nothing. Just take it and enjoy it." He moved to lean against a couch. "Look, Alex is my best friend, and between you and me, I haven't seen him much since you came into the picture."

I could feel myself shrinking inside. The one thing I never wanted Alex to do was lose his friends because of me.

He continued, "And I'm not trying to say that to you to make you feel bad, but if you are going to be in his life, then you are going to be in my life too." He smiled wide. "I just don't want to lose my best friend. So it would help if you could be friends with Amanda and I also."

Hell no.

The thought of being friends with Amanda was not something I was open to.

"What are you guys doing?"

Alex's accusatory voice sounded behind me, and I turned, the dress still in my arms. His eyes moved from me to Jon to the dress. He was dripping water all over the floor like he had jumped out of the pool and run straight inside.

"Hey, man," Jon piped up, straightening from his spot by the couch. "I got you guys some things." Jon moved to the bags and picked one up that was overflowing.

Alex took it hesitantly, pulling out a sweatshirt and some other things.

"Thanks. . ." Alex glanced up at me, his eyes skating down my form before he set the bag down.

"Amanda picked those out for you since she knows all your

favorites." He waved to the other bags. "I also got some things for Wren since you mentioned she didn't have anything."

"Wow, Jon, that's really great of you." A smile split Alex's face as he walked over to the bags. His mood switched so fast that I had to really watch him. One second, I thought he was angry, the next he was his normal self.

He picked up a bag and pulled out another dress, and held up some jeans and shorts. "This is great, Wren." His warm brown eyes were on me, and all I could do was nod.

Jon ended up giving us a ride home. Gloria had already left for work. Alex carried all the bags into the house himself, not letting me help. I slipped into the bathroom and showered, cleaning myself of the sunscreen and chlorine. I emerged wearing some shorts and a tank top, my hair still damp.

Alex had laid out all the clothes in a neat pile on the bed. There was only one small bag sitting on the bed. He stood there, staring down at the pile, a hand running through his hair.

"I. . . Uhm. . . I wanted to get all the bags down to the dumpster before Ma saw. She sometimes feels guilty when she sees that Jon has bought stuff. But, uhm. . . I figured I'd let you go through that last bag."

Confused, I walked farther into the room, about to look in the bag.

"I'm gonna go shower." Abruptly, Alex left the room.

I reached into the bag, feeling a scratchy material. "What the. . ." I pulled out what looked like a scrap of cloth. Picking the other end of it up, I realized what it was.

A thong!? His sister picked out a thong for me?

It was a scrap of bright pink lace. I sneered at the offending clothing and dropped it on the bed. I turned over the bag, and out fell more scraps of pinks and purples, cream white and blue.

I would rather go commando than wear half this crap. I scooped everything up and shoved it back into the bag before hauling it outside and tossing it into the dumpster.

Yeah fucking right, Amanda and I would never be friends.

Back inside, I hung up what I could in the closet, the rest I folded and put on the closet floor where there was room.

I sat cross-legged on the bed, a book open. When I heard the shower turn off, I tried to keep my composure. It took like what seemed forever for Alex to come back into the room, dressed in his favorite sweats and a T-shirt. He stood there, a damp ring around his shoulders from where his hair was dripping.

"Your hair is still soaked," I stated.

"Yeah, I forgot my towel." He moved to the closet where we normally hung them up. Pulled his out and started drying his hair.

I tried not to look up at him. Still embarrassed, I flipped through the poisonous plant book absently.

"So... uh. . ." He started.

"Nope." I stopped him. "I threw them away, and we aren't talking about it."

CHAPTER 17

WREN

ALEX AND I SAT IN A BOOTH ALONG THE BACK WALL OF Tony's, the diner that Gloria worked at. The diner was old, and it smelled like pancakes and grease. I was wearing cutoffs with a black tank top and had to keep adjusting to peel the backs of my legs off the fake leather seat.

"Here you two go." Gloria set down two milkshakes in front of us. Strawberry for me, chocolate for Alex.

"Thank you," we said in unison, bringing the bendy straw to our lips and sucking deeply.

It was a Friday night, and the diner was moderately busy. It was August and hot in the late summer months and the apartment just wouldn't cool down. We were escaping here tonight for a while. Gloria rolled her eyes when I asked for a coloring page and some crayons, but she gave them to me anyways, and I colored the pig with the cowboy hat that said *Tony's* across the top of it. She even gave one to Alex, who worked on his for a bit before folding the page into a football, and now we were flicking it back and forth. Each holding our hands up like they were goalies and trying to see who could make the most and not get our eyes poked out.

"So, where are you two going tonight again?" Gloria sat down next to me in the booth between tables. I laid my head on her shoulder, and she brought her hand up, cupping my cheek. I could faintly smell cigarettes on her. I had been smelling it more and more lately. I wasn't sure if she just started smoking or if it was something I hadn't noticed at first.

I loved Gloria.

I loved Gloria more than I'd loved anyone else ever before. She was the mother I never had. She braided my hair for me and then taught me how to braid it myself. Every Sunday she volunteered down at the shelter and would bring things home for me. Everything she said included me. Even though I felt like a burden to her, another mouth to feed when she could already barely feed Alex and herself.

The only thing that made it better was she finally started to receive checks for my care.

"There's a party that a bunch of our friends are going to. It's at Teddy Clark's place," Alex said around a spoonful of milkshake.

It amazed me how honest Alex always was with his mom. From the beginning, he never lied to her. As far as I could tell, he was always up-front and honest with her. I thought back to his confession of not wanting to ask for more from her. He didn't want to see her working more.

Alex and I had tried to get summer jobs. We wanted to contribute more, be able to get Gloria something special for her birthday and Mother's Day, but Gloria wouldn't hear of it.

You two will work when you are adults. Once you start working, it never stops. I want you two to enjoy your last few summers.

"Well, you two be careful and look out for each other." She kissed the top of my head before scooching out of the booth, kissing Alex's cheek, then pointing to him with a hitched brow. "Watch after our girl."

Alex grinned, his eyes sliding over to me. "I got her, Ma, don't you worry about that."

We could hear the music from Teddy Clark's driveway. He and his parents lived on the outskirts of town in an old two-story farmhouse. His parents had gone on some kind of vacation, so this gave him the opportunity to throw a party.

The gravel crunched under our feet as we walked up the driveway.

"I'm nervous." I started to chew on the side of my thumb. "I've never been to a party before."

"Stop it." Alex grabbed my hand, preventing me from chewing on my thumbnail. "You have been to a party and it's going to be fine. It's like a giant hang out with music."

"That was just Jon's *birthday* party. That's not a high school *drinking* party."

I didn't know what to do or how to act at something like this. I stopped in my tracks, causing Alex to stop. "Let's not do this."

His thumb caressed the back of my hand in small circles, a thoughtful look on his face. "If you really don't want to go, we won't."

I knew he meant it. I knew if I told him I wanted to go home, go back to the apartment and hang out in our room, reading or playing another game of Uno, he would. He would take me home and not say another thing about it.

There was a thought that tickled the back of my mind. Did Alex go to parties before me? What was his life like before he brought me into it? Did he hang out with friends and drink and just relax? Who was he before me?

These were answers I wanted, but didn't know how to ask.

"Just for a little while," I conceded.

A smile spread across his lips. "You don't have to have to drink. If you do, pace yourself." He tugged me along and we weaved between the parked cars up to the porch.

"Hey, Harper!" Some guy in a gray beanie slapped Alex's shoulders as we walked up the steps. "It's been a while, where ya been, man?"

"Hey," Alex greeted. I stood halfway behind him. The guy looked at our joined hands, then back up to us. "This your girl?"

"Yeah." He tugged me up next to him. "This is Wren."

The guy nodded at me, not really seeming to care. Alex was still letting me hide behind those words, *my girl*. The more I heard him say it, the more I liked it. There was something about belonging to someone. Someone wanted me and that felt good, even if they were just pretty words for right now.

"Booze is in the kitchen."

Alex weaved us through the house, his hand tight on mine. People were gathered in the living room, some dancing, some standing in corners talking. I saw one couple on the couch making out.

Once we were in the kitchen, Alex asked, "Do you want a drink?" He had to lean in close and almost yell to be heard over the loud house music.

I looked at the mess of liquor bottles on the counter and the punch bowl filled with red liquid. I could feel my shoes sticking to the floor. "Sure."

He ladled the juice into a red solo cup, taking a sip, and he made a face. "Woah. It's really spiked." He filled up another cup halfway and then cracked a can of sprite, filling it up the rest of the way. "It's cut, so it shouldn't hit as hard." He handed it to me. I took a sip; it was sweet, bubbly, but the alcohol still hit harder than I expected. "Just pace yourself."

"Hey, pour me one of those." Juni was there with her bright, freshly-dyed turquoise hair. She looked at me. "I didn't know you were coming." Her shoulder bumped against mine. Juni was beautiful. Her makeup was fully done, with dark liner around her eyes and eyeshadow to match her teal hair. There was a little part of me that was jealous of Juni.

I had never had makeup before. I vaguely remembered playing with some of my mother's when I was little. A ghost of a memory brushed my mind, of my father's face. I got my black, wavy hair from him, along with my green eyes. I'd always thought I got my fair skin from my mom, but the longer I lived with the Harpers, the more my skin started to warm with color. I had filled out this summer. After the embarrassment of getting my period for the first time, I spent a few days at our local library using their computers for research.

Apparently, malnutrition can delay a girl's period and puberty all together. The birth control and massive amounts of Plan B my mom had made me take hadn't helped either.

"Here I am." I tried to say it with more confidence than I felt. I felt like a fish out of water, like everyone knew I didn't belong here.

Juni could sense my unease. "After a few drinks of Teddy's punch, you will loosen up." She shimmied at me in tune with the music, reaching around me for her drink from Alex.

"Cheers!" Juni prompted us to raise our cups, and we did, all taking a drink together.

"Do you want to dance?" Alex took my hand and started to tug me to the living room.

"What? No. I don't know how to dance." I shook my head.

Alex chuckled. "I'll teach you."

My groan couldn't be heard over the music. He tugged me to the living room, where there were groups of people dancing. I didn't recognize the song.

I had never been one to dance, not even alone in my room.

Alex and Juni moved us into our own tight circle. They both started to dance on their own, Juni moving her hips and bringing her arms above her head. Alex's moves were all in his shoulders and arms. I think he was copying some old eighties dance with the peace signs over his eyes.

They both had big smiles on their faces while they danced around me. I was smiling too. Alex's moves had me giggling.

"Alex!" a girl shouted from out in the living room. I couldn't see her through the crowd, but Alex did. He tilted his head.

"Go, I got her." Juni threw her arm over my shoulder. I looked back to Alex and gave him a nod. I didn't want him to have to babysit me all the time. I would be fine without him for a little while.

He looked between us before nodding. "I'll be right back." He took my hand for a moment, squeezing it lightly. I watched as he pushed past a group of people and disappeared into the crowd.

"Are you two dating yet?"

She said it so loud that I looked around, worried other people overheard her. The last thing I needed was to be the topic of the rumor mill again.

"Juni!" I shook my head. "No, Alex and I are not dating."

She pursed her lips and looked past me. "That's too bad. I hear Amanda is trying to hook up with him tonight." She sighed dramatically. "I guess there's nothing stopping him then."

My cheeks flushed and Juni laughed at me. Now I realized that the voice was Amanda's. "Come on, I have my bag stored in Teddy's room upstairs." She tugged me through the crowd to the staircase. With the bedroom door closed, the music was muted.

"What are we doing, Juni?" I sighed the words out.

She motioned for me to sit on the edge of the bed.

"Can I put makeup on you?" She pulled a small zipper bag out of her purse. "Just a little." She held up a small pencil looking thing. "If you don't like it, you can take it off in the bathroom. No harm done."

Without much reservation, I agreed to it, closing my eyes as she brushed something over the lids, adding liner and then prompting me to look up while she attempted to put mascara on my lashes.

"Done." She opened a small compact to show me.

"Woah."

"I know! Right? It was just the right amount." She clapped happily while I stared at my reflection. She'd easily created a smoky look that made my eyes pop. "Here." She handed me a tube of lip gloss. "Just a little and you are good to go."

"Wow, Juni. You should go into beauty when we get out of school."

"You think?" She hummed a little as I put the gloss on. "Maybe I will."

We downed our drinks and then headed downstairs. I could feel the buzz start; it did exactly as she said it would, loosened me up. Juni and I melted into the crowd with our drinks refilled and started dancing, our bodies grinding up against each other in rhythm of the music. Juni guided me, holding my hips and showing me what to do. I mimicked her.

Hands came around my waist and they pulled me back into a hard body. Juni pushed closer to me and put her hands over me. Eventually the song ended, and we were a laughing, giggling mess.

"Having fun?"

I tipped my head up and looked into icy blue eyes. I froze. I had thought Alex was the one behind me.

"Jonathan?"

"The one and only." He tipped his head, looking into my empty cup. "You girls need a refill?"

"Yes!" Juni plucked my cup out of my hand and handed it to him, then shooed him away. "Girl, did you see the way he looked at you?"

"What? N-no." I huffed out a nervous breath. "Juniper, why wouldn't you tell me it was Jon behind me?"

"What? Come on, we were having fun and he loved having you rub up against him. I think he's into you." She continued to dance as she waggled her brows at me.

"Jesus Juni, stop it. We are just friends. Barely. Alex and him are friends. I'm just kind of there." It was hard to get the words out. I scanned the living room, looking for Alex.

"You could be more than frieeends."

"Girl, he had his sister buy me thongs," I said, the words coming out unfiltered. "Absolutely not."

"Here you ladies are." Jon doled out two red solo cups between Juni and me. We both straightened. I gave her eyes, silently telling her to keep her mouth shut.

"Juuuniiiii." Teddy did some kind of dance move toward her

that involved thrusting his hips, getting her attention. "I've got something for you out back."

There was a smell of weed that chronically traveled with Teddy. He grabbed Juni by the hand, and they headed toward the back door without another glance. We watched her go, and I hid inside my cup of punch. Awkwardly, I smiled up at Jon before trying to squeeze my way out of the living room.

"Hey, where do you think you're going?" His hand was gentle around my wrist.

"Oh, uhm. . . I was going to go find Alex." I took a drink of the punch; an overwhelming taste of liquor hit me.

Oh shit, is this straight vodka?

I went to pull the cup away from my lips, but then there's his hand. Jon tipped the cup up farther back, causing me to take a big swallow. I did my best to choke it down, trying not to spit it out all over his neat clothes.

"There you go." He nodded his approval. His thumb brushed the corner of my mouth, then he pressed it to his tongue. "Don't want to waste a drop of that."

I froze, a blush creeping up my neck. Juni's words echoed in my head.

Is Jon into me?

"Well." Fingers ran up the center of my palm before he laced our fingers together. "How about I get one more dance." His arm came around my waist, pulling me flush against his chest. He trapped our hips together and swayed. My feet tripped and stumbled as he took the lead. He guided my hand around his neck. "Shh. Just relax, follow me."

We danced and swayed in the crowded room. Eventually the tension left my body and the mix of alcohol loosened me up enough to not be a nervous mess with him. Finally, when the third song ended, I stepped back from him.

"I should really go find Alex." I was hot; I could feel the perspiration building between my shoulder blades.

Jon nodded toward the stairs. "I think I saw him go upstairs."

I looked over my shoulder at the stairs. "Thanks."

"Come back for another dance." His smile was unreadable, or maybe it was the alcohol. "I like dancing with you."

I headed upstairs slowly, my grip on the railing tight. I pushed the first two doors open, but no one was there. The last room on the left, the one Juni and I were in earlier, was slightly ajar. I pushed it open a little more, my eyes adjusting to the dark. There was movement by the floor of the bed, and then I froze.

Amanda was on her knees, eyes closed. I could just make out the bobbing of her head. Alex was leaned up against the corner of the bed, his side profile presented to me, head lulled back, eyes closed. Pleasure evident on his face.

When I looked back at Amanda, it wasn't her anymore.

It was me.

The world tilted on its axis and he had his hand fisted in my hair, my hands duct taped behind my back, choking on him. My chest tightened and I couldn't get in a deep breath.

I can't breathe.

I pulled the door shut and ran.

Back downstairs, I pushed through the crowd of bodies until I got out the back door, the muggy air finally hitting my face. I struggled to bring in a deep breath.

"Wren?"

I heard someone behind me, but the panic put me in a vice grip, and I still couldn't breathe. My hands clawed at my throat, wanting to tear it open so I could just get a breath.

Someone pounded on my back, and it startled me so much I was finally able to drag in air.

"You alright, Wren?" Jon, another boy, and Juni were all staring at me, wide-eyed.

"I think she's having a panic attack," Juni said.

"I-I'm fine," I stuttered out.

"Sure you are. Chance, can you go grab her a drink?" Juni's hand was on my back now and I didn't have the fight in me to ask her to stop. I couldn't tell her that being touched just made it worse.

I thought I was going to get through tonight without having a freaking breakdown.

"What happened, girl?"

I shook my head, bending over and holding my knees. "Nothing. . . It just got. . .way too fucking hot in there," I lied.

The smell of weed hit me hard, and I finally looked up and noticed the blunt in her hand, Teddy hovering a few feet behind her, watching us.

"Are you okay?" She took a drag, blowing the smoke away from me.

I nodded at her. "Just. . .peachy." My words were stretched, and I teetered on my feet.

"Woah, there." A hand at my back steadied me.

"Here." I accepted the refill from Chance.

"Did you find Alex?" Jon asked.

"Mhm," I hummed. "He's. . .busy." I took in another breath, but the air was mingled with smoke and a cough ripped through me.

Jon laughed, seeming to know my meaning. He waved his hand through the air, trying to bat away the smoke that was coming from Juni and Teddy. "Yeah, I bet he is. Come on." He and Chance steered me away from Juni to the opposite corner of the yard. There was a plastic table with matching white chairs. Jon eased me into the seat, taking one across from me, and Chance stood to the side, looking down at his phone.

I took a drink and winced. The alcohol seemed stronger in this one.

"So, I guess that answers that question for me." Jon relaxed back as much as the flimsy chair would allow.

"What are you talking about?" I pushed my hair out of my face.

"Whether or not you two are dating," Jon said, and I looked up at him.

I rolled my eyes and set the cup down on the table. "Alex already told you that we aren't dating."

"No. He just avoids the question every time. It's never, 'No, we aren't dating.' It's always a change of topic."

"Well, maybe it's an annoying question."

Jon laughed. "Oh, so there is some bite in you."

I didn't have any bite in me. I was just reeling from what I'd witnessed, my stupid brain putting myself into a situation that I wasn't even in.

Not anymore.

Never again.

I looked down at my drink again and wished it was water. Jon seemed to read my expression and stood.

"Chance, you should have gotten her water, you idiot."

"How the fuck was I supposed to know what to get her? We are at a party," he said, as if that explained everything.

Jon smacked the back of his head, and Chance whined.

"I'll get you a bottle of water. Be right back." Jon shoved his hands in his pockets and walks off.

I watched him until he disappeared through the door. Chance was now sitting in the chair across from me.

"So, you're the girl Alex has been hanging out with now."

"That's me." I stated, not sure how else to respond to him. I wished Jon hadn't left me with this guy. I didn't know him. I brought the drink back to my lips. I looked into my cup, I could smell the strength of the liquor, but the sips came easier now. I couldn't taste the alcohol, only the sweetness of the punch. It pushed the memory away, let me feel like I wasn't in my abused body anymore.

It never happened to this Wren.

Chance tucked his phone away. "What grade are you in?"

"I'll be a senior this year."

"Interesting." He leaned back in the chair, crossing his arms. "We're in the same grade, but I hadn't noticed you before."

I held back the urge to roll my eyes.

"Why'd you freak out in there? Having a bad trip or something?"

I leaned forward, resting my elbows on my knees, dropping my head between my shoulders. The cool air felt good on my clammy skin. "There were just too many bodies in there," I answered. I didn't know this guy, but I didn't want him to think I was weird, and I really didn't want this to get back to Alex.

I wanted to move on and live a normal teenage life. This was something normal kids my age had done. Parties were normal. I had half a mind to go over to Juni and try the weed she was smoking.

But I would never try drugs.

My dad used them to lessen his pain, and I didn't want to follow in his footsteps.

Chance leaned forward, mirroring my position, his own drink in his hands. I felt his eyes roam over me, and suddenly I was thankful for the alcohol in my system, giving me confidence to not shrink away from his gaze.

I stared at him for a minute, my brain fuzzy. My eyes looked over him in appreciation. Chance was cute in a boyish way. His blond hair was cut short. He was wearing a seafoam-green collared shirt that made his eyes pop with a stronger hazel color, with a pair of light wash jeans. I felt like this was the first time I'd noticed how good-looking a guy could be.

Lies. You've noticed Alex.

The alcohol seemed to be affecting more than just my coordination, allowing wayward thoughts of Alex to come to the front of my mind, but I tried to push them back and focus on the boy sitting in front of me.

I realized I'd been staring at him a little too intently. He leaned in closer, and I froze. He was a breath away now and he paused, his eyes staring into me. His soft palm slid along the back of my neck, and panic once again gripped me.

I put my hand to his chest, halting him. "Stop!"

"WHAT THE FUCK ARE YOU DOING?" Alex's voice boomed behind me.

I fastened my belt back in place. The water was running in the ensuite bathroom, Amanda rinsing her mouth out. I ran a hand through my hair and leaned against the bed. Amanda had pulled me aside and wanted to talk. I entertained her just long enough for her to pull me upstairs. Then I was in a position I hadn't intended on being in tonight.

I scrubbed my hand down my face. I felt like an ass.

Wren does not want to date you. You did nothing wrong.

I would be reminding myself this over and over. Since the lunchroom conversation, I'd stopped letting myself think that Wren and I would ever be something more. I didn't treat her any differently than I had before. I still welcomed her into my arms whenever she wanted to be there. I just had to remind myself that this would always just be this. A friendship. A platonic friendship.

Wren had been through so much that it only made sense that she would never want to be in a relationship. In a position to have sex with someone.

No shit, dumbass.

Amanda stood in the doorway of the bathroom, wiping her mouth with a towel. "Well, that was fun."

I rolled my eyes, shaking my head. "Amanda, we shouldn't

have done that." It felt wrong to be up here with Amanda when I had just left Wren downstairs.

"What do you mean?" She batted her eyes at me, trying to force the look of innocence. "You didn't do anything that I didn't want."

I shook my head at her again. "That's never going to happen again." I had stopped anything that could have happened between us the day that she called the police. I couldn't trust her to keep her head down on my side of town.

Her face fell and she crossed her arms, knowing exactly what I was thinking. "Alex, what would you have had me do in that situation? She was literally screaming at the top of her lungs like a crazy person."

"I had it handled."

"Yeah, well, you shouldn't have been the one to handle it. That was a police situation. She had a mental breakdown right there."

Amanda wasn't going to understand. She didn't grow up where we did. She didn't understand that you were to keep your head down and let things play out. You never called the cops. Amanda had been a nice distraction for a while, but I didn't want anything more with her, and I knew she didn't want anything with me. She just didn't like that someone else had my attention.

I went to leave, but her voice stopped me.

"Well, at least we gave your friend a show."

Confused, I turned back to her. "What are you talking about?"

"You know, your, girl *friend*." She smirked at me. "Yeah, she must have been looking for you 'cause she popped her head in a little bit ago before realizing the position I had you in and then scampered off." She laughed. "Her face looked like she had seen a ghost."

My heart dropped out of my chest, and I pulled the door open, rushing out of the room. Standing at the top of the stairs, I looked down at the throng of people and tried to find Wren.

When I couldn't spot her from there, I got down, pushing through people and going room by room. I still couldn't find her and I felt the panic start to bubble up in me. I shouldn't have left her alone. I wasn't supposed to be gone this long. I entered the kitchen and Jon was standing there, pulling a bottle of water out of the fridge.

"Hey, where's Wren?"

"Out on the lawn. I was grabbing this." He held up the water.

I ran a hand through my hair and sigh. "How's she doing?"

More people pushed their way into the kitchen, so we moved to the other side of the island.

"She got too hot inside and kinda looked like she had a panic attack." He shrugged. "She's had a little too much alcohol I think. It's probably time for us to take her home."

Guilt hit me and I gripped the edge of the sink, hanging my head.

"Dude, what's wrong?" Jon tipped his head to look at me.

"I messed up, man. Amanda and I were upstairs when—"

I looked up through the window above the sink and saw Wren sitting with Chance.

"You left her with fucking Chance?!" I barked at him, pushing past him out the back door. He was close behind me when we both heard her voice.

"Stop!" Her hand was on Chance's chest. I didn't think, I just moved.

"WHAT THE FUCK ARE YOU DOING?" I grabbed Chance by the front of his shirt with both fists, pulling him eye level to me. I just saw red, my arm pulled back.

"Alex, stop!" I felt a hand around my arm, holding back my attempt to bash his face in. "Stop, please. It's not his fault."

Still holding him by his shirt, I looked down at Wren. My eyes moved over her.

"What the fuck, man!?" Chance said. "I was just making sure she was okay."

I turned my glare to him. "That didn't look like you were *just* making sure she was okay." I shoved him back, and he caught himself. "Did she fucking ask you to fucking kiss her?"

"How would you fucking know? Maybe she did!" Chance shoved me back.

My fist connected with his face before I even thought twice about it. Chance fell back, breaking the plastic chair. Blood gushed from his nose and he cried out in pain.

"You're a fucking liar! Wren wouldn't fucking ask you to kiss her." I was on him again, my fist connecting with his face. I knew Wren, and the fact that he was going to spout lies about her infuriated me.

"Alex, please, stop!" Her voice was the only thing capable of pulling me out of the blind rage I felt.

I paused, heaving a breath. Wren reached for me, but Jon had her around the waist.

I looked back down at Chance, shoving my finger in his face.

"If you come near her again, not even she will be able to stop me." I said the words with all the malice I could muster. "I will fucking kill you." I whispered the last words so only he could hear. His eyes were wide and he nodded his head. I dropped him, standing and moving to her. She was in my arms then, and I held her close to me.

"I'm sorry," I whispered to her.

She was pulling at my shirt, and I could see the tears building in her eyes. "Come on, I just want to go home." Her voice broke.

I took her by the hand and started to the side of the house.

I kept my feet moving so I didn't turn around, because I didn't know what I would do if I got my hands on him. I didn't realize how hard I was pulling her until she spoke up.

"Alex, you're going too fast." Her voice was barely above a whisper.

I dropped her hand and turned to her; we'd made it about halfway up the driveway. "Sorry," I muttered, dragging my hands through my hair, pausing. I felt bad for scaring her. That's when I really looked at her. She has makeup on.

"What happened to your face?" I didn't mean for it to sound the way it did. She looked. . .good. The makeup made her eyes pop more than normal, but it seemed to have started to smudge a bit.

"Juni did it," she said, a flush creeping up her cheeks.

"Oh." I didn't know what else to say. I looked up the driveway and then back to her. "Come on, we have a long way to go." It was several miles back home, and I was suddenly wishing I would have asked to borrow Ma's car.

We heard the crunch of gravel and moved to the side of the road, turning to see Jon pulling up behind us.

"Come on." I took her by the hand and opened the back seat door, letting her slide in first.

Jon drove for a while in silence; not even the radio was on. He glanced in the rearview mirror several times. Wren had laid her head in my lap and tucked her legs underneath her, falling asleep.

"I'm sorry, man. . . I shouldn't have left her alone with him. I wasn't thinking."

"You're right. You didn't think," I whispered back harshly.

I heard the stress of the leather wheel beneath his palms. That's when I noticed the blood on his knuckles as the streetlamps illuminated the cab.

I sighed heavily, reaching forward carefully to not disturb Wren, and clasped his shoulder. Our eyes connected in the mirror and an understanding passed between us.

"It won't happen again." And if I didn't believe anything Jon had ever said before, this was the one thing I did believe.

Jon came to a stop outside our apartment. Gently, I woke Wren. She mumbled a thank you to Jon and we got out. When she tripped stepping up onto the sidewalk, I scooped her up in my arms and carried her the rest of the way to the door, only setting her down to get the keys out of my pocket.

Once inside, she headed straight to the bathroom. I stood in the kitchen taking in a deep breath, just glad to have gotten her home. I took a cup down and filled it up, chugging it down before refilling it and setting it on her bedside table.

The room seemed smaller now. We took out the desk that used to be in here and moved it into the living room. One day there was a moving truck in the parking lot, and we watched it, wondering if it was coming or going. It was going. We watched for hours as they hauled stuff out of the apartment and to the dumpster. One of those items was a mattress. Once the truck left, we ran out to it before anyone else could take the mattress. Took it around back and hosed it down with some dish soap, let it dry out in the bathroom. Took turns trying to dry it faster with Ma's hair dryer.

The bathroom door opened, and I turned to see her in her chosen pj's. One of my old shirts and basketball shorts. Her hair was tied up and her face was washed clean of the makeup. I took a seat on the bed, pulled my shoes off, and tucked them under the bed. She fell onto the blankets behind me. I glanced over my shoulder at her and she was facedown.

I fought the embarrassment off and spoke up.

"I'm sorry I wasn't there." I paused, catching her shoulder gently. She peaked up at me.

"It's fine," she mumbled into the bed. "It was just my brain being stupid."

I shifted on my feet, the awkward feeling growing. I had to say something.

"Amanda may have mentioned. . .you saw. . ." I paused, not sure how to finish the sentence.

"Yeah. . ." She burrowed her face deeper into the bed, trying to hide. "I'm sorry. . .I was just looking for you and. . .well, I opened the door and. . .saw." She rolled over, grabbing the thin pillow and covering her face with it. "I had a flashback to when they. . .forced me to do that."

My stomach dropped, and I felt sick. I lowered my head, clutching my hands together.

Wren hadn't told me in detail what Kevin had done to her, and if I could help it, I didn't wonder much. I had never known anger like the anger that was instilled in me at the knowledge that she had been violated every day while living just next door to me.

After she came home from the hospital, she wouldn't talk to me much. She just wanted to sleep.

So, we let her sleep.

Occasionally, we would get lost in talking about memories, and something would slip out. I would do my best to not react. Not make a face or show her how angry it made me.

When I failed at concealing my feelings, I had to tell her over and over again that it wasn't at her. It was at him.

Sometimes I didn't think she believed me.

"Are you mad at Jon?"

"No, Jon and I are good." I stood.

"What about you and Chance?"

I paused in the middle of pulling off my shirt. "Why do you ask?"

She pulled the pillow down and stared up at the ceiling. "Because he's your friend, and it's not his fault. He doesn't know." She brushed her hand under her eyes. "It was just me being dumb. Guys kiss girls at parties. It's normal. I'm just. . . I'm just not ready. I don't think I will ever be ready."

"Chance is not my friend. He never was and never will be. He's just a pest that followed Jon around all the time, and after the shit he pulled tonight, I better never see him again." I finished pulling off my shirt. "I'm going to go take a shower."

I took my time. Letting the hot water run down me. My split knuckles burned and I watched the water turn pink around my feet. I thought about Dad and Ma and the love I witnessed growing up. It made me sad to think that Wren may never let herself experience that kind of love.

The thought hit me hard.

I didn't want just *anyone* to be the one who showed Wren what love could be like.

That was something only I wanted to do. I wanted to shower her in affection. I wanted to be the one who took care of her.

I wanted to be her first kiss.

I tortured myself with these thoughts, but then something else hit me, making the blood run cold in my veins.

They. . .forced me to do that. . .

They.

It wasn't just Kevin who raped Wren.

I couldn't sleep. Wren was dead to the world, her body pressed up against the wall. Faintly, I could hear her soft snores. Usually, I would listen to her sleep sounds and eventually I would fall asleep too.

But not tonight.

The events of the party ran through my head over and over again. Her words.

At this moment, I didn't feel like I knew anything about her.

There was so much about the hell she lived in that I didn't know. I always thought that maybe one day she would open up and tell me in her own time. I never wanted to pressure her into telling me anything. My curiosity didn't matter, only her comfort.

Sighing, I slipped out of bed, replacing my body with my pillow in hopes that she wouldn't wake in my absence. Slipping on the first T-shirt I grabbed, I got a cup of water from the kitchen and went outside, sitting at the base of the stairs. It was in the early morning and I had been lying in bed wide awake for a few hours.

I ran both my hands through my hair, resting my elbows on my knees and staring down at the cracked concrete.

Soon, the birds would be chirping and it would be a new day, but I was still stuck in yesterday.

"What are you doing out here?"

Ma's voice startled me. If I had a watch, I would look at it. It was too early for her to be home.

"I could say the same to you." She raised a brow at me, and I laughed, putting my hands up. "Just jokin', Ma."

She pursed her lips and hummed. "Mhm, that's what I thought. Now, answer me, young man."

I let my head hang. "I messed up."

"Oh no. Not my perfect son." I could hear the sarcasm in her voice as she leaned against the stair railing. "What did you do?"

My cheeks flushed and I stayed silent. I wasn't going to tell her about Amanda and what Wren saw. I scrubbed my hands down my face and groaned. There were just some things Ma didn't need to know.

"I. . .started to let myself think that Wren and I could be. . .more than friends." I hesitated.

"Oh, sweetie." I felt her hand on the top of my head. She tugged at my hair, forcing me to look up at her. "I know Wren has been your lifeline these last eight months, and I'm not surprised you developed some feelings for her. Have you told her how you feel?"

I shook my head. "I don't want to mess up what we have. I don't want to rush her or make her feel pressured or ruin anything. Her friend at school teased her the other day about us and she kind of had a come apart on her. Saying how she would never date anyone."

"Well, I can't say I blame her." Her words had me curling in on myself. Like even thinking we could have more was wrong given what she'd been through. "Alexander, you had an amazing role model." Her hand dropped to my face and cupped my cheek. Her rough thumb brushed it softly. "Your father loved you and I with everything in him, and he loved hard. We were all he wanted in this world, and he showed it to us every day." Her face fell. "Wren has not experienced that kind of love. She has experienced some of the most vile people on this planet. If she never dates, never falls in *that* kind of love with someone, I hate to say it, but I understand why."

"I wish she felt like she could talk to me about what happened. She has told me some things here and there, but not everything."

Ma sighed heavily. "When I took her to the hospital that first day, I sat in the room while she gave a report of everything that had happened. . ." Her face became pinched, and she swallowed hard. "Sweetie, I couldn't. . . I couldn't sit and listen to everything. It was too much for me to handle. She spoke about it. . ." I watched as she tried to find the words, ". . .like it was normal. Like what happened to her was an everyday thing for you and I. Logically, she knew it was wrong, but it's what happened and she was very matter-of-fact about it." She bit the inside of her cheek. "She might not want you to know her in that kind of light."

My stomach turned from her words. "I know, I just. . . I can't help the way I feel. It was stupid to hope her and I might be anything more, I know."

"Alexander James." Ma's voice was stern. "Falling in love is never stupid. You can love her, but you just have to understand that she may never love you the same way back. All's you can do is treat her right, give her the things she deserves. Be there for her."

I stared up at her. The sun had risen higher and the birds were waking up. She smiled down at me, and I realized how much I had missed talking to her like this. When I was younger, I used to fall asleep in her bed and try to stay up until she got home. She would climb into her bed after a long night and smell of pancake syrup and bacon. She would hold me tight and tell me how much she loved me. We would stay like that for a few hours before I would have to get up and get ready for school. I didn't remember when I stopped doing that.

I stood. I was taller than her now and had to look down. I hugged her tight. "I love you, Ma. I'm going to take care of both of you one day. I'm going to get us out of this shithole and one day you won't have to work so much." I expected her to scold me for my language, but she just hugged me tighter.

"How are you feeling, Wren?" Laurel sat cross-legged, her elbow on the arm of her chair, chin in her hand.

I took a deep breath and leaned back, hugging one of her decorative pillows to my chest. I thought about my words.

How *was* I feeling?

"Honestly, kind of anxious. It kind of feels like I'm leaving something behind." I mulled over my words some more. "But I'm also excited."

She nodded at me with a soft smile on her lips. "You have come a long way since our first session. You aren't leaving this behind. You know you can always schedule another appointment. We can touch base. Remember your breathing techniques."

The nightmares had gotten worse during senior year of high school. Panic attacks became a weekly thing for me once I started college. I had started to isolate myself away from everyone except for Gloria and Alex. Then the paranoia started. I kept thinking I saw Kevin waiting for me out in the parking lot. I thought I got glimpses of him in stores. It was never him, though, just my brain playing tricks on me.

Alex had tried to get me to talk to him about things, and I would. I didn't mind telling him. I even wanted to tell him things. I didn't like keeping anything from him.

Except for how angry he would get on my behalf.

Being able to tell Laurel and have her have very little reaction helped me a lot. It was like being nauseous all day, every day, and the only way to feel any better was to allow yourself to throw up. Get everything out until there was no reason to be nauseous anymore.

I had finally gotten everything out.

"So, you have officially graduated college with a business degree and a minor in human resources. You have been at your job for a year now." She grabbed her notebook and flipped it open. "You bought a car, and Alex has closed on a house you are all moving into and getting away from the apartment complex where everything happened." The more she ticked off my accomplishments and life changes, the greater the excitement grew in my chest. "That is really wonderful, Wren," she praised.

I squeezed the pillow tighter and grinned. Last night we had packed up every last item in the apartment. We've been making trips back and forth, dropping all the boxes in the little detached garage of our new home.

But I had been distracted for a while. I had been hitting all these milestones, but one thing kept eating away at me.

"I want to have sex," I blurted out. "But I'm still. . . nervous."

Her eyebrows raised a hair in surprise before she schooled her expression. "That's a big step in your life, Wren." Laurel sat back in her chair, a cup of coffee in her hands. "What has made you open yourself to this? The reason I ask is because, when you came to me two years ago, you were adamant about never wanting to have sex."

I shifted on the couch, trying to pinpoint the moment I had decided this for myself.

I had been seeing Laurel for about two years. At first, our sessions were every other day of the week, and soon they leveled out to weekly, then biweekly. When I enrolled in college, I found out that the campus had therapists available. I ventured my way over and signed up. Laurel specialized in childhood sexual abuse.

I shrugged my shoulders, feeling embarrassed, but I pushed through the emotion.

"I'm twenty-one and the only sexual experience I have is from my mom selling me for cigarettes and rent." The words came out flippantly. I took a deep breath, trying to not hide behind sarcasm. "I want to experience it. I want to understand what it's like to have an. . .enjoyable experience."

There was a little voice in the back of my head that told me that wanting to have sex now was like justifying what was done to me. Logic pushed through: what was done to me was not okay.

I had been a child.

"That's perfectly natural, Wren, and there is nothing to be ashamed of," she said, clearly seeing my thought process on my face.

"I just don't know what to do. How to start." I shook my head. "I feel like I am so far behind everyone else my age."

"Keep in mind that there are other people out in the world, even ones with no sexual trauma, who have decided to never have sex. This isn't a milestone based on age, this is one based on your own deciding factors." She adjusted in her seat. "Have you experimented on your own?"

I picked at my cuticles, not looking up at her. I was comfortable with Laurel, but this topic was always difficult for me.

It felt like I was powerless.

"I tried watching porn a few weeks ago and it just seemed. . .like a lot."

"Well, that's understandable. Porn is a good way to introduce yourself to sex; it's generally how most people are introduced to it. It could be too much, especially if you don't understand what you are clicking on. You could always tread lighter and try watching some romance movies that have sex in them." She reached over to her desk, picking up her notebook, jotting some things down. "Here are some movies off the top of my head that have some explicit scenes in them." She ripped the page out of her book, leaning forward and handing it to me. I glanced at it before folding it and stashing it into my purse. "You may benefit from going the more clinical route."

"What do you mean?"

"Maybe picking up an anatomy book?"

I shook my head. "I've done that already. I was thirteen." And had the library at my fingertips.

"Are you still struggling with the same thought process?"

I sighed. "Yes. Sometimes when I get caught up in my thoughts, I start to scold myself. That voice in my head tells me that if I go through with this then I am saying that everything he did to me is okay, because I'm sexually active now."

"And what do you do when that voice starts to talk to you?"

"I remind myself that what he did to me will never be okay, no matter what I do with my life. That it will and always has been wrong."

"Good." She smiled approvingly. "That's what matters. Don't let that voice take over." She nodded her head, seeming to contemplate something, and checked her watch. "Do you have any plans after this?"

"None that can't be moved."

"Well, you aren't the only person I have sat with who has sexual trauma. I would like to introduce you to someone, if you are okay with it?"

I nodded, and Laurel got up, picking up her phone. She made a phone call and, once she was done, turned back to me. "Okay, here is the address. Go here, and you will meet Riley. Chat with her, and I'm sure she can get you in the right direction."

I left Laurel's office with nervous butterflies. I programmed the address into my phone and followed the guided GPS. It took a lot for me to talk to her about this. After I had decided this was something I wanted to pursue, I threw up for a week.

Sex never felt like something that was for me to enjoy. It felt like it was something for someone else to use me for pleasure, because that was what Kevin always told me.

I was a fuck toy to be used and was only meant to give him pleasure.

It wasn't my hole; it was his hole to use as he pleased. All of my holes.

I pulled into the parking lot and rolled down my windows. There was only a slight breeze, but I would take what I could get. I took in a few deep breaths. I was outside of a shop called Aphrodite's Desires.

The building was painted black, and all the windows had coverings on them.

"Okay, Wren. Let's go into our first sex store," I said aloud, trying to hype myself up.

I got out of my Geo and pushed through the doors. As soon as I walked in, there was a chime throughout the store.

"Hi, welcome in!" a women's voice called out.

"H. . .hello?" I walked in farther, and off to my right was a long counter and a beautiful redhead standing behind it.

She walked over to me.

"Are you Wren?"

I nodded.

"Hello." She gave me a wide smile. "I'm Riley. Laurel called and let me know you were coming." Riley walked behind me and flipped her sign to CLOSED, untied some blinds that were at the top of the door and let them drop, blocking anyone from seeing in. "Now, we have the whole store to ourselves." She turned around, her braided hair flipping over her shoulder.

"Oh, you didn't need to do that," I said shyly.

"Oh, yes, I did." She waved me off. "It's easier to feel more comfortable looking around when you don't have to worry about others coming in. Come on over, let's chat."

I followed her to a seating area by what looked like dressing rooms. The couch was velvet and hot pink. In front of it was a colorful coffee table with two drinks on it.

"I hope you like iced coffee." She picked up a cup and handed it to me.

I stared at her, confused. "Why are you being so nice?"

She laughed, kicking off her shoes and sitting down on the couch, picking up her own drink. "I'm going to be honest with you." She patted the seat next to her, but I didn't move. "Laurel was my therapist a long time ago. So, when she calls and says she's sending someone down here, I can only assume that something happened in your past to make coming here kind of a big deal. Don't get me wrong, coming to a sex shop is always a big deal when its someone's first time, but when Laurel calls. . ." She shrugged. "I just want to make this as comfortable as possible for you."

Riley sipped her drink and then continued, "You don't have to tell me anything you don't want to. I can leave you alone, you can browse with all your heart's desire and pick out whatever you want, or you can give me a little information about what you are looking for, what kind of experience you want, and I will do everything I can to find what suits your needs."

I took a seat down next to her, a little overwhelmed. I took a drink of the iced coffee, and a sweetness washed over my tongue.

"This is delicious," I commented.

"Right? It's my favorite." She swirled the ice in her already half-gone cup.

The only person I had ever gone into detail about what they did to me was with Laurel. Alex knew a lot, but he didn't know everything. I didn't have a girlfriend to tell these things to, but with Riley's own confession, knowing I wasn't the only person in the room who had been through this, it suddenly gave me a loose tongue. I wanted to have a girlfriend I could talk to. With my feelings building as of late, I found myself clamming up whenever Alex and I talked.

"My dad got hurt in an accident. I had accidentally hit the shift lever into neutral and it rolled over him while he was working on it. He got addicted to painkillers and eventually overdosed. To punish me, my mom basically sold me to our downstairs neighbor and the landlord, so she didn't have to pay for rent. I was eleven." I kept my head down, staring at the coffee cup. Watching the condensation roll down the side of the cup and to my hand. I forced myself to look up at her. She had a thoughtful look on her face, and I was grateful to see anything other than pity. "Anyway, I got out five years ago with the help of some really amazing people who have treated me like family from day one. I've done the work and come out on the other side. I have a really good life. Other than that, I have no sexual experience." The words rushed out, I felt like I was word vomiting all over this person I just met.

"And that's the only reason for today? Just. . .curiosity?" Riley asked, no annoyance in her tone at all.

I could feel my cheeks flush.

"Oooh." She moved closer, a smile splitting her face. "Tell me more."

"It's not just some guy." I fought with my words before I gave up, finally sighing and falling into the pent-up thoughts that had been circling my head for the last year. "He's my best friend. And I'm so nervous about telling him."

I spent the afternoon telling Riley about Alex. Really, I gushed about him. The prospect of it all was new, and I had no idea how to navigate these feelings.

How would I have told him about my feelings in a different life? All ideas came up blank. I had no idea how to tell someone my feelings. I had never looked at men—or women for that matter—in a way of finding them attractive enough to want to say something or having feelings for them.

I didn't know when I fell for him. I couldn't pin down the moment my brain went from survival mode to enjoying life. I'd spent many nights sleeping in the safety of his arms. He would hold me through my nightmares, and when they passed, we would stay up and he would listen as I relayed them. If I closed my eyes and thought about it, I could feel his hand brushing the top of my head, a gesture that was always comforting.

He took my mood swings in stride. There would be days that

I would fly off the handle at the oddest moments. Something would make me angry and I would scream and yell at him.

He never yelled. He never got upset. He let me scream, cry, and hate the world. When I had exhausted myself from the rush of emotions, he would be there. Understanding and always welcoming me into his arms.

I'd seen Alex angry. I'd seen him fly off the handle and start fights with men in bars because they looked at me wrong, but there wasn't anything I could ever do or say that would make him upset with me.

I was sad to admit that I'd tried. I tried to push him away. I tried to make him hate me. My own mother hated me, so he would too eventually, right?

Wrong. Alex wasn't capable of harboring hate, at least not for me.

Riley showed me her shop and introduced me to different things like vibrators, books on sex, and erogenous zones. I about had a heart attack when she showed me a display of edible panties and nipple clamps. I had no idea that such things existed.

"Hey, some of us like a little pain with our pleasure." Riley coyly brought the clamps to her breasts and showed me, over her clothes, how they would hang.

I picked out a few, less intimidating looking things and she bagged them up for me.

"I'm not suggesting getting drunk and having sex, buuuut," she dragged out the word, a smile on her lips, "having a couple shots before playing with these toys alone will help you not feel so weird during it."

I grinned at her. It had honestly been a fun afternoon and Riley was such a free spirit. She didn't make me feel weird or awkward from not understanding half of this. "Thank you so much." I finished paying and she walked me to the front door.

"Anytime. I hope you come back," she said, and I could hear how genuine she was.

At her words, I paused. Before I could second-guess myself, I brought out my phone. Riley seemed to already know what I was going to ask, because she took my phone and added her number. I texted her with my name.

"Text me anytime. We will go out for coffee or something."

CHAPTER 20

WREN

I walk out of Riley's store and head to the parking lot where I parked my little teal Geo Metro.

I felt my phone ring in my pocket and pulled it out, answering.

"Helloooo."

"Hey, where you been all day?" I could hear Alex's smile over the phone.

"My session went longer than normal." It wasn't a lie. "But it's over now. What's up?"

"Pizza. Wanna bring some home for the party tonight?"

"I'm not sure I would call moving places a 'party.'" I laughed, setting the bags into the passenger side.

"Oh no, it's a party. Gavin and Troy are going to stop by too." I could hear the guys say something in the background. "Troy says he wants anchovies."

"Ew. If he can have anchovies, I can have pineapple on my pizza."

"Wren, you can have whatever you want, except for that. That is disgusting."

"It's a delicacy." I started the car. "Okay, I'll bring pizza and beer home. Anything else?"

"Nope, I think we are good. See you there."

I hung up the phone and plugged the aux cord in and started my playlist. I turned the music up louder. I rolled my dry lips and reached back to my bag to find my chap stick. Movement from the car next to me caught my attention. The tint was too dark to see who was in it, but I could faintly see the outline of someone sitting in the driver seat.

A sliver of fear ran its way up my back, and I looked away, grabbing the steering wheel, forcing myself to take a deep breath.

The paranoia had started when I started at the community college. There were so many new faces that I didn't know, and sometimes I would feel like someone was watching me. I had convinced myself that Kevin was following me again, that he was after me.

There were times I thought I saw him in a store. Alex would walk up and down every aisle looking for him, and not once did he ever see him.

Alex never made me feel crazy. He would always be on the lookout for my boogeyman.

I opened my eyes and forced myself to put the Geo in reverse and drive slowly out of the parking lot. I focused on the music heading to our favorite pizza joint and, when I got there, I went inside and ordered three large pizzas. Troy and Gavin could eat anyone out of house and home.

After I got the pizza, I ran to a convenience store, picked the guys up some beer, and finally was on my way home.

I pulled up the alleyway into the driveway and parked in front of the detached garage at the back of the house. It was on a corner, so the property was larger than the neighbor's house. Most of the houses on this block had been foreclosed on and no one was living in it, so for the most part, the neighborhood was quiet. Alex had talked about installing an automatic door opener on the garage so I could just hit a button and pull right in, then walk through the garage to get into the yard. As it was right now, I had to open the gate, bring all my stuff into the house, run back outside, and close the gate.

Balancing the pizzas in one hand and the beer in the other, bags on my arms, I managed to get myself in through the back-door and into the kitchen.

"Honey, I'm home!" I hollered through the house.

"Oh, darling!" Gavin's voice rang through the house in a high-pitched tone.

"Shove a sock in it, Gavin," I could hear Alex say.

"Yeah, Gavin, sock it." Troy spoke up.

"I'll sock you!" Gavin retaliated.

"Ow, damn it, Gavin, that hurt!" Troy whined.

Troy and Gavin wrestled their way into the kitchen. Troy had Gavin in a headlock, and Gavin had Troy around the waist, trying to pick him up. Alex followed behind the two knuckleheads.

"Not in the house!" Alex had his hands on his hips, shaking his head, doing an amazing Gloria impersonation. Alex started working for Dan's Construction as soon as we graduated high school. Gavin and Troy had started a few months after him. The three of them had been inseparable since.

They were goofballs who just liked to joke around and play pranks on one another.

"Okay, you three." I set the pizzas down onto the counter and Alex took the beer from my other hand, putting them in the fridge. "We don't need someone breaking something already."

I maneuvered my way around the boys and the boxes.

"Hey, what else did you get us?" Troy said as I tried leaving the kitchen.

I still had ahold of the black bag that had the sex toys in it. I knew if I made a run for it now, Troy and Gavin would both chase after me until they got their hands on whatever I had. Troy and Gavin were like the brothers I never had. Teasing and tormenting me to no end.

With flushed cheeks, I turned around, holding the bag out. "Oh, I didn't know you also used tampons, here," I offered.

Gavin and Alex busted out laughing, and Troy's face turned several shades of red.

"Didn't think so." Before he could make a move, I turned around and ran up the stairs.

My room was right across from Alex's, last door on the right. We had both bought brand-new mattresses and upgraded ourselves from the twin we had been sharing to full sizes. The beds were delivered this morning. I set my purse down on my desk and pushed the bag underneath my bed. Grabbed a hair tie, throwing my hair up into a messy bun. I had let my hair grow out since moving in with the Harpers; now it fell around my waist. I loved it.

Back downstairs and in the kitchen, they already had a pizza open, and half the thing was gone.

"Jesus." I went to a box that was labeled FRAGILE and opened it to find some glasses. I filled it up with tap water and took a long drink.

"Don't judge us. We're growing boys," Troy said around a mouthful.

Out of my peripheral Alex handed me a slice of pizza. "Thank you." I took it, taking a bite and pulling it away the cheese stretching from my mouth to the pizza. I had to break it with two fingers. "Mmm," I hummed my approval.

"What's the game plan?" Alex leaned against the counter and bumped into my shoulder.

"Kitchen and bathrooms first, then our rooms." We really didn't have much stuff but had been buying more every time we saw something. Yard sales were our favorite things on weekends lately. "Where's Ma?"

"She and Candy had to go get their hair done." Alex grinned. "I told her that we could handle unpacking the rest of it. She unpacked her room this morning." Gloria had been able to move to part-time from working at Tony's. We didn't see her a lot lately, she had been going out with her friends and even started up on a bowling league.

The house had three bedrooms and two bathrooms. Two

bedrooms and a bathroom upstairs, the other downstairs. It even had central heating and air.

Alex was adamant about not living in a place with baseboard heaters.

"What's in the bags?" Alex nodded to the floor where I had left the bags from my solo shopping trip.

"Sheets sized to fit our beds." I had been saving all my money for the last year. My only expenses were the necessary ones. I had a nice little cushion now to go a little crazy to get the things we needed for the house, like new sheets for all three of us.

Alex bent down, opening the bag. He pulled out the sheets I had picked out for him—navy blue—a deep purple for Ma, and a deep forest green for me. "Wow, Wren, you didn't need to do that." He smiled down at me, and I grinned, pleased he liked them. "And guess what?"

"Hmm?" I said around a mouthful.

Alex leaned down to my ear and loudly whispered, "We have a laundry room." We had spent many nights hauling clothes baskets to the closest laundromat on laundry days. Now, we had our own.

It was odd to be excited over something as simple as our own washer and dryer.

Troy whispered loudly, "Now kiss."

Alex looked to the ceiling and rolled his eyes. "If you two are done stuffing your faces, why don't you go unload the truck." He picked up a dishrag and tossed it at them.

"Ah, Troy, you made Mom and Dad mad at us again. Come on." Gavin grabbed Troy in a headlock and dragged him out of the kitchen.

"I love those two." I smiled after them. Troy and Gavin brought a different kind of lightheartedness that I wasn't capable of. They joked and played with each other like nothing could bring them down. I loved to watch them.

When Alex didn't say anything, I looked up at him. His warm brown eyes were on me, a gentleness to them that I was familiar with. Alex had become my world. He was my rock in a storm, always keeping me above water.

He reached out, and I didn't flinch when he tucked loose strands of hair behind my ear. His rough thumb brushed down my cheek.

"You are so beautiful when you smile." His hand rested on my cheek a little longer before he pulled me into a hug. I buried my face into his chest, letting his woodsy amber scent envelop me.

I had fallen so deeply in love with Alex. I wasn't sure when it happened. I wasn't really even sure of the emotion. I had discussed it with Laurel at length, describing my feelings about him, how he made me happy.

For the longest time, I thought it was a trauma bond with him. That he was the first person who treated me with kindness, who helped me get out of the situation I was in. That there was a part of me that decided I just needed him to breathe. But after talking to Laurel, we dissected it and gave it a name.

Love.

The radio we had brought from the apartment was plugged in and sitting on top of the fridge. Alex reached up, turning the song up louder. He stole my pizza crust, popping it into his mouth in one bite. He took one of my hands and guided it to his neck, taking my other hand and holding it. We danced around the small space of the kitchen to the song. He had me doing turns and dipping me back. I laughed, not a care in the world.

"Well, look at you two."

As Alex spun me, I got a glimpse of Jon standing in the doorway. Alex didn't falter in his step, keeping us moving in the small kitchen.

"Hey, Jon," I greeted him, breathless.

"My turn," he said.

Alex put me in a spin right into Jon's arms.

Jon guided me in his own dance, a little faster than Alex's. The song ended shortly after.

"I didn't know you were coming over tonight."

"Alex texted me earlier. I managed to get out of the last few meetings of the day." He grinned, reaching up and loosening his tie. "Pays to be the boss's son."

As soon as we graduated from high school, Jon had started working for his dad's law firm.

"The whole plan is for me to take over one day," Jon had said one day the summer after high school. All I could think about is what it would be like to have parents who had your whole life planned out for you. It sounded amazing.

"Glad you could make it," Alex said, walking up behind me and wrapping his arms around my shoulders, chin resting on my head.

The butterflies erupted in my belly.

This wasn't something new that Alex did, but now that I had feelings for him, it seemed so different.

After my college graduation, Jon had taken us all out to a really nice dinner. Gloria passed on the invite, so it was just the three of us. He brought a pink bouquet of roses, a beautiful necklace, and a very sweet congratulations card.

Alex had been quiet that night. I tried asking him what was wrong, but he denied anything was wrong and we never talked about it again.

"How's work been?" Jon asked Alex.

"Good." A smile split Alex's face and he looked down at me. "Dan promoted me. I get to run my own crew."

"Congratulations!" I beamed for him. "That's amazing, Alex."

"Good job, man. You are coming up in the world." Jon slapped Alex's shoulder.

A weird tension seemed to build between them in that moment. I looked between them, about ready to ask what was wrong, when Gavin spoke up.

"Hey, where do you want these?" Gavin carried a box in. Alex stepped forward and grabbed the box that had my name on it.

"Here, I got this one. Troy, that one goes to my room."

We watched them go, and I realized how late it had gotten. I wanted to get the new sheets washed before we went to bed. I picked up the bags and brought them to the back of the house. I pulled the sheets out, stripping them of their packaging and the cardboard inserts before opening the top of the washing machine and getting a load started.

Jon reached around me, taking the garbage and getting it out of my way. "How was your day?" he asked as he unbuttoned his cuffs and rolled his sleeves up.

"Good." I started the load and closed the washer.

The laundry room was long and narrow. It was wide enough to fit the washer and dryer next to each other and even had a utility sink in it.

I turned around. Jon had found the garbage bags under the sink and was shaking one out. He threw away the empty pizza box and started to clear off the counter for us.

"Hey, Jon?"

"Yes, Wren?"

I chewed on my lip, working up the courage to ask Jon what had been going on with the two of them lately. There had been too many tense moments to continue to ignore it. Normally, I would always go to Alex first, about anything and everything. But if he wasn't going to tell me what was going on, I'd find out another way.

I felt on edge today.

I had a lot going on. Therapy, moving into the new house. Whatever weird shit was going on with these two. Jon and Alex had been friends for so long that their tension was starting to worry me.

But was it really my business? I had always been careful about not coming between the two of them.

I shook my head and moved to the boxes, pulling out more glasses and putting them up in the cabinets.

"Hey." He moved to stand in front of me. "You know you can ask me anything." He reached out, giving me a reassuring squeeze.

"I know, I just. . ." I glanced to the door, making sure Alex wasn't on his way back. "Something just seems off about you and Alex lately. Are you guys okay?"

He leaned against the counter, looking me over curiously. "Alex hasn't told you anything?"

"Told me about what?"

Jon sighed, running a hand through his neatly styled hair. "I shouldn't say anything."

On reflex, I reached out, touching his forearm. "Jon, you're making me worried. What's going on that I don't know? Is he okay?"

"Uh, Alex. . ." He took a deep breath. "He has a thing for a girl. And I've been telling him he needs to make a move before someone else does."

I couldn't hide my shock.

"You didn't know?" He tilted his head.

I shook my head.

"I'm sorry, Wren, I figured you of all people knew."

"I didn't know he was even seeing anyone," I whispered, and turned to the kitchen sink, disappointment rolling through me. I didn't know why I was so surprised. Alex had been relatively popular our senior year. After high school, when we all were able to get into bars, it wasn't a new thing for him to be approached or for a phone number to be slipped into his pocket. I had never thought much of it because I thought he was always throwing them away.

Stupid girl, did you think he would wait for you or something?

"You like him, don't you?"

I could feel my cheeks flush and frustrated tears burned my eyes. I nodded, afraid if I voiced the words I might fall apart.

"You should tell him, Wren," Jon encouraged.

"What?" I tried to laugh it off. "No. If there's someone he's interested in, I'm not going to make things weird by confessing my feelings." I looked to the ceiling and tried to blink away the tears. "Fuck," I whispered when I couldn't get them to stop.

"Come here." Jon pulled me to him and gave me a hug, patting my back. "I'm sorry, Wren, I shouldn't have said anything."

"No, I'm glad you did say something before I made a fool of myself by telling him. I don't think I'm ready for rejection." I gave myself a moment to just feel Jon's warmth. It soothed my jilted feelings. Jon smelled crisp and clean.

I just let myself be held while my heart broke over the love I would probably never have.

CHAPTER 21

ALEX

THE LAST FOUR YEARS SIMULTANEOUSLY FELT LIKE they flew by but also dragged on. As soon as we had graduated high school, I was applying to jobs like crazy, finally landing one at Dan's Construction. Wren spent months ensuring she had all the right documentation to apply to our local college while also working with Ma at Tony's. She spent endless hours talking to the school's financial department and finding every resource she could to go to college without having to pay for it. She had been a straight-A student and had one of the highest GPAs in our graduating class. I felt so proud of her when she stood up on the stage as it was announced she was on the honor roll.

Jon was accepted at a university and spent most of his time away, but every chance he could, he was calling us—and then video calling us once Wren and I had both saved up enough money to get smartphones. He always came home to celebrate our birthdays and any big milestone we hit. New phones. New-to-us cars. He was always there. Wren and Jon became closer, able to find their own common ground, both attending college. I was glad they became closer. The guilt from avoiding Jon those first couple of months Wren came into my life had faded away. Now they were friends and I was glad for it.

Well, I was glad.

"Night, guys, thanks for helping!" I waved at Troy and Gavin from the front porch. While Jon and Wren were unpacking the kitchen, we had hauled the remaining boxes into the house and put them in their respective rooms, making things easier for unpacking.

Troy had gotten a call and needed to go, and since Gavin always rode with him, he had to leave too.

They got into their little pickup and drove off. I took a deep breath in the cool night air, getting ready to go back inside. Jon had been pushing me to tell Wren my feelings for her. To tell her that I wanted to be more than friends.

"Are you ever going to tell Wren how you feel about her?" Jon's words had caught me off guard. We were playing basketball one day a month ago, just catching up.

"What are you talking about?"

"Come on Alex, It's obvious that you love her." He tossed the ball to me and I caught it at my chest. "You're buying a house for her. What are you going to do, live with her as friends for the rest of your life?"

"You don't know what you are talking about." I tossed the ball at him, a little harder than necessary. I had accepted that Wren and I would never be anything more than what we were. But that didn't make the feelings go away.

"Wren is beautiful. She's sweet and funny, and there is going to be guys that come along and want to date her eventually. Someone is going to scoop her up before you realize it."

"Wren doesn't want to date anyone. You don't know anything, Jon. Her mom's boyfriend did terrible things, and she has sworn to never date anyone."

"Alex, don't be ridiculous. She said that when we were still in high school. She's graduated college. We are adults now, and things change. She obviously knows not all men are pieces of shit like him. There will be someone who pursues her one day, and I don't want to see you regret not saying anything sooner." He tossed the ball back to me, just as hard.

I walked up the court and dribbled, wanting this conversation to end. "Why the hell are you buggin' about this? I don't see any guy around her. Troy and Gavin think of her like their little sister, so they aren't looking at her like that, and I—"

"Well, maybe I want something more with her."

I froze mid-shot, turning to him and frowning. He crossed his arms and stared me down. "You don't—"

"Yes, I do, Alex. I like her. I've liked her for years, and I've been waiting for you to finally make your move. I've been trying to be respectful. You are my best friend, but I'm tired of waiting. If you aren't going to say something to her, then I will."

"Jon, you don't know a damn thing about her."

Oh, give me a fucking break, Alex. I know she was abused. I just had to pay closer attention to her. I know it was bad and I also know her mom could give two shits less about her. That's why you and your mom took her in. I don't know the exact details. But I want to know. Only if she wants to tell me. And you know what, that doesn't even matter. I want to take care of her. I want more with her if she wants it with me too."

Since that day, Jon and I hadn't been the same.

Wren hadn't caught onto his feelings yet, but I didn't know how many more times I could dodge her questioning about what had happened between him and I.

As far as I could tell, he hadn't said anything to her. He'd always bought her things since the beginning. I never said anything about it because she deserved to have the world at her feet. It's what I'd always wanted to do, but I'd had to work hard to give it to her.

Jon could give her things without breaking a sweat at the checkout line. He never had to worry about his card declining and the embarrassment that came with it.

But Wren didn't care about that stuff. She was just happy to be living outside the hell that was those people.

She gave me a different outlook on life, a grateful one. Wren had taught me to appreciate the little things. The things that were in my control. She never wanted for more than what she had.

Food, water, freedom to go outside and do what we wanted. The days we spent inside reading during a downpour. Those were the things she truly enjoyed.

And now Jon wanted to be a part of that with her.

If you aren't going to make a move, then I will.

His words echoed in my head, flipping a switch in me.

With those words, I had realized just how possessive I was of Wren.

She wasn't my girlfriend, and I had never thought of her like a sister. She was always just Wren to me.

Just a friend.

Who I would burn someone alive for.

Who I would start fights over when someone dared talk badly about her or upset her even in the slightest.

Who I would do anything for, just to see her smiling.

She was smiling a lot these days.

And Jonathan had noticed.

I saw the way he looked at Wren when she wasn't looking. And I saw the way he looked at me when he thought I wasn't paying attention.

I had started to notice that Jon made it a point to invite only Wren to his family events now. His wording was always, *you're invited* rather than *you're both invited*.

Jon didn't dare say that the invite was only for Wren. We both knew she likely wouldn't go without me. I liked watching him struggle with her; Wren didn't have a clue that he liked her. She didn't see people like that. She didn't dissect everything that he said to get to the meaning behind it.

Wren wasn't mine, and I had no right to interfere. If she wanted to date him, I should just stand aside and let it happen.

That's what I should do out of respect for my best friend and her.

But I came to realize that I wasn't going to stand aside and let Jon be her first. Or let him be anything more than just her friend.

I shook my head at the thought, but a part of me wanted to whip my dick out and mark her as if I was a fucking dog who just caught another trying to claim her.

I shoved my hands in my pockets and went back inside. Wren was elbow-deep in suds, washing dishes while Jon was drying and stacking them to the side.

I looked between them and quickly realized that something was off here, but I wasn't going to press whatever was going on. Wren seemed sad, and that made something itch inside me. Whatever it was, I wanted to fix it.

"Gav and Troy had to go, but we got the boxes in."

Wren didn't look my way. "Oh, okay."

I picked up the plates Jon had been stacking and put them in the cabinet.

Suddenly, Jon went on a tangent about his schooling and how he was the top of his class.

"That's good, Jon. It sounds like you really love your classes," Wren commented absently. Jon was two years deep into his law school now. We had seen less of him because of it, which didn't bother me any.

Jon looked over his shoulder at me, a smile on his face as he dried his hands off. He walked over and clasped my shoulder.

"I'm happy for you, man."

I raised a brow at him, confused by his behavior. He was acting like we hadn't been at odds for a while.

"Thank you?" I didn't get his meaning.

He leaned against the counter with me and gestured around the room. "You bought a house, got a car, have a job." He folded his arms over his chest and looked ahead at Wren. "You aren't getting your clothes from the senior center anymore, and you guys aren't living from paycheck to paycheck. Now you're taking care of your mom and Wren."

I frowned at him, not sure where he was going with this.

"You don't need me anymore." The back door opened suddenly, and Ma walked through. "Hey, kids."

"Hey, Ma," Wren and I said in unison. Wren snapped out of whatever thoughts had her tied up before.

"Hey, Gloria." Jon took the dish towel and wiped the counter down. "Well, I should probably head home. I've got a mock trial I am prepping for."

Wren turned off the water and took the towel, drying her hands. "Well, thanks for stopping by. It was nice of you to help."

Watching them had the hair on the back of my neck standing. Wren hugged him and he hugged her back. It wasn't quick; they lingered longer than normal.

Jon locked eyes with me as he leaned down and kissed her cheek. "Sleep well." He straightened, and I could see his intentions clearly. I clenched my fists at my side, fighting the urge to throw him out of the house.

"Nice to see you, Gloria." He stooped down to hug her and slapped my shoulder as he passed. "Night, man."

"Yeah. Night."

The door closed behind him, but I didn't move.

"Dear?" Ma said, looking up at me.

My eyes were on Wren as she looked down and took a deep breath, forcing a smile to her lips before she turned to Ma. "Welcome home." She walked over to her, giving her a hug. "Your hair looks nice."

"Oh, thank you, dear. I let Charlie have fun with it this time. I saw all the boxes piled in the alley, you two sure did get a lot done." Ma coughed into her hand, clearing her throat.

"That was Gavin and Troy's doing. When they aren't wrestling throughout the entire house, they get shit done." I grabbed a glass from the cupboard and filled it up, giving myself something to do. "Here Ma,"

"Thank you, sweetheart." She took a sip, clearing her throat again. "Well, I am honestly so tired from all this excitement today, kids, I think I'll go to bed. Night, you two."

We watched as Ma left the kitchen and headed down the hall. I turned back to Wren, still fired up about Jon.

"No one should do anything to you without your permission. Do you understand me?" My heart was still racing in my chest, the anger growing. "No one has the right to touch you without your permission. Not even me. Do you understand?"

"Alex, Jon is our friend. Whatever is going on between you two, leave me the hell out of it." She tore her gaze away from me. She was leaning back against the counter, her hands gripping the edge.

Something about her words made me feel betrayed. Like she was choosing him over me.

"I need to take a walk," I muttered, heading out through the laundry room and out the back door. I was careful not to slam the door. I walked in circles out in our yard.

Had I ever needed Jon? Yeah, he had always been generous. Helping me out even though I never asked. Giving me things, even though I never asked. I thought that was just who he was though. We grew up in different ways. He wanted for nothing and I got by with what I had.

As a kid, I was lonely, but then Wren came along and things got better.

I paced for a while, letting my thoughts spin, before finally sitting on the stoop.

The door opened and then softly closed. Wren took a seat next to me. She bumped her shoulder into me, before handing me a beer.

"Are you okay?"

"Yeah," I sighed, accepting it.

She took a long drink of her own beer, staring out across the yard. We were still at the edge of the city, but it was a lot quieter over here. Horns could still be heard honking in the distance. The radio filtered out from inside the house.

"How was your session today?" I wanted to lighten the mood, and Wren always seemed better after her appointments.

"It was good." She looked down, picking at the label on her beer.

"What?" I asked, confused as to why she got quiet all of a sudden.

"I. . .uh. . .talked to Laurel about starting to date. . ."

Her words had me freezing in place.

Dating?

"I thought you never wanted to date?"

She continued to pick at the label. "Come on, Alex. I said that when I was sixteen." She shook her head. "I've just been thinking about it lately. I'm done with college. I'm working full-time now." She shrugged her shoulders. "I think I'm ready to put myself out there."

That possessive beast seemed to unfurl within me. Stretching and clicking his claws in my mind. I could feel that urge to take what's mine. Claim it and make sure everyone knew. Make sure *she* knew.

It felt like the sky was falling around me and Jon knew it before I did.

What the actual fuck was happening here?

I had so many questions. Why was she thinking of this all of a sudden? Who made her want to date? Was she interested in someone?

Was she interested in Jon?

Before I could lay into her with questions, I brought the beer to my lips, tipping my head back and draining it.

Her hand faltered over her bottle. Her throat bobbed up and down with the swallow.

We hadn't talked about sex since she caught me and Amanda at that party. I had never felt dirty about any of my sexual escapades until that moment. Until she vocalized that she was forced to give head to men.

Them.

The word still echoed in my mind from that night. That was the night that I had the realization that I only knew a small amount of what Wren had been through. She hadn't been trying to make me feel bad about it, but I did anyway.

"So, are you thinking about having. . .sex with someone?" I looked forward across the alleyway, choosing my words carefully, but I wasn't going to beat around the bush. I wanted to make sure she had thought everything through.

"Possibly." Her voice was small, a red flush creeping up her neck. "Are. . .you seeing anyone?" She peeked at me. I was caught off guard by her question, stumbling to come up with something before she continued. "Come on, Alexander, I'm not stupid. I know you aren't celibate." She said the last sentence in a light-hearted tone, a small smile formed on the corner of her lips. "I could hear you when you left the apartment at night. Or when you would come home late."

I had gone out a few times with some of the guys after work. I wasn't hiding it from her, but I wasn't going to talk about it with Wren. I never wanted to bring up sex. I didn't want to bring up unwanted memories. I was just careful about it. I didn't want her to know what I was heading out to do, because I was worried she would be at home thinking about what was done to her.

What she was forced to do.

"I. . .uhm. . ." I floundered, and she started laughing.

"Alex, really, it's fine." She bumped my shoulder with hers. "So," she shrugged her shoulders, looking at me expectantly, "do I get to meet her?"

"Meet who?" I was lost at this point, trying to hide my confusion by taking a drink of my already-empty beer.

"Your girlfriend."

I choked on nothing. Coughing so hard I had to stand and walk around until it cleared.

"God, Wren, no." She stared at me, confused. "I'm not dating anyone." I ran a hand through my hair, wishing I didn't have to say this. "It's just sex. That's all."

"Just sex?" She straightened.

"Yes. Just sex. People can have just sex. No emotions

involved." She looked away from me, thinking something over. Nerves filled me. I wished I was in her head. I wished I knew what she was thinking. "Wren, you're killing me here."

"I'm processing it, Alex," she bit out.

"What is there to process?"

"I just didn't think you were capable of. . ." She trailed off again.

"You didn't think I was capable of *what*?" I did my best not to shout, but I was so amped up over the awkwardness of the entire conversation that I was getting mad. Did she think I had been secretly dating someone this whole time?

Did Jon make her think that?

"Of having sex with no feelings." She pushed the words out quickly, her cheeks flushing red.

I stared at her, dumbfounded. "Why would you think that?"

"Come on, Alex, you're a romantic." She looked at me like I had a clue to what she was saying. "You know, the story of your parents, watching them love each other. Dancing in the kitchen."

I rubbed my face with both my hands. I had been a romantic when I was younger, but I had also been lonely. The reality of it was, I only wanted to be romantic with Wren.

"You know what," Wren stood, waving her hand, "it doesn't matter. Just know that you don't have to sneak around me." She gave a tight smile. "I'm heading to bed."

And with that, she turned around and went inside, leaving me to figure out what the hell had just happened.

I went inside, locked the doors, and turned off all the lights. At the top of the stairs, I looked at Wren's closed door. We no longer shared a room, and I wasn't sure how I felt about it. Before, we would lie in opposite beds talking until one of us fell asleep. Sometimes, we would fall asleep in each other's bed.

The move was good for us. I wanted to get her out of those apartments. In all my excitement, I hadn't realized that I was putting us in two different rooms. I tried to reason with myself. We were adults now. We needed to have our own rooms, but the gain of a new home had me feeling like I lost something more.

Wren's closed door felt like she was closing herself off to me.

Sighing, I went into my room, closing my own door. I stripped out of my clothes. I used to sleep in shorts and a T-shirt. It only felt right because of our proximity. Now, I had my own room. I could go back to wearing nothing if I wanted.

I crawled into bed. Wren had made my bed up with the new sheets. I let the sheet drape over my hips, lacing my fingers behind my head, staring up at the ceiling.

I replayed the conversation over and over in my head.

Wren was thinking about dating.

About having sex.

That thought alone had my cock pulsing to life, tenting the sheet. I tightened my fingers behind my head, refusing to touch myself to thoughts of her.

This wasn't the first time this had happened. Wren had been living with us for about two years when I started to obsessively think about her. My unsated sexual desires ran rampant at night. I would wake to my hand already fisting my cock at the thoughts of her. The way she smiled, or the sliver of skin that would show between her shirt and shorts. That's when I started going out at night.

I had fought with shame, thinking of her in that way even though I knew what she had been through.

But she wanted to have sex. She wanted to start dating.

I wanted to be her choice. I didn't want anyone else to have her.

The thought of pursuing her and ruining our friendship was the only thing that was stopping me. What would happen if she didn't feel the same thing for me? What if she did, and things went south?

Was it worth potentially losing her completely?

CHAPTER 22

ALEX

T̲HE HEAT WAS STILL BAD LATE S̲EPTEMBER. T̲HE CREW and I were sheeting a roof on a house, the speaker was blasting rock, and we were working as fast as we could to get it done.

"I can't wait to punch out and go down to Dave's and have a drink," Troy said as he tacked in a sheet. "You will be there tonight, right?"

Wren and I had been in a weird spot for the last week. After our talk the other night, I couldn't stop thinking of her in ways I shouldn't.

"Alex?"

Suddenly, I was imagining her in all sorts of different positions. During the day, I had a hold of my thoughts. It was night that had me struggling. Now the floodgates were open and I couldn't stop. It didn't even occur to me that she would ever be in a relationship with anyone. I had spent so much time taking the heat off her every time someone asked about us or what she was to me.

Something hard hit me in the head.

"Hey, what the fuck, man?" I looked to Troy as a nail hit the sheet and rolled down off the roof.

"Well, I've been talking to you for the last twenty minutes and you're off in fucking la-la land." He shook his head at me. "Being on a fucking roof is the last place you need to be daydreaming.

I could hear the seriousness in Troy's tone. Troy was never serious. He and Gavin were always playing jokes on each other, but he took safety precautions seriously.

"Sorry, man, off in my head."

"I can fucking see that." He grumbled some more before he shook his head, finishing tacking in the sheet. "So, are you coming to Dave's tonight with us or not?"

"Yeah, I'll be there," I confirmed, wiping the back of my arm over my forehead. "I need to shower first."

"Our angel is here!" Gavin shouted from inside the house.

We turned to the road to see a company pickup pulling up to the site, causing dust to fly all over the place. A few of the other guys hooted and hollered in excitement.

"Lunchtime," Troy piped up, walking the roofline to the ladder and heading down. Wren got out of the truck, rounded the back of it, and dropped the tailgate. Her hair was down in a mass of unruly curls. I could still remember the excitement she had when she found hair products that were meant for curly hair and could afford them. Splurging on the small luxuries was a win. Every paycheck we got was a win. Every present we surprised Ma with was a win.

With the heat being so bad these days, they had been sending her out of the office with water refills and lunch. The last thing any of us wanted was for someone to have a heatstroke and be sent to the hospital. I got down off the roof and headed over to the water spicket, running it, washing my hands, and splashing my face.

The rest of the guys grabbed their lunch and headed into the tool trailer where we had an AC unit running inside. Troy and Gav stood around the pickup with her. Slowly, I walked up. They were asking her out to the bar tonight. It wasn't an unusual thing, Wren joined us out most of the time, but now that I knew she was thinking about dating, I didn't like it.

"Yeah. Sounds like a good time." She smiled at them. She finally looked at me. "Hey, you." She wrinkled her nose at me. "You smell."

"Well, hello to you too." I paused, my hands on my hips, feigning hurt, before I lurched forward, snatching her up in a hug and spinning her. She shrieked, and to me it sounded like trilling bells. I loved the sound of her laughter. I loved seeing her happy.

"Alexander James! Now I'm going to smell like your sweaty ass all day," she grumbled, but there was still a smile on her face.

"Now you are just hurting my feelings."

She rolled her eyes at me before handing me my sandwich. "You guys need anything else?" Gavin reached in the back of her truck, picking up the watercooler.

"Nah, I think we are good."

"Oh, Gav, is it okay if I invite a friend to the bar tonight?"

I saw the way Troy and Gavin looked at each other, then glanced at me. "Nope. It's an open invitation."

I was struck by how odd it was that she was asking them. She wasn't even looking at me.

"Great. See you guys there then."

Without even glancing my way, she got into the truck and drove off.

What. The. Fuck.

"Oooh," Gavin whispered to Troy as we watched her drive down the road. "Mom is mad at Dad."

I spent the rest of the day in a mood and all the guys knew it, so they avoided me. When we finished cleaning up the site, I sped back to the office to confront Wren, but by the time I got there, she had already left.

"Yeah, she left early to go pick her friend up or something," Bonnie, the other bookkeeper, said. Bonnie was a gum chewer and snapped her gum constantly. She had a lot of personality and was fun, but she didn't come out with us much because of her son Sam.

I hopped into my truck and headed home. "Wren?" I hollered through the house. When no one answered, I headed upstairs and into my room, stripping from my work clothes and jumping in the shower.

Once I was out, I realized I didn't have a towel in here.

"Fuck." I wicked as much water off as I could before I stepped out and headed into the hall to my room. No towel was in there, so I walked across the hall and pushed open Wren's door, hoping she might have some unfolded laundry in her room. "Ah hah!" Hanging off of her desk chair was a towel. I pulled it up, and something fell and clattered on the floor. "Dammit." I wrapped the towel around my waist and bent down, feeling under her desk.

My hand touched something soft and smooth. It was black and oblong.

"What the. . ." I turned it over in my hand, found two small bumps, and pressed one. Nothing happened until it started to vibrate in my hand.

A vibrator.

What the fuck was Wren doing with a vibrator?

I pulled out the chair and got down on my hands and knees, looking for what else I heard fell. Under the desk was a black plastic sack. I pulled it out and opened it.

Condoms, lube, a book on sex, and a vibrator.

The only thing that kept my sanity in place was the fact that the seal on the condom box had not been opened. I put everything back on her chair, leaving her room.

I finished getting dressed and then locked up the house, heading to the bar.

It had only been a week since Wren and I talked about her dating people, and I swear it has been the worst week of my life. My temper was flaring more these days and now I find sex shit in her room.

Sex toys that she could be using with someone else.

Fuck that.

The floodgates were open now. Knowing she was ready to start dating flipped a switch in my brain. She was ready to date. She wanted to have sex. Her words gave me permission to think of her as more than just my friend, and it was driving me mad.

Wren Jacobson was mine.

Troy and Gavin had carpooled to Dave's bar together. I pulled into the lot and parked next to them. As soon as I walked inside, I started looking for her, but I didn't see her. While I was searching, Gavin motioned for me to come over.

"So, what did you do?" Troy said as he handed me a beer while I was walking up to the table he'd procured.

"What are you talking about?"

Troy gestured around us. "You're joking, right?"

"*Seriously*, Alex, what did you do?" Gavin spoke up now.

"You two are *seriously* getting on my nerves." I took a drink. "I didn't do anything."

"Yeah, right. She's going to bring one of her friends? All her friends are right here. There is no one else allowed in our little group other than Bonnie, and Bonnie has Sammie, so she's never out with us. So, what did you do?"

"I'm telling you guys; I didn't do anything," I growled out.

"Do you think he asked her out finally?" Troy said.

"Yeah, that has to be what happened." Gavin slapped his hand to his head dramatically.

"She totally turned him down."

"Had to have, that's why he's been so pissy this week."

"And spacey," Troy said. The two of them formed a half-circle and were loudly whispering to each other but were also making sure I heard everything.

It was hard to stay mad with them here. A smile pushed its way to my face and I shook my head. "Alright, you two, let's get a game going." Gavin racked the balls and Troy grabbed some pool sticks.

We got through two rounds before I heard familiar giggling.

My eyes landed on Wren as she walked up. She had clearly already been drinking. I stood there, shocked. She hadn't gotten drunk in years.

"There she is!" Troy set his pool stick down and rushed over to her, throwing an arm over her shoulder. "You look like you have already had some drinks."

Wren laid her head on his shoulder, laughing. "Hey, Troy." She giggled again and used him to keep herself upright.

"Okay, we need to sit you down."

Gavin strode up on her other side and threw his arm around her. All three of them sat down on a bench.

Wren was all smiles, which was contagious to the rest of us. They all stayed where they were at, arms thrown over her.

"Soooo." Troy looked to me. "Where is this friend of yours?"

"Riley? Oh. . .bathroom." Wren looked to me and her cheeks visibly flushed. I wasn't sure if it was the alcohol or if she was thinking about whatever the two of them had been doing before they got here.

I felt the possessive beast unfurl again. Urging me to claim what was mine.

"You know," Gavin leaned into her, eyeing me, "whatever guy you are introducing us to is going to get the third-degree from your sons."

"Yeah, we have to approve of our new stepdaddy." Troy winked at me, and I wanted to shove my pool stick up his—

"As long as you call me 'daddy,' I'll be sure to take good care of you boys."

A redhead who was only a few inches shorter than me stepped up with two glasses of water in her hands. She breezed past me and handed the water to Wren.

"Here, babe. Drink up or else you will have a hangover." The redhead turned and looked to me, a smirk on her freckled face.

"You must be Alex." She held her hand out to me. I shook it, confused. Rather than watching me suffer a moment longer, she spared me. "I'm Riley."

Laughter bubbled up and spilled out of me. I had to take a few breaths before I could say anything. "Of course, you're Riley." I pointed at the bench. "Those two dumbasses with their mouths hanging open are Gavin and Troy. I see you have treated my best friend to a good night, and you know what, I think I need to take her home now." Still chuckling at my own stupidity, I reached for Wren, who took my hand, a smile still plastered on her face.

"Thanks for the advice, Riley." She giggled. "Sorry I'm such a lightweight."

Riley hugged Wren, giving her a wink before turning to Gav and Troy, who were still sitting dumbfounded. She pointed at the two of them and said, "Whatever the story is here, I like it. How long have you two been dating?"

"Dating!? We aren't dating!" Gavin and Troy said in unison.

"Oh, come on boys, no need to be shy." Riley laughed.

"I think they finally met someone to match their ridiculousness." Wren giggled as we headed out of the bar together.

THE COOL AIR ON MY FACE FELT NICE. ALEX HAD practically carried me to his truck and buckled me in, and now we were on our way home.

I had left work with every intention of meeting up with Riley and bringing her out for a drink with the guys.

Talking with her the week before had been fun and I wanted more girl time with her. She was so carefree and didn't blink at anything I said.

She had brought out some vodka and started mixing drinks for us. I had admitted to her that I hadn't played with any of the toys I purchased from her store.

I was nervous. Riley called it the *mental embarrassment block*. She said that was a fault of the human brain, the embarrassment emotion. There was no point in it, and it constantly ruined so many things. Hence, the vodka. She brought out the alcohol in hopes it would help me loosen up. She didn't realize I really didn't drink hard liquor. I had two drinks before I was way more than buzzed. She drove me to the bar and the rest was history.

"So, what did you think of Riley?" I rolled my head to look at him. Alex had had a grin on his face since we left.

"Honestly, I didn't think much of her, just glad she was a *she.*"

I screwed my face in confusion, analyzing his words. "You thought Riley was a guy?"

"Yes. Yes, I did." He glanced at me before looking back to the road. "Look, you brought up dating, having sex, and then suddenly you are bringing your 'friend' to pool night?" He shook his head. "I absolutely thought you were introducing all of us to your new boyfriend."

"You're such a dork." I reached out, poking his side. "I never brought up having sex. You did." I looked back out the window. "I barely brought it up with you, and you thought in the span of a week I met some guy and was already going to let you meet him?" I giggled and shook my head. I let myself believe that maybe Alex was jealous. I really wanted him to be jealous. I wanted him to think about us too. I didn't want to be the only one wondering if something more could be here. "It will be a cold day in hell before I bring a guy home to meet you," I murmured against the window.

Silence filled the car.

"Do you really mean that?" His tone had changed. I turned to look at him and could see him white knuckle the steering wheel. Was he. . .mad?

I watched him. I was so confused. Jon said Alex liked someone; Alex told me that it was just sex. I had no idea what to believe anymore. And why was he acting this way?

"Do I need to?" I asked.

"It's not about you needing to, it's about you wanting to." He aggressively flipped the indicator to turn.

"Well, if you want to know who and where I meet everyone, then I should tell you that I met Riley at a sex shop." The words fell out of my mouth unintentionally. The liquor gave me loose lips. I tried to muster up shame or embarrassment, but the alcohol covered that up for me.

Alex slammed on the brakes, pulling over to the side of the road. He turned to me and I could see the shock written all over his face, the streetlights the only illumination provided.

"Why the fuck were you at a sex shop, Wren?"

The shock in his eyes had me laughing. Typically, Alex was the one pushing my buttons to get reactions out of me. Him giving the big reactions was something new. "Because my therapist recommended it."

"For what reason?" He sounded bewildered.

"Oh my god, Alex, what reason do you think?" I was still laughing. "Because I don't know how to have sex!" I threw my hands up in what little space we had together. "I have never had sex before. Not consensual. I don't have a clue as to how it's supposed to be like. I just know how to lie there and take it." The crassness of my words had him flinching. The more I spoke, the angrier I became. "I don't have firsts. I have never been kissed by a guy I liked. I don't know what it's like to lie in the arms of someone who loves me. I don't know what an orgasm feels like. I don't even know how to touch myself! I don't fucking know anything!"

My throat was raw from shouting. The alcohol had burned up in my anger. Somehow, admitting all this out loud to him in the heat of the moment, and not in a controlled environment like Laurel's office, made me angry.

I was so angry.

I had missed out on something that should have been normal, and now I was struggling with how to take my first step. Since I decided I wanted to try, it felt like a ticking time bomb. Like if I didn't get to it soon, it would never happen for me.

Or Alex would find someone he wanted to be with.

Quietly, Alex put the car in drive and took us home. I missed my buzz and was grateful that Riley had slipped the rest of a bottle in my bag.

We got home and I managed to stay upright long enough to open the fridge, pull a can of soda out, and head upstairs, shutting the door behind me.

I stripped out of my clothes, pulling on one of my sleep shirts before I dug the bottle of vodka out of my purse and cracked the soda open. I took a few swigs before chasing it with the soda and set everything down on my desk.

I was going to do it tonight. I pulled out the items from where I had stashed them on my desk chair and pulled out the double-headed vibrator and the lube, leaving the other items in the bag. Moving to my bed, I chased another shot of vodka down, slowly feeling it warm my blood and loosen me up.

I peeled the foil protectant off the lube and put a little dab on my finger, massaging it between the two. It was smooth and had a warming effect.

"Oh," I whispered in wonder.

I dabbed a little on the smaller head of the vibrator, rolling it between my fingers to coat it completely. I leaned back on my pillows, pulled my shirt up around my waist, sans panties, and turned it on. The vibrator was quiet. Gently, I glided it down my center, jerking it away at the sensation.

"Woah." Settling back down, I softly moved the head between my legs. I played with it, discovering the more sensitive areas of my center.

My skin heated in a flush and sensations built. I didn't understand what they were, so when it got too much for me to handle, I pulled it away.

Preparing myself, I took the smooth drumming head and place it at the top, finding a spot next to my clitoris where it wasn't so sensitive that I would explode on impact.

A moan escaped me, and my knees started to shake. I clasped my free hand over my mouth and decreased the pressure slightly.

Holy shit!

Right as I felt like I was about to crest a hill, my door swung open. A startled squeak slipped out of me and I shot up, fumbling with the buttons to turn it off.

"Wh-What the fuck Alex!"

Only the streetlamp illuminated my room in an amber hue. It cut across his chest. Slowly, he walked into my room and I was grateful that the shirt fell around my hips, hiding my lack of panties.

"What are you doing?" His words were slow and even.

"Nothing!" I said too fast, and I swear I saw a smirk on his face.

"Wren." His knees hit my bed and he kneeled. His hand wrapped around my foot. "I know about the vibrator."

My cheeks were hot and I felt mortified. I was breathing heavily, and I could honestly kill him for interrupting me.

I understand what they meant by *sexual frustration* now.

"How do you know about it?"

He chuckled softly. "One, I can hear that thing through the walls." My cheeks flushed hotter. "Two, I may have discovered it earlier today when I was looking for a towel."

I looked to the chair and was only just realizing the towel I had laid over everything this morning was missing.

Oh god.

"Let me be your first."

My eyes widened on him. My hands balled in my sheets.

"What?" The words came out in a whisper.

"I want to be your first, Wren." His thumb traced circles on the top of my foot. "After all these years, do you trust me?" His eyes searched mine. "There isn't another man on this planet that cares about you more than me. I would never hurt you. Not intentionally."

"Alex, I thought there was someone else. I thought. . ." I almost let it slip what Jon had said to me.

He shook his head. "Wren, there is no one else. There is only you for me."

Uncertainty had me gnawing at my lip.

"But Alex." I had to voice it. I had to. "What happens if—"

"If things go bad? I know. I've thought about that, too, but I know if this isn't what you want, I'm not going to force you into anything. I'm not going to resent you. If this happens once and you never want it to happen again, that's your choice and I respect it. I would never treat you otherwise."

"What if. . . *I'm* not what *you* want?"

The tension seemed to leave him. He laughed softly, his head dipping down, head shaking, before he looked up, a gentle look in his eyes. "Wren, what have I told you?" His other hand came up, cupping my cheek. "You are the *only* thing I have ever asked for. The only one I have ever wanted."

His eyes in the streetlight seemed to be on fire, matching the fire that was burning inside me.

I crawled to the edge of the bed. My eyes dropped to his lips and then back up to his eyes.

"I want you to be my first." My voice was steady, true. I wanted this. I wanted him.

And that's what this was. Alex would be my first. Nothing before him ever happened.

He rose up, his lips a breath away from mine. I took the last inch, my lips softly brushing against his. Testing the feel of his lips against mine.

His lips were softer than I had imagined. Alex held still, letting me kiss him. Slowly, his lips moved against mine and he took control. I followed his lead. His rough hand brushed my hair back and he pulled away. I craned my head up to look up at him at his full height. I was only now realizing it, but he was just in his boxers.

He closed my door and pushed the button lock on it. Crawling on the bed, I rose up on my knees, unsure of what to do.

"If I do anything you don't like, just tell me to stop, okay?"

I nodded. We were both kneeling on the bed, my hands fisted in my shirt.

Alex took them to his chest. He nodded down at me, and tenderly I ran my hands over the hard muscles of his chest. His breath shuddered. My hands explored further, running down his hard stomach and up his sides.

He leaned in and I closed the distance to kiss him. Feeling more confident this time. He tipped his head and I felt his tongue brush the seam of my lips, the feeling foreign. I parted my lips and he tasted me, deepening the kiss. My hands moved around and tangled in his hair. He moaned at my tightening fingers. The sound caused a thrill to run through me.

I had never been turned on by a man's reaction before. I tightened my fingers more and he hissed in pleasure.

His hand swept under my sleep shirt, fingers grazing up the soft flesh of my inner thighs. I shamelessly widened my knees farther apart, inviting his hand. It climbed higher until I was tensing in anticipation, my clit throbbing, wanting his attention.

"Alex," I breathed against his lips.

"Tell me you want me to do it, Wren."

I opened my eyes and looked into his brown hues. This felt significant to him. Important. His eyes spoke to me and I pulled his lips down to mine. Nipping at his lower lip.

"I want you, Alex. Please, touch me."

He stroked my center.

"Oh." I gasped at the feeling.

He slid his fingers through my wetness, coating them before carefully sliding one digit into me. My eyes closed and my head fell against his shoulder at the unbearable feeling. One finger and it almost felt like it was too much. He pulled out and gently thrust back into me. His thumb rolled over my clit and I involuntarily bucked against his hand.

"You're so tight. I need to get you ready."

"Hmm?" I hummed, dizzy with pleasure.

Chuckling, he reached down, picking up the hem of my shirt. His eyes asked the question, and I nodded my answer. Lifting my arms over my head, he took my only scrap of clothing off of me. I was bared to him.

"You are so beautiful." But his eyes weren't looking down at my body, only at my face. He held my stare for another moment before his eyes finally dropped.

His breath seemed to catch in his throat.

"Fuck."

Alex dipped his head down and captured my nipple between his lips. His tongue rolled over the hard nub. I found myself panting. He sucked hard before pulling away, causing a *pop* to sound as he released my breast.

With one hand braced behind me, he lay me down. I was so overwhelmed with everything that I didn't realize what he was doing until he licked up my center.

"Oh god!" I gripped his shoulders and struggled. He lapped at me, paying close attention to my most sensitive spot. I felt his finger insert in again and he rolled it upwards, causing blinding pleasure to hit. My first orgasm rolled through me. I bucked and writhed against his mouth.

"Fuck." The word slipped from my lips and Alex chuckled as he pulled away. He moved away from me and I heard the tearing of foil. He rolled the condom onto himself and settled between my legs.

I swallowed hard, the apprehensiveness building. I wanted this, I did. I didn't have to convince myself, but the nerves were there.

It's Alex. You have nothing to worry about, I reminded myself.

"You tell me if you want to stop. Okay?"

I nodded, and he lined himself with my entrance. Slowly, he pressed into me. Both our gazes were fixated on this, watching as he pressed inside of me. Slowly, inch by excruciating inch. My throat clogged. It wasn't painful, but the pressure building had my nails sinking into his forearms.

"A–Alex. . ." I was trying to fight to breathe. He stilled, watching me.

"Does it hurt?" he asked, his breath heavy.

"S-sort of." I couldn't articulate the way it felt.

"Do you want me to stop?"

I shook my head. "I just need a minute."

His hand moved to my side, and soon I heard the low thrumming of the vibrator. "Let's try this." He handed it to me, nodding down to where our bodies joined. "Put it where it feels the best." Nervously, I moved it between us, finding the spot that felt the best. Pleasure entwined with the pressure, and I could feel myself relax.

"F-fuck!" Alex 's arms started to shake and I pulled it back, startled.

"Are you okay?" I asked nervously.

His head dropped and he let out a breathy laugh. "Yeah. It's just a lot. It's fine, put it back."

I did again and relaxed. "Move." It came out as a whine, and I rolled my hips, trying to get some friction.

He pushed in slowly to the hilt.

"Is that okay?"

I gripped his hip, trying to encourage him to move. "Yes, god, Alex, don't stop."

He moved slowly, but then his pace built.

"Wren, between your grip on me and that vibrator, this isn't going to last long. You tell me when you are about to come."

Our sweat-drenched bodies caused my handling of the vibrator to move. It made direct contact with my clit and I clenched around him.

"Yes," he strained the words out. He pulled almost all the way out before he pushed back in, the pleasure heightened.

"I think I'm about to. . ." I gasped. "Oh god."

"That's my girl."

And that did it. I let go of all the building pressure, riding the waves and pulling the vibrator away when it all became too much.

"Wren. . ." I felt Alex's release inside me, his hips jerk and move with the last of his own pleasure. His arms gave out, and he dropped his weight onto me.

My tired arms came up and ran up and down his back. The only sound was our heavy breathing. He nuzzled into my neck, placing kisses there.

CHAPTER 24

WREN

THE SUN CAST THROUGH THE WINDOWS, WAKING ME. The clock radio on my bedside table played quietly. I mentally took inventory of my body. I was sore. I stretched my legs, feeling Alex's tangled with mine. His arm wrapped around my waist and pulled me to him. His body was warm against mine and I felt at home.

His lips pressed against my forehead. I nuzzled into his neck, kissing his throat.

"Hmm, morning." I could feel the vibration from his hum on my lips. "How do you feel?" He pulled his head back, looking me over. Rough hands moved over my hips, pulling my thigh up to hook my ankle around him. We were still naked, and I could feel his arousal at my center, but he didn't push. Didn't probe. Just held me.

"Sore." I smiled up at him. His brown eyes searched my face; a crease in his brow formed. "But good. I feel good. Happy." Really, I was on cloud nine. I didn't know sex could feel this way. I didn't know it would feel good. The frown disappeared and he smiled at me.

"Good." He came closer, his lips ghosting over mine. I led the way, deepening the kiss. Alex rolled me on my back, putting a minimal amount of weight on me. His lips moved down my neck, over my collarbone, to my breasts and down to my stomach. I felt my insides twist, a heat moving into them, when my stomach growled. Loudly.

Alex laughed, placing his head on my stomach. I covered my face with my hands, groaning. "Not again."

He laughed harder then. "I should know by now that I am to feed you before anything else."

He sat up on his knees. I squirmed, a little shy to be bared to him, but I didn't move to cover myself, and he didn't cover himself. His want for me was standing at full attention. Alex was strong, and you could see it on him, broad shoulders with muscles that moved with him. His waist tapered down to his hips. He didn't have defined abs like I would see on models in magazines, but his stomach was hard with muscle.

"I'm going to run and get us some food."

"No, I can make us something." I went to get up, but he dropped down onto all fours, making me lie back down.

"We haven't gone grocery shopping. There's nothing here unless you want cold pizza, and I think Jon ate the last of it." He pressed another kiss to my lips. It was languid, sensual, and I never wanted it to end. "Don't you dare get up, we are eating in bed and sleeping all day."

"Just sleeping?" I questioned with mirth in my eyes.

He chuckled, slipped off the bed, and walked his bare naked ass across the hall, coming back dressed in a pair of jeans that had paint on them and pulling on a white T-shirt. "Any special requests?"

"Dealer's choice." I pulled the sheet up around myself, sitting up cross-legged. I reached over to the bedside table and grabbed a hair tie, pulling my hair up into a bun. Alex leaned against the doorframe, arms crossed, watching me.

I watched him, a smirk on my lips. For some reason, I felt powerful with his eyes on me. He made me feel powerful. I could see all the love, want, need evident on his face. The feelings were overwhelming in my chest, and I felt like I was going to burst.

"What?"

His arms lifted and fell as he took in a breath. "I just never thought that drowning could feel this good, till I was drowning in you."

"I love you." The words were out and I couldn't take them back. I didn't want them back. I wanted him to know. I wanted to make him feel the same way I did.

"I love you."

He strode over to me in three steps. His hands grasped my face, and he kissed the sense out of me, ending it with a few pecks. "This is what I want, Wren—you, and me for the rest of our lives. I want to be your first and last. I want to wake up to you, go to sleep with you, work with you, listen to you sing, watch you get ready. I just want you, Wren. For the rest of forever."

"Yes, I want this too. I want you for the rest of our lives."

Alex brushed a few strands out of my face, kissing the sense out of me one last time. "Be back soon."

I fell back onto the bed, the sun still casting through the windows. I had thought about getting some curtains, but I loved the morning light. I loved everything about this room, this house. My life. Everything was falling into place. I had a good job; Alex, Gloria, and I had made it out of the apartment. We weren't living paycheck to paycheck anymore. We were actually able to live a little. Splurge a little.

I rolled over pulling the pillow under my chest and holding myself up on my elbows and scrolling through my phone. The radio played a song I recognized. I reached over and turned it up a bit, humming along, noticing Alex's necklace on my bedside table. He must have taken it off last night. I worked on a shopping list, writing out things we needed for the house.

The minutes ticked by and I bathed in the warmth of the sunlit room; the sheet had fallen around my hips, but I didn't care. I patiently waited for Alex to return with food. Maybe we could go to the library, update our address, get some books, and spend the day reading in bed like we used to.

Behind me, I heard the squeak of the stairs and smiled.

"So, what did you get? Something from Tony's?" I heard the click of the bedroom door behind me and laughed, "What, afraid Ma is going to come home and see us? She is going to have a field day when we tell her, but she is going to be happy for us."

I felt the bed dip at my feet and locked the screen of my phone, setting it on the bedside table. The sheet slowly pulled down my back and I lay my head back down. "I thought you wanted to feed me first."

The overwhelming stench of cigarettes and body odor hit me. My body locked up. Alarm bells sounded in my head. I don't turn around, my eyes shifting to my phone that was just in my hands.

No.

No.

No.

A rough hand wrapped around my ankle and jerked me down the bed, breaking me out of my frozen state.

"NO!" I screamed, kicked, and tried pushing myself off the bed. I reached for my phone, but his hand gripped my hair and shoved my face into the bed. His fist came down and a ringing sound split my head.

"I finally fucking found you." His oily voice was directly in my ear.

My vision doubled before everything aligned back together.

Kevin.

But he didn't look like Kevin. He's bald now. His skin was extra shiny. It rippled. Half his face was leathery, the result from the burns he'd sustained.

"HELP!" I finally found my voice and screamed as loud as I could manage. I grabbed his hand still holding my face and ripped at it with my nails, kicking and screaming with everything I had. My throat went raw before he punched me again, the bite of metal along my face from his ring. Everything went still and his weight was pulled off me. Through the haze and ringing, I heard the clink of his belt, the sound of his pants dropping.

I found myself wishing he would have hit me harder. I wished I would have blacked out, so I didn't have to be aware in this moment.

Then his weight was there again, and I felt his spit hit my ass, sliding down. His dick was there, pushing and prodding around until he found what he's looking for. In one thrust, he buried himself in my ass. I screamed, his hand pushing my head into the bed, muffling the sound. Pain ripped through me, blinding me. He pumped himself two, three, four times till he pulled out. And then he was pushing into my center, ripping through every good moment I had with Alex up until now. I squeezed my eyes shut and tried to go back to last night.

Alex's rough hands on my hips, his soft hand in my hair. His weight on me, his woodsy amber scent that I could drown in. I tried wrapping myself in every memory of him. Alex would make it better. This would be over and he would make everything okay again.

Kevin's hot breath was in my ear. "You thought you got away, didn't you?" His hand ripped at my hair, pulling my head up. His hot tongue licked up the side of my face, swirled in my ear. I tried not to react. Tried not to shudder, but I couldn't block out the feeling. I did and he groaned his pleasure into my ear. "That tight fucking cunt loves my dick."

It felt like forever. He beat me, slapped every part of my exposed skin, punching my back. His fingers dug into my fleshy ass. He pulled my head up and shoving his fingers in my mouth. I tried to bite down but he dug his fingers into the joint, keeping my mouth open as he thrust into me. He was leaving his mark. With each hit, I flinched, tensed, and Kevin groaned. It felt never-ending. "There's so much more to you now with some meat on your bones."

I wanted to die.

Like my brain knew exactly what to do, like I hadn't spent the last four blissful years healing and recovering from the last four, I found a spot on the wall and focused on that. Hot tears spilling out of my eyes. The numbness never fully took over. I couldn't disconnect from my body and come back when it was over. I felt every thrust.

Alex.
Alex. Where are you?
I need you.
Come home.

CHAPTER 25

ALEX

"Yeah, man, you can come by and see if it's here. I didn't see it this morning, but I wasn't really looking." I tried to hide my disappointment from Jon over the phone. I was almost back to the house when he called. He thought he'd left his suit jacket at the house and needed to come pick it up before some meeting.

"That's why I called Wren first. She probably would have noticed. I wonder why she didn't answer the phone. She always answers."

I rolled my eyes and refrained from telling him she was naked in bed waiting for me to come home. Not that I would ever shove that in his face, out of respect for Wren, but he was constantly shoving her at me like they were something when they only were in his head. "She might be in the shower or something. We were up late. . .unpacking." A smile pressed its way to my lips. He was going to flip out when he eventually found out about us.

I just wanted to keep her to myself for a while longer.

I was on cloud fucking nine.

"Well, are you almost back? Would you check? I have a brief to get to this afternoon. I'm already on my way there. I'm about five minutes out."

"On a Saturday?" I turned up the next block, my eyes

catching on a figure walking down the sidewalk, distracting me from Jon's words.

He had a hat pulled low on his head but his face looked. . .disfigured, and I strangely felt like I knew him.

"Alex?" Jon disrupted my thoughts.

I pulled up to the house and turned off my truck, grabbing the sack of food and getting out. "I just pulled up. I'll check in a minute." I moved fast, taking the porch steps two at a time, unlocking the door. I was eager to get him off the phone and continue where Wren and I left off.

"I'm in the kitchen and I don't see it." I looked in the laundry room and on the counters.

"Well, can you ask Wren?" Jon said impatiently.

"Don't you have like five suit jackets?" I tried not to sound irritated. "Yeah, let me ask her." I bounded up the steps, walking into her room.

"Hey, Jon is on the phone, he's asking if—" I froze at the door. Wren wasn't in bed where I left her. Her sheets were a mess. "Wren?" I turned around and looked in the open bathroom, but she wasn't there either.

"Dude, the house isn't big enough for you to lose her in." He laughed at his own joke.

I didn't respond. I looked back to her bed, and that's when I noticed them. The dark patches on her brand-new sheets. I walk farther into her room, pinching the sheets between two fingers and pulling them up. "What the. . ." Then I saw her. She was on the far side of the bed on the floor in a ball, her head tucked on top of her knees. I froze. She was still naked, and shaking.

Bruises were already forming over her entire body. I could see the handprints on her arm.

"Wren!" She flinched and I dropped the phone, hearing it clatter to the ground. I rounded the bed and kneeled down beside her, my hands hovering over her body. She looked up at me. Her face was swollen, hair matted with blood. Cuts across her cheek. One eye was swollen shut.

No!

My stomach fell out from under me. I didn't want to believe it. I didn't want to think about it. But it was all right there in front of me, the evidence littered over her body and on the floor, trickling out from between her legs.

"H. . .he found me." Her voice was barely a whisper. "Kevin."

The figure walking on the sidewalk came back to me. The whole world tilted, and rage blurred my vision. He found her.

Even after all these years. After getting her out of the apartments, moving eight miles away from where it all happened, he found her. I had hoped the fire would have killed him, but it didn't. I had known it didn't kill him, but I thought that maybe the damage to his body would have been bad enough he wouldn't be able to go out and do much, but he did. He had.

I failed her.

I didn't have long.

I moved away from her, picking up the phone. "Where are you?"

"Just pulled outside. What's going on? What's with the shouting?"

I hung up the phone and look back to Wren. "I'll be back."

"Alex, no! Don't leave me!" Her voice broke, and the thought of her being raped by him, screaming with no one to hear—without me to be there for her—only ripped me apart.

"Jon just got here." I moved to her closet and pulled a large hoodie down, quickly, and as gently as possible dressed her in it. She whimpered and cried in pain with every movement she made. With each sound, the anger intensified. "I have to go. I don't have much time." I grazed her bloodied swollen cheek with the back of my hand.

"Alex, no, I need you to stay." Her voice was hoarse and my eyes dropped to her neck. A red ring circled it. Her fists balled into my shirt as she tried to keep me to her.

"Did he. . .did he choke you?" The tips of my fingers grazed the welts, and she hissed in pain.

"Alex, please just stay." She stood on shaky legs and wrapped her arms around me. My resolve was breaking. The need to find him was overwhelming. Once I killed him, I could tend to Wren, but only after he was dead.

"Never again." I shook my head, doing everything I could to keep my voice level. I wasn't going to be the one to scare her. Gently, I unwound her arms from me, but she got up and followed me.

Jon was just walking into the house as we got downstairs. Wren was still on my heels. I turned and wrapped an arm around her, passing her to Jon. He took her, confused.

"Don't let her follow me."

"Alex! Please!" She was trying to pull herself away from Jon.

"Don't let her follow me! You keep her safe!"

"Alex, what is going on?" His hand lashed out and grabbed my arm. I jerked away from him.

"Just fucking stay here! And make sure she's okay." I sprinted out of the house and headed in the direction I saw him going. Looking up and down each street as I passed. I jumped fences and sprinted through people's yards. Dogs barked, people yelled, but I didn't stop. I had to find him. My lungs burned and I could taste the blood from the exertion.

I ended up in a business district. It was a strip mall with all glass fronts, and half of them had paper or dark tint in the windows, still closed. Still, I pulled on the door of each one I walked past, just in case.

I combed through the streets, finding the bare lots that the homeless have set up camp in. I asked around. They either didn't know who I'm talking about or weren't in the right state of mind to answer me. Kevin had to have lived close by. It wasn't a situation where he just happened to see her.

I was not in the right state of mind to be looking for him. I didn't have my cell phone on me, so I couldn't call Jon and check in on Wren. With my hands in my pocket, I gripped the cool metal in my pocket.

I would find him.

The morning came and went. By late afternoon, my patience was wearing thin.

I couldn't go back to the house. I couldn't face her again unless I could tell her that he was dead.

I walked into my sixth bar. But I wasn't going to be here long.

That's when I saw him. He was sitting up at the bar with a beer in hand and a shit-eating grin on his face, talking to someone else. I took a step forward, but a hand was on my shoulder before I could move.

"Hey," a voice sounded. I turned, about ready to rip the guy's arm off. "I don't know what's going on, but if you're here to cause trouble, then just leave." He pulled his hand off my shoulder and I glimpse something.

A black band around his wrist.

I reached into my back pocket and pulled out my wallet, grabbing all the cash I had. It was seventy-five dollars.

"The guy with the fucked up face at the bar, can you throw him out into the alleyway?" I held out the cash to him. He looked down at it, then back up to me.

"What did he do?"

My eyes fell back to the black hair tie around his wrist. I had been known to keep a hair tie on my wrist for Wren. It never failed that she would want to throw her hair up and never had one. I liked being able to always hand her one.

So, I took a chance that he was the same way.

"You know the worst thing men can do to women?" Understanding hardened his eyes. "That."

He looked over my shoulder then back down to the cash. "Keep it. I'll give you five minutes to get back there."

"Hey, what the fuck did I do!?" The emergency door opened and Kevin was kicked out, landing on his ass.

"Fuckin' ugly bastard," the security guard said before the door was slammed shut. Kevin threw himself up against it and pounded at the door, yelling.

"Hey!" I shouted, getting his attention.

I was almost on him, dragging a pipe I had found along the ground. Kevin turned toward me, and as soon as I saw recognition in his face, I swung.

I connected with his stomach. He doubled over, groaning. I swung the pipe again, lower this time, catching his shins. I thought I heard the crack of a bone in his leg.

He cried out in pain.

I tossed the pipe to the side, letting it clank and roll along the ground.

His leathery face split into a smile when he looked up at me, like he knew who I was. Blood was trickling out the corner of his mouth, the sickening grin heightening my anger.

Like he knew who she was to me.

I kneeled down on his chest, pinning his arms down. Rage blinded me as I threw punch after punch at him. Turning his face into something unrecognizable. He gurgled up a laugh, and even when I couldn't hear him anymore, I kept punching, beating. I stopped and his head turned, spitting out more blood and even a tooth. He wheezed as I wrapped my fists around his throat and squeezed, bearing all my weight down onto my hands. I watched his eyes widen. I was straddling his chest, my knees on his arms so he couldn't even try to stop me. I was twice as big as him. He kicked and flailed his legs, then slowed. I could hear his heels digging into the gravel. Blood vessels in his wide eyes popped. He stopped fighting, but I still held his throat.

Only when I felt the thread of his pulse stop did I let go. I continued to sit on his chest, letting the seconds and minutes tick by, watching for any sign of life. He didn't move. Didn't breathe. Still, the sick look of satisfaction seemed to remain on his face, even in death. Even when you could barely tell he was human.

Only then did I finally get up, leaving him in the alley and heading back to the house. My limbs were heavy.

I needed to get back to her.

I could finally go to her.

Back at the house, I looked through the first floor. I took the stairs one at a time. At the top, Jon was standing there at Wren's door. His eyes widened.

"Alex? What the fuck happened to you?" Jon's words were guarded, hesitant. He took a step back.

I look over his shoulder into the open bathroom. I could see my reflection in the mirror. My white shirt was stained with blood. My face had Kevin's blood splattered all over it. I didn't look like the man I was when I woke up this morning.

This morning seemed like a lifetime ago. Funny how the course of one's life can change in an instant.

I failed her. I promised her over and over that I would never let it happen to her again, and it did.

All because I'd failed to kill him in the fire the first time.

I looked away from Jon, ignoring the fear in his eyes. Wren's door was wide open. The evidence of what transpired in there evident. I looked across the hall to my closed door. I knocked softly on it. Leaving behind blood spots.

"She won't come out. I've been trying since you left." I could hear the apprehension in his voice.

"Wren, it's me." My voice didn't even sound like my own.

Soft footsteps, and then the door pulled open. She looked me up and down. Both of us were covered in blood. She was still in the hoodie I left her in. Her face more swollen. She hadn't cleaned herself up all day.

Anger split her face, and she slapped me. The sound was deafening. The sharp pain in my face didn't come close to the pain I felt for her. Slowly, I turned my head back to look at her. Tears were streaming down her face.

"You fucking left me!" Her hands turned to fists, and she

pounded on my chest. "You left me!" Sobs racked her body. Her hits slowed, and soon she was gripping my shirt. Her head bowed as she cried.

"I'm sorry." My own sob cracked my voice.

"Is he dead?" she asked, her voice tired.

"I took care of him," I said, conveying my meaning to her.

She lifted her head and hit me with angry greens.

"Wren, I'm *so* sorry."

Her face contorted then, and she grabbed onto me. Her wails rang out and I held her, picking her up as gently as I could. I sat on the bed with her cradled in my arms and let her cry. She did it all: cried and screamed as loud as her voice could manage. I knew I would never be able to unhear those sounds. They would be the sounds of my nightmares for the rest of my life. I held her to my chest. Rocked her and kissed her forehead, murmuring the words I should have been able to tell her years ago.

"He's dead, sweetheart. He's never coming back. I made sure of it."

It felt like I held her for hours. Jon eventually disappeared, but I didn't know where he went. I didn't care.

Then the cops came.

"Alexander Harper, you are under arrest for the murder of Kevin Whitman. You have the right to remain silent; anything you say can and will be used against you in a court of law. You have the right to an attorney, and if you cannot afford one, one will be provided for you."

Six years later

CHAPTER 26
WREN, 26 YEARS OLD

"Come on, you can hit harder than that!" Mario yelled, his voice echoing off the gym walls. We were causing a scene; there were people lined up around the mat. When two instructors went at each other, it was always a show. "Come on, Wren, my fucking grandma can kick harder than you!"

I threw two more jabs at his mitts. Mario was good, but he got into a rhythm and tended to repeat the same moves when we were just training like this. Knowing when he was about ready to sweep my feet, I jumped, landing two blows simultaneously on his chest when I touched the mat.

"OOF!" A puff of air left him. I dropped down into a crouch and swept his feet out from under him, knocking him on his ass.

"There we go!" Marshall clapped his hands together from the sidelines. "See, that's how it's done!" I took a few steps back away from Mario before reaching down and helping him up.

"Maybe if you would stop talking and actually fight, you wouldn't always end up on your ass," I huffed out.

"Good job, Wren." Mario nodded, a chuckle on his lips. I nodded back, bracing my hands on my hips and walking a circle on the mat to catch my breath.

"That's a wrap for the day," Marshall said. He was the gym owner. I'd joined four years ago, and I was here every other day, either training or teaching. I crossed the mat and unwrapped my hands, heading to my bag, balling the blood-stained fabric up and shoving it away. I turned my phone on and set it down while the messages pinged in. Grabbed my water bottle and took a deep drink.

"Coming from behind," Mario warned, and I moved so I could see him. It wouldn't be the first time I took someone to the ground for sneaking up behind me. "Good job today. I think next week we will work on ground defense."

I nodded, swallowing the last of my water. "Sounds good." I dragged in a breath, the perspiration clinging to my skin. Mario was only telling me so I could prepare myself.

"What's the plan tonight?"

"We have that thing tonight, right?" Typically, Mario and I went out for drinks on Fridays after a training session. It wasn't something that was expected, but it was something that we did if we were both up for it. I met Mario years ago when I was in high school. He and Marshall partnered to open this gym, and now he taught classes here as a personal trainer. He was tall, strong with a lithe body, muscular but not bulky.

"You showering first?"

"Yeah. Just a quick one. Will you wait for me?"

"Okay." Mario nodded. "Make it fast."

I headed to the showers, tying my hair up and quickly showering. I dried off in the shower stall and threw on a black T-shirt and jeans.

"Mine or yours?" Mario asked as I emerged from the showers. His face was turned down to his phone. Most of the lights were turned off in the building now.

"Yours." I didn't know why he even asked anymore; we always took his, but I did appreciate the gesture. He stood, pocketing his phone. "Let's go."

The bar was only a few miles from the gym. We parked and headed inside, seeing some other people who took classes from us.

"Here." Mario passed me cash. "For the coin machine. We can do a few rounds of pool. I'll grab drinks. Your usual?"

"Yes, please." I took the cash and headed to the coin machine. Once the coins were in hand, I scored us a pool table at the back corner of the bar. The balls rolled out the bottom and I racked them, lining them up for break.

"Here you go." Mario handed me a well whiskey on ice, and I sipped it.

"Thank you."

We played a few quick rounds in silence. Mario and I had been working together for the last five years. We had a pretty good flow.

After the third round, he cursed. "Why are you so fucking good at everything you do?"

I placed the end of the pool stick on my shoe, laughing. "I'm not good, you're just really bad."

"Tell that to those awards on my uniform at home."

Mario had retired from the military and was a detective here locally. He was in his late thirties but had enlisted shortly after his eighteenth birthday.

He was done with the party life and wanted to be someone of importance. Going into the military had given him the advantage of free schooling. He went through post, graduated top of his class, and got on the police force, working his way to detective status.

He worked in the drug unit now.

I'd joined the gym shortly after Alex's sentencing.

At the memory of Alex, I drained my drink. "I'll get us another round." I gave a tight-lipped smile and headed up to the bar. It wasn't a busy night. A few people were scattered throughout the building. Some loners were sitting up at the bar end. The jukebox continued to play old rock.

I smiled at Barry as he walked over. "What can I get for you, my dear?"

"Your well whiskey on ice and a stout."

"You got it." He tapped the bar top with his knuckle before heading off.

I rolled my head, the tension building in my neck. I was going to be sore tomorrow and was looking forward to a hot bath in my clawfoot bathtub at home. I turned to survey the bar. Mario was leaning against the pool table, his face lit up by his phone.

Even when he was off duty, he wasn't really. "I think you need this. Here, drink." I looked to my left, where a man had saddled up to the barstool next to me.

"You think so, huh?"

"I do." I glanced down at the red drink. Vodka cranberry from what I could guess. My eyes narrowed at it.

"No, thank you. I've got my own drinks." I dismissed him, turning my head from his putrid breath. He smelled and I had a strong guess he was an over-the-road trucker. I didn't make a habit of taking drinks from strangers.

"You really going to turn down a drink?"

"Here you go, dear."

I picked up both the drinks, arranging them so I could hold them with one hand, passing a bill to Barry. "Keep the change."

Barry nodded to me before he looked at my unwanted companion.

"And thank you for the drink, sir," I added in a sickly sweet voice, snagging the drink without it spilling and heading away from him.

I could hear the guy's curses as I walked away.

Mario looked up as I approached him, his expression lifting and falling when he spotted the red drink. "You switching it up on me?"

I got up in his personal space, gesturing for him to take our two drinks from my hand.

"Don't look, but do you see that greasy guy up at the bar? Probably still talking to Barry and glaring at me?"

Mario quickly caught my drift and brought his drink to his lips, only looking to the bar with his eyes. From this angle to anyone else, Mario and I probably look like we were a couple having an intimate conversation.

"Mhm."

"I think he roofied this drink." I brought it up between us, turning and tipping my head back so the guy would think I was drinking it. "See the bubbles coming up from the bottom, and that white film?"

"I see it." Mario sets his and my drink down on the table by us. "You ready?"

I nodded.

He started patting his pockets like he forgot something. He walked around me, and started walking backwards, and from here, I knew the drill.

"Where are you going, babe?" I said, louder than necessary.

"Forgot something out in the truck." He winked at me. "Be right back."

I turned my back to him and the bar, picking up my whiskey and taking a long drink. I went through the motions of re-racking the balls, making sure to sway and shake my head, gradually getting worse. I picked the red drink back up, turning toward the bar, my body angled to the door like I was watching for Mario to come back. I faked taking a drink, letting it spill down my front.

"Fuck." I set the drink down on the table, wiping the spilled liquid off my chest before heading toward the bathrooms, making sure to sway and catch myself on the wall.

In the bathroom, I stood at the sink, turning it on, waiting for the door to open.

The fucker would follow. He thought he was a predator and I was his prey.

On cue, the door slowly opened, and I did my part, playing like the drugs were kicking in.

"Are you okay? His stench rolled into the small space. I did my best to not wince.

"Hmm?"

"Oh, let me help you." He took the paper towel I'd wet,

tossing it to the side before guiding me out the bathroom door. Turning right, he ushered me out the back exit. I didn't make it easy for him, dragging my feet and forcing him to support my weight.

I could tell that he'd done this before. The thought of other girls going through this made my stomach drop.

He started steering me toward a truck.

"Let her go! Put your hands behind your head!" Mario's voice boomed out. The guy's grip on my wrist tightened and I felt something press into my back.

"You fucking bitch," he spit out, realizing I'd stood to my full five-foot-four height, no longer dragging my feet.

"Better let me go." He pushed whatever was in his hand farther into my back.

Police cars started to roll into the parking lot, several coming up behind the building. Lights were flashing, and now a whole scene had been made.

"I'll fucking shoot her!" he yelled. "I'll do it!"

"Stand down!" Mario raised his gun; the officers surrounding us did the same.

I took a deep breath, centering myself before moving. I grabbed his wrist, twisting it. Something dropped in the gravel, and I kept twisting till I was at an angle to sweep his feet out from under him, making him land on his ass.

He tried to scramble up, but Mario was already there, kneeling on his back and cuffing him.

"It was just a knife." I kicked the silver thing away from them. A butterfly knife that was still folded together lay on the ground. I shook my head. This guy had underestimated the wrong girl.

Forty-five minutes later, I leaned against Mario's truck while he finished up with the other officers.

"So much for a day off." He walked up to me. "Good eye."

I shrugged. "All that training with you paid off."

"Here, let me take you back to your car."

"Wren?" A familiar voice caused me to look away from Mario.

Jonathan jogged up to me, his arms out, a concerned look on his face. "Are you okay?" He enveloped me in a hug. One arm banded across my back, the other cupping the back of my head. I took in a deep breath of his clean, crisp scent. He pulled back, looking down at me. "What the hell happened?"

I looked up into his handsome face, disheveled blond hair and light blue eyes. "I'm fine, Jon." I gave him a reassuring smile.

He gestured around us to all the police cars. "This doesn't look like everything is fine. Tell me what happened?"

"A guy tried to drug her, but she caught it before it happened. Helped get him out of the building before he could get anyone else involved," Mario explained. There was a hint of pride in his voice.

"Why is she helping you? She's not law enforcement. That's your job!" Jonathan's voice continued to rise the more he spoke.

"Jon," I interrupted, stepping in to take the heat off Mario. "I'm fine. I can handle myself."

He closed his eyes, and I could tell he was counting to ten. His icy eyes leveled me with a look that told me he was going to argue.

"Jon, you need to stop treating me like glass." My temper flared hot and I could already see that he was melting. Jon hated to fight with me, which had been something we did off and on for the last few years.

He had been treating me like I was going to break, but what he didn't realize is that I had broken a long time ago.

Now when someone fucked with me, they ended up bleeding.

"I'm sorry." He looked between me and Mario before he cupped my face in both of his hands. "Alex would never forgive me if something happened to you."

His words were heavy, and I could see the weight of them. After everything that had happened, Jon took it upon himself to take care of me. He stepped into Alex's role like it had always been his responsibility.

I tried to convince him that I was fine, that I would be fine, but he wouldn't have it. I think it was his way of comforting himself, so I allowed it.

"Come on, let me take you home." Jonathan's eyes pleaded with me.

I nodded before looking at Mario. "I'll see you on Monday."

Jon's arm came around my shoulders, guiding me to his car. He opened the door for me and even reached in, buckling me before pressing a kiss to my forehead.

He stood outside his car door, seemingly talking to himself before he got in, turning to me. "Are you crazy?"

I couldn't help but laugh at his worry. Jon was wary of the way I had chosen to cope with everything. I had joined every mixed martial artist class there was to offer. I gained the strength and the confidence to never let myself be put in a position where I was going to end up the victim.

"Just a little."

Shaking his head, he started the car.

"My car is at the gym."

"No, no, I'm taking you home. I'll pick you up tomorrow for breakfast and we will visit Gloria and *then* I will take you to your car."

"And Alex," I said softly.

He reached over, grabbing my hand and kissing the back of it. "And Alex."

CHAPTER 27

WREN

THE NEXT MORNING, AFTER BREAKFAST AT TONY'S Diner, Jon took me to see Gloria and Alex. The tires of his car crunched under the gravel road, and I rolled down his window, letting the warm summer morning air into the car. It smelled like fresh cut grass, and I could hear the sprinklers on in the distance. He found a place to park and got out, rounding the car to open my door.

I had put on a forest-green sundress with sandals, thinking that Alex would love this dress on me. I wore a light amount of makeup, keeping today simple.

I was going to do my best not to ruin my makeup with the tears I was sure would fall. We quietly walked the path to a shaded area underneath a mature oak tree.

Jon smiled softly, handing me the flowers we had picked out for today.

"How you doing, Ma?" I said, placing the flowers in the permanent vase incorporated into her headstone. I took a water bottle from my purse and filled the vase up. I brushed some fallen leaves away from the base and picked a few weeds that were poking through.

"You picked a beautiful headstone," Jon commented. He was

used to my routine now. Maintaining Gloria's resting place was important to me. She took care of me without a second thought, and now I would take care of her, even in death.

I smiled at his words, wishing Alex had been here to help me with everything for his mother. Finding his father's resting place had been hard on its own. Neither of them had ever brought me here before. I had to call every funeral home in town before someone finally found his resting place.

"Thank you." I fought back tears as they clogged my throat.

Gloria died of lung cancer five years ago. We were so caught up in Alex's court hearings that the diagnosis came too late, and there was nothing doctors could do but keep her comfortable. She didn't want to fight it. Losing her husband so early in life, and then Alex, she spoke of death like it would be a kindness. She would get to see her boys again.

I looked to the right, at the bare space next to her.

"Has the state said anything about releasing Alex's body?" Saying the words out loud had the tears spilling over. I knew the answer already, but I couldn't help but ask.

"No, sweetheart." He gentle placed his hand on my shoulder. "They still won't release him to anyone except next of kin."

Alex had committed suicide after he got news of his mom. Jon had been the only one allowed to visit him after his sentencing. Alex hadn't taken well to prison. He had gotten into fights, thrown into solitary confinement for weeks on end. Then he got the news of his mother and hanged himself in his cell.

"The guilt was too much for him. What happened to you, then losing his mother. He blamed himself." Jonathan's words echoed in my mind. *"You know he swore to protect you, and he felt like he failed you."*

"I know it's been almost five years, but it's still all so surreal," I forced the words out, standing and wiping the tears away. "I keep hoping I'll turn the corner, and he will just be there. With his big smile and his arms wide open like he was waiting on me." I wrapped my arms around myself, the emptiness still too much to handle.

"Shh. I know, honey." He enveloped me in his arms, and I buried my head into his chest. "Alex wouldn't want you to cry. He would be so proud of the life you have built. You know he's up there cheering you on."

I wasn't a religious person. After their deaths, I tried to be. I tried to find reason. The universe took the two most important people away from me so close together. I had been angry for a long time. I was still angry, but I refused to be angry here. I just wanted be grateful for them. Grateful for the life and safety they had given me. .

If it wasn't for Alex, Kevin would still be out there.

"I know." I turned my head, looking at the empty plot next to his mother and father, which I had purchased for him as soon as I had the money. "I'm going to call the cemetery on Monday. Get a headstone made up for him. Even if I can't lay him here, I want it to feel like they are all together," I decide.

"Whatever you need, Wren, we will do whatever you need." He pressed a kiss to my forehead and gave me another squeeze. "You ready?"

I nodded and Jon guided me back to his car.

Jonathan had been my biggest support after their passing. Jon had lost his best friend too. We mourned the loss, finding comfort in the stories we recalled together. We had been there for each other.

He dropped me off at my car, having me promise to go out to dinner with him sometime this week before he headed off. I sat there for a minute, trying to compose myself.

My heart ached for Alex. I missed him so much that some days it was hard to get out of bed. I couldn't work daily at Dan's Construction anymore. Being there had me falling apart. Now, I worked part time. I went in on payroll days, got the checks made out and got out of there as soon as possible.

I stopped off at the bar some evenings and caught up with Gavin and Troy. They were still thick as thieves, but even they had a little less sparkle since Alex's passing.

They had been so much support after everything.

After Kevin.

I shook my head, slapping the steering wheel. Nope, I wasn't going to spiral today. I reached into my purse and pulled out my phone, dialing the one person who could pull me out of any mood.

"Hey, baby cakes!" Riley said, her upbeat attitude infectious. "What are you up to?"

"I need a girl's day. What are you doing?" I tried to mask my mood.

"That sounds like exactly what I need, but I'm working the shop today. Trish called out sick."

"How about I pick us up some treats and come help you stock up dildos?" I couldn't help but grin.

"You know the way to my heart. See you soon!" Riley hung up.

In better spirits, I headed off to a local coffee shop, picking up a few baked treats and our iced coffee orders. The store parking lot was empty when I pulled in. Juggling the drinks in hand, I pushed my way into the store.

"I'm here!" I hollered, heading to the counter to set everything down.

"Hey, cakes." Riley appeared, walking out of the back room. She hugged me tight.

"How the hell do you always look so freaking cute?" I held her at arm's length. Riley wore coveralls that were loose fit, a black long-sleeve shirt underneath. Her red hair was braided into two French braids that sat forward on her shoulders.

She grinned and did a little twirl. "Thank you. I knew it would be a slow day, so I dressed to stock shelves." She picked up her drink, took a sip, and hummed her approval. "So why do I have the pleasure of seeing you on this beautiful Saturday afternoon?”

“Oh, Jon and I had breakfast and then went to visit Gloria.” I lifted one shoulder. “I was too sad to just head home.”

Riley squeezed my shoulder, giving me a sympathetic smile. “How are you doing with everything? It’s coming up on the five-year anniversary for both of them, right?”

“Yeah.” I picked up my own drink, taking a sip. I shook my head, clearing the thoughts of him away. “Nope, not doing this today. Come on, let’s stock some whips and chains.”

We spent the rest of the afternoon stocking the store, laughing and listening to music. Riley was like sunshine, warm and just happy. She had been my rock after everything had happened. She let me crash at her place while I looked for a new house. I couldn’t be in that place without recalling every moment of what had happened. Her, Gavin and Troy all helped pack up the house on the corner and got me moved while I was at the hospital by Gloria’s side day and night.

Once she passed, they helped me with the funeral planning and did things like make sure I ate and checked in on me.

Everyone knew what happened in that house after that day. Even though I wanted to keep it private. I wanted to just tell everyone that it was a robbery gone wrong, but I couldn’t. I had to give the gory details to the police, trying to prove that Alex had done it in self-defense.

Self-defense by proxy, to be exact.

But Alex had hunted Kevin down. So, they wouldn’t allow me to testify.

I think my friends thought I might follow in Alex’s footsteps. I had lost both people I loved most in this world in the span of weeks.

I wanted to drown, and I did for a while. I drowned in the emotions. The sadness, the anger, the guilt. I went through it. I had thoughts of ending it all. What was the point of living when everyone who ever loved me was gone?

But I could never allow myself to drown. I had always known how to swim.

Jonathan was there to pick up the pieces, and when he wasn't, Riley, Troy and Gavin were.

No one left me alone for an extended amount of time. All took shifts in watching over me. Some days they would all be there, cooking dinner, doing laundry, or just existing with me.

I don't know where I would be without them.

The afternoon went by quickly, and Riley and I said our goodbyes. I headed out of the store and was walking along the sidewalk when I glanced across the street, a figure catching my attention. I froze.

A man in dark wash jeans and a black T-shirt, his hair shaved close to his head and his arms covered in black ink, stood with his hands in his pockets. Watching me. He brought something to his lips.

"Alex."

I whispered the word, my heart falling out of my chest. I blinked once. Twice. He was still standing there, eyes still on me. I took a step in his direction, about to step out into the road when a box truck hit its horn as it sped past me. I screamed and spun back onto the sidewalk. With my hand clutched to my chest, I looked back to the man, but he was gone.

"Wren!" Riley rushed out to me, grabbing my arm and pulling me farther back on the sidewalk. "Girl, what the hell!?"

I kept staring across the street, searching for him. "I thought I saw. . . He was. . ." I struggled to find the words.

I finally looked away, staring into terrified blue eyes. I was going to tell her that I thought I saw him. I tried to say his name but, it wasn't possible.

"I'm sorry." I pushed out. "I just thought I saw someone I knew, and I didn't look both ways."

Her eyes searched mine before she let out a nervous laugh. "Jesus, Wren, you scared the shit out of me." She clutched her chest before she bent over, laughing more. I tried to laugh with her, but I was spooked. I had dreamed of Alex regularly after everything, but I had never actually hallucinated him.

"I better get home," I told her.

"Send me a text when you get home, okay?" Her eye met mine and the guilt hit me. She was still worried about me.

"I will."

CHAPTER 28

WREN

I WAS NECK-DEEP IN MY CLAWFOOT BATHTUB, submerged in hot water with a tequila perched on the little side table I'd purchased just for that purpose. I had music going softly in the background and I was trying to relax and reason with myself. The steam rose and clung to the walls of the bathroom. My skin was tinged red. I always made the water as hot as I could stand it.

I loved taking hot baths. I imagined Alex crawling in behind me, telling me how I looked like a lobster and drawing circles on my skin.

I imagined a whole life with him. Sometimes I even talked aloud in the house, as if he was in another room. I wondered if we would have fought, and what about. Would he have been the type of lover to be overbearing? See me wearing shorts and a tank and not allow me to go into town wearing something that showed too much skin, like in the movies I had watched?

Or would he have been the type to let me wear what I wanted and be proud that I was his?

I could never figure out what version I liked more.

I imagined a simple life with him. One where we were content with it being just the two of us. Fucking until the early hours of the morning and then sleeping till noon just to get up and do it again.

I closed my eyes and took in a deep breath before sliding down under the water.

Alex is dead. He hanged himself in his cell.

Jonathan identified his body.

The state would release his ashes to me here in a few months, and then I could put him to rest next to his mother.

Then I could move on.

There was no moving on from Alex, but I had to stop letting myself wade in the stagnant water.

Alex is dead.

I said the words over and over in my head, but when I closed my eyes, he was there. His messy brown hair, warm brown eyes, wide smile. That's how I remembered him. His strength and the lengths he would go for me.

He killed for me.

I had to keep kicking.

I stayed underwater as long as I could, letting my lungs burn until I couldn't hold it any longer.

I forced myself to come up for air slowly, taking in slow breaths.

Once the water had gone lukewarm and my tequila ran dry, I drained the bath, drying off before tying a robe around me. As I opened the bathroom door, two large German shepherds scrambled to get up.

"Hi, guys." I smiled down at my Velcro dogs.

Gavin and Troy hadn't been able to help themselves, bringing me home two puppies to keep me company after everyone had finally gone back to their own homes. King and Queen had been the best things to happen to me since.

I had focused all my energy into training them, getting help from Mario and some of the guys down at the station who worked with police dogs.

No one could step foot onto my property without these two knowing.

I managed to step around them and get to my bedroom, dressing in an old T-shirt and sweats. We headed downstairs, and I planned to force myself to make dinner.

I lived out of town, down a long dirt road. The property had several acres to it. It was an old farmhouse with a barn that had been converted to a shop by one of the previous owners.

The house was perfect, with a wraparound porch, hardwood floors, decent-sized kitchen and a laundry room.

I had the property fenced and a gate put at the entrance of the driveway. If the wind even blew the gate too hard and the chain rattled, the pups would hear it and take off down that way.

They didn't take too kindly to strangers.

I paused outside my office door, staring at the glass door that had paper taped to the inside of it. I turned the doorknob and pushed it open gently, flicking on the light.

The room was a mess. It had papers taped up all over the walls. In the center of the room was an easel with a piece of paper pinned to the board. His eyes stared at me.

The tips of my fingers tingled while I stared at the image I had worked on for hours.

I had no pictures of Alex. I'd torn through boxes of his mother's things after I had packed them all up. There were a few pictures of him as a child, but none of him as the Alex I knew.

Once I realized that, the anxiety started. What if I forgot his face? The flecks of golds and greens in his warm brown eyes. The way the sides of his forehead crinkled when he was concerned about me. The freckle just below his left ear.

I had gone to an art store and picked up different mediums. Acrylics, oils, watercolors. I grabbed everything I could get my hands on, determined to recreate him from memory.

I failed at all of them.

That was, until I got my hands on charcoal. Something about it made sense to me, and I had been working with it ever since.

I closed the door, heading to the kitchen.

I made quick work of some boiled noodles and a jar of alfredo sauce. I even went as far as to put some butter and garlic seasoning on some bread, toasting it in the oven.

I fed the pups their meal, which consisted of high-end ground meat that I made for them. Their meals cost more than mine did.

They sat in the kitchen, drooling puddles, when both their ears perked up. In the next breath, they had both launched themselves out the dog door.

I moved to the window above the sink. The motion-sensor floodlights had kicked on. Straining to see anything out the window, I left the kitchen and headed to the front of the house. In my front hallway, I opened the drawer of the entryway table, pulling out a .38 revolver and checking the cylinder before heading to the front door. Holding the gun had my adrenaline spiking. I steadied my breath, forcing myself to maintain a clear head.

I stared out as far as the lights illuminated but couldn't make anything out. The longest minute passed before King and Queen emerged, a ball in King's mouth and his tail wagging happily.

The stress melted away and I shook my head, only pausing when Queen stopped and turned her head back, tail high in alert mode.

I unlocked the door, opening it but keeping the storm door in place.

"Whatcha think, Queen?" She looked at me, snorting before she disappeared around the house. Moments later I heard the dog door open and close, two sets of paws on the hardwood. I stared out into the darkness for another beat; it wasn't rare for a critter from the dense woods to hang out around the property. I always tried to remind myself of that. Locking the door, I double-checked all the windows before I went to bed.

A BLACK SEDAN PULLED UP JUST AS I STEPPED OUT OF the confines of prison as a free man. The sun beating down on me was too bright. The air smelled too clean. Not enough like the blood, sweat, and shit I had dealt with for the last six years. I stared at the sedan, eyebrows quirked, hands shoved in my pocket. The only things I owned were on my back. The passenger window rolled down halfway.

"Alexander Harper?"

"What's it to you?"

"Nikolas said you needed a ride."

I stared at the sunglasses-shielded eyes for a moment longer before I looked over my shoulder. A guard stood there, his arms crossed, staring at me, a pissed look on his face. Tilting my head back, I looked to the barred windows I had been staring through the last six years. Faintly, I could see a figure standing in the window, his head nodding.

Giving the figure a two-finger salute, I gave my attention back to the sedan, pulling open the passenger door and sliding onto the leather seat. Looking back to the guard that was watching us, I flipped him off.

"Tint's too dark," the driver said, chuckling.

I proceeded to roll the window down and flipped him off again. "There you go."

The guy threw it in drive and peeled out of the dirt parking lot, kicking dust and rocks at the guard. We started down the long winding road till he braked at a stop sign.

"So, you going to ask who I am?"

"I learned a long time ago that it's better to not ask questions. Less you know the better off you are." I kept my eyes forward. Out of my peripheral vision, the guy was wearing an expensive looking suit, watch, and sunglasses. The car itself screamed *money*, and I wouldn't be surprised if the entire thing was bulletproof.

I didn't know much about Nikolas, but my instincts had told me he was dangerous. I would rather be on the devil's side than against him.

The guy turned in his seat to look at me, pulling off his sunglasses, showing ocean-blue eyes. Eyes that were eerily familiar.

"You protected my brother."

I weighed my words before I spoke them. "Can't survive in there being the only one watching your own back. He had my back, and I had his."

The guy pursed his lips. "You had my brother's back in there, I have yours out here." He held his hand out to me, and I shook it. "I'm Ezekiel." His eyes dropped to my hand, reading my knuckles. "This must be her."

I pulled my hand out of his grip, eyeing him. "What did Niko tell you about me?"

"He said he owed you his life. He said you killed a man with your bare hands for her." He nodded to my tattooed knuckles.

I flexed my hand. "I did. And I would do it again."

Ezekiel seemed unphased by my declaration. "Tell me, Alexander, do you like to kill?"

I thought about it. Did I like killing? I had enough blood on my hands to be escorted to hell by the devil himself. My world changed being in prison, and I'd had to adapt if I wanted to survive.

"It's not about liking it for me. He deserved to die."

"Did those other men you killed deserve to die?"

"They started it." The words almost felt childish coming out of my mouth. As if they had stolen my toys or something. "If they didn't want to die, they shouldn't have picked a fight."

My entire driving force was to survive in prison to get back to Wren.

I had to know why she abandoned me.

"What do you need from me?" Ezekiel asked.

"What kind of pull do you have in there?" I nodded my head back in the direction of the prison.

He chuckled. "Well, you saw what I could get in and out of there. Why?"

I did know what he could get in there, but I didn't care to know how he did it; I was only grateful he could. "I need people to still think I'm in there for a while longer. That guard that watched us leave will be a problem."

He shrugged. "Okay. I'll make phone calls." He reached behind the seat, pulling a duffel bag out and dropping it on my lap. "This is for you." I unzipped the top as he turned onto the road. "Nikolas said you needed things to get started on your new life, so here you go."

Inside the bag were some clothes, a phone, and shoes. I kept digging through it. At the bottom were several envelopes of cash. "What am I going to owe you for this?" No one did anything out of the goodness of their own heart. There was always a favor to be owed.

"No favor. You are a part of the family now. We take care of our own." *Family* had little meaning to me these days.

"I need to get back home."

"To her." He gave me a sideways glance. "If you go home, they'll know you are out. Plus, she hasn't spoken to you since you have been in there, right?"

I pulled out the phone and turned it on, working my way through the menus to get it activated. It was a little eerie how much this guy knew about me when I knew Nikolas didn't take phone calls, didn't have visitors, nor did he ever get mail. "If she thinks after all these years, I'm getting out of here and walking the other way, she has another thing coming to her."

I'd been in the dark for six years. *Six years*, I'd waited for a letter, a visit, or a phone call. Something, and I had received nothing.

My mother hadn't reached out, Wren hadn't reached out. Troy, Gavin. Not one person I called my friend. My family.

Except for Jonathan.

Jonathan had been there in the beginning. He hadn't been a lawyer yet for my trial, but he did his best to get me someone who could help me.

His father wouldn't let anyone from his firm take on the case. A murder with witnesses, something that was sure to lose, wasn't something the man wanted on his docket.

Jon's visits became fewer and fewer every year that passed. It'd been eighteen months since I last saw him.

The letters I sent were never returned.

Every person had abandoned me.

And I wanted to know why.

Wren Jacobson was going to look me in the eye and tell me she wanted nothing to do with me. She would face me, rather than running like a coward.

The sedan accelerated as we merged onto the interstate. I dialed the only phone number I knew by heart, just to have an automated voice tell me the phone number was no longer in service.

CHAPTER 30

ALEX

James David Harper
Gloria Elaine Harper
Beloved Mother and Father
Gone but never forgotten.

I READ THE GRAVESTONE ONCE, TWICE, THREE TIMES. I read it over and over, waiting for the tears to fall. Waiting to feel something other than anger.

My mother was dead.

Pure, unbridled rage filled me. *No one told me.* No one gave me the courtesy of letting me know that she died. I pulled the manila envelope out from under my arm, ripping it open and pulling out the file that Foster, the PI that Ezekiel had connected me with, sent me.

Medical documents. A diagnosis of the stage-four lung cancer that took her life within four months. The dates on her death certificate showed that it happened shortly after my sentencing. Turning the page to the nurses' notes, I saw documentation of every time Wren had checked in and out to visit her. Days went by before she checked out. Even Jon, Troy, and Gavin's names appeared on the forms. The next few pages were pictures of Wren at the graveside. Pictures of her cleaning it, sitting with her back to it, her mouth open like she was talking. There was even a picture of her lying in the grass.

A sliver of sentiment wormed its way through me. Memories of her and my mother talking and laughing together flashed through my mind. I was angry with her. I had tried to reason with myself, but I hated her for moving on with her life like I meant nothing. Still, there wasn't a doubt in my mind that she loved my mother and did everything she could for her in her last moments.

My father had an unmarked grave for years, and now my mother lied beside him, both their names on a headstone. A beautiful, black marble headstone. It looked expensive. Ma could never afford one for Dad. She could barely afford the funeral costs.

I knew Wren was the reason behind this. I placed my hand on the top of the stone, the cold seeping in. Seeing the stone melted the ice I had built around my heart, but it immediately froze again. There was no excuse for this.

Not one person told me that she died. What right did they have to not tell me?

Guilt ripped through me. I had been angry at my mother. At first, there was understanding. Wren had just been raped. I couldn't imagine the aftermath of it. I had taken care of the problem I should have taken care of years before. For the first several years, I made excuses for them. Making up reasons as to why they hadn't reached out.

I couldn't imagine what my mother thought of her only son murdering a man with his bare hands. I hadn't gotten the chance to talk to her. To tell her I was sorry.

I wasn't sorry for what I did though. I didn't regret it at all. The only thing I regretted was not being able to be there for Wren afterwards.

I had imagined that Ma would have at the very least understood.

It never even occurred to me that she had died.

I had been out of prison for a month now and learned something new every day. I rolled my neck atop my shoulders; the tattoos were barely healed but the skin was still healing and itched. There was nothing to be said. I patted the top of the grave one more time before following the path out of the cemetery.

I remembered every detail of that day up until the moment they took me away. I still had nightmares of the screams that ripped through Wren when they pulled her out of my arms.

I had already been by the house on the corner. A different family lived there now. I walked by the apartments, which were all vacant. The parking lot had potholes everywhere and the weeds were overgrown. The place looked abandoned.

There was no trace of my life anywhere.

I had tried my bank card, but it was declined. My account had been closed. The only thing that saved my ass was Nikolas and his brother.

"Fuck." This was only a minor setback though. Being cut off from the world for so long made me turn to some unorthodox methods to make sure I had something when I got out.

My cell phone rang. I answered, "Yeah?" Only two people had my phone number.

"Did you look at the file?"

"Most of it." I opened the car I was borrowing from Ezekiel, sliding into the driver's seat, tossing the documents on the passenger's seat.

"We have eyes on her."

I paused. "Where is she?"

"She just entered Aphrodite's Desires off 16th street. Looks like she's going to be there a while."

"Interesting." I turned the car on and my phone automatically connected to the Bluetooth, Foster's voice surrounding me over the intercom. "I think she has a friend who works there." The redhead I'd met once flashed through my mind. "Must still be in contact with her."

"What do you want us to do?"

"Nothing. I'll head that way." I put the car in drive. "Just keep eyes on her till I get there. I saw the pictures and the medical records, what else is in the file?"

I can hear paper shuffling on the other end. "Troy Lawson and Gavin Hayes share an apartment together off of cherrywood. They still work for the same construction company."

"What about Jonathan Smith?"

"He took over his dad's law firm as soon as he passed the bar exam. There is some paperwork showing ownership transfer."

"What happened to his father?'

"I didn't look in his direction, but I will pull some information on it." I could hear something squeak in the background, like a chair. I hadn't met Foster in person, but the PI was efficient. "The rest of that file has dates for when she sold the corner house, bought a house on the outskirts of town, and a gym she has been going to for the last four years."

"Anything else? Is she married?" The words rushed out of me. That was the unknown information that had plagued me in prison. I was convinced that she managed to move on without me. That she'd met the love of her life, gotten married, and had a kid while I was rotting in prison. Living her best life without me in it.

That's why she never wrote to me. Why she disconnected her phone, moved without a forwarding address.

"There's no marriage certificate recorded in the courthouse, She's not wearing a ring in any of the photos, either, but we can't get a good idea on if she is dating anyone. There are pictures in there of her with two different men. They are in the file." I pulled up to a stop sign and reached over, tossing the files I had seen to the floorboard until I found more pictures.

One picture was her with Jonathan. He had an arm around her waist, smiling down at her.

The other was a picture of her with a man I didn't recognize.

She was wearing shorts and a tank top, holding a water bottle while he stood with a hand on her shoulder. It looked intimate.

"Who's the other guy?"

"His name is Mario Vitale. He works at the gym she trains at, and he's also on the police force."

The shop came into view. It was different from all the other buildings surrounding it. Painted black and a deep purple, it was obvious what it was. I parked across the street and stared at the building.

"Call your guy out of the area. I want more information on those men next time you call me." I cut the call, pocketing my phone.

She was right there. I could walk across the street, go inside, and see her for the first time in years. There was an awareness that buzzed through me. The fact that she was right there. So close I could almost smell her sweet honey scent.

I had been cut off from the one person I cared about, and now that I was out, I was going to fix that. First, I had to get my affairs in order. The last month had been torture. Being out but not being near her. All trust in her had withered away.

I didn't know her life anymore.

I'd watched men find God in prison. Find a religion that spoke to them. I think it was about forgiveness or needing a purpose. Something greater in the unknown. Not every person that you meet in prison is a cold-blooded murderer. Sometimes they were just at the wrong place at the wrong time. Fell asleep at the wheel, one mistake that changed the course of their life.

I didn't need prison to find my purpose. To find my religion.

I had mine, and her name was Wren Jacobson. She was mine, even if she didn't think she was anymore.

Even if she didn't want to be.

Pushing my sunglasses up my nose, I stepped out onto the sidewalk, still facing the shop. I pulled out a pack of cigarettes and lit one, taking a deep pull. The irony hit me then; my mother died of lung cancer, and I had picked up her one bad habit while I was in prison.

I knew she had started smoking after Dad died. I found a pack in her coat pocket when I was looking for change one day. There had always been a faint smell of cigarettes on her, but I had always thought it was just from being at the diner where other people were. I knew Candy smoked. When I found the cigarettes when I was fourteen, it confirmed what I already knew.

I'm not sure how long I stood there just watching the shop, but I did, letting scenarios play in my head on how she would react if she saw me.

Maybe she wasn't there just for a visit with the redhead. Maybe she was there to buy some lacy nighty for Mario or Jon.

Visions of the one and only night we'd spent together flashed through my mind. The way she felt wrapped around my cock had me twitching. The way she moaned when I brought the vibrator to her clit, and the way she shook with pleasure as she shattered around me.

Then what happened afterwards was like throwing ice-cold water on me.

I took another drag, letting the nicotine settle me.

I opened the car door, about to slide in and drive down the street, when I heard the ringing of bells. Looking across the street, I saw her.

Wren.

She was in a green dress. To my displeasure, her hair was straightened. She was thinner than I remembered, the dress loose on what little curves she had now.

I could see the soft smile on her lips. She looked down to the bag slung over her body, went to dig in it, when she stopped in her tracks.

Our eyes locked, and I felt that current through my body. The magnetic pull that I had to fight against, grateful the car was in my way. I pulled on the cigarette again. Curious as to what she would do.

She looked like she had seen a ghost.

Good.

I saw her move to step off the street, when a truck broke our connection. I dropped into the seat, closing the door. I didn't wait. I started the car and drove off.

If I stayed any longer, I would go to her.

I didn't have the resolve I needed to approach her now and find out what I needed to know.

CHAPTER 31

ALEX

"Is this all you do with your time?" Ezekiel shelled another pistachio, tossing the shell to the ground. He was dressed in another high-dollar suit, his hair slicked back.

I rolled my neck, trying to ease the tension there.

I was used to structure. Wake up at the same time every day, eat at the same time, go out into the yard at the same time, shower on a set schedule, and just hope no one stabbed you while you were washing your ass.

The scar on my side ached at the memory.

"Do you need something, Ezekiel?" I asked as I shuffled through more paperwork that Foster had sent over.

My phone vibrated on the table, flashing Foster's name, but I ignored it while Ezekiel was in the room. I didn't fully trust Ezekiel, but I didn't feel threatened by him either. I think he missed his brother.

"No," another shell of a pistachio was tossed to the ground, "I was just coming by to see if you were comfortable. I'm sorry the arrangements couldn't be more luxurious." He gestured to the room.

I was staying in his warehouse. There was a mezzanine he had fashioned into a room with a full bath attached to it. It was cold and rusty, but it worked. It was better than the jail cell.

Every few days someone would show up to the warehouse, Ezekiel would warn me beforehand. They would bring in pallets of boxes in and then after a few days, they would leave. It was an irregular thing. I ignored it. It wasn't my business, and I wasn't going to piss him off by being nosy.

My phone lit up with an incoming text. Foster, again.

"It's fine. I'm grateful for what you have given me." And I meant it. I hadn't expected this, but it gave me a chance to adjust to being out along with keeping an eye on Wren. Figuring out all her lies before she told them to my face.

Before I made her tell me.

I reached for the phone, turning to face him, eyeing the pile of shells on the floor for a moment before looking up to him.

"I will send maid." Every so often when he spoke, an accent that I couldn't quite distinguish came through. I had heard it from Nikolas, too, but never questioned it.

I shook my head, "No. I don't want anyone in my space."

"Okay, so I get you broom."

I didn't respond to him. My eyes reading over the text from Foster.

> Kevin had a storage unit that you are going to want to see.

Another incoming text gave me an address, and a sickening thought came to me.

Before I could delve further into the depraved place my mind was going, I grabbed the keys off the desk and went to leave. "I need to borrow the car again."

"Where are we going?" He had fallen into step behind me. I didn't argue with him. If he wanted to come, fine. It was his car, his place I was staying in.

"Foster found something I need to look at."

As soon as we were in the car, my phone rang again, and I connected it.

"How does he still have a storage unit?" Kevin had been dead for years.

"I checked his bank records; he received insurance money after the fire. A good amount. The storage unit is set up on auto payment," Foster explained.

Ezekiel rolled the window down, tossing more shells out. "How is Foster?" he said, that accent coming through.

There was a pause on the line before Foster continued, ignoring him, "My guys got the unit opened. It's a shady place, no security, and since Kevin isn't around to complain, you shouldn't have any issues."

"Have they gone through anything?" I white knuckled the steering wheel; given who owned it, whatever was in there couldn't be good. I didn't want anyone other than me laying eyes on the contents of those boxes.

I was pissed with Wren. I was so past hurt, and on that fine line of hatred and obsession. She consumed my thoughts day in and day out. I almost let the guilt eat me alive. I almost relented and let her go. She deserved a life with someone who hadn't broken promises to her.

Someone who could have protected her.

But I was already too far gone. She was ingrained into my being and I couldn't carve her out.

"I had them open one box. I didn't want to bother you with it if it wasn't anything important and well. . . it's not good, Harper."

I ended the call, and we drove the rest of the way in silence. The storage unit was south of town, close to the apartment complex we had lived in. We pulled through the opened gates to the back row. One unit was opened, and a car was parked in front of it. As we pulled up, the car pulled farther up. I headed straight for the unit. Ezekiel walked to the car, talking to the driver.

It was a small unit, but it was filled with banker boxes.

I opened the box closest to me.

Right on top, light pink sheets with a character printed on them.

Bloody, pink sheets.

I swallowed hard, my stomach rolling. Sickness rippled through me, and I had to take a deep breath to keep from throwing up. These were Wren's sheets.

I let the anger seep in, creating a wall for the nausea to beat against but get nowhere.

I moved to another box and opened it. The box was full of pictures, all of Wren smiling. It looked like she was on campus in her college days. Pictures of her and Juni. Pictures of her through a window. I recognized the building, the house on the corner. He had been watching her the *entire time.* I opened box after box. They were all filled with her. Clothes that had to have been from when she was little.

I realized then that Kevin was obsessed. It had been a convenient thing for him in the beginning and something he grew to obsess over. He had been watching her for years.

I wanted to bring him back to life just to kill him again. What I gave him had been a mercy killing. It was too quick.

Another wave of guilt hit me. Sixteen-year-old me trying to kill her monster and failing. If I had succeeded, things could have been different.

She never deserved what they did to her.

I pulled out my phone and shot Foster a text.

Where is she?

The response was immediate.

Gym.

I dropped the pictures back into the box.

I needed to lay my eyes on her. I needed to see she was fine. That she was in one piece.

I clenched my fists at my sides, but I couldn't hold it in anymore. I kicked the box to the back of the unit, grabbing another and chucking it across the room. Grabbing anything I could get my hands on and ripping it apart. A guttural roar bubbled out of my chest and ripped up my throat.

She was just a little girl, and her mother sold her to a monster. *They.*

The word echoed in my head again, in her voice. I could hear her say it like it was yesterday.

My chest heaved and I wiped my hand down my face, exhausted.

I was so angry. I was angry with her. Angry *for* her. There wasn't a thing I wouldn't do to ensure that every last person who'd ever laid their hands on her was obliterated.

Even I should be on that list, for failing her.
Twice.
Dead wasn't enough.

But I had to find out who these other people were, and the only way to do that was to confront Wren.

It was time.

"I can send someone here to clean up this mess and take it to the warehouse if you want," Ezekiel said. There was no emotion in his voice. Just a statement. He didn't react to the episode he just witnessed.

"Fine," I bit out.

I closed the unit, not bothering to lock it, given the padlock had been cut. Once we were in the car, Ezekiel made a call, talking in another language, while I drove us out of the place.

"It's done." He pocketed his phone and patted his suit. "God dammit." He started to frantically look around the car.

"What?" I glanced at him before focusing on the road again.

"I think that fucking Foster's goon stole my pistachios," he grumbled.

I snorted, finding slight amusement in it.

"What's the deal with you and Foster anyway?" I asked, trying to distract myself.

"Oh, you know. She hates me, I love her." He shrugs, grinning. "It's complicated." He waved his hand, ending the conversation. "Where are we going? I need more pistachios."

"One more stop, then we will get you your damn pistachios."

"You know, when you are done handling your business, you should come work for me."

"Doing what?" I watched him from my peripheral.

"I'm sure we could find something for you to do in the business."

I PULLED THE HEM OF MY SHORTS DOWN, ADJUSTING MY clothes. We were grappling today, and loose-fit clothes weren't allowed. I tied my hair back then slid on fingerless gloves. The people who were taking our class today were all dressed similarly.

We all went through the motions of stretching, warming up. Mario and I paired each student up with someone who was sized similarly, giving them places on the mats to spread out. None of them were newbies, and we worked our way through the class, watching and critiquing their positioning.

I got in the rhythm of the day. Staying busy enough so my mind didn't wander away from what was right in front of me. This was a coed class. Sometimes we had all women's days and all men's days. We liked to mix them together occasionally, and only if everyone was up for it.

"There is no way I can take him down," Pam said, pointing at Daren.

"Why can't you?" I walked toward them, my hands clasped behind my back. Pam wasn't new to the class, but she wasn't consistent either. She had shown up maybe twice a month for the last six months.

"Because he's a man," she stated blandly.

I fought the urge to roll my eyes. Not that he was bigger than her, not that he was potentially stronger than her, just because he was a man.

"So, because you are a woman, you don't have the strength to take him down?" I countered.

"Men are biologically stronger than women." She said it like it wasn't something I had known my entire life.

It was an argument I had heard before, time and time again. I couldn't help the expression on my face and turned to Adam.

Adam was a good six inches taller than me, and he was built like a linebacker. He had only recently started grappling class.

"Okay, Pam, step off the mat. Adam, I want you to put me on my back."

"You want me to do what?" He gaped at me.

"Put me on my back. Take me down."

The pairs surrounding us were faltering in their moves, their curiosity getting the better of them. Good. I wanted them to see.

I stepped up on the mat, my hands still clasped behind my back, relaxed. He stood at the edge of the mat before he rushed me. He crossed the mat in five steps, and just as his hands went for my shoulder, I spun away from him, stepping behind him and gently kicking him in the back of the knee, causing him to stumble.

My steps were sure. I never stumbled.

"See, Pam, he may be stronger, but I'm faster." I raised my voice for all to hear. "Your attacker may be bigger than you, but you could be faster. Kicking them in the side or back of the knee can get them on the ground. In a life-or-death situation, once they are on the ground, you grab the heaviest object you can get your hands on, I don't care if it's a rock, a solid ashtray, a candle—you hit them on the head."

Pam shook her head and turned away from me. I didn't know why she was even taking this class when it was obvious where her mindset was.

"How many times should we hit them?" Cary, another girl who had joined a few years after me, asked.

"Depends."

Her eyes were steady with mine. "On?"

Cary was a quiet girl. *Haunted* was the look in her eyes. She'd showed up one day and had taken every class she could get into ever since. First, she would just stand back and watch. Slowly she got comfortable enough to start working one-on-one. I had my suspicions about her. I kept my eyes on her. Searching for the signs.

"On if you want to keep fighting that demon forever. Or if you want it to stop. My suggestion, hit them until their face is caved in."

The class went on longer. Eventually some people left, and a mat opened. Mario and I stepped up to it. We always ended each class with a demonstration, showing what all the skills we were teaching would look like when they became proficient.

People started to surround the mat, a good crowd forming. We circled each other, hands out in front of us. This time, I made the first move, stepping in and throwing some jabs at him, trying to get an opening where I could force him to the ground. He easily maneuvered his way out of it.

"Gonna actually get me to the ground this time?" I jeered at him, a grin on my face. Fighting was a rush that I loved. It made me feel powerful for just a little while. Like my past never happened.

"I'll get you on your back, you'll see." Mario smirked and I rolled my eyes.

Mario stepped first and I managed to sidestep him. My first instinct was always to go on the defense. Block, evade. It took a few moves to get myself ready to go on attack.

Out of the corner of my eye, a large figure stood taller than anyone in the crowd. Without thinking, I turned my head, locking eyes with Alex.

Pure hatred was on his face.

And then Mario took the opening to kick me right in my stomach.

All the air left me, and my vision went fuzzy.

"Wren!" I heard my name, followed by shouting.

Everything blurred. Mario loomed over me. "Fuck, are you okay?"

A loud ringing started in my ears. I turned my head and saw the figure's back. He was walking away.

It can't be him. He can't be here. Alex is dead.

———

Twenty minutes later and I was finally sitting up, sipping water. The students had filtered their way out once the chaos had ended.

"Wren, talk to me." Mario was crouched in front of me, concern filling his face.

Marshall, the gym owner, was there too. "What happened?"

"We were just going at it on the mat, and she didn't block my kick. Knocked her out," Mario explained.

"Wren?"

I looked up at Marshall, and a red blinking light caught my attention.

"Cameras. I need to see the security footage," I wheezed the words out, still trying to catch my breath from the blow.

I felt like I was going insane. Not once in the five years since Alex's death did I see him or hallucinate him. Sure, there had been times I hoped that maybe he would walk around the corner like this whole mess never happened, but I never actually saw him.

Mario and Marshall looked at each other, but they didn't argue.

I stood behind Marshall as he pulled up the footage on the office computer. He rewound it till we saw Mario and I step up to the mat.

On the screen, I stared at the crowd carefully while Mario and I circled each other. I looked about ready to give up when, on the edge of the feed, someone's shoulder appeared just as I got kicked to the ground.

"See that!" I point to the edge of the screen. "Rewind it."

"I didn't see anything," Marshall said, but he complied.

The camera didn't have the capability to go frame by frame, but no matter how many times we watched it, they didn't see what I saw.

"Wren, are you okay?" Concern laced Mario's tone.

I dug the heel of my palm into my forehead, massaging the pulsing headache that was forming. I felt like I was going insane. How could I tell them that this was the second time I thought I saw my dead best friend, clear as day? As if he'd manifested right in front of me?

"Yeah." I rolled my head over my shoulders. "I'm going to get out of here." I headed for the locker rooms and changed into some jeans and a white T-shirt.

I left the gym and drove aimlessly in town. Normally, I avoided being in town at all costs, only staying as long as it took me to get groceries and run whatever errands I couldn't put off any longer.

But I didn't want to go home to my empty house and listen to every creak and groan thinking someone would be there. I had a bad history of being paranoid and letting my imagination get the best of me.

So, I parked my car at Jon's law office, entering the building and waving to the receptionist. Carla smiled and waved back as she picked up the phone, answering it in her perfected customer service voice.

"Go on back," she whispered, covering the receiver of the phone.

Jon had taken over his father's law firm some years ago. With Alex's death, he'd buried himself in his work, but he had come out on the other side of everything, showing everyone just how capable he was.

I hadn't a clue about his job, but I listened the best I could. It was hard to though; it always put me back to the night our lives imploded.

"Wren, I need you to tell me what happened." Jon hovered in Alex's bedroom doorway, his phone in one hand and the other pushing his blond hair out of his face for the thousandth time. He had tried to sit down next to me, he'd tried to comfort me, but every time he tried I just screamed.

It was a visceral reaction. One I couldn't seem to control.

I didn't know how much time had passed since they took Alex. They had walked into the room, reading him his rights. Alex picked me up and set me on the bed, but I wouldn't let go of him. I clung around his neck for dear life.

I was safe in his arms.

No one could hurt me in his arms.

"It's going to be okay now, Wren, you're safe. I prom..." But he couldn't finish that sentence and I knew why. Was I really safe? He couldn't guarantee it last time, so how could he now?

When the cops noticed the blood on me, one walked over to me too fast and I panicked, screaming. Alex put himself in front of me.

"Don't you fucking touch her!" Alex moved and both the cops unleashed their tasers on him. He dropped to the ground and then they cuffed him, taking him out of the house.

"I'm sorry, Wren. I'm so sorry."

Those were the last words I had heard from him before he was gone.

I was still huddled on his bed.

Jon knelt next to the bed, dipping his head so he could catch my gaze. "Wren, I need to know what he did so I can figure out what kind of lawyer he needs. Alex needs you right now."

At that, I finally told him.

"Kevin came back."

"Who's Kevin?"

"My mom's boyfriend." I swallowed hard; even saying his name made me want to throw up. I was sore. Still raw, and if I *moved the wrong way there would be new blood spots on the navy blue sheets I had bought for Alex.*

Another thing I'd ruined.

"Kevin came back and raped me again."

Again. It happened again. How cruel could the universe be to me? Give me everything I ever wanted, get me so close to the sun before the waves took me under again.

I finally focused on Jon's face. His brow was furrowed, and I could see the cogs turning.

"You didn't move in because of the fire, did you?"

I shook my head. "I ran away."

"Because. . .this happened before?"

"For five years."

I could see the moment the words hit Jon. His body seemed to cave in on itself as he settled to the ground.

"Wren. . ."

"Don't." I could see the pity on his face clear as day. "Don't focus on that, you focus on Alex. You get him back for me because I can't. . ." The words were right there. The ones that evaded me so much as a child. I could feel the canal's current drag me under again, and this time, I didn't want to kick. I didn't want to swim.

I can't go on without him.

"I'll do everything I can, Wren."

"Wren!" Melissa's excited voice pulled me from the memory. I looked up at her, dazed, but she didn't seem to notice. "What a nice surprise!"

I glanced around, realizing I had been standing in the foyer before going back to the lawyers' offices.

"Hey, Mel." I smiled at her.

Melissa was Jon's paralegal. Melissa and I met at one of Jon's parties. She had been new to the firm and was standing in a corner sipping on something. I'd taken pity on her, as I always hated new spaces and feeling awkward, so I started up a conversation that never seemed to stop. Afterwards, she had found me at every function and glued herself to me. Melissa liked to talk a lot.

She's a pretty blonde with blue eyes and long legs. Men stared at her everywhere she went, and she loved to be the center of attention.

I was pretty sure they had slept together for a stint. I suspected she wanted more, but Jon didn't keep steady girlfriends. At least none that I knew about.

Because he's waiting for you.

The thought took me off guard, but I couldn't think about it too much before Melissa spoke.

"It's great that you came to visit, but," she made a face, "he's in a bad mood today." She was standing behind her desk, looking down the hall at his corner office.

"What's wrong?" I had rarely ever seen Jon in a bad mood. He was always cool and composed when we were teens.

"No clue. Something about someone not answering his phone calls. I tried getting him to tell me who it was, and I would work on it, you know, 'cause that's basically my job," she rolled her eyes, "but he's adamant that he needs to be the one to make this call. I don't know. Maybe seeing you will get him to pull out that stick he's had up his ass all day."

I laughed. Melissa had no filter, and it was one of the things that was refreshing about her.

"I'll see what I can do." I smiled and headed down the hall. Each office was lined with glass. I pulled open Jon's door and watched his thumbs hit the screen of his phone hard.

"Whatever it is, Melissa, it can wait," he growled out.

"Are you sure?" I teased.

His head shot up and his ice blue eyes were on me. When we were in high school, it had been hard to look him in the eyes. They were so much like Kevin's that I couldn't not think of him.

Now I could see the dark blue ring that was around his irises and the fleck of green that was only in his left eye.

"Wren, what a nice surprise." He leaned back in his chair, and I stepped into the room and took a seat in one of his brown leather chairs across from the desk.

"Just thought I would pop by and say hi while I was in town."

He chuckled, coming around his desk to lean against it. "I love that you're here, but in all these years this might be the first time you've come by without notice." He put his hands up. "I'm not mad, I actually love that you are here, but something tells me that there's more to this than what you are letting on." He gripped the edge of the desk.

I pressed my lips together, debating telling him the truth, that I thought I was seeing our dead best friend in the flesh, but I thought better of it. If I told him that I was seeing things, he was just going to worry and ruin his back sleeping on my couch again. Convincing him I was fine after I moved had been hard enough; I didn't want to worry him and everyone else.

"Oh, come on, I'm not that much of a hermit." I sat back and crossed my arms.

"Ha! Yes, you are. It's a fight to get you to go out anywhere." Jon relaxed, moving to the chair next to me. He smiled. "It really is nice that you stopped by. You were just what I needed after today."

"Mel said you were dealing with a pesky client?"

"Something like that." He brushed it off. "Really, Wren, are you okay?"

"Yes, Jonathan, I'm okay. It's just. . ." I sighed. "It's just one of those days I guess."

"I know, baby."

I tried not to react to the endearment, but chills ran up my spine. I couldn't help but feel Kevin's breath on the back of my neck. Hear his voice when it was said.

"Have you called the cemetery yet?"

"Yeah." I pushed away the revulsion. "They still have the stone I picked out for him originally and are going to start working on it." Jon reached out for me, and I took his hand. He gave it a squeeze.

"That's good, Wren. That's a big step. Alex would want that for you."

I nodded, trying not to dwell on it.

"Jon, your next appointment is in the conference room," Melissa said from the doorway.

Jon walked me out into the foyer.

"I love that you stopped by. You should do it more often." He winked at me.

"Oh!" Melissa started. "Wren, I've been meaning to ask you to go on a double date with me!"

"Huh?" Her question took me off guard. Jon chuckled beside me like he already knew what I was in for.

"I promise, I tried to get you out of it," he loudly whispered in my ear.

"Oh, stop it," Mel chided him. "I met this guy online, and he wants to go out for dinner next week, but I'm too nervous to meet him alone, so I've been trying to convince Jon to ask you to be his date. I'll text you the details, but I expect you there!" She pushed Jon into the conference room, and I was left there, shaking my head.

Of course, she would rope me into something like this.

CHAPTER 33

WREN

THE HOSTESS GREETED ME AS I ENTERED THE restaurant.

"Good evening, ma'am, can I get the name of your reservation?"

"It's under Jonathan Smith." I tucked my hair behind my ear and scanned the dining area. It was packed in here and too loud for my own comfort. The tables were all set with tablecloths, candles and wineglasses. I scanned the room, but I didn't spot him.

Melissa had spent the last week texting me incessantly to make sure I was coming to her double date thing. I thought about canceling almost every day, but I didn't want to disappoint her, and this was falling nicely into the "normalcy" plan I had been working at for ages.

Ages being about seventy-two hours, but I was on a mission to convince my brain that we were not going to let ourselves go crazy. And crazy is what I'd felt for the past two weeks.

I swore I could smell his woodsy amber scent again.

Jonathan had been thrilled when I texted him and confirmed.

I guess this meant I was his only double date option.

This is going to be a weird first date for whatever schmuck Melissa is bringing, the poor guy.

"Yes, ma'am, part of your party is already here, right this way." She guided me through the dining room, turning the corner into a little alcove with our own candlelit table.

Jon stood. "Wren, you made it." He beamed, looking me up and down, approving of my outfit choice before kissing my cheek and pulling out the chair next to him. I wore strappy heels and a fitted black sleeveless dress that had a high neckline. It stopped about mid-thigh. Classy enough to wear to whatever event Jon wanted to drag me to, and it also wasn't so revealing that I was crawling out of my skin.

I took time getting ready today, doing an everything shower and putting an ungodly amount of product into my hair to combat the frizz before straightening it, which I rarely ever did.

Alex had liked it curly.

But Alex was dead, and Jon liked it straight.

I was here with Jon and would stay focused on him tonight.

I knew Jon had been waiting for me. He had been waiting for me every day for the last five years.

And Alex would want me with Jon. Alex trusted Jon and would be happy for me in whatever choice I made.

"Can I interest you in wine?" The waitress went to fill my glass, but I stopped her before a drop could spill.

"No, thank you, just water."

She smiled politely and set the bottle back down on the table. "Would you like to order anything, or are you waiting for your other guests?"

"We will wait for the guests, thank you," Jon answered before turning to me. He slung an arm over the back of the chair, and I tried to keep myself from bowing away from his touch on my upper back.

Jon is not a threat. Jon is a friend.

Breathe.

"You look amazing. Those workout classes have done wonders for you."

My body had filled out. I gone from having no food to a habit of munching and snacking. I was always eating something. I didn't have the self-control to stop. I also didn't think I needed to stop. I had loved the way I looked seven years ago. I wasn't all sharp edges and bruises. Now that I spent three days a week at the gym, I had thinned out. I was trim but muscled.

Now, I could take down any full-grown man that dared to see me as his next victim.

I loved my body then, and I loved it now.

"Thank you." Jon wasn't a threat to me; he had done so much to help me, and I was eternally grateful to him, but there would always be a small part of me that felt like I was betraying Alex. "How's work?"

Jon went into a long speech about the court system and whatever case he was working on. I did my best to keep up, but I kept looking around the room, people-watching. Listening to a lawyer talk just reminded me of the hell I'd experienced for the first year after Alex's arrest.

Jon couldn't be Alex's lawyer at the time but got him someone he said would do what he could to keep Alex from getting a life sentence.

All my letters were sent back. My requests for visitation were denied.

Then Gloria got sick.

I'd had more imperative things to worry about then. I mentally shook my head, clearing my thoughts and blinking away the tears that threatened to fall.

Right then, Melissa rounded the corner wearing a beautiful maroon dress that was fitted and had a high slit. Jon and I stood, hugging and greeting her.

"Where's this date?" Jon asked, looking behind her.

"He's parking the car; it started raining so he dropped me off out front." Her eyes went wide as she looked at me. "Oh my god —he is hotter in person! The tattoos were a little shocking, but I could get used to them on a man like that."

I laughed; Melissa was a serial dater. She was hellbent on

finding a husband in the next year. "Well hopefully he's a good one." She sat across from Jon and the hostess poured wine for her. She immediately snatched it up, taking a huge swallow. "I think no matter how this ends tonight, I'm taking him home."

"Oh really?" I didn't conceal my laughter, leaning back in the chair. "Please do tell."

"He is so hot! And it's been a long time since I've gotten laid. Blame my boss," she said cheekily.

"Hey now." Jon gave her a faked stern look.

Jon rested his arm across the back of my chair while he and Melissa caught up. His fingers grazed my arm lightly. I fought myself to not pull away from his touch.

I took in a deep breath. I had gone out with Jon and Melissa before, but I was fidgety. Jon had never been forward with me. He had always been relatively respectful and able to gauge my reaction, but tonight I kept thinking of Alex.

Being out with Jon felt like I was betraying him. Which was unfair to Jon. He hadn't done anything wrong. He had only ever done things with my comfort in mind.

I knew this.

"Melissa, I think your date is here." My attention was diverted to the figure walking toward us.

Who stole my breath away.

"Alex."

I froze, wide-eyed, horror, panic, and disbelief all flooding through me at once.

I blinked again and again but he was still there, staring down at me.

Anger surged in me, and I had to fight it back, balling my hands into fists. The night he left me to go hunt Kevin down hit me blow for blow. I had to fight to keep myself together.

Brown eyes were on me, but I didn't see the warmth in them any longer—no, there was fire behind those eyes now. The world tilted on its axis, and I could faintly hear Melissa introducing us to her date.

Alex was her date.

I tore my eyes from him and looked at Melissa. She could see him too?

But he's dead. He's not supposed to be here.

Alex was in front of me, his large and very tattooed hands gripping the back of Melissa's chair as he helped tuck her under the table.

The gesture flared something inside me.

Jealousy?

I looked at Jon as Alex moved to him, reaching across the

table. Jon mechanically gave him his hand, shaking it. I could faintly see Jon wince at the contact.

"But you're. . ." The words died on my lips. The betrayal rolled in slowly.

I was still awestruck at the sight of him. Blatantly staring at him. He was dressed in a well-fitted suit, a forest-green dress shirt underneath, and even wore deep green and gold cufflinks. A part of me wondered if he did that intentionally.

With every move he made his muscles contracted under his clothes. His hair was cut shorter now, not the messy mop I remembered.

Then the waitress was there.

"Can I get you something to drink?" She directed the question to Alex, but I jumped in.

"Yeah, whiskey on ice, a double."

"Make that two," Alex said, a wicked look in his eyes.

"Three. Make that three," I said. I needed the alcohol, because how the hell was this man here, now, sitting across from me?

"Yes, ma'am." The waitress escaped the awkwardness, and Melissa finally piped in: "Come on, Wren, sit down. I know I told you he was hot, but you don't need to gawk like that."

Everyone else had sat down. Melissa wasn't reading the room, her flirtation still just as strong as ever, even though she couldn't see past her own nose.

"Oh, it's okay, Melissa. We are all old friends here." Alex looked between Jon and I.

The look wasn't friendly or happy. No, there was something else there now. Something that I didn't think I had ever seen on his face.

"Wait, you know them?" She turned in her chair. I watched as she twirled a lock of her blond hair around her finger, giving him her full attention, breasts pushed out, brushing his arm.

"Oh, yeah, we all go way back." Slowly, I took my seat, watching Alex as if he were a ghost.

"No one wants to tell the story?" he asked, and after a split second said, "Alright, fine. I will." In a sarcastic tone. He turned toward Melissa, sitting back relaxed in his chair. "We all went to high school together. Wren and I lived together in high school and through her college days. Jon and I have been best friends since elementary school. Or, should I say, *were* best friends."

My eyes didn't leave Melissa's breasts, still pushing up against his arm.

The most unhinged part of my brain wanted to take the knife on the table and deflate her silicone boobs.

The thought took me off guard. I had never been hostile toward her, ever.

"Really?" Melissa's mouth was in the shape of an O. "I knew these two went back, but I didn't realize it was that far back. I thought they met in college or something. You know, neither of them talks about themselves much. Well, actually, Jon talks about himself a lot, but not in the way to give you history on him." Melissa continued to ramble while I felt like I was gut punched.

Our waitress was back, setting drinks down. Before she could leave, I tossed back the first one, handing her the glass.

"That's my girl," Alex said the words loud and clear.

I froze, a mixture of emotions flashing through me. I was still so shocked I couldn't process any of it.

"Uh, excuse me?" Melissa said, an awkward laugh following her words.

"Melissa, I have to confess something, you see." He laid his arm over the back of her chair, and I watched as one of his fingers trailed up her shoulder. "You are kind of the pawn in this situation, and I apologize for that."

Melissa was trapped in Alex's heated gaze, inching her way closer to him.

I tore my eyes from the exchange and looked at Jon.

Jon was white as a sheet. He looked like he was going to be sick.

"Jon?" His blue eyes snapped to me at my words. "What the fuck is going on?"

"Wren," he shook his head, "I'm so—" He moved in close to me, putting his hand on the back of my neck. I was frozen in place, those icy blues were just as confused and shocked as I was.

"Get your fucking hand off of her," Alex growled, "before I break it." Alex stood in one fluid motion, both hands on the table. "I don't care if it puts me back in prison."

"P-Prison?" Melissa stuttered.

I ignored her and stood. I turned my venomous gaze on Alex, but I was at a loss for words. Jon slowly stood, his hands out like he was trying to calm a snake before it struck.

"Wren, I—" Jon stuttered, but I cut him off.

"Who do you think you are?" I turned to Alex. "Coming here on a false pretense that you are on a date with our friend? To what? Corner us? Act like *we are the liars?*" Alex's only reaction was a raised eyebrow. He sat coolly in his chair, watching me. "What the fuck is this?" My voice rattled. I felt anger like I had never felt before. I could see Jon staring at me in the corner of my eye. This wasn't the same Alex we had known growing up. This wasn't the boy who gave me snacks in between classes or walked me home from school.

I didn't know this man.

How dare he yell at Jon when Jon had been doing exactly what he promised? He was taking care of me.

Even now, Jon was thinking of my feelings before his own, trying to console me.

I reached down, grabbing my drink, gripping it tightly just to stop my hand from shaking. My hand gripped my glass so hard I thought it might shatter. I stared down at the amber liquid. Alex's hand came up and rested around his own glass, and I finally noticed the tattoo across his knuckles.

W-R-E-N.

"A reckoning."

CHAPTER 35

ALEX

HER BROW FURROWED AT MY WORDS FOR ONLY A moment.

She was the most beautiful thing I had ever seen. It had been years since I laid my eyes on her up close. She looked the same, but different. Her hair was straightened, and I wanted to take her to a shower just to watch it frizz and curl.

I loved her curly hair and hated this straightened version of it. This wasn't her.

This wasn't *my* Wren.

She left you there to rot.

Betrayal lashed through me like a lightning bolt, allowing me to lock down my wayward feelings for her.

I thought I had put them all in a box and taped it shut, but seeing her now was like a wave soaking the measly cardboard container I had put them in, and it was disintegrating before my very eyes.

I didn't want to be here. I didn't want to do this to her here. I wanted to confront her someplace without onlookers. But when Foster had admitted to making a fake dating account using my photo to get closer to Melissa and presented me with the opportunity of seeing Wren, I'd taken it.

It was reckless and stupid on my part, but after seeing the

things in that unit, I needed to be close to her. My stupid fucking heart still wanted to protect her.

I still had no idea what fucking reason could have my *heart* avoiding me for the last five years. I needed this moment with her in front of him. I needed to see both of their faces. Gauge both their reactions.

I watched her. Her emotions were rapid, horror and shock most prevalent.

I didn't know what to expect when I confronted her. There was a small part of me that thought maybe she would run into my arms, excited to see me. And if she did that, it would erase the years of betrayal I felt.

But it wasn't excitement in her eyes. They kept drifting down to my arm, where I was hyperaware of the blonde's fake tits pushed against my elbow.

I didn't move away from them, though, a sickly satisfied part of me relishing in the. . . What? Was that jealousy I saw?

She tossed back the remaining drink in her glass and for just a moment, her eyes flicked back to me, widening slightly.

I wasn't going to wait any longer. Watching Jon fidget satisfied a part of me, but I didn't have a lot of time before he or Wren would bolt. "Melissa, I didn't make that dating account that you found me on. The PI I hired did." I said this while watching Wren. I laid it all out for them. A part of me wanted her to know it hadn't been me looking for an actual date. It was just another way to get closer to her. I sipped my drink. I was trying to savor this. I watched Jon's face over the rim of my glass. He was getting angry.

Good.

"You work for Jon. I needed to get close to him because I knew, even after all these years, even after Wren turned him down two, three times now, he wouldn't give up on her. His pride wouldn't let him."

"That's none of your business." Wren spoke with bite in her

tone. Her emerald green eyes narrowed on me, but they flicked over to Jon, who sat as still as a statue.

Her defending Jon agitated me, and I rolled my shoulders.

Wren's trust in me had been everything, and I had worked my entire early adulthood to ensure she trusted me.

Now, I could tell her the sky was blue and she wouldn't believe me.

"See. I was right. Anyway, Wren." I called her attention to me, wanting it to all be on me. She hadn't left yet, so that told me she knew something was happening, if only subconsciously, my smart girl. "Did you know I was transferred ten different times?"

She stiffly shook her head.

"Well, I was. That first year after my sentence was the most. I was bounced all over the state."

"You were bounced all over because you couldn't be contained. You started fights everywhere you went." Jon's outburst was exactly what I wanted. I watched as Wren tore her eyes off me and to Jon. Out of every person on this planet, dead or alive, she knew me, she had to believe me.

Used to know me, I told myself.

I had never been much of a fighter before her. I didn't start shit for no reason. If I was throwing a punch, someone else started it and I was just there to finish it.

The only fight I ever started in high school was over Wren.

Wren's eyes softened on Jon, and I watched as she lifted her hand and squeezed Jon's forearm, comforting *him*.

Melissa stared between the three of us. I gave her a wink and her cheeks flushed. She was just a bystander in this whole situation, but there was something more there that I was going to have to figure out at a later date.

"Stop." Wren's voice was low and angry. I almost had to lean in to hear her. "I don't know how you did it, Alex, or even why you would do it, but I'm not going to sit here and be lied to after six years."

Jon stumbled over his words. "W-Wren has been through enough of your mind games. You need to leave."

Wren watched Jon as he spoke. Her forehead crinkled with confusion. I could see the distrust in her eyes; it was minor, but it was there.

"Jon was never there. At any of the hearings. He said he would be, but every time they brought me out, I looked for him." I tossed back my drink, feeling like this was about to end. "I had some lawyer who didn't know his head from his ass. He's lying to you."

"He's lying to me? You want to argue that *he* was the one lying to me when you. . ." Her words trailed off and she shook her head. Something passed between her and Jon. Something that I wanted to understand. "He's been here, Alex. Where the fuck have you been?" She stood, gathering her purse. "I can't believe I trusted you." Wren shot daggers at me before she rushed past me. The sweet scent of honey and spices followed behind her.

I took my time, staring at Jon. His face was hard and filled with hatred. I really wished he would drop dead right then and there. I wanted to poke at him, see what he would do, but my reason for everything was leaving, and I needed to follow.

Slowly, I rose from my seat, chuckling, relishing the anger written all over Jon's face. "I'll be seeing you, Jon." I turned to leave, then paused. "Oh, and by the way." I narrowed my eyes, lowering myself across the table to get right in his face. He shrank into the chair. "I know *everything*. And soon, Wren will too."

I left the restaurant, picking up the pace, looking up and down the sidewalk for Wren, but I didn't see her.

"Dammit," I muttered, choosing a direction and following it. I got about a half a block up when I heard her.

"Alex."

I stopped and turned around. She was behind me, holding her heels by their straps in one hand.

How the hell is she behind me?

We stood there, staring at each other. I watched her eyes roam over me, and I knew we were feeling the same thing. Looking at a stranger we were supposed to know. Feeling familiarity but not being able to act how we used to. It looked like she might come to me. I felt goosebumps at the thought of her wrapping her arms around me. Burying my face in her hair, holding her again.

She fucking abandoned you.

But did she? Not once did I see shame or regret on her face.

I could just reach out and grab her, pull her to me, and God I wanted to, but I clenched my fists at my sides.

"Alex, I—"

I put my hand out, silencing her. She wrung her hands together nervously.

"So, I get out of prison, and this is how I find you? Shacking up with the jackass who ruined my life."

I threw the poisonous words out at her. Her face screwed up, mouth popping open. Her hands stopped fidgeting, crossing over her chest in defense, a hip popping out.

"Ruined your life? You have got to be fucking kidding me." She laughed darkly. "This is how you get my attention? Ambush me at dinner by going on a date with my friend?"

I shoved my hands into my pockets. "You're pissed at me?" I chuckled humorlessly. I walked in a small circle, needing to do something. "You fucking abandoned me as soon as I went to jail. For what? So you could finally get with Jon?"

She looked like I had slapped her but recovered quickly. "So, that's what this is? Tit for tat?"

"Had to get your attention somehow. You obviously only pay attention to the things that are conveniently in front of you." This wasn't how I wanted this to go but the words kept coming out.

"Are you fucking kidding me? You're the one who tried to make me go fucking crazy, by *stalking* me, letting me see you for just a second before you tuck your fucking tail between your legs and run?!"

I sneered. "This was the only way I could—"

"Could what, Alexander James?! Find me? This was the only way you could do this?" She laughed, her hand moving to her hips. "You really think so little of me now? You don't think that if you had gone to Danny and gotten my phone number that you couldn't have called me and said, 'Hey, let's meet up and talk,' that I would have just shut you down? Told you to go fuck yourself and went on with my life?"

I relished the sound of my whole name on her tongue. She was the only person that could make me savor my own name. It was obviously a habit she couldn't filter out in the heat of this moment. "How was I going to find you, Wren!? You fucking up and moved your life to who fucking knows where. I didn't know how to get ahold of you. You don't live in that house anymore." I realized my mistake immediately. Smacking my hand to my face and dragging it down.

Stupid mouth.

I had always been so careful with what I said to her before. Evaluating my words before saying anything to make sure I didn't say something that would remind her of before.

"What did you expect me to do! Did you want me to continue to live in that fucking house? Just go in there and clean the blood up off the floor and throw the sheets in the wash, continue like nothing happened?" She covered her mouth with her hand, head subtly shaking. Her voice softened. I could clearly see her now. The look on her face was that same look she gave me when she asked me for help. It was a scared, horror-filled look. "Alex, I thought you were. . ." She shook her head, eyes hardening. "You know what, no. I don't have to tell you shit. You come here to accuse me? Call me a whore?"

"Hey!" My voice shot out in the night. I lowered it, not trying to cause more of a scene than we already had. Several people were loitering on the sidewalks, watching the fight play out.

I took a step toward her. "I never called you a whore."

"No? That's not what you were implying? Fuck you, Alex."

She brushed past me and continued up the sidewalk, her pace quickening.

I followed behind her. "Wren! Stop." I stared at her bare feet on the street, and the memories of that day came back to me. I reached out without thinking, grabbing her by her arm to pull her to a stop. In one motion she turned, connected her foot to my balls.

"Ah! Fuck!" I doubled over grabbing myself.

"Don't you fucking touch me!" She turned away from me, and started to head up the street.

"Fuck." I managed to keep from crumpling to my knees, leaning against the brick wall of a building. "You thought I was what?" I managed to say through the pain, stopping in her tracks.

She turned back to me, her hands on her hips. For a moment, her eyes softened and there was concern in her eyes.

"I thought you were dead."

ALEX THREW HIS HEAD BACK AND LAUGHED.

He fucking *laughed*.

It wasn't even one of those shocked chuckles. It was full-bellied; he had to lean against the brick wall to support himself laugh.

"You have got to be shitting me." He straightened, pushed himself off the brick wall to stand in front of me. He dragged a hand down his face. "So that's it? I'm suppose to believe that you thought I was dead?"

I opened my mouth to speak, but he cut me off.

"You know, Wren, I could have believed a lot of things, but this? This is just fucking ridiculous." He turned his back to me and started to walk away.

This was the angriest I had ever been with him. He turned his back on me, wouldn't even give me the benefit of the doubt?

I chucked my heel at him, nailing him in the back of the head. He grabbed the back of his head, looking at me with wide eyes.

"Fuck you, Alex!" I threw my other heel at him but he dodged it. "After *everything* we have been through, you want to call me a liar?" I shook my head. "I didn't know you were the type to ask for proof, but fine." I reached for the necklace that was tucked behind my high neckline dress, tugging hard to snap the cord, then I tossed it at him. He didn't catch it, but the sound of metal on concrete could be heard as it pinged to the ground.

The necklace he left on my bedside table that day. His father's wedding band.

He crouched down and picked it up. His face softened at the sight of it.

"There's your fucking proof." I let the information sink in a bit. Once he looked up at me, I didn't give him a chance to speak. "If I really 'forgot' you, I wouldn't have been wearing that every day for the last six years, now would I?"

I turned my back to him and walked barefoot to my car. "Get in your car and follow me. I have more *proof* at home."

I shouldn't have been behind the wheel. I broke every traffic law on my way home. A few times, I thought I had lost him, but once we were out on the back roads and turned down my gravel drive, bright led lights shown in my rearview mirror.

I was only a few steps ahead of him the whole time. I pushed my way into the house, flipping on the lights as I went. The dog door opened and I told the dogs to go to their beds before one of them bit Alex.

At this rate, he'd deserve it.

"I tried to visit you but my request was denied every time. They told me you were in solitary confinement for weeks. Then they told me you had restricted visitation rights only to your lawyer. I sent letters for a while and I never got anything back from you. Then," I paused, swallowing hard, "your mom got sick and I was with her day and night." I didn't turn to look at him. I couldn't. I stared down the hall of my home while he hovered in the doorway behind me.

I needed to calm down. I needed to get it together and breathe through this, but I couldn't believe the man behind me.

I wanted to reach for him. My hands ached to touch him. "I

relied on Jon to keep me updated after that. Gloria needed me and—"

Alex scoffed. I turned to look at him and saw the slight shake to his head. As if everything I told him was a pathetic excuse.

It hit me like a sack of bricks. The anger overthrew any control I had gained on the drive over. It bubbled up like a soda that someone kept shaking.

I exploded.

"I THOUGHT YOU WERE DEAD!" I screamed the words, rushing him. I was a breath away from him. I needed him to understand the gravity of what I had thought.

He stilled, slowly raising his head to look at me, the fire in his eyes smoldering.

At least he had the decency to look confused. I shook my head, an almost manic laugh rising up through me. I stormed my way through the house into the den where I had a drawer of files set up with important paperwork. I pulled out the file labeled *Alexander James Harper*, flipping through it until I found what I was looking for. I turned, not surprised he followed me. I tossed the paper in his direction. I was so fed up at this point. The only thing I could do was explain and defend myself.

He didn't bother to catch it. Just watched it as it floated down to his feet. He stared at me for another beat before dropping his eyes. I saw a small crinkle forming in his brow before he bent to pick it up.

"That's your *death* certificate. Jon brought it to me." I turned and reached for another file labeled with his mother's name, pulling out her death certificate. "That's your mothers. They are exactly the same. I had no reason to doubt it, Alex." My hands were on my hips, and I dug my fingers in to keep from shaking. I couldn't dim the anger even for a moment. I was done reasoning with his anger. It was time he knew mine. "I mourned you, Alex. I grieved for you. So fine, be pissed at me. Be angry at Jon, but we thought you were dead. Think that every reason I give you is a pathetic excuse." I wiped the tears away angrily. "I had no reason to think that it wasn't the truth." I shook my head. "So why don't *you* explain to me why you faked your death."

Saying it all out loud to him now made me feel like an idiot. I should have tried harder. I should have been down at the prison every day fighting to see him, but I relied on someone else. Someone I had no reason to not trust.

How could he think of Jon and I this way?

The thought was cut short when I felt his hand on the back of my neck and was pulled forward into his chest. I froze, unsure what to do. Another beat passed before I felt his arm band across my back, pulling me flush to his hard body.

"I'm sorry." His voice rumbled in his chest. His fingers laced up the back of my neck and into my hair. He held so tight it was almost painful, but that pain held me in this moment.

I brought my hands up and balled them into his shirt. His woodsy amber scent filled my nose as I buried my face into his chest. My defenses fell and I was in the arms of the boy who saved me.

The man I had once loved.

I was finally home.

He dipped down, leveling his gaze with mine. "I would never willingly leave you. That includes taking my own life."

His lips pressed hard to the side of my head. Before he abruptly released me, leaving me cold as he turned and headed out the front door. The storm door slammed, causing me to jump.

Uncontrolled sobs racked my body and I caught myself on the edge of the couch.

Alex is here. He's home.

I covered my mouth and took a deep breath. I tracked him through the window as he paced out in the front yard, worried he might leave.

King nosed my hand, and I ran my nails over his head. I could see the concern in the shepherd's eyes.

"It's going to be okay, King," I said, more for myself than him.

I gave myself another moment to calm down before I headed out the front door, not able to stay away now. That red string of fate tied itself tighter around my heart and pulled me in his direction. Alex was pacing back and forth, his black boots kicking at the gravel.

I leaned against one of the posts of the porch, my arms crossed. I watched as he pulled his phone out, thumbs moving quickly across the screen, and I heard the sound of a text being sent. He put the phone away and then stood there, staring at me.

I could see the anger in his eyes. Anger that would come and go in our younger years, but seemed to have taken root now.

"All these years," he shook his head, "I thought you just moved on without me."

"No, Alex. I never moved on from you. I would never move on from you." I allowed myself to feel his pain. The thought of him moving on from me, it hurt deep in my bones. An unyielding pain.

He ran his hand through his hair and I missed the length he used to have. The way his hair would start to curl at the nape of his neck. I could imagine the way it felt wrapped around my fingers.

What would it be like to come back and not have a home, your family?

I stepped off of the porch and tentatively reached my hand to him. He looked at it, then back up to me.

"I want to show you something," I explained, trying to push down the dejected feeling.

He continued to stare at my hand, and just before I started to pull away, he took it in his own. I pulled him toward the side of the house, following the overgrown path out to the shop around back.

We went through the side door, and I flicked the fluorescent lights on. At the back of the shop, boxes piled high.

"What is this?" he asked, releasing my hand and walking in front of me.

"It's all your things from the house." I wrapped my arms around myself. I rarely came out here, only when I needed to get another bag of dog food or some yard tools. "You can go through it if you want." He looked to our right, where a tarp was covering something large.

"What's that?"

I grabbed the dusty tarp and lifting it to show the tailgate of his truck. I never had the heart to get rid of it and I couldn't drive it without sobbing every time I was in it.

"You kept it?" His eyebrows lifted high, a glimpse of his younger self coming through.

"I kept everything, Alex. I didn't get rid of anything that wasn't solely mine."

I couldn't. I wasn't strong enough then and I wasn't now.

He ran his hand over the pickup's tailgate before heading back to the boxes. He pulled a pocketknife out and cut the tape, opening it up and pulling out a shirt that I could immediately tell wouldn't fit him anymore. The boy I once knew was now a man. Reddish brown stubble covered his strong jaw.

"Everyone helped me after you were taken. After Gloria's diagnosis. Troy, Gavin, Dan, and Jon."

"Stop." His voice was stern. "I don't want to hear about Jon right now, Wren."

I stood there quietly, unsure what to do. His hands dropped to his sides and his palms opened and closed. I watched as the muscle's in his arms flexed while he stared down at his boxed belongings.

I wanted to stay and watch him, but a part of me didn't feel like I had that privilege anymore. This man in front of me wasn't the same boy I grew to love so many years ago. He was a different person now. I didn't know him.

Quietly, I slipped out of the shop and headed back into the house. Without giving it much thought, I headed into my studio. I unclipped my work in progress from the easel and set it in a folder before placing a blank page up on it.

I took a whole piece and started to add color, using my fingers to smudge parts out, adding texture where it needed it. I lost track of time while I was working on it. King's hungry whine caused me to realize it was dark outside. I closed the room and headed to the kitchen, fixing him and Queen their meals. Queen was nowhere to be found, which was unusual for her.

I decided that I wanted a quick dinner. I made grilled cheese sandwiches with a can of tomato soup. I plated everything and stared down at the two plates. I wanted to take one out to Alex. A peace offering. I was still trying to wrap my head around everything.

I took it out to the shop.

Alex had cleared the back of the shop out, moving his old mattress out from behind everything and placing it on the ground, sitting on it while he read through something. Surprisingly, Queen was lying behind him on the mattress, raising her head as I walked in. I was a little shocked to find that neither of the dogs had any issues with Alex, but then I really thought about it.

I still had one of Alex's blankets from when we were kids. It was the blanket I pulled out on cold mornings. It was folded up on the end of my bed now. It had lost the smell of him years ago, but the dogs slept on it for years. Maybe they recognized him.

I stopped, waiting for him to look up at me.

For a moment, I got a glimpse of the boy I used to know. His face was soft, like his guard had dropped.

Queen's tail thumped on the ground, and she stood, stretching lazily before walking over to me, her nose in the air taking interest in the food in my hands.

"I was wondering where you were," I said to her. I walked over to Alex, holding the plate with the sandwich and a soup bowl out to him. He took it, nodding to me. I moved to the tailgate of his truck, sitting on it.

King sat down on the ground where my feet dangled and stared at Alex.

"Yeah, buddy, that's Alex." I dropped my gaze to King, reaching down and patted his head.

"How would he know me?" Alex asked.

I looked up into his eyes through my lashes. The words were on the tip of my tongue. *Because I told him about you. I cried for you. I slept in your clothes for years as I mourned the loss of you.*

I sat there for a moment before I took a bite. "Who knows."

Alex's words still rang in my head, the hurt he caused me out on the sidewalk and the fact that he didn't believe me.

I never thought I would have to convince this man of anything.

I had stopped trying to convince people to believe me at a young age. Alex was the first person to believe what I told him. Now, I was trying to convince him that what I said was the truth. I didn't think he believed me yet, so my guard was still up.

When Alex didn't say anything, I second guessed my presence. Maybe I needed to give him some space.

"I didn't know my mom kept a journal."

His words hit me hard. When we were kids, he never referenced her as *my mom*. It was never possessive. It was always just *Ma, our Ma* or *did you see that Mom. . .* It felt like there was a wall there now.

I swallowed hard.

"I found them in her drawers when we were packing everything up."

"Did you read them?"

I shook my head. "No." I tried to find my words. "I opened them just to see what they were, and when I saw her handwriting, I closed them up." I stared down at the plate in my lap, "She had gotten the diagnosis and was hospitalized shortly afterwards. I was packing her a bag and she asked me to make sure I grabbed her journal. So, I did. She wrote in it every day until she was in so much pain that she was medicated to sleep." The memory lanced through me. Watching the strongest women I had ever known deteriorate into nothing was awful. I was glad Alex hadn't seen his mother like that.

Alex closed the journal and picked up his own plate, eating the sandwich in two bites before bringing the bowl up to his lips and drinking the soup straight from it.

He still ate like we were starving. I bit the inside of my cheek to keep from smiling. I may not know this man anymore, but the boy I did know shone through every so often.

"You mind if I stay and keep looking through these things?"

"You can do whatever you want, Alex." I meant the words. Alex had a power that I never granted another human being. He could come and go as he pleased. He could walk into my life, make decisions, and I wouldn't question his motives. The trust I had in this man even after all these years astounded me, but I knew in the marrow of my bones that he would never hurt me.

I looked back down to my plate. Normally I would have scarfed it down already, but I was eating slowly. A silent excuse to stay longer. Queen had taken up residence at his side again.

"It looks like Queen has taken a liking to you." He glanced behind her. She raised her head, watching him watch her. "She doesn't normally act that way to. . ." The words died on my lips.

"Strangers?" Alex said, his amber eyes on me for the first time since I walked in.

I looked away, not willing to acknowledge out loud that he was, in fact, a stranger.

"Well," I said, sliding off the tailgate. He handed me his plate, and I got another glimpse of my name across his knuckles. A thrill ran through me. He had branded his body with my name. The ink looked fresh.

Questions surfaced but I bit them down, taking his plate from him. "I'll make up the guest room for you. You can stay if you want. It's up the stairs and to the left. The back door is unlocked." I moved away from him, turning back and looking at Queen, "Come on, girl." She looked from me to Alex before reluctantly getting up and following me.

I HADN'T BEEN ABLE TO SLEEP. I LISTENED HARD, trying to hear the door open, but Alex hadn't come in. I rolled over and pulled the sheet up under my neck, trying to shut my mind off long enough to fall asleep.

"Fuck it." I kicked the sheets off and got out of bed.

Jon had texted and called me so many times that I finally had to turn my phone off before I threw it across the room. I couldn't talk to him right now. I was hinging on believing he made a mistake when he went down to the morgue to identify Alex's body at the jail.

I headed downstairs and turned on a small lamp in the kitchen, then started some coffee while I stared out the window. There were no windows to the shop, so I couldn't even tell if Alex was awake or not.

It was strange, him being alive, and not feeling like I could go to him.

"Quit it." I stared down at King, who kept pawing at my leg. He was a needy guy and still acted like a puppy at four years old. I sighed and scratched his head. He laid his ears back and had a very pleased look on his face. His girlfriend, Queen, was missing, and I knew she had snuck out and gone back down to Alex. "Traitor," I mumbled. Neither of them were ever far from me until now.

It was one in the morning. I walked out the back door and sat out back on the deck of the farmhouse.

The crickets chirped; frogs croaked; our resident owl hooted in the night somewhere. King turned his head away from me, looking out into the tree-lined barrier I had around the place.

The farmhouse was my sanctuary. The property had several acres surrounded by trees and was crossed by a creek that fed into the lake. It had a large dock built by the previous owners that was larger at the end. I had a chair out there to sit on. It was one of my favorite places. I was in the middle of nowhere. I had no neighbors, no light pollution from the city.

I loved being here.

I hated being alone.

Alex was alive.

The realization of it all was finally settling in. I hadn't been going crazy; I had really seen him.

Gloria was still dead.

My heart ached at the thought of her. She'd died too soon.

I wish I would have seen the signs. I wish I would have been able to pay attention to more than myself. Maybe we would have seen the signs sooner. Gotten a diagnosis quicker.

I took a sip of my coffee. It was the dead of summer and even at night the temperature didn't drop. I sat in a sports bra and shorts, feeling comfortable only because I knew no one was around.

And if someone dared come onto the property, King and Queen would let me know.

There were only a handful of people who knew where I lived now. I had gone to great lengths to stay as anonymous as I could. I opened an LLC and purchased the house under that. I had a PO Box set up in town to keep the mail trucks from coming out here.

I tried quitting Dan's Construction, but Dan wouldn't let me. Now, I showed up twice a month to run payroll. Bonnie verified everyone's time cards were correct and turned in on time. I showed up in the early morning, got everyone's checks either printed or direct deposited, then got the hell out of there.

Bonnie and I met up for coffee every other week to catch up. She was good about not asking too many questions. She talked a lot about her baby daddy and her kiddo. I loved talking to her. She gave me a perspective on a life I was never going to experience.

I picked my phone up off the deck next to me and turned it back on, flipping the toggle to silence it. Once it was booted up, I dialed.

"What in the hell are you doing up this early?" Mario's groggy voice filled the line.

"Come on, you know I don't sleep much." I sipped my coffee. "Why are *you* still asleep?"

I could hear the shifting of sheets over the line. He groaned. "Some of us actually like to sleep."

"Oh, suck it up."

Mario chuckled. "What's wrong, kid?"

"Can't sleep."

"Well, that's obvious."

I ran my index finger around the rim of my cup. "How likely is it for someone to identify a body wrong?"

"What?" He was awake now.

"Is it possible?"

"I mean, yeah. Depends on the situation, though, and how identifiable the body is." He paused. "What's going on? Is this about Alex?"

How did I tell him that the best friend who I told him died was alive? How did I tell anyone?

"When he committed suicide, Jon was the one to identify him. Jon was the one to file the paperwork, get the death certificate. Jon did everything."

"To get the death certificate, the death has to be reported, then filed with the local jurisdiction. . ."

"How are bodies identified?"

"Lots of different ways. DNA, dental records, next of kin." He sighed. "Wren, what's going on?"

He's alive.

But I didn't say the words. I wasn't ready. If I told Mario, he would start looking into it, and I wasn't ready for the truth yet.

My stomach filled with dread.

"I just wasn't a part of the process and wanted to know about it is all," I lied.

I could hear Mario expel his breath. "Just thinking about it because of the anniversary is coming up?"

"Yeah. Sorry to bother you with it, Mario."

"Don't apologize. Call me anytime." He paused. "Aside from that, how was the dinner thing?"

I scratched under King's chin. "It was. . ." I sighed. "It was a lot."

"Wanna talk about it?"

"Nah. It is what it is. I'm good."

"See you Wednesday."

Mario ended the call. I laid the phone in my lap and looked around the porch. Sighing, I stood, turning and heading back into the house. Before I turned my phone back off, I made one more phone call.

"Riley, I need you."

"Say that again?"

"You heard me the first time."

"No, ma'am, because what I thought you said is, *Alex is alive.*" Riley's red hair was in her signature braid, and it whipped back and forth, smacking her in the face as she vigorously shook her head. Her teal-blue eyes widened.

As soon as I'd called her, she sped over to my house. It was still dark out, but she didn't hesitate. She was dressed in a T-shirt and sweats, with her clamshell slippers.

I nodded at her. "He's alive, Ri."

"How is that possible?"

"I don't know. I want to believe that there was some kind of mistake, but. . ." I thought about Jon's face at dinner. He'd been just as shocked as me.

"Fuck Jon right now. Tell me again. Alex called you a whore?"

I tried to remember the first time Jon and Riley met. It had to of been after Gloria got sick. The moment didn't stand out for me. Jon, Riley, Troy and Gavin had worked together to get me moved out from the corner house and into this house. She never spoke badly about him, but she didn't go out of her way to be friends with him either.

I never thought much about it, but what did she sense in Jon that I didn't?

I sat back on the couch, groaning. "Not straight out, but he said I had been shacking up with Jon, the prick." I was still so angry and hurt that he would say those things to me.

The memory of him leaving me that night hit me again. I had always fought with the anger I felt for him. He left to protect me. But I'd needed him more than anything at that moment. I could still remember begging him to stay, but he left anyway.

If he hadn't, Kevin would still be out there.

Riley held my hands and bit her lip. "Can I play devil's advocate here?" I sighed and nodded. She squeezed my hands tighter.

"Wren, he's *alive.*" She stressed the word. "This is your second chance. Think about it from his perspective. He had no contact with you for years. Yes, you were told he died. His lawyer was the only person who could identify him because of whatever fucking bullshit reason Jon spilled to you, but let's forget that. You were mourning him, and he thought you were ignoring him. I can understand him getting out and being pissed off. So, maybe, you should give him a chance? Forget the chaos of that first meeting and try talking to him. Explain what happened. His anger is misplaced. It should all be on Jon, not you, cakes."

Hot tears streamed down my cheeks as she spoke. She was

right, but I still wasn't sure it was Jon's fault. Emotions were running high back then; he could have just simply made a mistake. Her words settled into me and I cried harder. My heart ached with too many emotions. He was alive, but Gloria was dead.

"Oh god." I pulled back, looking to her. "Riley, Jon told me that Alex committed suicide because his mother died."

Riley nodded, knowing this, but she didn't seem to be catching on to what I was saying.

"Ri, when Alex came into the house, I showed him her death certificate. What if he hadn't known his mom died?"

Her brows shot up to her hairline and her mouth popped open. "Oh shit," she whispered.

I pulled my hands from hers, covering my face. "What if that's how he found out?" A flood of memories hit me. Watching him and Gloria together, laughing. Her griping at him about something he did or didn't do. The pride that'd shone in her eyes at her son.

"Cakes, you're the best person to tell him. You're his best friend. Almost more if that night had never happened."

The pain of that night always felt like it had just happened, overshadowing the good that had occurred since. What could have been between Alex and I?

I shook my head. I wasn't going to dwell on what had never happened. I needed to push my feelings aside and talk to Alex about his mother.

CHAPTER 38

ALEX

I wasn't sure what time I had fallen asleep on that mattress in Wren's shop, but I woke to Queen licking my cheek.

"Come on, girl, quit it." I groaned as I rolled away from her. I had been using an old sweatshirt balled up as a pillow. The bed felt huge to me. Even though I shared it all night with the dog. Not long after Wren had left with her, Queen came back, scratching at the door till I opened it. Growing up, sharing that XL twin mattress with Wren had been cramped, but not once did we complain about it. In prison, the bed was the same size, only less comfortable and had stains that I'd tried not to think about too much.

I felt like a kid, staying up all night with a story, reading from a flashlight. Only this time the flashlight was from my phone. Doing so had drained the battery dry.

Ma had written mostly about me and everything I told her I did at school that day. She wrote down her grievances with me and talked about how much she missed my dad. She worried about not being there enough for me and things she planned on doing to make more money to make up for not being around much. Reading her journals was a lot like going down memory lane. Her handwriting was sharp and sometimes messy, like she had to get it all out in a short amount of time.

When the journal entries of Wren started, I read them like I had been starving for information. Some things surprised me.

Ma had almost taken Wren to the police station.

I planned on taking her to the police station today. Candy and I have been talking and she's right. If her mother puts out a missing persons notice and they track her to our house, I could get thrown in jail for kidnapping. I can't let anything happen to my son or myself. I have to be there for him.

But when I came home early today, Alex was smiling. I don't think I've seen him smile like that since his father died. He's been doing better in school and he looks happy. I feel guilty, because of course my son has been lonely. I have been so worried about making sure the power and water stayed on that I never thought about how he must be lonely all the time.

Now he has Wren, and I'll be damned if I take that away from him. Wren is a sweet girl and I think she needs Alex as much as he needs her. I still can't believe the horrors that were happening just next door to us. I can't help but feel guilty. If I had just been home and noticed the things that had been happening. Of course I heard them fighting a lot, but I would just ignore it. People fight all the time and I was too tired to deal with anything more.

Maybe I could have done something to help the poor girl.

I can't separate them now. Alex would never forgive me. She will be eighteen in a year and then there's nothing anyone can do.

If something happens to me, at least they have each other.

I sat up. The mattress cover Wren had it stored in crackled, causing Queen to groan. I could tell it was early. I closed Ma's journal, set it in the box closest to me and stood, throwing my shirt over my shoulder. It was hot and muggy in here and I had stripped down to my boxers sometime in the middle of the night.

Ma's journal didn't surprise me at all. I wouldn't have forgiven her if she took Wren away. Nobody could have guaranteed her safety except for us. We kept her safe. We gave her a home and the time to help her heal.

I pulled the cover from my old truck, a warm feeling growing in me. I had saved up every paycheck I could to buy this thing, worked day and night to make the necessary repairs, and had figured it had been long gone. The keys sat on the dash. I grabbed them and tried to turn the ignition over. It ticked before it died. I popped the hood, noting the battery was probably dead. I rounded it and opened the gas tank, shoving my nose close to it and inhaling. The gas had gone bad. I wanted to get it up and running as soon as possible, and to do that, I needed to get into town and buy a battery and get some gas.

I pulled my jeans back on and slipped into my boots, leaving them unlaced. I headed out of the shop, Queen following close behind. It was just barely dawn, the birds started chirping, and the sky started to brighten. It was hot outside still; even the night couldn't dampen the hot nights, but I could feel a slight breeze as I walked to the house.

Every step I took had boards creaking. I thought about the tools I would need to fix it. I used the downstairs bathroom before heading to the kitchen, opening the cupboards till I found a glass and filling it up from the tap, drinking greedily.

Queen joined in on the drinking, lapping up her bowl of water. I remembered when Wren and I had found a litter of puppies abandoned by the train tracks. We had wanted to keep one so badly but didn't dare try. We both knew money was extremely tight, and adding another mouth to feed would have just been selfish on our part.

I was glad she had dogs now. Glad she had someone to keep her company.

Nails clacked on the floor, and soon King was downstairs, his tail high before he laid eyes on the two of us. Queen chuffed and King relaxed, his tail wagging.

"Where's your mom?" I asked King. The shepherd stared at me before turning around and leaving the kitchen.

I started up the coffee machine and poured two cups, then hesitated; did she still take it black? Before I could question it any longer, I took the two mugs toward the front of the house.

In the living room, Wren lay out on the couch, her arms crossed and head tilted against it. King was lying on the floor by her.

I was surprised to find her asleep. Her hair was a mess. It splayed across the cushion in messy curls. Her lips were slightly parted, and her chest was rising and falling.

When she first moved in with me and Ma, she'd slept for a week straight. After she had rested, she became restless. Even the slightest noise would wake her. The nightmares would keep her up.

I wondered how bad they had been over the last six years.

Wren startled awake, shooting upward, causing even King to jump.

"Shit, Alex!" She clutched her chest, steadying her breath.

"I'm sorry." I raised the mugs in my hand. "I didn't think you slept this long."

She grabbed her phone off the coffee table and looked at the time. It was only seven in the morning; I had already been up for two hours, still used to prison wake-up.

"I didn't sleep much," she said, her voice groggy.

"Why are you out on the couch?" I handed her the mug. She clasped it with both hands, taking a sip, humming her appreciation. It satisfied me that I still knew how she took her coffee.

She rubbed her eyes with one hand. Something in me softened at the sight. Even six years later, this was familiar. She was wearing shorts and an oversized T-shirt with the neck cut out. Disappointment slashed through me when I didn't recognize the shirt.

"I was waiting for you to come in. I wanted to talk to you about. . .everything." She turned so she sat right on the couch. "Must have fallen asleep out here. Did you come in last night? How was the guest room?" She stood and moved around the couch. King followed her to the window, where she opened the blinds, letting the sun in.

"It was fine," I lied.

Her nipples pebbled beneath the shirt, making it obvious that she wasn't wearing a bra. Before, I would look away. I never wanted her to feel self-conscious or like she needed to cover up from me. I was respectful of her and never wanted her to feel uncomfortable.

Now, I blatantly stared.

Looking away from her beauty would be a crime in itself.

I cocked an eyebrow at her as she sat cross-legged back on the couch, the confusion clear on her face before she looked down, seeing what I saw.

The ghost of a memory landed on my tongue. The first and last time I tasted her. I could hear her moan at the back of my mind when I sucked harder or ran my teeth over her nipples.

"Not as gentlemanly, I see." She covered herself with her arms. I dropped my gaze, taking a sip of my coffee. "Those years in prison didn't do much for your manners." I could hear the smile in her voice and almost choked on the coffee.

"You give me too much credit. I was never a gentleman. I was just a nervous kid."

"I don't remember you being nervous at all."

"Oh, how do you remember me?"

"Alex, we need to talk."

"Answer me."

She leaned forward, her elbows on her knees. "You were. . .my rock. You were always there no matter what. You took all my panic attacks and sleepless nights in stride. You never complained. Never made me feel like I wasn't worth something." Her voice softened. "You were my everything, Alex."

I took that in.

I was her everything.

She had never said those words growing up. I knew I was

important to her. Knew I was her comfort, but it was different to hear now.

You were. Past tense.

Meaning I wasn't her everything now.

"What do you want to talk about?" I took a seat on the chair across from her, needing to move my thoughts along. There were a thousand things I wanted to talk about, but I wanted her to lead the conversation.

She set the coffee down on the table between us before she rubbed her face. I waited for her to continue. She brought her hand to her mouth and started to chew on the edge of her thumb. I wanted to pull it away. I remembered how she would chew her thumb raw, and holding her hand was the only way to make her stop.

"Wren." I shifted my eyes from hers to her hand. Realization struck and she folded her them in front of her.

"I realized last night that I dropped a bomb on you." She sighed the words.

My brow crinkled and I waited for her to continue.

"Alex, your mom. . ."

"Is dead. I know. I found out shortly after I got out." I spoke the words, feeling nothing. Mom was dead and there was nothing I could do about it. Wren hadn't known I knew, but that wasn't what I wanted to talk about right now.

"How did you find out?"

"How I found out doesn't matter right now, Wren." I knew she was going to be pissed when she learned I hired a PI to look into her whereabouts. That was a fight for another day.

She wrapped her arms around her middle and stared at the floor. I softened. Talking about Mom had to be hard for her. I hadn't gone through watching my mother die. Wren had.

"Hungry?" she asked suddenly, standing.

"Starving."

For you.

"Come on."

Wren pointed. "Living room is obviously there. Library is through there; bathroom is under the stairs." I followed her, passing the staircase. "Kitchen is back here."

Her kitchen was in the back corner of the house. Skylights basked the room in natural light, and it was wall-to-wall windows. Looking out the back window, I could see the glimmer of a lake.

"Nice place," I commented. I already knew these things; I just wanted to soothe her nerves.

"Thank you." She opened the fridge, pulling out a carton of eggs and taking them to the stove. She started to fuss about, looking for a pan.

"Sit." She motioned to the kitchen table.

I did as I was told, slightly amused watching her. I leaned back and took a long drink of my coffee.

"Wren, stop it."

"Stop what?"

"Stop fussing. Frankly, you're agitating me."

"Why the hell would my fussing agitate you?"

"Because you're acting like you're scared of me!" My temper flared but she didn't flinch like she used to.

"I'm not scared of you! You just," she grabbed the edge of the counter and hung her head, "you make me nervous."

"Wren, just sit down and fill me in on the last six years," I said more gently.

"We're just going to jump into it? Just like that?"

"Yeah, Wren, just like that," I deadpanned. "What I need to know is why no one ever wrote me."

She took a deep breath. "I did write you, Alex. I wrote you hundreds of letters, but they were all—"

"Nope." I took another swig of my coffee. "I didn't get one damn letter from you." I was being hostile, I knew it, but I couldn't soften my tone.

Wren stood up so quickly she knocked her chair over. She headed down the hall, coming back with a basket of envelopes in her hand. She dropped the basket on the table and pointed to them.

"These are just some of the letters I sent you." She picked the chair back up before dropping back down into it. "I wrote you all the time, Alex, they either went unanswered or were returned to me." She reached over, shuffling through them before plucking one out. "I sent you hundreds of letters and not once did I get anything back."

It seemed like the fight was leaving her. She looked exhausted.

I sat forward, my elbows on my knees. "After the hearing, they bounced me around to a few different places. I finally settled in at a prison north of the state." I shook my head before looking up at her.

Wren wasn't looking at me but past me. She was lost in thought, and I knew she was thinking of my mother. I wanted to reach out to her, cup her face, and bring those emeralds back to me. I wanted to comfort her.

But I hadn't been the one to comfort her in a long time.

Unwanted images flashed in my mind. Her being comforted by men. Specifically, Jon comforting her. Jon sleeping with her. I clenched my jaw and looked to the ceiling, trying to calm the annoyance that started to brew at the thoughts.

That fucking prick.

"What's wrong?" she asked.

"Nothing," I said too fast.

"Bullshit," she said, straightening in her seat, apparently reading me easily still. "Tell me," she demanded.

The woman before me wasn't the same girl I knew. Wren hadn't been demanding in the past. She'd accepted what I said and didn't ask me twice.

"I need to get a battery and gas for the truck," I tried.

Her eyes narrowed. She stood, moving away from me to lean against the kitchen counter, and crossed her arms. "Alex, I have spent the last five years thinking you were dead. The last time we were together. . ." She paused. "Before that, we were happy. We were. . ." She laughed softly. "We were in love."

Her words hit me hard. We *were* in love. I was wildly in love with her. Addicted to her, and in those moments, I'd planned on spending every moment with her, forever. I had always planned on being with her forever, whether I was just her friend or more, but that was the moment we both agreed to be more.

And it was all ripped away from us.

"Alex, I never stopped loving you. Not for one moment." She held my gaze before breaking eye contact. "I understand that you thought I abandoned you, and I understand if your feelings have changed, but—"

I was across the room in an instant.

I cupped her face and crushed my lips to hers. She sucked in a breath before her fingers were at the back of my neck, pulling my mouth harder down on hers. I turned my head so I could deepen the kiss, tasting her. I drank from her. She was a never-ending spring, and I was dying of thirst. Dragging my lips down her neck. A thrill traveled up my spine.

I pulled away just enough to rest my forehead against hers. "I spent years convincing myself you had moved on. That you were married with this whole new life away from me. That you broke away from your past. I thought you left me behind. I tortured myself with images of you with other men." I tucked her hair behind her ear. "You are not the same woman I fell in love with all those years ago. You are different, and I can't help but wonder who was there for you when I couldn't be."

Her eyes searched mine, and I could see the hurt there. Was she thinking of me with other women?

"You were thinking about me with other men?"

I had tried to simply hope that she was being taken care of. Hope that no one was hurting her, and she had a good life. Hope that she was smiling every day. But I was a selfish bastard when it came to her, and I wanted to be the only one for her.

"Yes. I thought about it every day. I tortured myself with the thoughts of you being with another man."

She shook her head. "Alex, I haven't. . . I've only ever been with you."

THE WORDS WERE OUT OF MY MOUTH BEFORE I COULD stop them. Heat crawled up my neck.

His eyes traveled up the length of me. I leaned in, wanting more. I wanted this. I wanted him. My heart pounded in anticipation.

I saw resistance in his gaze before he spoke.

"Wren, there's something I need to show you." He breathed the words against my lips before pulling away. His hand brushed my cheek and came around to the back of my neck, his favorite handle.

I tried to pull away, but he held me in place. I felt rejected and embarrassed. "Wren, please. I want this with you, but I need to show you something first."

"Okay," I said meekly. "Let me get ready and we can go."

He kissed my forehead before letting me go. I headed upstairs, closing the door gently behind him. I collapsed back on the bed, a frustrated breath escaping me.

"What the hell did you think would happen?" I grumbled to the ceiling before getting out of bed and getting dressed. The moment he said he had been thinking of me with other men, I wanted to erase those thoughts from his mind. I wanted him to know that I had never even come close to slipping into bed with someone.

I had thought about it. Ripping the Band-Aid off, having a one-night stand with a stranger in a bar just to break that last connection I had with him, but I couldn't do it. The weight of Alex's and my first time was too great. I needed more than just a body to sleep with.

Alex had ruined me for anyone else. He had taken me, mind, body and soul.

There was no other person for me.

I dropped my face into my hands, the realization hitting me.

For years, I knew Jon wanted more. Even though he had never said it out loud, I knew he had been waiting for me to be ready to be with someone else. And I knew that *someone else* in his mind was going to be him. I had let my resolve break down over the years and I was going to settle for him.

Alex's best friend.

The best friend who may have betrayed us.

Suddenly, I felt sick.

I shot out of my room and ran to the bathroom, putting up the toilet seat and hanging my head over it. Nausea washed over me and I fought to keep the coffee down.

Once I fought it down, I went to the sink, cupping water to my mouth.

I chose jeans and a black tank top before heading across the hall and spraying my hair with my water and leave-in conditioner to bring some life back to my curls. Once I was satisfied with my hair, I went ahead and applied some light makeup.

Alex was sitting on my front porch when I came downstairs. Queen was laying close behind him while he was tossing a ball for King. I shook my head at them. The pups had been glued to me since the beginning, Alex had been here for a day, and they were already attached to him.

Just as attached as I was.

I pushed open the storm door and the smell of cigarettes hit me.

"Ready?" Alex stood, turning around, and I saw the culprit hanging from his lips. I walked forward and ripped it from his mouth, taking it to the birdbath in my flower bed and putting it out before I whirled on him.

"Your mother died of lung cancer and you picked up her one bad habit!? Are you fucking kidding me, Alexander!"

His eyebrows rose and he put his hands up in surrender. "Woah, I'm sorry. I won't smoke around you."

"You won't fucking smoke! Period! I lost one person I loved to this shit; I won't lose you too! Not again!"

He slowly walked toward me, hands still up like he was trying to calm a wild animal.

"You aren't going to lose me, Wren." His fiery brown eyes were on me.

"Like I wasn't going to lose you before? You forget, Alex, I thought you were dead for five years. I mourned you once. I can't do it again." My voice broke.

"Okay, I won't smoke."

"Promise me." It was a demand that I didn't care if I had the right to make.

"I promise."

I let him drive my car. I sat in the passenger seat with the radio on. We drove in silence. The ash trees passed by my window on our way into town, thinning out as we got closer to town until there were none at all.

He drove us to the industrial district, parking outside a huge warehouse.

"Where are we?"

"This is where I've been staying since I got out."

I closed the car door behind me. The building was nice

compared to everything else around. The other buildings were older, rundown, with graffiti everywhere.

"You've been staying here?" I asked, confused.

It looked like another prison to me.

We went inside. The place was empty except for some boxes stacked at the back of the building. The door closing echoed in the empty space. I looked around, a chill running down my spine.

"This place is creepy," I muttered.

"At least it's quiet," Alex mumbled.

In the center of the huge warehouse were rows of boxes stacked four high each. He stopped in front of them.

"What am I looking at?" I asked when he didn't say anything.

Alex sighed, shoving his hands in his pockets, and paced. "I really wished I hadn't agreed to stop smoking."

I crossed my arms and glared at him.

"When I got out, I met someone who helped me get back on my feet. I didn't know what to expect when I got out, but I expected the worst. I wanted to know what you were up to. What everyone was up to really. I didn't understand why every person in my life stopped talking to me. So, Ezekiel got me into contact with a private investigator."

"Who's Ezekiel?'

"He's who owns this building."

"How did you meet him?"

"I met his brother in prison."

"That doesn't tell me how you met *him*."

Alex threw his hands up, stopping me. "Wren, please."

I took a deep breath and nodded, motioning for him to continue.

"I told the private investigator our story. I told them about Kevin. When the PI, Foster, looked into him, they found he had a storage unit."

A loud ringing started in my ears, and I felt the room teeter. I turned away from Alex. I could hear the shutter in my head. The whirl of the polaroid's printing.

The boxes were Kevin's.

"Oh god," I whispered. Horrified that anything from those years still existed. I thought they had been destroyed in the fire. I never imagined he had kept them elsewhere. I hadn't said anything about them to anyone because I didn't want anyone to find them.

I thought I was done with this. I thought that there wasn't any more evidence of what he had done to me.

I felt Alex's hand on my back, and I shoved him away.

"NO!" My voice echoed in the warehouse. I put my hand up. "Just. . .give me a minute."

I tried to push the invading images away. The memory of the pain ripping through my body. The smell of his sweat on me, the feel of his hot breath in my ear.

Relax, baby girl.

I swallowed hard. "Have you. . .opened them?"

"Yes."

"Did you see. . .everything?" My voice shook.

"Yes."

I raised my face to the ceiling, taking in a deep breath. I could feel the angry tears welling up.

"Tell me what you want me to do, Wren, and I'll do it." His voice was soft.

I walked up to him and took the pocket knife on his hip. I grabbed a box and opened it up. I recognized the dress immediately. It was orange with black ribbon detail. It had been one of my father's favorites; he had called me *pumpkin* whenever I wore it. I pushed the box to the side and opened another one. There were the Polaroids. I couldn't look at them. I could still feel everything that Kevin did to my body—I didn't need to see it in my nightmares too.

I moved to another box, and then another, until my entire childhood was splayed out in front of me. I had moved on from this part of my life. I went to therapy, and I got through this. I didn't want any of this to ever show up in my path again.

"Is this everything?"

Alex was at my side then. "Yeah. This was everything. The only reason it was found was because no one closed out his bank account and it was on autopayments."

I nodded, moving to the last box. I pulled out child drawings, not looking them over. I already knew what they were. The images depicted my dead father and my mom with her new boyfriend. I crumpled the pages, tossing them one by one on the pile I created.

Without even looking at me, Alex moved closer to the mess, pulling out a small bottle and squirting it on everything till it ran out. He tossed the empty tin down.

He knew what I wanted to do.

I thought he might stop me. Tell me this wasn't the place for it, but he reached into his pocket, pulled out a Zippo, and ignited it.

I took the lighter and tossed it on the pile. The flames ate away at the path he'd created with the lighter fluid. Slowly, the fire engulfed everything. Alex tenderly wrapped an arm around my waist, pulling me farther from the flames.

There was something cathartic about watching my worst memories turn to ash. Disintegrating into nothing.

No longer existing anywhere but inside my head.

I used to pretend it'd never happened, but not anymore. It happened. I was raped. I was raped hundreds of times, and it was done violently. Sometimes, I could still feel the phantom pains from it. The flames danced and licked higher, the smoke billowed up and threatened to choke me before it funneled out of the building from the roof vents.

It was cleansing.

We stayed until it was only smoldering. Before leaving, Alex walked over to the burned mess and stomped the remaining embers out. I watched as his foot dragged the soot along the darkened concrete.

It would probably stain this spot forever.

We left the warehouse unaware that it had been storming. The wind whipped through the ash trees and pushed my car all over the road. Alex held my hand on the center console the whole way back to my place.

Once home, I headed straight to the bathroom without a word, stripping out of my clothes. I smelled like a campfire and wanted to wash it all away. As soon as I stepped inside the shower, thunder boomed around me. The bathroom light flickered and then cut out.

I stood under the cascading water, turning the temperature up as hot as I could stand it. This wasn't the first time a summer storm took out my power.

I heard the click of the bathroom door opening. Alex was there, lighting a candle and setting it on the small table next to the bathtub. Even in the soft glow, I caught his gaze. I didn't want him to go. I reached for the door and opened it slightly in silent invitation.

I implored him with my eyes, hoping to convey that I wanted this. I wanted him. I wanted him closer. There was six years of distance between us, and I wanted to get rid of it.

He scrubbed a hand down his face, and I knew I'd won. I heard the bathroom door shut. I watched as he pulled his shirt off, letting it fall to the floor. He kicked his shoes off, and then pulled off his socks. I wondered if he was waiting for me to change my mind.

I would never change my mind when it came to him.

He reached for his belt, and even though the room was slowly fogging up with steam, I didn't miss the way he grabbed his belt buckle, so it didn't jingle.

He still remembered.

I went to turn toward him, but he stopped me with both hands on my shoulders.

"Alex. . ."

"Shh, just let me have this, give me the satisfaction of taking care of you."

I relented.

He lathered up my loofah and washed me slowly, methodically. Pushing my hair over my shoulder, he washed my back, lifted my arms and washed from the tips of my fingers to my shoulders. His strong hands rubbed my palms, working between each finger.

His palms skirted around my breasts before moving down my body. I placed my hands on the wall to support myself, my head hung. I was already panting.

"Alex. . ."

He didn't say anything. Just moved lower, washing down my stomach till he got to my hips. His thumb grazed across the top of my mound.

I moaned in frustration. I couldn't tell if he was doing this on purpose to get a rise out of me, or if he didn't realize what he was doing to me.

That's when I felt his length graze my backside before it pulled away.

Tempted, I reach for the bodywash, pumping some into my own hand before I lathered it, turning in his arms.

"Wren," he warned.

If he thought he was the only one who got to do some touching, he had another thing coming to him.

I started with his shoulders, mimicking his own movements, only I worked the lather in with just my hands. My thumb found the hard muscles of his shoulders and massaged them. I working my hands across his shoulders and down his arms, stopping them from working his own magic into me. I repeated his actions, massaging between each of his fingers before I moved back to his chest.

I turned and traced over the lines of his tattoo, admiring them. One of these days I would ask him about them, but for now I traced them down his chest, over the hard lines of his abdomen.

While he was working his way up my back, I reached behind. Boldly, I gripped him at his base, stroking his length.

"Fuck." He shuddered, his head dropping to my shoulder, his hand clamping around my wrist.

"Alex, please. . ." I panted, frustrated.

"Spread your legs." The loofah disappeared and his arm pulled me, my back flush against his chest. He angled us so the water hit him, only the overspray catching me.

I parted my legs and stroked him again while his hand dipped between my thighs. His finger found the ball of nerves.

"Oh!" I moaned, leaning my head back against his shoulder. He was the one supporting my weight now. His fingers swirled over the bud before dipping lower to my opening, coaxing my need out.

I wanted to touch him. Feel him. I pushed off him and went to turn. He ripped his hand away from my center, leaving me bereft.

I reached around his neck, pulling his mouth down to me.

"Please," I begged.

"Are you sure?" His voice was barely a whisper. He was wrung taut. I knew if I said no, he would respect that. He wouldn't be mad, he wouldn't call me a tease, and something about knowing I was in complete control of this situation made me need him so much more.

"Yes."

He turned the water off and we stepped out of the shower. I reached for a towel, but I was pulled back, turned, and lifted. I yelped in surprise, my legs circling his waist automatically.

"Alex, I'm all wet."

"And?"

He set me down on the vanity next to the sink. My hands trailed up his chest before making their way around to the back of his neck. My fingers danced at his nape, wishing for his longer hair again.

I brought my lips to his and he devoured me. I got caught up in the kiss and nipped his bottom lip, feeling his cock jump against my leg.

He groaned. "Fuck, Wren."

I loved my name on his lips.

He kissed down my jaw, teeth skimming my throat before I was arching my back, thrusting my chest up toward his mouth. He teased me with his tongue before he finally took me into his mouth. I gasped at the sensation of his tongue lapping over me. His other hand came up to my other breast. He massaged and rolled my nipple gently between two fingers.

I was at risk of falling apart.

"More," I moaned.

I felt his cool breath on me and heard a faint chuckle. If I had half a mind, I'd have felt embarrassed, but I didn't. I wanted this. I wanted him. I had only ever wanted him.

"Anything for my girl."

Alex lowered himself between my legs. Before I could comprehend what he was about to do, he dragged his tongue excruciatingly slowly up my center.

"Ohh." I rested my weight on my hands, leaning until my back hit the mirror behind me.

Alex worked his magic. I tried to stay put, but I couldn't. My body involuntarily moved with each stroke of his tongue. I could feel my ass sliding to the edge of the vanity. I didn't say anything. My skin buzzed and static started in my ears as he brought my orgasm closer and closer, but then he stopped.

"Alex, don't stop," I cried.

He was laughing as he carried me to my room before tossing me on the bed and resuming his tongue thrashing. Our shadows danced on the walls in the candlelight.

He built me higher and higher before the stars exploded and I was shuddering with pleasure. He teased and licked until he had rung me of every last wave I was capable of.

His lips were on mine again and I could taste my arousal on his tongue. It was tangy and unlike anything I had ever tasted before. He crawled over my body, and I almost couldn't open my eyes, exhaustion hitting me, making my lids heavy from the onslaught of pleasure I'd just received.

I thought I heard my name on his lips so I reached up, my palm caressing his stubbled cheek while my other hand reached between us, stroking him. My thumb glided over the head and I slicked his precum over it.

His pleasure spurred me on and I stroked him from root to tip, loving the control I had. I opened my eyes just in time to see his arm shake in the amber glow.

"Sweetheart, if you keep that up, I won't last. It's been too long." His warm eyes were full of want and need.

"You haven't. . .?" I let the words hang between us without saying more. Of course, I had wondered if he had been with anyone else since being out, but I hadn't really thought about it until this moment.

He shook his head, and I knew the unasked question in his eyes.

"I haven't. . . I was tested after. . ." I couldn't say the words; it was like dipping my toes in ice cold water, unpleasant chills sent down me. I shivered, wishing we could go back to our hot shower.

He dipped his head, taking my lips again. I took over the kiss, demanding more. I tasted him, devoured him, wanting to be consumed by him.

With my hand still holding him between my thighs, I gripped his hip with my other, urging him to enter me. I rolled his head through my wetness before settling him at my entrance.

"Alex, fuck me now," I whispered against his lips. He pressed into me, pulling back and pressing in again, working his length into me until he was fully sheathed.

I had to breathe through it, allowing my body to stretch to accommodate his size.

"Are you okay?" he asked breathlessly.

My hand was in his hair, nails biting into his shoulder as I adjusted.

"Yes," I panted.

He dropped from his hands to his elbows, more of his weight pressing down on my chest. A hand caressed my breast and I tried to focus on his fingers tweaking my nipple and the pleasurable pain that needled through me. He moved his hips and pleasure built again.

I pulled my lips away from his and he kissed my neck. My eyes flew open, and I stared up at our shadows on the ceiling.

Breathe, it's okay, baby.

His voice was in my head now, and I squeezed my eyes shut, trying to block it out. I focused on Alex's pants, his shudders when he almost pulled all the way out before gliding back in.

My temple started to thrum in line with my heart rate and I could feel the panic working its way up my throat. My hand pressed against his chest. I couldn't breathe.

Alex must have seen the panic on my face because I felt his hips jerk back, almost pulling out before my hands shot to his hips, nails sinking in so he didn't leave me.

"No!" I shouted. "Don't. . . I just. . ." His weight was taken off me and I took in a gasp, heaving air in and out. "I want this. Please, I want this, I just couldn't breathe."

Alex's brow furrowed before understanding bled into his expression. Suddenly, still inside me, he moves us so I was on top, straddling him.

I felt the cool air hit my body and relief flooded me. My head sagged back as I took a moment, calming my heart rate. When I was ready, I looked down at him.

Concern was still etched in his face.

"Is that better?"

"Yes." I nodded.

I was very aware of the new position I was put in.

"Come here." He held his hands out and I leaned down. He cupped my face and softly kissed me, his thumb brushing my cheek gently. It's slow, endearing. He kissed me until my lips felt swollen. He pulled back and looked up at me.

"You are in control here. Take what you need from me."

I sit up, placing my hands on his chest and adjusting so I could get some leverage.

I moved up, and Alex's eyes fluttered close, his head relaxing back against the pillow just as I moved down again.

It felt good, but having the control felt even better. I repeated the motion but lifting higher, until it felt like he might slip out, before dropping back down.

"Fuck!" His eyes shot open, and I moaned when I felt his fingertips bite into my hips. "I'm all yours, Wren." The words were clipped, like he was fighting for control.

With that, I moved faster. Sensations built inside me and I tipped my head back before rolling my body forward, the change in position hitting a new spot inside me.

I was taken off guard and fell forward, catching myself on his chest. When I blinked away the stars, he laced our hands together and I realized what he was doing. I used his hands as leverage to roll my body back and forth repeatedly, hitting the spot I liked over and over. I was trembling and could feel myself getting closer.

"Alex, I-I'm. . ." I stuttered out the words but it was too late. My second orgasm hit me and my hips jolted sporadically. Alex pressed up and I felt his own release spill inside. I fell forward onto his chest.

My face found the spot I loved between his neck and jaw. His breath heaved, and it was no longer water coating our skin but sweat. I couldn't form words, but I felt him move my hair to the side and his fingertips traced down my back, causing me to shiver.

WREN STRADDLED ME IN JUST A TANK AND PANTIES. The sun slashed into her room across her, setting her aglow. I couldn't keep my hands off her. I massaged her thighs, working my way up. I ran my thumbs under the hem of her shirt.

She leaned back, stretching her arms above her head, groaning a little as she did. Her muscles bunched and moved under my hands.

"Keep it up and I'll never let you out of this bed." She purposely rolled her hips right over me, causing more friction to strain my control.

I could lie in bed with her all day.

She smiled down at me, tucking her hair behind her ear. "Maybe that was my whole plan." She teasingly kissed my lips, running her tongue at the seam.

My thumbs circled over the scars I had seen on her when she was on the mat. I had wanted to ask her about them before but hadn't found the right time.

"What are these?" Softly, I ran my thumbs over them again.

Her expression dropped, and she cupped her hands over mine.

"Scars."

I could see she didn't want to talk about them, but I pressed further. "From what, Wren?" They were thin raised scars with little white pinpricks above and below them. From stitches, I assumed.

She swallowed hard. "After that day. . . I did several STI tests. I needed to be sure I didn't get anything from him. On my six-week exam, they told me I was pregnant."

I froze, staring at those scars. "You were pregnant?"

She nodded again, her hands dipping below mine to block my touch. My world flipped and my mind started to run.

She was pregnant.

Pregnant.

"Don't." She cupped my face, bringing my eyes to hers. "I did the same thing. I wondered if maybe, just maybe, it wasn't his. I tried convincing myself it was yours." She shook her head harder. "But I wasn't willing to risk it. I wasn't willing to hope, because if that baby got here, and it didn't have your eyes, and your smile." She took a steadying breath. "I wouldn't be able to do it. I didn't want a reminder of what had been done to me." She let go of me, sitting up, her arms clutched across her body. "So, I had them terminate the pregnancy, and I asked to be sterilized."

My first reaction was to be pissed. Not because of her decision, but because of my failure. If I would have just made sure he died in that fire. If I had stabbed him or something, maybe, just maybe she wouldn't have had to go through this. I stared at those scars and thought of all the things they took away from us. All the possibilities we could have had.

"Is that what you wanted?" I just spoke the honest truth. "If that's what you wanted then I support you." Wren hadn't ever had control over her body, and I imagined that was something she had been fighting for her whole life. I wasn't going to insert my wants onto her. I had never thought about being a father. It wasn't something that had ever crossed my mind, and I didn't want it to think about it now, just because I never would be.

"It is, but," she waved her hand between the two of us, "Alex, the choice, for me, was an easy one. I didn't want to be pregnant.

The thought of raising a child in the same world I grew up in, if I couldn't protect them. . . If I took away something that you wanted, I understand if this. . ."

"Wren." I sat up, holding her in my lap and banding one arm around her, cupping the back of her head with my other hand, keeping her in place. "The only thing I have ever wanted in my life is you. You are the only thing I have ever asked for, and if you still want me, too, you are all I need."

She kissed me deeply before pushing down on my chest, planting me back on the bed. Adjusting her positioning, she moved the sheet down, exposing the scar on my right side. Above the scar, in jagged tattooed ink, read *nice try*.

"What happened here?" Her fingers brushed over the rough raised flesh.

I smirked. "A guy with a shiv got me in the showers one day."

"Wait, you were stabbed?" She reared back, sitting up.

I shook my head. "No, I moved just in time, it was only a flesh wound."

"Why the fuck would someone go after you? That doesn't make sense."

"Prison is a whole other world, darlin'." I moved my hands back to her thighs. "You just look at someone too long and it's on." Fear crossed over her face. I had my theories on who sent guys after me, but I wasn't ready to talk to her about it.

"Did I almost lose you while you were in there?" she asked softly.

"No, you were never close to losing me. I'll always crawl home to you."

I could see the words settle into her.

"Tell me about the tattoo on your back. Is it a scale?"

"It's a justice scale."

"With. . .two eyeballs on it?"

I sat up, and she yelped as I moved her easily off me. I turned my back to her.

"An eye for an eye." I turned my head to watch her face. "I

believe in an eye for an eye. Kevin took your childhood and part of your adulthood. So I took his life."

The tattoo spanned across my back, with the scales hanging from each end and an eyeball on each side. It was my largest tattoo. I waited for her to say something. I expected her to tell me the same thing I knew Ma would have said.

An eye for an eye will make the whole world blind.

Then the world would know not to fuck with *my* Wren.

"Sounds fair to me," she whispered.

I shuddered when I felt her lips on my back. She kissed both sides of the scale, and then her lips pressed at the back of my neck. I pulled her back into my lap. She took my hands and ran her fingers over each digit. Each letter of her name.

"Why did you do this?"

"These hands will do anything for you."

"Anything?" she asked.

She placed her palm against mine. Wren's fingers were long but dainty, only reaching as far as the top crease of my own fingers. "Yes."

Her fingers trailed up to the tops of my hands where I had two different styled birds on them.

"These are wrens?"

"They are."

"Alex, you. . . You branded yourself with me and you didn't even know if I would be here for you when you got out." I could hear the hesitation in her voice.

"You have been ingrained in me since the day we met; I'm just showing the world who I belong to." I moved my left leg out from under the blanket and twisted so she could see the side of my calf. The inked dandelions. She touched the tattoo tenderly, her eyes watering, and I reached up, catching her tears.

We spent the day in bed indulging in one another. She told me what it was like raising two puppies at the same time and how she had to spray things down with apple cider vinegar just to keep them from chewing on the legs of the furniture. She told me about how she broke her ankle the first time she went up against Marshall at the gym. She told me about the sleepless nights, and how she started up charcoal drawings to keep herself occupied when she started having nightmares about forgetting my face.

"Are you going to go back and work for Dan?" she asked, her voice heavy with sleep.

"No. I have a job." Ezekiel had some things lined up for me. When I was ready, he would put me to work, but for now, I wanted to eat, sleep, and breathe Wren for a while longer.

Wren was asleep in my arms by midafternoon. She slept on her side, hands tucked up underneath her chin. I traced the scar along her jaw from the time her mother backhanded her with her wedding ring. This was before her mother had pawned it off for money, I was told. The scar had faded as the years passed, but it was still there and a part of her.

"I'm sorry," I whispered to her. "I'm so sorry for thinking you were anything except the person I always knew you as." Guilt flooded me. The things she went through without me. None of it was her fault, and I had every intention of dealing with Jon.

But the things I wanted to do to him would put me right back in jail and I couldn't let that happen.

Not yet.

CHAPTER 41

ALEX

WE PULLED UP TO DAN'S CONSTRUCTION YARD MONDAY morning, finding a space to park in. Everything was soaked from the rain over the weekend. The building was painted new colors; they had new logos on the trucks. More employee parking. I still hadn't fully wrapped my brain around the fact that everyone's lives had continued without me.

I didn't regret what I had done or the time I spent in jail. Not for a damn second.

Wren squeezed my hand, bringing my attention back to her. I brought her hand up and kissed the back of it.

"Are you ready?" Wren had to work today, so we decided it was time I show my face. I was coming to Dan's with her to see everyone.

"You go in without me."

She nodded, before leaning across the center console and kissing me softly.

She got out of the car and opened the back seat for King to get out as well. She had insisted on bringing him, and I wasn't going to argue. I watched as they walked inside the office. She still brought donuts in, which made me smile.

I just needed a minute. I just needed to get my bearings.

She abandoned me.

They all did.

But they hadn't. Like some sick joke, they had all thought I was dead. Wren and I talked about it into the early hours of the morning. She told me about my funeral. The one where they had nothing to bury and could only stand next to the freshly buried grave of my mother, who they had put to rest a week before they got the news of me.

The lies of me.

Trucks started to pull in. Workers climbed out in their Carhartts and work boots. I watched everyone, looking for two familiar faces. I got out, leaning against the hood of a car. I wanted to light a cigarette as I waited for them, but I didn't. I wasn't going to be the one to ever break a promise to Wren.

Not on purpose.

Foster's paperwork said Troy and Gavin still worked here, but they had never been known for their punctuality. Always stumbling in the door at the last minute.

A little black pickup came into the parking lot, parking across the way from me. Their doors were thrown open at the same time, and they were already bickering at each other.

"If you would have gotten your ass out of bed, we could have gotten breakfast," Troy hollered, a coffee cup in his hand.

"If you wouldn't have spent the entire night snoring, maybe I would have been able to wake up this morning," Gavin said.

"I have a deviated septum. It's not my fault."

I shook my head, holding back a laugh. They were still the same goofballs. I wanted to give them the benefit of the doubt. I wanted to believe that there was a reason why they didn't come around.

I found myself feeling guilty for thinking the worst of them.

"Troy! Gavin!" I yelled at them. They both looked around until Troy's eyes landed on me. He dropped his cup.

"Nice, dude, you aren't getting mine." Gavin said. I watched as Troy reached out, and gripped Gavin's face with one hand, turning his head to me.

"Alex. . . ?" In Gavin fashion, he didn't hesitate. He dropped his own cup and ran to me, slowing only when he reached me.

Troy followed closely behind. "How is this possible?"

"Who fucking cares!" Gavin said as he clasped me around my back, hugging me tight.

I hugged him back. Troy pushed his way into the hug and I watched as Gavin turned, seemingly wiping tears out of his eyes.

"Why are you guys acting like you thought I was dead?"

Troy pulled away, looking up at me and then to Gavin. They exchanged a look. It was a cruel joke.

"Because—" Gavin started, but Troy cut him off.

"Have you seen Wren?" Troy held his hand over Gavin's mouth.

"Over here, boys." Wren called, coming out of the office.

She walked out onto the asphalt and Gavin broke away from us, crossed the parking lot, and hugged her. King excitedly wagged his tail next to them, but Gavin didn't let her go. He stooped down to hug her tight, and I could see the way her hands fisted into his shirt.

I had met Troy and Gavin first, befriended them first, but I was witnessing a friendship that I wasn't familiar with.

"We all thought you were dead." Troy leaned back, looking me over.

I didn't know what to say or how to explain things. I had my suspicions but I wasn't ready to tell others yet.

"Mix up in the paperwork," I stated, exasperated. I was exhausted. I was tired of being angry. Tired of not having the answers.

"That's one hell of a mix up, man, but I'm glad it was a mix up."

Troy looked to me, slapping me on the back. "This is the best fucking day ever."

King ran over then, and Troy crouched down to pet him. "Hey, buddy." He whined and licked him on the face, his head dropping low to sniff my leg.

My attention went back to Wren and Gavin. She was wiping her face and Gavin was shaking his head, bringing her in again for a hug.

"It's been a few months since we've seen her," Troy said from the ground. "She doesn't come out that often. This is the first time she's been here during the day in years."

"What happened?"

Troy sighed heavily. "She couldn't handle being around anyone for a while in the beginning. Tried to quit working for Dan, but they figured things out so that she could come in for payroll early in the morning. She gets to come in and have the place to herself, get her work done, and leave before anyone else gets here."

"She's been alone most of the time?" I asked. Wren seemed put together on paper. She had a routine, met up with friends on occasion, was at the gym twice a week, sometimes more. But that was just on paper.

We both turned and watched her with Gavin.

"She was lost for a long time. We took shifts after your. . . you know." He sighed. "Made sure she had food in the house, cooked for her. There was a time when. . ." He trailed off.

"When what?"

"We thought we were going to lose her. She would wake up in the middle of the night and no one could find her. We would search the entire house until we found her standing out on the dock, looking out into the lake."

I couldn't hide the panic on my face.

"It freaked us out for a while, I don't think she was actually going to jump in. Gav and I got her the pups shortly after that and she was easier to find 'cause they wouldn't leave her side."

"Thanks for looking out for her."

"Always."

Wren headed back inside, giving me one last look over her shoulder before she went inside.

"So, Alex. Did you just eat spinach and work out the entire

time you were gone?" Gavin asked, bumping his shoulder into me as we walked back out into the parking lot.

I chuckled, "Bout all there is to do."

Wren

I pulled back from Gavin, giving him another reassuring squeeze, then went back into the office with King.

If I was coming into town for some errands, I normally brought King with me. He was the best-behaved out of the two of them. Queen was more territorial and aggressive to what she deemed hers. The car being one of them.

I would never discourage the behavior though; that was the reason I had them.

I sat at my desk with a fresh cup of coffee, turning on the computer and loading the programs. While the boys were outside, I ran through the time cards and made any adjustments I needed for overtime or for people who took time off before hitting submit on everyone's paychecks.

Seeing Gavin cry broke my heart, but he was more concerned about me.

"Wren, what's happening?"

"I know, Gav. It's been a lot for me to process. But he's alive and here and we wanted you guys to know."

Looking at Alex was like looking at a stranger. I knew him, but I didn't really know him.

But we were working on that. We had all the time in the world now, right? We could start from scratch.

Once I started hearing people get louder, I called King to me and had him stay behind my desk.

"Oh, my days, is that Wren?" Bonnie smiled, dropping her bag on her table and coming over to me. I stood and we hugged. "What's the surprise for? Something the matter?"

"You'll see." I smiled. Bonnie always came in from the front, and not the back where the field workers were, so she missed the show.

"Hmm." Bonnie moved to her desk. "But it's good to see your face in here anyways."

"How's Sammy?"

Bonnie gave me the rundown of her seven-year-old starting a fight at school and getting detention for the next week.

"Sounds like his mother." I grinned into my coffee mug.

Our shared door gave me a perfect view of anyone who walked in. Every time the door opened and closed, I couldn't help looking that way. I didn't know if he would come inside or not.

I recognized most of the guys who came in. Danny didn't go through a lot of workers. Most of them had been hired right around the time Alex had been hired, so I knew them through him.

The office got louder while everyone started to move to the main room.

"You coming out for the meeting?" Bonnie stood, a notebook in her hand.

"I'll pop my head in, in a bit." I waved her off.

Outside of my office, Dan started the meeting, the crew gathered around him. "Alright, guys, today we are splitting you up to two different sites. . ."

I listened for a bit as he got through everything he needed to say before directing things to the team leads. I still hadn't seen Alex or the boys come in and I hated the disappointment I felt. I wanted Alex to come in and see Dan, but understood that this might all be too much for him. Both he and his wife Frannie had been at his funeral. They both loved him as if he were their own son.

I stood and King followed, sitting down next to me as I leaned against my office doorframe, listening. Everyone had their back to my office.

"While we are all here," Dan called attention back to himself, "please say hello to Wren." Dan directed everyone to look at me, and I couldn't help but smirk. Of course I hadn't gotten in without him noticing. "She is the reason the coffee is already brewed and there are donuts in the breakroom. She is also the person who does payroll. Don't piss her off." His tone was sarcastic, and I couldn't help but laugh and raise my mug to him. He looked around and frowned. "Where the hell are Gavin and Troy?"

Right on cue, the door opened, and Gavin, Troy, and Alex walked in.

"The whole family is here today!" Gavin announced.

The room was quiet, and the three of us turned to see Alex still standing by the door, his hands shoved into his dark wash jeans.

I looked across the room to Dan, whose eyes were wide in shock.

"This can't be. . ."

"How you been, Dan?"

Dan moved across the room with wonder on his face before he hugged Alex, slapping his back and holding him tight. He looked how I was sure I had. Like a loved one came back from the grave.

I watched the exchange between the two men. Gavin joined me, and I rested my head on Gavin's shoulder, who then rested his head against mine.

I couldn't imagine the change Alex saw in his mentor.

Dan had aged considerably since Alex's fictitious death. The stubble on his face was practically pure white. He seemed shorter now, with more wrinkles around his eyes.

And that was it. Several of the others who recognized him all surrounded Alex, talking over each other. I only relaxed when a smile broke across Alex's face.

See, Alex, no one forgot about you.

CHAPTER 42

ALEX

WHEN WE GOT BACK HOME, I OPENED THE BACK OF THE SUV and King barreled out and disappeared around the side of the house. "I'm going to go see if I can get my truck running." I pulled out a box of things from the back of the SUV.

"Okay." Wren sounded disappointed.

I walked over and kissed her cheek, before heading down the path to the shop.

I pulled the tarp off the truck and popped the hood. I had figured at the very least the battery needed to be replaced, fresh gas and an oil change.

For some reason, Wren really had kept everything from the old house. I found the old radio and plugged it in, putting on a station that wasn't pure static and cranked it up. I needed to get out of my own head.

Seeing everyone today was jarring. There wasn't one person who was disappointed in my "miraculous resurrection." Everyone had been happy to see me. In any other universe, it would be great.

But it wasn't what I'd expected.

Manual labor was what I needed. I got lost in digging around the old shop, surprised that there were as many tools as there were. It was an old building, the concrete not quite level, and if you didn't pay attention you could trip. I was able to change the oil, siphon out the gas, and put in new gas. I installed the battery last.

I opened the roll-up door and, as I did, I spotted Wren heading down the driveway with King and Queen in tow. Queen stopped when she heard the door. I had locked her out, not wanting to worry about her getting into any of the chems I had laying around. She was about ready to head my way when a high-pitched whistle sounded, and she continued to follow Wren.

Absently, I wondered what she was doing, but assumed she was just going for a walk. I loved how she had so much space to just be herself in. We took lots of walks growing up, but we never really walked far. Always to the same grove or along the canal. Avoiding people the best we could.

Now she could walk as far and as long as she wanted, and it was on the safety of her own property.

I climbed into the truck and turned the engine over. It cranked but sputtered out.

"Come on," I muttered. I pumped the gas a few more times before it finally rumbled to life.

"Ah ha!" I let it idle and hopped out, closing the hood. I dug around the shop a little more and found a few old rags, went outside to the spigot, filling a bucket up with water and wiping the dust off the windows and mirrors. It needed a thorough cleaning, but this was good enough.

I heard the screen door open and slam shut. Glancing out of the shop, Queen was barreling toward me with something shoved under her collar.

Pizza up at the house.

I grinned at Wren's messaging tactic. I found an old contractor's pencil and wrote back under her line.

Be up in a bit.

I told Queen to head back to the house and she did, King meeting her halfway. I pulled the truck out of the shop and carefully drove it to the driveway, taking it out for a quick spin and listened to see if there was anything else I needed to do to it.

It was dark by the time I got back to the house. I hadn't meant to drive as long as I did, but once I got out onto the main road and rolled the windows down, I just kept on driving to the edge of the county line.

What would happen if we left Ashwood?

Leaving was tempting. I wondered what Wren would say to that.

I was quickly realizing she had more ties to this place than I did. She had friends. A family even. A group of people who looked out for her and loved her. She had more than just Ma and I.

Thinking of all the time I missed made me angry.

I turned the truck off and got out. The screen door squeaked, reminding me to take care of it.

"Wren? I'm back!" I hollered into the house, kicking my boots off at the front of the house and heading in. I headed back to the kitchen. No one was there, a pizza box sitting on the counter. I went to the sink and used the bar of soap to scrub my hands and forearms, getting the grease and grime off. After drying my hands, I flipped the box open and pulled out a slice. It was cold but I bit into it. Cold pizza was better anyway.

"Wren?" I walked through the lower floor from room to room. I paused for a minute in her studio, flipping on the lights. The room was a chaotic mess. There were papers on every surface. Smudges of charcoal on the wall. Small bins of paper towels with charcoal dust on them.

I walked farther into the room and opened a folder. There was an image of a girl with her knees to her chest and her head tucked into them. Shadows of bruises along her back. I flipped to another page that looked like a self-portrait. It showed Wren's face, eyes closed, head turned up as if she was looking at the sky. More shadows of bruises along her face.

Nothing in Foster's paperwork said she went back to therapy, but I started to think that art was her therapy this time around.

I closed the folder and left the room the way I found it. I took the stairs two at a time, finishing my slice at the top. King and Queen were lying outside one of the doors.

"Wren?"

"Come in."

I pushed open the door to find her in the tub. Her hair was pinned on her head, stray tresses drenched around her neck. I could see bits of steam rising from the water.

"Hot enough for you?" I asked, a smirk on my lips.

"Eh. Could be hotter." She grinned. "Where you been?"

"Got the truck running." I shrugged. "Went for a drive."

She nodded, the water rippled around her. "Feel any better?"

I shrugged again. I didn't know how I felt.

"Join me?"

"Pretty sure I'll melt." I chuckled.

"Don't be a wuss."

I shut the door and pulled my shirt off, kicking out of my jeans. If Wren wanted me in the tub, I'd get in the tub. There were too many years between us without me being able to give her exactly what she wanted. She leaned forward in the tub and I slid in behind her.

I tried to hold it in, but the farther in I sank the more I hissed. "God damn, woman, you trying to burn my flesh off?"

She laughed and it was a beautiful sound. I didn't think about the pain anymore, I just wanted to listen to her laugh more. She leaned back against me, laying her head back against my shoulder.

A slight breeze came in through the cracked window and a

radio droned on in the corner. She started to hum along to a song I didn't recognize.

I thought back to our early years, when she first came to live with us. There were some days the fighting from next door was so loud that she would sit in the opposite part of the apartment, with her hands over her ears, trying to block out the sound.

I had stolen someone's MP3 player and slipped headphones on her to help her block out the sound. It worked for a while, until the battery died and I didn't have any batteries to replace it.

On the edge of the tub, a washcloth was laid on the edge. I tugged it off and dipped it in the water before running it over the tops of her shoulders.

"Talk to me, Alex, what's going through your head?"

I methodically washed her shoulders, trailing down to the tops of her hands while I tried to put my thoughts into words.

"None of this is what I expected," I said simply.

"You thought, *everyone* abandoned you?"

It sounded bad. It sounded like I didn't have faith in a single soul.

"I did something that no one thought I would do. My own mother wasn't speaking to me." I shrugged my shoulders, hating feeling like I'd lost faith in everyone. Like I was the one who gave up on them.

"It's okay, Alex." She tipped her head back, looking up at me. "Alex, we love you. We are all just thankful you are here, and we aren't going to take this second chance for granted."

Tuesday morning felt surreal. I had woken up to a vase of flowers that had been picked from my garden and a note from Alex letting me know he had gone to town to drop off the car he had been borrowing.

Alex is alive.

I would be saying this to myself over and over again, probably for the rest of my life. I kept expecting to wake up and realize it was all a dream.

I had been a little disappointed to wake up and find he wasn't around, but at the same time, it gave me a minute to breathe, center myself with this reality.

Alex is alive, he's back, we slept together, now what?

I had no idea where we were at. We spent the weekend in bed. Exploring each other, asking questions, rediscovering. It was a mix of bliss and confusion, because where did we go from here?

I couldn't get Alex to talk much last night, so after our bath we ended up watching *The Outsiders* until we crawled into bed.

I got in a quick workout at the gym and now I was heading to the grocery store. Since living on my own, I had been bad about keeping much food in the house. Alex had been suffering. We'd had spaghetti two nights in a row, and even though he didn't complain, I was sure he would like more of a variety.

I made my rounds, picking up some essentials and choosing a few old recipes to make.

I chewed on my lip, second-guessing some of my choices. Rather than letting my mind get the better of me, I pulled out my phone and shot Alex a text.

W: I'm at the store. Anything you don't like?
A: I'm not picky. I'll eat whatever you make.

I let out a frustrated sigh. His response wasn't helpful.

I typed out, *See you at home.* But I stopped myself from sending it. Was my place home for him? Did he plan on going back to the warehouse and staying there?

I felt like I was standing on a log in the middle of the ocean. I didn't have my balance. I didn't know what was up and down.

Six years ago, I was solid in knowing him. Knowing where we were going, and I knew back then I could make simple decisions without second-guessing myself.

Now, I didn't even know if he still liked red apples over green ones.

I went with my gut. I picked green. I even bought a container of caramel, because the green apples always went well with caramel, and I couldn't remember the last time I had any.

Standing in the chip aisle, a thought came to me, and I called Riley.

"Hey, Riley, I have an idea. . ."

Riley and I chatted quickly. She was on board with my plan, and I had a few more errands to run to get everything into place. As I was loading things into the cooler that I kept in the back of my SUV, my phone rang.

"Hello?"

"Wren, I need to talk to you." Melissa's voice was stressed. I was a little shocked to hear from her. I hadn't spoken to her since the night Alex showed up, and I honestly didn't know if I wanted to talk to her.

I liked Melissa, but I wasn't deluded enough to think that she would choose me over Jon. Jon had given her a job and she'd had an obvious crush on him for years.

"Hey, Mel. What's up?" I asked hesitantly, still loading things into the car.

"Are you in town? Can you meet me at the sandwich shop?"

I wanted to tell her no. Jon's messages had finally stopped coming in, and I wasn't ready to see him yet. This seemed like an obvious ploy to get me in the same place as him. I imagined showing up to find him sitting there with her.

I don't know if I ever wanted to see him again. Alex and I needed to talk about him. I still wanted to believe it was all a mistake and that he hadn't betrayed me. That he hadn't come up with some scheme to make me believe Alex was dead. There was no way I would ever forgive him.

"Melissa, I don't want to see Jon."

"Jon is missing."

Twenty minutes later I was sitting out on the patio of a local sandwich shop with a glass of lemonade as Melissa tapped her long, manicured nails on the edge of the plate.

"He hasn't been to work since that night. He's not answering calls and I can't get up to his condo. The doorman won't let me inside." She took a huge bite of her sandwich. "I can't keep covering for him at work. He's missing court hearings, and I can't get anyone to handle his cases anymore." She took a long drink of her soda. "Please," she practically begged, "please go check on him."

I sat back in my chair and looked down at my phone. "Melissa, he lied to me." I shook my head. "He told me that my best friend, that *his* best friend, was dead. For six years, he played into this fucking lie. How do you explain that?"

"Wren, I understand." She paused mid-bite. "Well, actually, I don't. I didn't even know that you two had a best friend outside the two of you. Not once did either of you ever mention Alex." She shook her head. "But that is besides the point. You need to be a better friend to him than he was to you. Two wrongs don't make a right."

I chewed on the edge of my thumb and sat back in my seat. I was a little irritated with her. How dare she tell me to be a better friend to him when I knew he didn't deserve it.

Did he?

Jon had been there for me from day one, but there would have never been a day one if he hadn't told me Alex was dead.

"Fine, I'll go check on him." I stood from the table and dropped a few bucks for my drink. "I'll text you."

I headed to my car. I wanted to text Alex, but something told me he wouldn't like me seeing Jon.

We hadn't talked about Jon at all.

Before I could get too deep in my thoughts, I headed to Jon's condo. I parked in the ten-minute spot to give myself an excuse to not stay long. Walking in, Berny greeted me.

"Hello, Miss Jacobson. It's been a while. Are you here to see Mr. Smith?" Berny was an older man with smile lines and graying hair. He tipped his hat to me and held the door open.

"I am. Have you seen him?"

"I have not seen him. I actually just got back from my honeymoon this week. Fifth time's the charm." He winked at me and I couldn't help but laugh.

"Well, congratulations, Berny." I headed into the building and into the elevator.

The anxiety built as the floor got higher. I didn't want to see Jon, but I didn't want him dead. I would just do a sign of life check and then I would leave and head home so I could get on with my day.

I exited the elevator and rang his doorbell. After a minute with no answer, I knocked.

Nothing.

Sighing, I pulled my keys out and unlocked his door, pushing through it.

"Jon?"

My eyebrows rose and my mouth fell open. It looked like a tornado had ripped through his place. There was broken glass everywhere, wood splintered apart, stuffing from his couch spread across the expansive space.

Alarm bells went off in my head. I was about to take another step in, then stopped myself. Something could have seriously been wrong in there, and I knew I didn't want to face it on my own.

I called Mario. He answered on the third ring.

"I need you to come to Jon's place." I explained what I was looking at.

Mario didn't hesitate. I could hear his car accelerate over the line and I was grateful I caught him when he wasn't already on a job.

I met Mario and two more police officers down in the lobby. We rode up the elevator and I explained the situation.

"Wait a minute. Alex is alive?" he asked, disbelief in his voice. The elevator doors slid open, and we all stepped out. "Is this why you called me the other night?"

I nodded. "I know, it's been a crazy last couple of days. I meant to tell you sooner. I really don't have an explanation except—"

Mario put his hand up, halting me from following them into the condo. "It's fine, Wren, we'll talk about it later. Just wait out here while we go take a look."

The officers announced their presence and went inside. I waited out in the foyer, my phone gripped tightly in my hand, mind running wild. I wanted to call Alex, but I knew he wouldn't be happy with me.

As the anxiety built, I made every excuse for Jon. Maybe he hadn't known Alex was alive either. Maybe he was so stricken with grief that the person on the table really had looked like Alex. Maybe there was just a mistake in the prison filing, and it really was an honest mistake, and I had been shutting him out for no reason.

But how did someone fuck up this badly? Why did none of Alex's letters get to me? There had to be an explanation for this. I was going to find out.

"Wren, he's back here."

The anxiety dissolved, and I headed inside, careful where I walked. The two officers have Jon sitting up on his bed. One crouched down in front of him.

"W-ren?" Jon said when he laid his bloodshot eyes on me. "Wren, I'm so s-s'ry."

"He's drunk," Mario said, and I could smell the alcohol permeating from his pores.

I took a step back; I didn't want to talk to him like this. I despised drunks, and I wouldn't even entertain this for a moment.

Jon tried to stand but swayed, so the officers put him back on the bed. His hair was a mess; he was wearing a white undershirt and blue boxers. I'd never seen him look so *not* put together before.

"Thank you, Mario."

I was too angry at Jon to feel sorry for him right now.

"Anytime. Come on, let's get you out of here."

"N-No, Wren. . . Come b-back," Jon stuttered.

I ignored Jon, leaving with Mario. I told Berny to let Melissa in the next time she came by and shot her a text, letting her know what I saw. I didn't want the responsibility of a drunk Jon on me. I had enough of my own shit to deal with, and this wasn't going to be another thing I added to my plate.

Mario walked me to my car, where of course there was a

parking ticket on it. Mario took the ticket and told me he would deal with it.

"What is this about Alex?"

"I really don't have all the answers, but Alex is alive. There must have been some kind of mess-up with the paperwork or—"

"Wren, that's a huge fuckup." Mario would know better than me.

"I know." I looked at the time on my phone. "You should come by my place this afternoon. I'm doing a thing and I'd like to introduce you two."

CHAPTER 44

ALEX

"Ezekiel, what do you and Nikolas do?" I walked around his study, looking at all the old paintings he had displayed.

"What do you mean?" he asked, shuffling through the papers on his dark cherrywood desk.

"What do you do for work?"

"Niko didn't tell you?" He chuckled. "We are just financial backers."

"I don't know what that is."

"Someone wants to buy something, start a business, but they don't have money. We support them financially for a cost."

"A cost?"

He put the papers down and leaned back in his chair. "Yes, a cost. It could be anything. A stake in the company, repayment plus interest, maybe they have something that has the same value, or—"

"Their firstborn?" I was only half-joking.

He belted out a laugh, leaning back in his high back chair.

"No, no, I don't like children." Ezekiel walked around the desk and gestured to the sofa, taking a seat. "Why do you ask, Alexander?"

I mulled over his words, taking a seat across from him in the large brown leather chair.

"Where do you see me in this mix? You offered me a job. I'd like to know what that entails."

"How strong is your moral compass?"

I weighed his words. Younger me wasn't on the straight and narrow. I broke rules and laws. I lived by just keeping my mother happy. What she didn't know didn't hurt her. I snuck out at night and went to parties, drank too young and tried my fair share of weed. I never wanted to stress her out more than she already was, so I just made sure she never knew. She did her best for me, and I had always known that. Even though there were times I was resentful for being the poor kid. I wished for name-brand clothes and nicer things. I always felt like I stuck out like a sore thumb in my hand-me-down clothes and Goodwill shoes.

It wasn't until Wren came into my life that I looked at life from a different perspective. I learned that things could be worse, and she showed me that there was beauty in simplicity. Ma provided us with the bare necessities because that's all she could do.

I could go back and work for Dan. Although it was long and hard days, he paid a livable wage—but I wanted more.

I wanted to give Wren more than she had before.

I had blood on my hands now. . . I didn't regret it. I didn't lose sleep over it. My moral compass pointed straight at Wren. Whatever benefited her, I would do.

I didn't care what it was, as long as it helped her.

He pursed his lips as he watched me. "I like you, Alexander. You have done a lot for me. You protected my brother when you had no reason to, but you don't know everything about Nikolas or I. And if you did know, I'm not sure you would want to be around us, let alone work for us."

I stared at him. There was weight in those words, and something told me I should ask him to explain. I should find out what he really meant by them, but I decided not to. Going against my better judgment.

"As long as you never hurt Wren, whatever business it is that you run, it never hurts her. Then whatever it is, I can get past it."

He had talked to me about a job before, and I hadn't taken him seriously on the offer. I was here for one thing—Wren. When I had finished, I hadn't expected to stay in town. I didn't know what I was going to do, but now I knew I was staying.

My phone chimed and I pulled it out, a smile pulling at my lips when Wren's sleeping form lit up my screen. I had snapped a picture of her this morning. She slept on her stomach naked. The sheet was down by her hips and her hair was a mess on the pillow.

It was the most beautiful I had seen her.

I swiped my thumb across the screen and opened her text.

> What are you up to?

I typed back quickly.

> Talking with Ezekiel about my job.

The bubbles started and stopped a few times before her message came through.

> Invite him to dinner tonight. I want to meet him.

"As long as Wren is safe, nothing else matters."

Ezekiel and I came to an understanding, and I passed along the invite. I looked at the clock; it was noon and I missed her. I opened my phone and sent her another text.

> What are you up to?

Her response was immediate.

A slow grin formed, and I stood up. "I need a ride."

Ezekiel dropped me off, and I scanned the parking lot till I found Wren's car. It was filled to the brim: a cooler, bags of groceries, some soil, and four bags of dog food.

I frowned, staring at everything piled in the back.

I wished I had known what she was doing today; I would have been there to help her. I just wanted to get Ezekiel's car back to him now that my truck was up and running.

I headed into the mall. The place was bigger than I remembered. I hadn't spent much time here as a kid, only going when Jon dragged me.

I pulled out my phone.

I glanced around the place and started to walk around, hoping to catch her. There was only one department store that sold just about everything if I remembered correctly.

I headed up to the second story, glancing around until I saw the mass of curls.

I only saw her side profile as she picked an item up, looking it over before her face visibly balked and she set it back down, shaking her head.

After she left the table, I picked the same item up. It was a golden German shepherd statute. On the bottom was a tag for forty dollars.

Well shit, I would have put it down too.

With my new job, and new credit limit, money didn't matter.

I picked the statue up and followed her.

She was gorgeous as always. She wore a thin gray long sleeve shirt, jeans, and her crossbody slung over her. Her hair was in a knot at the top of her head, loose tendrils framing her face, headphones in.

I took pleasure in just watching her, staying out of her line of sight. I had never seen her shop before. We had gone and gotten groceries, but she never window-shopped. She never had her eyes on things we couldn't have.

She picked things up, then set them back down. Soon we were in the lingerie section, and she was dragging her fingertips over some silk nightdress. I watched her shoulders lift and drop before she moved on, heading to a checkout counter.

When she was far enough away, I went to it. It had black lace over the neck of it and at the hem. It was a deep forest-green color, my favorite. I picked it up along with the handful of other things she had touched.

One thing I had never been able to do was spoil her, and now I would be able to.

I left the store and headed out to wait next to her car, placing the items I had bought for her in the back so she wouldn't see them. It wasn't long after that she walked out.

"Hey, darlin'." I grinned at her as she walked out with one bag in hand, her free hand shading her eyes from the sun.

I took the bag from her and wrapped an arm around her before dipping down and taking her lips. She stood there, wide-eyed and dazed. I grinned, pleased with myself.

She hummed her approval at my greeting. "I could get used to that."

"I'll load the car," I said.

She pulled the keys out of her purse, handing them to me. I went about unlocking the door and guiding her to the passenger seat, opening the door and buckling her in.

After placing her things in the back, I climbed into the car, starting it.

"Anyplace else you need to go to?" I asked.

"No. I'm ready to go home."

"Okay, sweetheart. Let's go home."

As soon as we hit the gate, I could hear the dogs barking. Wren was quiet most of the way back to her place. Pulling out her phone and texting someone off and on. I couldn't quite make out her mood, but every time she looked at me, she had a smile on her face.

"What's got you all smilin'?" I reached for her, brushing the small hairs at the nape of her neck away before I settled my hand there, gently massaging. I just wanted to have my hands on her.

"I don't know what you're talking about," she answered in a sing-song voice.

"Bullshit. You have the same look on your face you did when you bought me those seat covers for my birthday."

"I do not!" she laughed, leaning back into my touch. "I'm just happy. Can't a girl just be happy?"

"Just happy, huh?" I gave her a sidelong look as we got off her driveway and into the clearing of her home. I slowed down quickly, confused. "Who's here?"

There was a small SUV parked off to the side, along with another car that I didn't recognize. When I looked to her, her face had fallen, and her eyes were wide.

"I didn't expect anyone." I hit the brakes and threw the car in park. King and Queen were nowhere to be seen, but I could hear them barking.

"Stay here." I got out of the still-running car and went inside. The dog's barking started to get louder, and I felt a breeze hit me through the house.

"What the. . ." I walked down the hall and through the kitchen to see balloons drift in the breeze through the kitchen window.

"Surprise!"

Voices shouted from all different directions. Gavin, Troy, and Riley stood together—and Mario too. There was a table set up with food, balloons on each side of it, with a WELCOME HOME banner set up.

"You have got to be kidding me." I grinned, turning around to see Wren leaning against the door frame with a shit-eating grin on her face.

"I'm better at keeping secrets now." Her eyes sparkled.

She walked down and took my hand, "Alex, I want you to meet Mario. Mario," she paused, looking up to him and tugging me closer, "*this* is Alex." She stressed the word, and I felt the meaning behind my own name.

Mario put his hand out and we shook hands. "It's. . .surreal to finally meet you." He gave a small laugh.

"Well, here I am in the flesh."

I tried keeping my face neutral. I knew all about this man from the information Foster had given me, but meeting him now, in-person, was another story.

He was clean shaven, tall and well-dressed. I glanced between him and Wren and could see something there that I was not privy to. He was someone to her that I wasn't. He had filled a void in her life that I wasn't a part of.

And stupidly, I hated it.

He meant something to her and I was jealous of it. For years I had been the main person in her life, her protector, now I shared the space with him.

Dan pressed his way between us, relieving me of the turmoil of emotions I felt. "I just can't believe it." He hugged me tight before pulling away, wiping his face. He had done a good job keeping himself together at the office, but he seemed just as amazed to see me now as he was then.

"Oh, I can't believe it." Frannie was freely crying. A tissue wadded up in her hand. I had to stoop to hug her. "I can't believe they made such a huge mess-up like this."

"That's the damn government for you!" Dan shouted while wiping his eyes.

Straightening, I smiled down at her. "It's good to see you, too, Frannie."

I had been telling everyone that the jail made a mistake. There was no other way for me to explain everything, so this would have to do for now.

Gavin and Troy were there then, handing me a beer and raising their bottles.

"It's about time we had a beer together," Troy said.

"You know, he could have quit while in prison," Gavin put in plainly. "You should be considerate of that."

"I promise, I didn't quit drinking while in prison." I raised my beer to him before I brought it to my lips, glancing over my shoulder at Wren. Riley was standing with her, rubbing her shoulder while Wren wiped a finger under her eyes. They both turned and went inside.

I wanted to follow her. I wanted to be the one who wiped her tears away. There was no reason she should be crying, but I stayed put out on the porch with everyone else.

I WAS FIXING THE DOGS' DINNER WITH RILEY WHILE the party continued outside. I set their bowls on the ground and let them eat so I didn't have to worry about them stealing anyone's food. I had texted Riley and the guys to get food out here and get things set up so I could surprise Alex. They surpassed my expectations completely, and I was so grateful. I took the time inside to pull myself together. I'd never thought this could happen. Alex and all our friends in this house. I was emotional.

I thought of Jon and how he was missing out on this. I needed to figure out what the hell his part in all this was, but I just wasn't ready. I was still angry with him. I wanted to understand. But I wasn't ready.

"You know, those boys can say one random-ass thing and go on talking for hours. You should have seen the three of us in the store. It was a mess, and then trying to set everything up here." Riley shook her head.

She had me smiling at that thought. "I bet it was nuts. Those two can go on for hours. I love it."

"Yeah." Riley paused, looking out the kitchen window. "Are you sure there isn't something between the two of them?" She brought her beer up to her lips.

I watched her watching them. "I've never wondered about it. Why?"

Her brows furrowed a bit, studying them. "Since the first time I met them, I. . . I don't know." She shook her head and waved her hand as if she was banishing the thought. "Nothing. Probably just my wild imagination." She waggled her brows at me before grabbing the chips we had brought in from the store and the pasta salad I made.

I listened to stories of her heading into the next town over and doing parties where she showed the different kinds of toys and demonstrations. She laughed hard at my face and then told me it was PG demonstrations.

Her little adult store had gotten bigger in recent years. She started to host bachelorette parties and teach sex education, primarily focusing on the female pleasure points. She loved it and I was happy for her.

She dated here and there, but there hadn't been anyone that she gushed about in particular. She had always told me that she didn't want anything less than "goddess" treatment. If her man wasn't obsessed with her, she didn't want it.

Seeing Jon earlier had me feeling off, and Riley noticed.

"What's going on, girl?"

I glanced out the window, seeing Alex out in the grass with everyone else. Quickly, I recounted the events of Jon and Riley made a face.

"What's with the face?"

She popped a grape in her mouth. "Nothing."

My eyebrow rose and I crossed my arms, "Spill it, Ri. I know you don't like Jon."

She sighed. "It's not that I don't like him it's just. . ." She looked away from me, out the window.

I put my hand on her arm, giving her a reassuring squeeze. "Riley, whatever it is, you can tell me."

I couldn't remember a moment in our friendship where I had

to work this hard to get her to tell me something. Typically, she was an open book, ready to spill anything.

"When you were taking care of Gloria in the hospital and we started to pack that house up to get you out of there," she took both my hands in hers, her blue eyes wide, "your room was the hardest room to walk into. The blood and the way it was left." She shook her head slightly. "Troy, Gavin, and I couldn't walk in there. It was too hard. It made all of us sick to go in there and see the remnants of what had happened to you. Gavin couldn't even go upstairs without getting emotional. But Jon. . ." She took in a deep breath. "Jon *wanted* to be in that room. For three days, all he did was walk up there and stare at everything. At first I thought he was in shock. I thought he was trying to process everything like the rest of us; you guys have history and it made sense. One day, he was coming down the stairs empty handed, and when I looked up at his face," she swallowed hard and a sick feeling rolled through me, "the only way I could describe it is that he was *satisfied*."

I pulled away, taken aback.

"It also could have been in my head, Wren," she rushed out. "It wasn't long after that Gloria passed away, and then Alex. It was just a glimpse, and I thought that maybe I had imagined it. He had always been by your side and helped you day or night. Please don't be mad at me." There was a tremor of panic in her voice.

"No, Riley, I'm glad you told me." I tried to shake off my unease. I stepped forward, pulling her into a tight hug. "You can always tell me anything. Now, come on, we have guests waiting."

"Thanks. Now. How are things with Alex?" she asked in a loud whisper as we headed outside. It was a warm summer evening with only a slight breeze. We stepped out onto the grass and walked our items to the table, and as I passed Alex, our eyes connected, and it erased my unease from what Riley told me. Alex and I would talk, we would get through this and figure out where we stood, then figure out what happened.

"Things are good." I smiled, arranging plastic cups and plates on the table.

"Aaaand?" Her shoulder bumped mine, trying to lighten the mood. "Are you guys picking up where you left off?"

Tongue in cheek, I gave her a look. "Maybe."

She squealed and grabbed my arm. "I'm so happy for you, babycakes." She hugged me tight.

"Thank you." I returned her affection. "I'm not quite sure where we are yet, but I'm sure we will have that conversation soon." I said to everyone else, "Alright, guys, food's ready."

Dan and Frannie had been working the grill, with hot dogs and hamburgers. Troy and Gavin were playing with the pups by the water.

"Did you two hear her?" Riley marched her way over to the guys. I laughed, turning to find Alex, missing him. I headed back into the house and when I didn't find him there, I looked out the front door.

There Alex was, standing with Mario and another woman.

I frowned. Mario hadn't shown up with a woman, and I didn't know her. Maybe he invited her here to introduce us? That didn't seem right. Mario would have given me a heads up. I took a step away from the window, pacing down the hallway.

I centered myself and went back to the front door. Alex looked pissed. From where I stood, the woman was beautiful. She had long brown hair and was tall and slender in suit pants, a cream-colored blouse, and a blue blazer. Her hands were folded in front of her, and she wasn't fazed by whatever Alex was saying. Then, the woman's eyes flicked to me and she put a hand on Alex's arm. He turned and looked at me, straightening. Guilt hit me. Like I was spying on them.

Why the hell was I watching them? This was my house, I had every right to look out my fucking window. I opened the door and took even strides out to them. My eyes only on Alex.

He met me halfway across the graveled front, Mario on his tail.

"Wren, what the hell were you thinking?"

"Excuse me?" I reared back at his demeanor. Alex never spoke to me like this.

"You saw Jon today. You went there alone," he said accusingly. "Again, I ask, what the fuck were you thinking?"

"Oh boy," Mario said behind him. "Here we go." Mario was used to my temper by now.

"Alexander James, I don't know who the fuck you think you are talking to like this, but it's not me. Who's she?" He could go fuck himself at this point. He didn't get any explanation from me until I knew who she was.

Alex straightened, his own confusion on his face. He looked back at the gorgeous woman and then back to me. Something crosses his expression. . .something like amusement?

He tucked his hands into his pockets, then looked up at the sky, seemingly counting to ten.

"Wren," he said, his voice back to normal. He placed a hand on my back and guided me to the woman. "This is Foster. She's the PI I hired that I told you about."

Understanding flooded through me. This was the woman who found the storage unit of Kevin's trinkets. A sort of melancholy hit me.

The jealousy dissolved. The woman reached her hand out, her face open and welcoming. There was no pity there. "Dylan Foster, it's nice to meet you, Ms. Jacobson."

"It's nice to meet you too."

"Wait a minute, you hired a private investigator to snoop around Wren?" Mario spoke. We all turned toward him.

"I did."

"For what reason?"

Alex's demeanor changed. "I spent six years in prison. Five of those years with no contact with her, because someone made it look like I had died. I didn't know what to expect when I got out."

"That doesn't give you the right to invade her privacy."

"What do you know about her privacy?" Alex hissed. "What do you know?"

Mario didn't budge at Alex's hostility. I could see Mario's detective side start to come through his stance.

"I know she went to great lengths to keep her life private, and for a fucking murder—"

"You're fucking right. I am a murderer." He took another step forward. "Did you read the reports?" He chuckled darkly. "Of course you did. Then you know I killed him slowly. Brutally. I took my time killing him. And you know what?" He dropped his voice. "I enjoyed killing him."

Alex turned and reached his hand out to me. We hadn't talked about that night. Not about the killing. I took his hand, lacing my fingers through his.

"I killed him, I served my time, and I don't regret it. I would do it again, if it meant that bastard never laid a hand on her again."

"Alex." Gently, I rested my palm on his chest, pulling his attention to me. His eyes were hard and full of fire until they landed on me. "I don't think Mario knows the whole story."

The anger I felt earlier dissipated, and I felt nothing but adoration for him.

A part of me always thought Mario knew, but over the years of working with him, sparring with him on the mat, he never looked at me differently. I never saw the pity in his eyes the way the other police officers had looked at me that day. The ones who knew my story. The lawyers and the judge reading over my statements. The medical reports I sent them.

"You never told him?"

I shook my head up at him. "I only told him that Kevin beat me. I didn't tell him anything more than that." I looked at Mario. "I kind of thought you might have read the reports. Gotten curious."

Mario shook his head, nodding to Alex. "I read Alex's reports, but not yours. I didn't want to invade your privacy like that." I could hear the insinuation in his voice while he eyed daggers at Alex.

I nodded at him, looking over to the very silent Foster. She knew enough already. I built up my resolve and spoke. "Kevin raped me. It started when I was eleven, until I was almost seventeen. Alex got me out, he and his mom hid me from them. I was safe for about five years. We didn't think he would ever come back, and then one day he did. That's the day Alex killed him." Alex pulled me tighter to his side. "He wasn't just my mom's abusive boyfriend. He was a pedophile. A rapist. He would have never stopped." It'd taken me over ten years to say these words out loud calmly.

Mario's face paled.

"I fought with the police, the courts, but because Kevin had left me at my home still alive, and there were reports of Alex 'hunting' him down, they deemed it a separate case. And since he was dead, there was nothing for me to do but 'move on.'" I remembered those days of fighting to be heard. To be seen. But if the jury knew the real reason behind Alex's action, then the city would have just looked bad in the papers for putting away a man who killed a rapist.

"Wren, I'm so. . ."

"Stop. I know. You don't have to say it. Just, give Alex some grace. Please."

Mario nodded at Alex. I knew it was going to take some time for Mario to wrap his head around everything.

Gravel crunched behind us. A black SUV pulled up the driveway.

"Ah, fuck," Foster spoke under her breath, disgust filling her expression.

The SUV pulled up next to the other cars, the door opened, closed, and around walked a man I hadn't seen before. He was dressed in a black suit, light blue undershirt with the top few buttons open. Sunglasses covered his eyes and everything about him seemed expensive. If I had met him on the street, I would cross it just to get away. There was something about him that made the hairs on the back of my neck stand.

"Alexander." The man smiled a toothy smile, showing his very white teeth. He and Alex greeted each other like friends.

Alex turned to me. "Ezekiel, this is Wren."

"Ah." He picked up my hand and kissed the back of it. "The girl that my friend would burn the world down for. It's so nice to finally meet you."

"Okay." Alex pulled me back from Ezekiel. "That's enough of that." There was humor in his voice, nothing told me I should be wary of Ezekiel, but. . .

"And you must be Mario." Ezekiel shook his hand. Even Mario frowned.

I tried to quell the storm in my mind. Something was off about the man and it scared me.

I hadn't been frightened like this in years.

"On that note, I'm out of here. Alex, I'll get you the rest of that information later." Foster kept her eyes on Ezekiel.

"Oh, come on now—" Ezekiel started.

"Ezekiel, let me introduce you to some friends of mine. Come on back here," Alex said.

Alex put his arm around the man's shoulder and guided him to the house. Mario followed them.

"Uh, Foster?" I began.

She turned.

"I'm sorry about my reaction earlier."

A smirk played on the corner of her lips. "It's fine. I would have the same reaction if it was my man. Sorry for ratting you out to him, but he's the one who pays me."

"Ah." I laughed. "That's how he found out. I thought Mario told him."

"Nope, all me." She went to turn, but I stopped her again.

"Hey. . . What's Ezekiel's story? Have any idea?"

Foster's brown eyes looked to my house. "Why?"

I took a deep breath. "He, uhm. . . Well. He gives me a bad feeling."

She chuckled. "Well, your nervous system is on point then. You should listen to it."

"Do I have anything to worry about?"

She sighed. "Ezekiel is a bear. If you threaten him or anything he values, he will kill you. But," she nodded to the house again, "he takes care of his own. From what I can tell, your man did something for him. Something big." Her shoulders lifted and fell. "He protects his own. Fiercely."

Foster walked to the black SUV, opened the passenger door, and pulled out a bag. "When you go back inside, do you mind telling Eze that I have his pistachios?"

I couldn't help but laugh. "Uh, sure?"

She winked at me, went to his back tire, and pulled out a knife from somewhere and stabbed the side walls. The tire hissed as the air escaped.

"You can also tell him that I did that." She grinned, got into her own car and drove off.

Still giggling to myself, I walked around the house, King and Queen immediately spotting me and running my way. I scratched their heads as I found Alex standing with Ezekiel and Mario. He put his arm around me.

"Everything okay?"

"Uhm." I looked up to Ezekiel, fighting down the tremor of warning my brain screamed. "Foster told me to let you know she has your pistachios?" His face fell and he looked like someone just told him Santa wasn't real. "Oh, and she may have. . .slashed your tires?"

The man who I thought was terrifying gaped, and he leaned back, looking to the sky, muttering, "That fucking brat."

CHAPTER 46

ALEX

WE HAD JUST ABOUT FINISHED PUTTING EVERYTHING up. Everyone had left, Ezekiel driving on the donut I'd put on. Troy and Gavin had gone only when Riley stated she wanted to go home, after the sun had dipped below the trees surrounding Wren's property.

Those two seemed more than eager to run at Riley's beck and call.

I had just come in from taking the trash out. Wren had changed into some shorts and a racerback tank top. King laid behind her on the kitchen rug, guarding her. I watched as she finished washing the dishes, the muscles on her now-defined back visible.

I felt the pride for her swell in me. After everything that had happened, she didn't lie down and give up. She came back stronger every time. I was proud of her, even a little sad that I hadn't been there to watch her. I was grateful to Mario for that, even if he seemingly did have a crush on her.

"Alright, all done," Wren said as she dried her hands off on the towel.

Stepping over King, I brushed the hair off the back of her neck and kissed down the slope of it. My tongue darted out to taste her.

She shivered at my touch. "Well, hello there."

I wrapped my hands gently around her wrists and moved them to the edge of the counter. She understood my meaning, keeping them there.

"You and I still need to talk," she whispered breathily.

"Yes, we do."

When Foster came today to deliver some documents on Jon, and then told me that the men she had tailing Jon had spotted Wren, I was furious with Wren. Mario had walked up to us during the conversation, and he explained what had transpired.

I had to reason with myself. Wren would call Mario. He was a cop, and he had been the one there for her for years. Of course, I wished she would have called me, but there were some things I was not going to do.

I wasn't going to get angry at her for calling someone she trusted to help her. I wouldn't do that to her.

"Alex." She turned her face into me, rubbing her cheek along mine. "Where do we stand?"

I paused at her words, pulling back and staring into her emerald irises. "What do you mean?"

She dropped her head, seeming to consider what she wanted to say. When a long minute passed with nothing, I turned her in my arms. "Sweetheart, what's going through your head?" I picked her up and set her up on the counter so I could be eye level with her. I made myself at home between her legs. Unable to keep my hands to myself, I ran them up and down, squeezing her thighs.

Her arms hooked around my shoulders. "I need you to tell me what we are. What are we doing?" She pulled back. "Today at the grocery store I almost said 'see you at home,' but then I realized that I didn't know if this was your home. If you intended on staying here. Before, we never got the chance to establish ourselves as boyfriend or girlfriend, and the way we talked that day. . .what you said. What we said. . ."

I could play that conversation on repeat. "Forever," I said. "I told you I want forever with you, and you wanted the same." I cupped her face, running my thumbs over the apples of her cheeks. "Wren, nothing has changed for me. I still want forever with you. I want everything with you."

"So. . .I'm your. . .girlfriend?" she asked hesitantly.

I chuckled. "Sure, Wren, you're my girlfriend. My fiancée, and soon to be my *wife*."

Her eyes went wide. "W-what?"

"I'm not wasting another minute. As soon as you are ready, I'm hauling your ass down to the courthouse and we are getting married. You are mine, Wren. The moment you asked me for help, you were mine. I claimed you and you claimed me. You always have been, and you will always be that—*mine*."

I watched her absorb my statement. In my youth, I had never been selfish with her. What she wanted had always come first for me. It was always at the front of my mind and I would do anything for her.

With this statement, I was being selfish.

Her eyes shone with unshed tears. I was ready to catch them. Ready to catch her at any moment. I had always been there for her when I could be. I wanted to be there for her for the rest of our lives. I had been prepared to do that as a platonic friend. Back then, didn't care which way I got her, as long as she wanted to be with me.

Now, I knew where I wanted to be in her life.

And she wanted me too.

If she wanted to define us, then she could use whatever label she wanted. We were all the things. She was my best friend, lover, my reason for breathing.

I needed to talk to her about Jon. About the things Foster had pulled up on him. We had his bank records, call log, and a phone call, a 911 recording, from the night I was picked up by the cops.

I tried to feel saddened by the information I had learned today. Tried to feel something for the man who at one point in time was my best friend.

It was a strange sort of detachment. I felt nothing for him.

The moment I knew he did things that hurt Wren emotionally, all attachment I had to him broke. I didn't care about him anymore. I didn't care if I ever saw him again or if he lived or died.

I needed to talk to her about it and prepare her for what was to come.

I didn't want to ruin this moment though. The shine in her eyes. I thought she knew my intentions. I would have to be better at telling her.

She wrapped her arms around my neck, her hands delving into her favorite spot in my hair. I knew she wanted me to grow it back out how it used to be when we were younger, and I was happy to let it grow if it made her happy.

"Before I take you up to *our* room in *our* bed," I said, "I need to talk to you about Jon."

Just like that, the sparkle faded.

"Look, if you're mad at me for calling Mario, then—" She started to pull away from me, but I caught her arms, keeping them in place.

"No, I'm not mad. I'm sorry I seemed that way earlier. I'm glad you called someone." She relaxed a bit. "I need you to stay away from him. Okay?" I could have gotten into the details. I could have told her that he was the one who called 911 on me, but that wouldn't have changed the outcome of that night. I still would have gone to jail. There were too many witnesses that night. I was loud and verbal about looking for Kevin Whitman, the man with the burned face. Someone would have told the cops when they found his body in the alleyway that night.

"He did it, didn't he?" She moved her hand to the scar along my side. "He's the one who tried to. . ." She couldn't even get the words out of her mouth.

"Yeah, honey, he did it."

It pained me to tell her this. That the person she thought had her best interest at heart had betrayed the both of us and lied to her for years.

CHAPTER 47

WREN

It'd been a while since insomnia hit me. Every time I closed my eyes I saw blues that stressed and softened between the icy color of my nightmares and the ones that were once my safety.

Alex's body heat was radiating off him. I peeled my cheek off his chest and sat up, grateful for the slight breeze coming through the open window. The moon gave off enough light to see his sleeping form. His chest expanded with each breath. I couldn't help myself; I leaned down and pressed a light kiss to his full lips and held back the urge to run my tongue over them.

Since Alex had taken up residency in my bed, I was realizing that I should invest in a bigger one. We'd spent every night since the bonfire tangled in each other's arms, and I had reveled in his presence, but right now the room felt too small and too hot. I needed more air. I'd gone from sleeping alone for the last six years to having him in my bed again. Even though I was so grateful for this second chance, my head was spinning with the changes.

I sat on the porch swing. In the distance I saw the moonlight shimmering off the lake. I settled myself in the serenity of my home. The frogs croaked and crickets chirped. King walked out onto the lawn and rolled around in the grass. Queen was walking around the edge of the property, checking her territory. I loved that I couldn't hear the city noise. I hadn't heard a gunshot in the middle of the night in years. Hadn't heard the loud rattling noise of the train passing by or the neighbors fighting out on the streets. This was my home, my sanctuary, and it was the place I was always meant to find.

Sometimes I wondered about fate and everything that needed to line up just right for me to end up where I was today. I wondered if there is an invisible red string tied around me, pulling me in the direction I was meant to end up. Then I cursed the Fates for the very same things.

"Wren?"

I jumped a little at Alex's panicked voice coming from the house.

"I'm out here," I called.

The storm door creaked and there he was. He was standing in his sleep shorts, a sheen of sweat across his forehead and chest. Immediately, my heart ached for him. I could see the worry all over his face. His eyes scanned me.

"Hey." I reached my hand out for him. As if I had a magnetic pull on him, he reached for me, too, lacing his fingers between mine and pulling me to him. He crushed me to his body and I allowed it. His nose was buried in my hair at the nape of my neck. I ran my fingers over his back in slow circles. "It's okay. I just needed some air."

"Did something wake you?"

I leaned back to look up at him. I wasn't used to this. I was not used to someone being there to talk to when there were too many sleepless nights. When the demons crawled out from under my bed and tormented me. I wanted to lie. I wanted to tell him that I just got up to use the bathroom and take the dogs outside. I didn't want to admit that what had kept me awake was the echoing of my own voice begging for him to stay. To hold me.

"I just couldn't sleep," I tried, but I could see it on his face.

The eyes that could still read me like I was a page of his favorite book. The six years of distance hadn't transformed me into an unreadable language to him.

"What's keeping you up, darlin'?"

He allowed me to slip free from his hold, and I set myself back down on the porch swing, tucking my feet underneath me. He ran a hand through his still too short hair before they settle on his hips expectantly. He was vibrating with nervous energy and it pained my heart to see. In the daylight, things seemed so right between us, but there was still so much unsaid.

The lie was on my lips when his amber eyes sharpened with the knowledge, like he's already read my mind, knowing I'm about to give him a lie to placate his anxiety.

"Wren. . ." He said in the same warning tone he used on me in the bathroom when I first exposed my bruised and emaciated back to him.

"I still have nightmares of that day, and they keep me up on occasion." I looked across the lawn to the trees. "So, when they would get to be too much, or the voice too loud, I would come out here and sit in silence. The voice isn't so loud out here." The words came out softly. Like I didn't want to disrupt the tranquility around us.

I could see the cogs turning in his head. He shifted on his bare feet, looking out at the scenery.

"You still hear his voice?" Alex asked, an edge to his tone.

I hesitated, once again wanting to lie to him.

"It's not his I hear."

"Then whose do you hear?"

I wanted to ask him to drop the subject. I wanted to go back upstairs and get lost in him. I wanted to erase this conversation from existence, but I wasn't blind. I saw the guilt on his face. I saw that he had been at war with himself, and I couldn't imagine the festering guilt and anger that he had been dealing with all these years. Had he had someone to talk to? Did they offer therapy in prison? I didn't have a clue.

I took a deep breath and loosened my hold on the words that I didn't want to say.

"I hear my voice. I hear my cries and my screams. I hear myself begging you to stay and watching you leave anyway."

He looked as if I'd reached out and slapped him. He even staggered back, catching himself on the post. I was rooted in place, watching him. We needed to talk about this, I knew we needed to, and there was no gentle way to pick at this scab.

"Do you. . .blame me for—"

"God, no, Alex." I couldn't even let him finish the sentence. "I don't blame you for anything." I shook my head, wishing he would look at me but also knowing his eyes would clog the words in my throat. "It's just, that day, I needed you. I needed you to stay. I needed you to be there for me, but you left me, and. . ." I took in a shaky breath. "I'm still angry that you left me."

He took the porch stairs and walked barefoot out on the lawn, turning back to me.

"I left you to go *kill* him." He gestured wide with his hands.

"I know, Alex. I know you did, and today, right now with you here in front of me, that is what needed to happen. I could not have gone on with him still walking this earth. No matter what happened that day, him being dead is the greatest gift you could ever give me." I was standing, moving down the steps to follow him. I didn't like the distance he'd created. The void between us was getting bigger by the second. "But that day, after everything he did to me, you still left *me*."

It was like I opened the dam and the words didn't stop. "You left me there bleeding and broken on the floor for someone else to pick up the pieces. Someone I never even wanted to be there in the first place."

"I came back to you, Wren. As soon as he was dead, I came back."

"Yes, you came back, and you were ripped away from me, tased and arrested." The words came out angrily.

His mouth parted to speak but I interrupted him.

"I had no time to heal, Alex. I immediately went to the ER and had another rape kit done because I wanted them to have the evidence to help you. I had them pull my first rape kit and had it run and evaluated because I wanted them to know that you did everything to save me. But of course, justice would never be on my side, because they didn't include what happened to me in that courtroom. They treated what he did to me and what you did to him as two totally separate things." I ran a hand through my hair, catching on the tangles. "Then we got the diagnosis of your mom, and then she died." I was walking in circles now, pausing only to catch his gaze. "And then, Alex." My voice rattled with the pain. Tears bloomed in my eyes and ran down my cheeks in hot rivers. "Then you died." Gloria's death hurt, but Alex's death wrecked me.

"Wren, I never died. I—"

"Yes you did!" I screamed the words that were swallowed up by the trees. "No matter the miracle of you standing here in front of me today, the universe still played its sickest joke on me! First, it gives me you, and you save me. Your mom takes me in and loves me like I am her own, and then the rug is ripped out from under me, and you and her both die within *months* of each other. I had no time to grieve her before you were dead, and then I was grieving the both of you." My hands dropped to my sides, exhaustion hitting me. "Then I was fighting the state to get your. . .your body. Jon had spun this story that because there was no living relative, I couldn't claim you, so they were holding your body for five years, and then I could collect your ashes and finally put you to rest with your mother." I pushed my hair out of my eyes, holding my throbbing head.

The anger that I thought I had a handle on was coming out of a bottomless pit. "I ordered your headstone, Alex. I had your name, your birthday, and your death date engraved. I was trying to figure out if I put *loving son and friend,* and my heart broke all over when I realized that there was no space for me to be buried next to you in the cemetery. That our names wouldn't be on the same headstone."

My body was limp and I just wanted to lie down. I wanted to go to him and be held, be comforted. "I'm not pissed at you, Alex, I'm just. . ." I fought for the right words. "It's just been a lot to take in this last month. Everything has happened so fast, and I just need to take some time to process everything."

I brought my eyes up to look at him again and he held my stare, his head shaking slightly.

"Wren, you *should* still be pissed at me." He pointed to himself, the gesture hitting him right in his own chest. "If I would have made sure he died in that fire, if I would have just finished him off ten years ago, you would have never gone through that again. It would have been over. But because I broke my promise, *that* happened again."

I heard the way he stressed that one particular word.

That.

"Rape."

He flinched, then cast his eyes down. I could see the disconnect now. The way he had been avoiding the word. Avoiding that night. Everything up until now had been about my abandoning him. Jon's betrayal to us.

We hadn't talked about that night, though. It was always him killing Kevin. Never Kevin raping me.

"Alex, say it."

He turned his back to me. It was then I could see the brick wall he'd built around himself. Around what had happened to me. Before, I had always kept a barrier around what had been done to me in the apartment. To me, it was another Tuesday, but to Alex, I could see the confusion and anger that hearing about my abuse caused him. I had always been careful about how I said things, I never wanted to upset him, but the fact of the matter was that it *should* be upsetting. It shouldn't be something that was tiptoed around, and I had set the path for tiptoeing.

"Alexander James Harper."

His head tilted back to the sky, and I watched as his shoulders lifted and dropped.

"Raped. I was raped that day." I walked around, forcing him to look at me. "He broke into our home, quietly came upstairs, closed the door, and he raped me." There was no way Alex knew everything. The word was a blanket statement. It gave no detail of what had actually happened that day.

"Wren. . . Stop. . ."

Just like in the police report, I had to be specific. I had to say exactly what had been done to me point blank. I couldn't leave room for his imagination.

"I was lying in bed, still naked waiting for you, he sodomized me, then vaginally raped me. He beat me and choked me. He left me alive only because he planned on finding me again and doing it all over." I could see his body vibrating with rage. His hands were fisted at his side and he wouldn't look at me. If I didn't know him, I would think he was about to reach out and hit me. "If you hadn't killed him, he would have come back and done it again."

"Wren." He rushed at me, cupping my face. I placed my hands over his. His amber eyes held mine. "You can tell me it wasn't my fault until you are blue in the face. You can make me say *rape* a million times, but you can never convince me that what happened to you that day wasn't my fault, because I failed you. I swore to protect you, and I failed. I broke that promise. It wasn't on purpose, but I broke it."

"You are holding yourself responsible for someone else's actions and that's not fair to you!"

He ripped his hands away from me. "How was it fair to you!? How was it fair that your own mother sold you to someone! I just. . ." He ran his hands down his face. "After all these years, I still can't fathom that kind of heartlessness."

"Because your mother loved you with her entire being and you can't, in any world, imagine her not loving you." I spoke the words and again approached him, laying my hand on his arm. We were at a wall that I didn't know how to scale. I didn't know how to get us around this. I couldn't let him carry the weight of this for the rest of his life.

This was going to be a fight that neither of us would ever win.

He tucked my hair behind my ear, his thumb grazing over my cheek. I could see the exhaustion in his face. "I'm sorry that my leaving you that day has hurt you, and I will spend every day for the rest of my life making it up to you, but I can't apologize for it. I needed to go. I needed to protect you so that never happened to you again."

"Would you do it again?" I didn't know why I was asking this question when I knew the answer, but some sick masochistic part of me had to hear him say it.

"In a heartbeat."

"Where do you think you're going?" I reached for his naked back, placing my hand on the hard muscles as they flexed. He had running shorts on and he was bent over, tying his shoes.

I glanced to the hanging clock; it was six in the morning. We had only gone back to bed a few hours ago, never really falling back asleep. Rising up on my knees, I wrapped myself around him, kissing down the side of his neck, letting my tongue trace along a sensitive spot.

I didn't want him to leave right now. I wanted him to stay so we could nurse the still raw feelings together.

"Fuck." He groaned and reached around, managing to pull me off of his back and onto his lap. "You are going to be the reason I'm out of shape."

I cupped his cheeks, the morning stubble rough against my palm. "Just stay in bed with me a little longer." I pushed out my bottom lip, trying my best to pout. Reached to his neck and played with his hair. It'd gotten longer in the last few weeks, and I was hoping he would let it grow back out.

"If you keep pouting I'm going to bite that lip."

"At least you would stay." I smirked.

His eyes sparkled, but he straightened and set me back on the bed.

"Where are King and Queen's leashes?"

"You're going to take them on your run?"

"I either take them on a run this morning, or I'm throwing the ball all day." He crawled onto the bed, over the top of me. "If I tire them out this morning then I'm all yours tonight." He kissed me softly. "Plus, I have plans for you."

A thrill coursed through me at his playfulness. After the heaviness of last night, we needed a little fun. "Downstairs in the coat closet," I whispered when he let me come up for air.

"I'll be back in an hour."

"Alex." He turned, his head tilted to the side as he took in my face.

I felt raw. Scared to let him walk out that door after the night we had. I had an unreasonable fear of him leaving me in bed again. "I'll walk out with you." I got up, grabbing my light summer robe and tying it off around my sleep shorts and shirt.

I watched as he clipped their leashes on. The two pups were overly excited, and I knew even though they were well trained, would give him a hard time with as much energy they had.

"I love you."

"I love you, Wren."

With one more toe-curling kiss, he turned to leave. I glanced down at my gym bag by the door.

"Oh shit." I palmed my face.

Alex stilled, turning to look at me. "What's up?"

"Mario is supposed to come by this morning for coffee. It's time to start planning the fundraiser we do for domestic violence victims every year."

"Okay, we will have our day after you two get done." Alex shrugged before he continued down the porch.

I watched as he and the dogs headed down the driveway.

I wandered into my studio. I hadn't been in here since Alex found it. I pulled down the project I had been working on and found a new file for it so it didn't smudge, putting on a piece of tissue paper to protect the charcoal.

I let myself get into the zone, taking a piece of charcoal sideways and adding dimension to it.

I realized I'd lost track of time and headed to the kitchen. I filled the coffee pot up and scooped some grounds into it. Trying to get the coffee started before Mario got here.

I heard the squeak of the storm door. "Shit, hey, Mario." I thought I had more time, glancing around the kitchen for my phone to see the time, but realizing I had left it upstairs.

I headed down the hallway, "I lost track of time, let me change and then we can—"

It wasn't Mario standing in my hallway.

It was Jon.

"Jon, what are you doing here?" I fought down the panic crawling up my throat.

"I needed to see you, Wren." His eyes were wide and bloodshot. He looked around the room like he was waiting for someone. "Where is he?"

I swallowed hard. "Where is who?"

"Don't fucking play with me, Wren!" He rushed forward and I took a few steps back. His eyes went wide, hands coming up, placating me.

"Alex isn't here, Jon," I said slowly, calmly. "He left this morning."

Alex had been taking the route around the lake for the last week, which usually took him about two hours.

Jon straightened and that's when I see it, my revolver in his hand.

I brought my eyes up to his, trying to keep my nerves at bay.

"How have you been? Are you f-feeling better?" A tremor

caught in my throat, but he didn't seem to notice. That gun was loaded, and I knew it. I always kept it loaded.

"No, Wren, I haven't been *feeling* better." He ran a frustrated hand through his hair.

Mentally I was cursing myself. My phone was upstairs, and even if I got outside and screamed, I didn't have neighbors for miles. I knew I could take him, I had the training, but even I knew I couldn't go up against a gun. Alex hadn't been gone very long, and I didn't expect him to walk through those doors anytime soon. I had to deal with Jon myself.

"Talk to me. Melissa said you haven't been going to work." I pushed the words out calmly. I was hyperaware of my barely dressed state. The thin material of my sleepwear and my light robe. I pulled it tightly around me.

"I can't go to work. They will find me." He moved past me and pushed the curtains open, looking outside. Before I could make a move for my knife drawer, he raised the gun at me.

My heart hammered in my chest, and I couldn't help the trembling in my hands.

"Who will find you?" I asked.

"The fucking loan sharks!" he yelled, moving away from the window. I had never seen Jon lose his temper before.

"Jon," I whispered. "I don't understand why you are doing this, why you lied about Ale—"

The gun collided with my cheek. My ears rang and I fell to the floor, stars bursting behind my eyes. I tried to blink them away quickly to catch my bearings.

"Fucking Alex! Oh my god, that's all you fucking think about! That's all anyone thinks about!"

I tried to push myself up off the floor when his hand gripped my hair and shoved me into a chair.

"If it wasn't for you, I would still have my life."

My face screwed up in confusion. I pushed my hair out of my way, watching him with my eyes as he paced back and forth. I felt hot blood trickle down my face. I reached up and touched it, my hand coming back red.

"Alex was miserable before you, but he was fun. He would come out to parties and look at me as if I hung the fucking moon. I could give him anything. Clothes, games, movies. Anything he wanted and he was still fucking miserable. That made me feel good because I fucking hated my life, too, but at least I had money and both my parents. And then you came around. . ." He approached me, his hand caressing my cheek, thumb roughly grazing over my lips. "I didn't get it. You were nothing to get a hard-on over. Fucking scared, dirty, skinny-ass thing. You always looked like someone was going to reach out and hit you." He pushed my face back, disgust in his voice. The person standing in front of me was not the same man who had been caring for me for the last six years. The person who'd been at my side through my heartache.

Jon spoke as if he was unhinged. His eyes darted all over the place. He moved to the back door, unlocking it and stepping outside. He whistled and looked around. "Where are the dogs?"

My stomach dropped. What would he do to them?

"Alex took them with him. . ."

Jon looked back outside before closing the door.

"I don't get it, Jon, if you hated me so much then why did you befriend me?" I asked, trying to distract him away from my dogs.

I wouldn't let him hurt them.

"Because he always wanted you around! And then suddenly, Alex was happy. He didn't want things anymore. It didn't matter what I bought or what event I invited him to, he didn't care. He just wanted to stay home all the time and be with you!" He laughed maniacally. "And then, I figured it out. He was happy because of you." He used the gun to point at me. I recoiled. "So, if you can't beat them, join them. I bought things for you instead, invited you instead. Then I thought to myself, what's so special about her? What about a girl could make the most miserable guy I knew happy? I waited for five fucking years for him to finally make his move on you. He never did. And you know what, I wanted a slice of the fucking cake. I wanted to know what it was about you." He scoffed. "Then my fucking dad just about gambled the entire family fortune away. He was going to run that fucking firm into the ground, and then I was going to be just as broke as Alex. I couldn't let that happen, so I did the only thing I could do: I went to a financial backer, and I got the money I needed to keep the firm. Forced him to sign it over to me and sent his ass to Florida for retirement with a nice little nest egg."

"I didn't realize that your parents were. . ."

"Deadbeats. My dad got lucky in the beginning with his trials. Made money fast and flaunted it. As he's gotten older, he's squandered most of it. My mother realized all he was good for was his money, and soon found herself a lover on the side. They fought like cats and dogs growing up. Neither were happy. So, me taking over the firm was the best thing that could happen for the both of them—and my sister. She still gets to live her cushy life, none the wiser. Of course, no one wants to work with the boss's son. We started losing clients. How the fuck was I supposed to pay back the fucking loan sharks without any income!"

He moved to the kitchen and yanking open the drawers one by one, searching for something. "So again, go back to the fucking sharks and pay them to plant easy evidence. Get my firm out there winning trials under my name. Easy, done, it's just money, and as long as business is thriving, money is easy to come by." He wiped a hand down his face. "Where the fuck is the duct tape?!"

I almost laughed. "I don't have any." I'd never kept it in my life.

As Jon rambled on, I kept glancing out the back window, hoping to catch Alex before he came back. I didn't want him rushing in here not realizing the danger he was in.

"What are you looking at?"

I jolted in surprise; Jon turned and looked back through the window.

The coffee pot hissed and sputtered as it finished brewing.

"The coffee! It's. . . It's done. C-can I pour you a cup?"

I didn't know what I was doing, but I didn't want him focusing on the outside. "Come on, Jon, you look tired, let me take care of you." I softened my tone. I was hoping that maybe if I pretended to care for him, he might relax.

"Yeah, coffee sounds nice." Jon's demeanor seemed to change at my offer. He relaxed his shoulders again, dropping the gun to his side.

I would use this to my advantage.

I stood cautiously. I pulled two mugs down and poured him a cup. Glancing over my shoulder, he was looking outside again. I opened the cabinet above the coffeepot and pulled down a small glass vial, pouring out the contents into my hand and grinding the brittle petals between my fingers into his mug. I opened the fridge, poured some milk, and added sugar into his cup, just how he liked it.

"So, tell me more. I want to understand." I handed him the mug. I held my own between my hands, letting the heat soak into them and tried to stop the trembling. I tried to arrange my face in a concerned look, giving him my full attention. I needed him to pay attention to me and not outside.

I can't lose Alex again.

He hesitated for a moment, taking a sip of the coffee. "Wren, you have to understand, at first, I hated you. You took the attention of my best friend. He wanted to be around you all the time like some love sick puppy. But eventually, I was able to understand why. I came to appreciate you just as much as, if not more than, him. That day when I came to the house. . . I was only trying to help you." He reached for me, his hand running down my arm before he squeezed my hand.

"What do you mean?"

"You wouldn't sleep. You weren't eating. I had to do something to get you to let go of him."

My stomach dropped. "What did you do?"

"I would have been the better choice, Wren. I could give you everything you ever wanted. Everything you ever dreamed of. I waited for you to let him go. I waited for you to move on, but you," he pointed his finger at me, "you stubborn woman, were going to wait for him to get out of there, and then what? What would that do for me? I needed to get rid of Alex so you could move on. Conveniently enough, the same loan sharks do shady shit like kill-for-hire."

I remembered Alex's scar, and contempt grew inside me, understanding settling.

"You. . .*hired someone* to kill him?"

"Yeah, but they fucking failed," he griped. I watched as he brought the mug up. Time seemed to slow as I watched the liquid almost touch his lips, then he pulled the mug away without taking a drink. "Of course, the guy they sent in there ran into someone who had a problem with him, and Alex, of all fucking people, saved the guy." Jon shook his head and muttered, "Who knew the fucking trailer trash knew how to fight."

Fuck.

"I should have paid more attention, but like Alex, you managed to fucking distract me."

He looked back to the mug before he set it down on the table. The hope I had fizzled out quickly. I glanced around the kitchen trying to find something to use. I took a drink of my own coffee, careful not to place my lips in the same area my hands touched. I had dealt with an unhinged man before. Jon was nothing compared to him.

I just needed to wait it out.

"So, you made up a story. Gave me a fake death certificate and watched me mourn the loss of *our* best friend for. . . years." I sighed the last word out. "What happened to all the letters I sent him? The ones he sent me?" I tried to keep my voice neutral, keeping my eyes on the clock and looking down at the gun still gripped in his hand.

"I had some friends in the mail room. Had them destroy them all. You needed to move on. You were unwell. I only did what was best for you." Jon sounded like he had convinced himself that everything he had done was in my best interest.

"Then you distracted me. I didn't ensure they had taken care of business. You finally were going to order the headstone, and I knew you were ready." He walked over to me. His hands came up, one still holding the gun, and cupped my face. "We could finally be together." He closed his eyes, his head tilting slightly like he was in pain. I glanced at the backdoor, noting it was unlocked.

"I. . .I never knew you felt that way." I tried to push down the fear that was building.

"C-can I get a refill?" I straightened as I regained the space I needed.

"Sure." His eyes were still closed and he motioned in the direction of the coffee pot.

Do it. This is your chance.

I turned to the carafe, grabbing it and tossing the hot coffee on him.

"FUCK!" he screamed.

The gun clattered. I smashed my mug over his head before rushing out of his reach, throwing the backdoor open and running. I hit the grass and slipped in the dew. I scrambled and kept running down the hill. Terror nipped at my heels.

The lake came into view.

I slipped into the water as calmly as possible, trying to ensure that the ripples didn't expose my hiding spot under the dock. I thought about swimming to the other side, calculating how long I could hold my breath, how deep I could get under the surface, but he would see me. I wasn't sure how good with a gun he was, and I wasn't willing to risk it.

I didn't move. Didn't breathe. Just listened.

"Wren!"

I could hear Jon screaming, and I worried that Alex or the dogs would hear him too.

Please no.

Footsteps sounded on the dock. I tried to look up between the wood slats but they were too tight together. I could only see a shadow.

It was quiet, and I thought I could see him retreating to the house.

A hand came down and grabbed me by my hair. I locked my arms around the post. He ripped at my hair, but I didn't let up.

"You fucking bitch!" He jumped down into the water, managing to pull me away from the post.

He dragged me from the water, onto the lake's edge, and loomed over me. "After everything I have done for you!"

Once we were on solid ground, I managed to twist around and kick him right in the groin. He dropped to his knees, and I scrambled away from him. My fingers dug into the soft marshy ground and I pulled myself away from him. His hand gripped my ankle, pulling me back. I turned in his hold and kicked him in the face.

I ran up the hill and back into the house. I dashed through the kitchen soaking wet. The broken glass sliced my foot open, the pain causing me to stumble and fall in the hall. I scrambled back up, lifting my foot and seeing the large shard I had stepped on.

I dug my nails around the shard and pulled it out, tossing it to the ground.

I looked up the stairs. If I went upstairs, I could get my phone and at least dial 911. Or, I could try to run and lose him in the brush.

I had wasted too much time deciding, so I ran out the front door, ready to run for my life.

Then everything went black.

CHAPTER 49

ALEX

King and Queen had no idea how to run on a leash. They spent most of their time getting tangled up together, forcing me to stop and unwind them.

So instead of running, we fast-walked.

I took a different route today, deciding I didn't want to fight King from going into the water. He loved the water, but I didn't want to spend the next few hours washing the mud off him and drying him. I wanted an afternoon of just Wren and I.

After last night's events, we needed it.

I reached into my pocket and pulled out the velvet green box I had found in my mother's things.

I was surprised to find it; she had given it to me so long ago, and I had stored it in a shoebox of things I kept of my dad's. It was still in there. I could only assume that everyone packed everything in a hurry, not bothering to look at anything. It was evident that Wren never went through the things. She didn't even pull out my old clothes.

I was grateful to find it.

I remember the day Ma gave it to me. She told me one day I would find the woman I wanted to spend the rest of my life with and she wanted me to have it.

I imagined she wanted Wren to have it too.

She had been right. I did. But I'd never thought I would be able to propose to her with it. Wren had still been adamant on never dating at that time.

I had planned to give it to Wren as a gift one year. Nothing expected of her, but I had always wanted her to have it. She was the only woman worthy of my mother's ring, even if it was just a platonic gift.

King whined and raised his head in the air. He was such a mama's boy, never liking to be away from her for too long.

"I know, boy, we are heading home." I put the box back in the safety of my shorts pocket.

We made our way out of the ash trees, stepping over fallen tree limbs, and made it to the gravel driveway. King and Queen's heads both rose, sniffing the air, and their tails stood high.

"What's the matter with you two?" They started to tug on the leashes, whining and barking. My scalp prickled with unease, and I picked up the pace with them.

Alarm bells rang loudly when we made it to the gate that was wide open.

Everyone knew to always close the gate, coming or going.

I dropped the leashes and ran fast as I could.

Something isn't right.

The clearing opened up as the house came into view. In the driveway was a BMW.

Jonathan.

I ran into the already opened front door.

"Wren!?" I ran up the stairs and she wasn't there. Back downstairs and into the kitchen, I saw the broken glass scattered across the floor.

King and Queen were on my heels, "Stay!" I commanded them like Wren showed me. I didn't want them in the glass and I couldn't worry about them and her.

A scream sounded from out the back door and it turned my gut.

Wren.

Jon had Wren by the hair. Her hands were locked around his wrist, and he was dragging her backwards down the hill.

She shrieked when he jerked her. I ran for her but Jon finally spotted me, bringing his other hand up, and then I was looking down the barrel of a gun. The gun fired, causing us both to flinch.

"No!" Wren screamed, clawing at his arm. She tried to bring her knee up to hit him but couldn't at her angle. I moved to lunge for her, but he moved the gun from pointing at me to her.

I froze.

"You better think twice, Alex," he warned, a sick smile on his face. "I have no problem shooting her." He jammed the gun into her cheek. He had me. He knew I wouldn't do anything with a gun pointed at her.

"Jon, she has nothing to do with this," I gritted out.

"She has everything to do with this!" He pushed the barrel of the gun until I could see Wren close her eyes, visibly in pain by the amount of pressure he was putting on it. "It's all her fucking fault."

I clenched my teeth. "What is?"

"If it wasn't for her, you and I would still be exactly where we were."

"What are you talking about, Jon?"

Wren's eyes were wide, staring up at me.

What the fuck am I gonna do?

"You met her and then you made your entire life about her!" He lifted his hand with the gun, using it to push his hair out of his eyes. Slowly, I moved closer, only stopping when the gun was back on her.

Come on, you spineless fuck. Point it at me.

"You used to need *me*, but she came into the picture and suddenly you needed *her.*" He pulled her down into the water, pushing her under and holding her there. He didn't take his eyes off me; he didn't pull the gun away from her.

I stood frozen. If I dove for him, he would shoot her. There was no guarantee I could get the gun away in time.

"Jon, just tell me what this is about! Why are you doing this to her?"

"I'm not doing this to her, I'm doing this to *you*." He pulled Wren up, and she sputtered and choked the water out, dragging in deep breaths of air.

"Then let me trade her spot!" I put my hands up, trying to show I wasn't going to harm him. I took slow steps, trying to get closer I was at the start of the dock now.

Jon laughed. "Oh no, I want to hurt you, Alex, and the best way to do that, is through her." He shoved Wren back under the water, pulled her back up and then pushed her under again before she could get in a breath.

"If you would have just minded your own fucking business, this wouldn't be happening right now. But no, you had to choose her over me."

He was in the water waist-deep, his blond hair too long and falling down around his eyes. His teeth were gritted, and Wren continued to struggle below him. A hand came up out of the water, clawing at his arms.

He pulled her up again and she sputtered, gasping for air. I could see exhaustion on her face; she couldn't handle much more of this.

A bark sounded from behind me, and everything slowed. I looked over my shoulder at the dogs barreling out of the house.

They were going for him.

I turned back to see Wren's eyes widen. Jon was already pulling the gun from her—to the dogs.

I moved, trying to put myself between the gun and them.

"No!" Wren screamed. She grabbed Jon's arm, pushing it up just as the gun fired. Jon let go of her hair. She moved, elbowing Jon in the stomach, and he doubled over. She twisted his wrist.

"FUCK!" Jon howled.

"Alex!" Wren choked my name out. Just as she was shoved back underwater, she tossed the gun.

It clattered at the end of the dock, and I ran for it. My shoe caught on a loose board, causing me to stumble and land on it.

"Jon!" I screamed his name, getting his attention. He had her under again. For a moment, it seemed like he was going to stand up, pull her up with him. His blue eyes locked on me.

My heart pounded in my ears.

Ba-dump.

The hand that clawed at his arm stilled, dropped under the water's surface.

Ba-dump.

Then his face hardened, and he pushed down harder while still holding my gaze.

I brought the gun up, aimed, and pulled the trigger.

I caught his eyes as they widened with realization before the bullet hit.

It shattered his face into something unrecognizable. Like it was in slow motion, he fell to the side, floating in the water. Blood pooled around his body. I jumped in and waded out into the lake, pulling Wren up and getting her to the shore.

"Come on, sweetheart, breathe." I patted her face a few times, but she didn't stir. Her lips were blue and there was a gash in her temple. Dread filled me.

Tipping her head back, I started CPR. "Come on, Wren."

One. . .two. . .three. . .

Breathe life into her.

One. . .two. . .three. . .

Force air into her lungs.

Clasping my hands on her chest, I press down over her heart again.

One. . .two. . . Crack!

There goes one rib.

Three.

She was breaking under my hands, but I wouldn't stop. I couldn't. This couldn't be the end.

"Please, God, I'll never let her out of my sight again. Please just give her back."

I can hear the whine of the dogs, my heart breaking as I looked down at her unnaturally pale face and blue lips.

"Fuck!"

I didn't stop, I wouldn't stop even if I had to cut my own heart out of my chest and put it in her. *Wren Jacobson will live.*

I cursed every god and deity there was, desperate to get my girl back and *finally*, she choked out a mouthful of water.

"Come on, Wren." I rolled her to her side, and she stopped coughing and took a deep breath. I looked to the sky, exhaustion taking over me. Tears ran hot down my face. I could barely keep King off her as she took in more deep ragged breaths.

She's alive.

"Alex!" I looked over my shoulder and Mario was running our way. He took in Jon's dead body and then looked down at Wren. "I heard the gunshots, what the hell happened?"

"I can't explain now, I need to get her to the hospital."

"Did she. . ." He couldn't say it. "How long was she. . .?"

"Too long."

Mario and turned back to Jon's body, where it floated on the surface before he looked back at me.

"Alex, you're bleeding."

I looked down at my left shoulder. That's when the pain registered, but I ignored it. "It's just a graze."

He was on his phone then, calling in for an ambulance.

I managed to scoop her up in my arms and carried her around the house, Mario following. "I'm going to meet them at the main road."

"Mario," I paused, looking over my shoulder at Jon's dead body.

I was a felon, and I'd just killed another man. It didn't matter that it was in self-defense. I knew what that meant.

Mario pushed me to get me to keep walking. "Just get her to

the road. She slipped off the dock and fell into the water. That's all you tell them." He turned and headed back around the house.

CHAPTER 50

ALEX

THE MONITORS BEEPED, SHOWING ME PROOF THAT SHE was still alive. I watched her heart line like it was my own. She was breathing, but she wasn't awake. I maneuvered my hands around the tubes and wires they had her hooked up to. Her face was pale, but her lips had color again.

We don't know the cognitive damage she might have due to her being down so long. Only time will tell.

The doctor's words echoed in my head.

I could feel the spiral pulling me under. It was the same thing over again. I failed her. I didn't keep my promise. I should have dealt with Jon sooner. I never should have waited.

I failed her.

I failed her *again.*

"Alex, I can watch her. You should get some—"

"No."

Mario sighed, moved to the other side of her. She had a blanket pulled up under her arms. Her hands laid on top of the blanket, palms up. He reached for her hand, squeezing it.

"Come on, kid, come back."

A part of me hated Mario. He had trained her. Showed her how to defend herself. He had been there for her when I couldn't be.

I was jealous.

He had a relationship with her like I did when we first met.

I wasn't the only one anymore.

But then there was the part of me that was grateful to him. Grateful that she hadn't only had Jon. That she had others there to care for her.

Troy, Gavin, and Riley had been here earlier. I had called them from her phone to ask them to check in on King and Queen. They were here an hour later, dropping off a change of clothes for the both of us.

"For when she's ready to come home," Gavin said with tears in his eyes.

Riley cried at her bedside, and the guys finally took her away. I only left Wren's side to change my shirt in the bathroom. I had managed to pass the blood on my clothes off as the blood from Wren's cut.

I was so tired, but every time a doctor or nurse came by and asked me if I wanted a break, I declined.

I promised heaven and hell I would never leave her side again. I'd be damned if I broke that promise on day one.

"Do you love her?" The words left my throat in a croak. I didn't know what I would do if he did. Did it really matter? I wasn't going to walk away from her. I wasn't going to let her go to him just because he hadn't made the mistake I did.

Mario at least gave me the dignity to not look at me like I was stupid.

"I do, but not in the way you think." His voice was resolute. Like he had resigned himself to losing her. "My sister died when I was seventeen. She was in a similar situation to Wren's. Committed suicide when she was fourteen." I watched as his throat bobbed up and down. "I'd like to think my sister would have turned out like Wren, if she could have gotten out sooner."

With his words, the jealousy evaporated.

The curtain behind me opened, and then a hand clasped me on the shoulder.

I could smell Ezekiel's cologne. It cut through the antiseptic smell of the hospital room like a knife. I brought my hand up and patted his.

"Whatever you need, brother, you just say the words."

That voice wasn't Ezekiel's though. I looked up to see Nikolas's face, concern in his eyes. More emotion was in them now than I had seen in all the years I'd spent in prison with him.

I stood and he clasped me on the back before holding me at arm's length. "It's good to see you. I'm sorry that this is the situation."

"I didn't know you were getting out so soon."

He shrugged his shoulders, eyes flicking over my shoulder. "I know a guy who knows a guy."

I took my seat again and placed Wren's hand back in mine.

"Alright, gentlemen, visiting hours are over. It's time to go." The head nurse made her way into the room, eyes taking a good look at each man that stood. They all stood about a foot taller than her. The brothers were equal in height. About four inches taller than Mario. She was older, with short curly hair and a wide frame. I thought her name was Connie.

She pumped some hand sanitizer on her hand, rubbing it together as she checked the monitors and wrote things down on her chart before leaving again. I looked at Mario, who was staring at Niko and Ezekiel.

"What do you need from us?" Niko asked.

"I want a complete security system installed at Wren's place. I don't want one square inch of that place to be without monitoring." I hadn't even started working for them, and I was already requesting things. Favors I had no business requesting. I didn't care.

Anything to protect her.

Niko and Ezekiel looked at each other. "I'll call Emery and get that started."

They left.

"I'll be by before my shift in the morning," Mario said, and started to leave.

"Mario." I got his attention. He shoved his hands in his pockets, turning to me. He knew what I was going to ask. I had been waiting for him to pull out his cuffs, take me in.

The suspense was killing me, and so was the guilt.

I was going back to jail, just as Wren and I were finally figuring things out.

She was going to lose me for a second time.

"It's been taken care of," Mario said.

My brows rose.

Mario pointed to Wren. "You just take care of her." Then he left.

I moved around the bed, crawling in and pulling Wren into my arms. She felt cold. I cradled her to my chest the best I could on the small bed. It was bigger than what we grew up sharing, but so was I.

"I'll be right here when you wake up, sweetheart. You just take your time. I've got you."

CHAPTER 51

WREN

The sun dances on the surface of the water above my head. I keep swimming, kicking my legs harder, but I can't come up for air. My lungs burn as if they are on fire. I fear I might burn from the inside out.

The edge of my vision blackens, I kick harder but I can't hold it anymore.

I can't keep swimming. I'm so tired.

Breathe, the voice tells me.

I can't!

You have to.

Pain. That's all I could feel. My chest felt like I had a cinder block dropped on it. My limbs were heavy and everything ached.

Faintly, I could hear machines whooshing, beeping and. . . was that. . .snoring?

Slowly, I opened my eyes. I had to blink a few times to focus on my surroundings. It was dark with only a faint light coming from around a curtain.

I'm in a hospital.

I turned my head and had to fight the groan. Pain exploded in my head and blurred my vision again.

"Shh. . . Wren, hold still." I felt Alex next to me. His face was pale, tired. Dark circles were under his eyes and even his cheeks looked thinner than I remembered. "Do you know where you are?"

"Hospital." My throat was hoarse. I tried to bring my hand up, but it pinched and I realized an IV was in it. "What happened to you?"

"You," he breathed, brushing my face.

"I'm the best thing that ever happened to you," I responded cheekily, managing to pull some humor through. I felt like I had been thrown into a trash compactor.

Alex smiled, I leaned into his touch. He dropped his head to my shoulder, his chuckle turning into a silent, body-shaking cry.

"Oh, my love." I buried my nose in his hair, inhaling his scent. I kissed his head and tried to comfort him the best I could. "I'm so sorry. I didn't mean to scare you."

His head jerked up, fire eyes on me. "No, Wren, I'm sorry. Once again I left you and you got hurt. I almost. . . You were. . ."

I understood his implications then.

"You weren't breathing. . . You were d—"

"Shh. I'm here, Alex. I'm here and I'm not going anywhere." He dipped his head down, his lips ghosting over mine.

"Mr. Harper, what did I tell you about being in the bed with Ms. Jacobson?" The curtain opened and a nurse came in. I winced at the bright light that flooded in, burying my face into his chest.

"And I told you, Ms. Connie, that you would have to pry my cold dead body out of this bed." He tightened his hold on me, he sounded serious and a smile broke across my lips.

God I loved him.

"Sir, that is my patient and—"

"This is my *wife*. I will not be getting out of this bed."

I jerked at his words, staring up at him. His eyes flicked down to me, giving me a look that said *not now*.

"Uh-huh. I still don't believe that." She moved to a computer mounted on the wall. A chair screeched across the tile. Alex leaned back and I got a glimpse of a huge man behind him who looked eerily familiar. I was now realizing this was the person behind the snoring.

"Good thing I brought in a copy of his marriage certificate." The man got up, pulling a paper out from somewhere, handing it to her.

She looked it over and gave a disapproving look. "Well, congratulations, *Mrs.* Harper." She handed the paper over to me. "You might want to work on getting your license updated."

"Yeah," I took the paper from her gingerly with my corded hand, flipping it over and staring at the words. "I'll get on it." Sure as shit, that was my signature, but I knew I hadn't signed this paper.

"Mrs. Harper, would you like me to update your emergency contact in the system?"

A laugh bubbled up, causing me to wince in pain. "Yeah, please update the information to my *husband*."

After Nurse Connie took my vitals and blinded me with lights, informing me that I had taken a nasty fall, she ordered a few more tests before she finally left.

"You forged my signature?" I said softly, once I knew we were out of earshot.

"Yes."

"How did you even know how I signed things?"

"I used to mimic your handwriting when you gave me back the biology homework. It's still a habit of mine."

"But why?"

"Why did I pick up the habit, or why did I forge your signature?"

"Obviously the signature." I would figure out the copying my handwriting later.

"They were trying to get ahold of your mom," he said softly. "I wasn't trying to take away having a wedding or proposing to you, sweetheart. I didn't want them to contact her. So much happened all at once and I needed a little control over it."

I held the marriage license up. "We are going to talk about this later." I set it down before saying, "She's dead."

"What?" His eyebrows rose in shock. "Foster never. . ."

"She wouldn't have found her. She dropped her married name and went back to her maiden name. She died three years ago." The words came out with no emotion. I didn't care then, and I still didn't now.

"I see."

The huge man cleared his throat next to us.

"Wren, this is Nikolas. We had each other's backs while we were both in prison. He's Ezekiel's brother," Alex explained.

He had a buzz cut and striking blue eyes. Scars along his face told me he had been in quite a few fights.

"It's nice to meet you, Mrs. Harper." There was an accent in his voice that I hadn't heard before. "If you ever need anything, please don't hesitate to reach out to me or my brother." He placed his hand over his chest in a sincere gesture. "Alex saved my life, and so I will spend mine repaying him. Since you are his life, you are included in that vow."

I didn't know what to do with that information. My head was killing me and it was a lot to take in.

"It's...nice to meet you too," I whispered.

I looked back to Alex. "Fall?"

"I'll explain everything once we get you home." Gently, he brushed my cheek with his thumb.

I was exhausted. I had questions, but I leaned my head back and closed my eyes.

"I think she's out."

"Yeah. Seems so." I felt his lips touch the crown of my head. I wanted to open my eyes, I wanted to talk to him more, but I couldn't muster the strength.

"I need to leave for a few hours. Anything you want me to get you?"

"Some clothes for her. I'm hoping to bring her home now that she's awake."

"Don't piss off the nurses and you might be able to get some- where with them. Try being charming." His voice was light, teasing.

"The only woman I'm ever going to be charming to is this one." His arms adjusted around me.

"Well, brother, you stink. The blood is starting to soak through your bandage and you need a shower. I'll bring you back some stuff and watch her while you shower."

"No. I'm never taking my eyes off her again."

"You haven't slept in three days."

"I'll sleep when I'm dead."

"If you really die, you won't be able to take care of her, so take care of yourself too."

Their voices faded out as I fell deeper into sleep.

<hr>

I woke up a few hours later. Alex was sitting in the chair next to me. Nikolas was nowhere in sight. I tried holding still while I watched him. He had ahold of my hand, running his thumb over my fingers.

That's when I felt it.

I tugged my hand away, holding it up to my face.

"Alex, this is—"

"Ma's ring."

Tears were already forming in my eyes. I had only ever seen Gloria's ring once. I noticed it when I had been living with them for about three months. I complimented it. Told her it was beauti- ful. I could tell she treasured it. She had told me how there were days when she almost pawned it so she could pay the bills, but could never bring herself to do it.

It was the one thing I was selfish with. I couldn't give it up.

It wasn't long after that I noticed she stopped wearing it. I was worried that she had pawned it and told her so.

No, sweet girl. It's tucked safely away. You'll see.

I never understood what she meant back then. I was just happy she hadn't pawned it because I was too much for her to care for.

The ring was a singular, circle cut diamond held on a gold band. The band had carvings around it that looked like vines. It was simple, but exquisite.

"This was the surprise I had for you that morning." He rubbed a hand down his stubbled face. "Remember the party when everything happened with Chance?"

I nodded, still stunned it was on my hand.

"I couldn't sleep that night. I laid awake all night while you slept. I couldn't lie there anymore, so I went outside. Ma came home early that morning. I had a lot on my mind and somehow, it was like she knew I needed her and she was there." A soft smile curved his lips. He took my hand again. "She gave me the ring that day. Told me that Dad would want me to have it and she wanted me to give it to the girl I decided to marry." His watery eyes looked up to me. "I think she knew it would be yours one day."

Another five days passed before I was released from the hospital. Ezekiel and Nikolas picked us up and drove us home. Alex sat in the back seat of the SUV with me. He opted for them to pick us up rather than Troy and Gav, stating that they could hold their emotions where Troy and Gavin couldn't. He had pulled me onto his lap and strapped the seatbelt over the both of us, rolling the window down when I asked so I could feel the wind on my face. Ezekiel and Nikolas talked quietly to each other while I fell asleep.

Alex carried me up the stairs to our room, which had a makeover. He had bought a king mattress that had all the bells and whistles: heating and cooling settings, plus a remote to raise the bed up like a chair. I was on bed rest for another few weeks before my next appointment, and Alex was adamant on having me listen to every tiny detail the doctors gave us.

"Hey," Riley whispered. She opened the door and slipped in quietly. I'd been home for three days now. I slept most of the time, Alex and the pups always close by, but today I was restless. I looked down at a sleeping Alex. His head was on my lap and I had been combing my fingers through his long-ish hair. The poor man hadn't been sleeping and had finally passed out in exhaustion on my lap. I didn't mind. It was nice seeing him sleep peacefully.

She carefully sat on the edge of the bed, whispering, "How are you feeling?"

I shrugged my shoulders. "I'm feeling fine. Tired, sore. Glad to be home."

"How's he been?" She nodded to Alex.

"A wreck," I sighed. "He's not sleeping, barely eating. I can hardly get him to go downstairs to answer the door."

"I noticed the fancy new security system coming in." She raised a brow at me.

I grabbed the iPad next to me and flashed it to her. I had a live feed of the entire property constantly recording. "Window sensors, door sensors, motion sensors, and an alarm if the wind blows the gate too hard." It was hard for me not to roll my eyes at the whole thing.

"Don't you think that's a little extreme?" Riley hedged in a hushed voice.

"She died." Alex pulled his head from my lap. Rolling off me and wiping his face. He moved to the edge of the bed, rubbing his beard. He hasn't shaved since I was hospitalized. He was full on mountain man mode. "I won't apologize for taking every precaution when it comes to her." He stood, leaning down and kissing my forehead gently. "I'll give you two some time alone." He left the room, surprising me.

"I wasn't trying to upset him."

"No, you're fine." I leaned over and patted her hand. "He's going through it."

"Do you think he has PTSD?"

"I think so. Give him some time."

"So." She lay down on her side, propping her head up on her hand. "Are you going to tell me about that diamond on your finger?"

I looked down at my ring, running my fingers over it.

"It's Gloria's." Riley knew what the weight of that meant.

I decided to keep my newly married status to myself. Still needed to process it.

Riley was able to distract me for a few hours. Alex would hover by the door every twenty minutes, but Ri didn't see him, her back being to the door. She told me about Gavin and Troy and how they wanted to throw a coming home party for me that she had to talk them down from.

"I love you, girl." Riley hugged me. "Stop getting into these shitty situations." Her voice was clogged with emotion. "I can't see my life without you."

"What can I say, the gods hate me." I squeezed her tighter. "Don't worry, I'm here for the long haul." I watched her go and heard the front door ding on the iPad next to me. I picked it up and pulled it onto my lap. I scanned each section until I found him and Queen.

He was down by the lake.

My heart ached for him. He had been blaming himself for what had happened, but I didn't blame him at all.

Jon had been raised in a house that was based around buying people's love. Being needed made him feel loved.

Jon tried to control people with it, but Alex never *needed*, and neither did I. He had just deluded himself into thinking we did.

It all made sense now.

I threw back the covers and slid out of bed.

King stood stretching, his tail wagging.

"Okay, buddy, let's go outside." I carefully made my way out of the house and down the porch steps, stopping every so often to let the dizziness dissipate. I got to the top of the slope and paused, watching him. He stood at the edge of the dock, hands in his pockets.

Queen spotted me. At her whine, Alex turned.

"Wren, you aren't supposed to be out of bed." He made his way to me, scooping me up in his arms. I laced my fingers behind his neck.

"Would you take me down there?" I nodded to the lake. I hadn't been back to it since he had pulled me from the water.

He hesitated, looking back at the body of water.

"Please?"

On that note, he took me back down the hill and onto the dock. He made no move to set me down until I wiggled. I saw it in his eyes, the fear. The way he wanted to leave this place and never return to it.

"Love." I cupped his face, brushed my thumbs over the wrinkles by the corner of his eyes. "Let's sit down."

Alex sat me between his legs, I let my feet brush the cold water. His arms were banded around my middle as if he was the only thing keeping me from falling back in.

"We should move, find a new place where nothing bad has ever happened."

"Did I ever tell you about the time I tried drowning?"

I could feel the tension building in his body, so I ran my hands up and down his thighs, trying to soothe him.

"I had just turned twelve. Kevin had been in my life for about eight months by that time. This was after I told my Aunt Katie what had been happening and she brought me back to them. I overheard my mom say something like, 'If her life is so bad then she would just kill herself. Until then, her life obviously isn't that bad.'

"I didn't know what suicide was. I didn't understand the concept of it, but at those words I thought, maybe if I tried to, maybe it would make everyone realize how bad things were. So on my way home from school one day I was crossing by the canal and I just jumped in." I shrugged, letting my toes graze into the water again, and watched as the ripples expanded to the middle of the lake until they dissipated. "The current took me under and pulled me a ways down. At some point, the canal widened, the current wasn't so fast, and I got myself to the edge. Climbed up on some rocks and got out. Back then, I just thought that I didn't drown because my dad taught me how to swim."

"What did you do after you got out?"

"I walked back home, soaking wet. Stripped out of my clothes in my room and changed into new ones. Tried hiding under the bed from Kevin. Life went on." I pressed my back into his chest. "I've never been a religious person, Alex, but I never missed the fact that the same place I had tried to end my life was the same place I ran into you, and my whole world changed. Maybe divine intervention does exist." I tried to catch his eyes but he buried his face in my neck. "After you went to jail, and Gloria got sick, I started looking for a new place. I couldn't stay in that house. I told the realtor that I wanted something outside of town, with a large property. I didn't care about the cost, I would make it work. I just wanted to be away from people. This place had been on the market for years. The previous owners had died in the house, I guess that made some people not want to live in it." I shrugged. "They died of old age and together. I liked that. So, I took it. It needed a lot of work, but I needed something to keep me busy."

He listened quietly, his hands loosening and then tightening on me every so often.

"I never really wanted to die before. Not until Jon had told me you were dead. After I got that news I threw myself off of this dock. I was drowning in my sadness, my anger, but I always knew how to swim. So I did. Every time it was too much to handle, I would swim laps in this lake until my arms and legs felt like they would fall off."

"So, you're telling me we aren't moving."

I tipped my head back to look at him. "Alex, I'll move if you really want to. I'll pack everything up and find a new home with you, but this lake healed me, and I think it could heal you too."

CHAPTER 52
WREN

One month later

I stood outside on the cracked sidewalks staring up at the nightmare I used to live in. The Cherry Wood apartments had been vacant for about two years now. They were falling apart. Trim was no longer just popped but had completely fallen off. There was graffiti on the sides of the buildings now; all the windows were smashed. Red signs were plastered on every door, sun-faded and nearly illegible.

VIOLATION

Listed were what I assumed were city codes and other things.

I didn't know how Alex did it, but he did. He'd managed to buy the property from the bank. I turned around just in time to see a truck and trailer with a backhoe chained onto it. Dan had let him borrow the equipment for the next few days.

Alex was never far away from me these days. Always staying within sight or ear shot of me. Riley had been right about his PTSD. He would wake me in the middle of the night, checking to see if I was still there, still breathing.

Alex got out of the truck and strode right over to me, wrapping me up in his arms and kissing me like it would be his last time. He wore my favorite worn jeans, the ones he would put on if he was going to be working outside. They used to be a dark wash but were faded now, with rips up on his thigh showing his tanned skin through with the smattering of dark hair. His signature black T-shirt stretched across his chest in its usual manor.

He still looked tired.

With recent events, he was a different man. I'd been trying to give him the time and the grace he needed to forgive himself. I didn't mind the kisses or the constant attention he gave me now, but I knew he was still beating himself up. There wasn't anything I could say or do to make him feel like it wasn't his fault.

It would take time, but I knew he could pull out of this.

"I missed you," he whispered against my lips.

I had only gotten here about five minutes before him; the only reason we got separated was because I got through a light before he did. "I missed you."

I wasn't going to tease him or admonish him for his newly clingy behavior. I wanted him to sleep at night, and if knowing my every move every day was what did it, I would give that to him.

The man who killed for me.

"You ready?"

"I will be." I reached up and twisted my fingers in the hair at the base of his neck.

Alex pulled back and looked me over. "Is something the matter?"

I sighed. I had been preparing to tell him for the last week, since he told me he closed on the property. I was resolute to the situation at hand. I didn't know how Alex would react. I wasn't worried or nervous, but I wasn't eager to tell him either.

"Do you trust me?"

"With everything." His answer was automatic.

"We need to call Mario."

"Why's that?"

"Because there's a body in unit 4B."

Alex looked up to the unit behind me, his brow furrowing. He let me go, took the stairs two at a time and opened the door. I was standing in just the right place to see him bring his hand up to cover his nose.

I didn't think the body smelled that bad. The last time I had checked on it, it had been right around day four, and it had smelled. . .awful.

It didn't take Mario long to arrive with the coroner. He and Alex stood to the side while I sat on the tailgate. I watched the two men talk to each other from a distance. Mario and Alex had bonded after the recent events. Mario seemed at ease around Alex now that Mario knew everything Alex did, he did for me.

I was glad. I wanted them to be friends.

"I'll let her know," Alex said as Mario took a phone call. "You doing okay?" He asked once he was back at my side.

"Yup." I laid my head on his shoulder. His hand rubbed gentle circles on my back.

"So," Mario hung up the phone, walking over to us, "the coroner thinks the body has been there for at least two years. They think it was a homeless person who curled up and died there. They will do DNA testing and take it from there."

"Can we take down the other apartments?" Alex asked.

"Yeah, just not that one. Just in case they need to come back for whatever reason. I'll let you know when I know."

It didn't take long, but they hauled the body off in the truck. Mario left too. As soon as they left the parking lot, I looked at Alex.

"Come on, let's go home. We can do this another day."

"It was Lloyd," I blurted out.

"Who was Lloyd?" Alex asked.

I nodded my head to the apartment.

"The dead body?"

I nodded.

"How do you know who it was? And who is Lloyd?"

"Remember the old fat greasy apartment owner?"

Alex shoved his hands in his pockets and shrugged his shoulders. "Barely."

"Well, that was Lloyd, and he was the other man that used to rape me. My mom let him so she didn't have to pay rent anymore."

I watched as his face took on several different emotions. He paced for a moment before he took a deep breath. His broad chest expanded. He tipped his head back to the sky and released the breath. "I've been trying to figure out how to ask you who the other guy was, since I realized it was more than one." I didn't respond. Slowly, he raised his head and looked at me. "Is there anything else I need to know?"

"I killed him." A crisp breeze pushed my hair out of my face. "And my mother."

He watched me. "Do I need to worry about you spending the next six years in prison?"

That made me laugh, but there was no humor on Alex's face. "I don't think so. Did you bring the spray?" I had asked Alex to bring a ground sterilant with him.

"Yeah. It's in the bed of the truck."

"Do you mind grabbing it?" He gave me a confused look but didn't argue. He followed in step with me. I laced my fingers with his free hand. "Remember when I told you I used to pretend to poison mom with dandelions?"

He nodded.

"Well, I spent a lot of time in the school library. Came across a book about poisonous flowers and discovered some." We walked around the back of the apartments, to the edge of the trees before the train tracks. Alex followed me quietly.

"I managed to find out that lily of the valley grows in our area. It likes growing under trees and is poisonous from flower to root. Lucky enough for me, Lloyd wasn't very good at maintaining the grounds. I found a spot where he wouldn't destroy the plant. I cared for them until I had a good understanding of how dangerous the plant could be. I only accidentally poisoned myself a few times." We ducked under some limbs, walking farther into the trees until the signature little bellflowers were there. "I would pick the flowers and dry them, put them into little glass jars and steep the dried bits in water. Then I would dilute the water into marked water bottles and give those ones to her. I poisoned her for a long time. Just enough to keep her constantly sick. She lived off of booze and cigarettes. She hated the doctors, so I was never worried about being found out."

I turned to him. "She died of renal failure. A side effect from long term exposure to the poison. Lloyd, on the other hand, got a lethal dose from an extract I made two years ago." Alex watched me. A jolt of unease shot through me, my insecurities getting the better of me.

I thought back to Jon. "I had made coffee the morning that Jon came for me. I kept a vial of leftover extract in the kitchen. I never had any plans for it. I don't know. It turned into a habit of mine to just keep some on hand. So, when Jon was distracted, I poured it into his coffee. Unfortunately, he didn't drink it."

I gently took the spray canister, wincing when I had the full weight of it. Immediately, Alex took it back.

"Do you want me to spray all the flowers?"

I nodded, leaning against the closest tree. I had always worried about someone stumbling into the area. A child who saw the pretty bell-shaped flowers and picking them was something that lived in my nightmares.

"Are you sure?"

I stared at the small flowers that littered the area. They had always been a comfort. A tool I had in my back pocket.

I didn't need this tool anymore.

I was strong enough without it.

"I'm sure."

He walked through the flowers and started farthest away, making long sweeping motions until the ground was saturated.

A poison killing a poison.

Without another word, he guided me out of the area. Once we were in the open space of the playground. I turned to him.

"Are you upset with me?"

"No."

"Do you think of me differently now?"

"What?" He scoffed. "No, Wren, get your ass over to the truck, and we are gonna talk."

My brows raised at his tone, but I didn't argue. Alex put the spray back into his truck and walked over to the water spigot, washing his hands before coming back to me. He picked me up gently, careful of my still sore ribs, and set me back up on the tailgate and stood between my thighs.

"Wren, I told you years ago that there was nothing that you could ever do that would make me hate you. I meant it."

I opened my mouth to argue with him, but he silenced me.

"Yes, when I thought you abandoned me, I was angry. I wanted to hate you, but I still loved you then, just as fiercely as I do now. Even if you told me you killed an entire monastery, I would still love you."

I quirked my brow, a smirk on my lips. "Why would I go after a monastery?"

He bowed his head, his forehead on my shoulder. I inhaled his scent. "What I'm trying to say is, if you had a reason for it, then it doesn't matter to me."

We were being so cavalier about death and murdering people. I had two people under my belt, and so did he.

"I know you started the fire when we were kids."

He didn't tense, didn't deny. "My biggest regret is not succeeding." I could hear it in his voice and it pulled at my heart. I wanted to take his guilt from him. I wanted to make him understand that I don't blame him.

"Obviously you need to work on your pyromania. How did you start the fire?" I asked instead, trying to lighten the mood.

He pulled back to look at me. "I lit the curtains hanging above the baseboard heaters on fire."

I narrowed my eyes. "I had those pinned up."

"Obviously not good enough." A smirk formed at the corner of his mouth. He sighed, his face sobering "There's one more thing. They found Jon's body. The other day."

I pulled back, absorbing what he said.

Once I had gotten out of the hospital, Alex told me what Mario did.

He took Jon's body and hid it somewhere. They had already had enough evidence that alluded to Jon's mental stability. Melissa talking to the doorman, worried about him. Reports from work stating he hadn't been in. Mario's report from when I found him drunk. Mario's plan was to spin it so that it looked like he committed suicide.

To any normal person, it would be scary. Scary to know how easily it is to manipulate a situation to benefit someone else. Mario had done this for me. He didn't want to see me live without Alex.

He did this for me.

"Are you okay?"

There was a part of me that wanted to be sad at the loss. Sad because the person who I trusted and cared for was gone, but somewhere between Alex coming back and Jon holding a gun to my head, all the feelings I had for him were gone.

Jon hadn't cared for me; he'd used me.

"We're better off without him."

I delved my hands into his hair, pulling tight to tip his head back. I kissed him slowly, languidly. I took my time and tasted him, until the heat in my belly was too much to bear.

"Do it," I told him, nodding to the nightmare that had been standing too long. Alex pulled out some safety glasses and slipped them on me.

For the next few hours, I sat on the back of the tailgate and watched Alex operate the backhoe and tear down apartment A.

He started at one corner and worked his way all the way through the building. I listened to the glass shatter, wood snap and break, until it was all rubble on the ground.

There was something light about this moment. Like there had been a balloon inside my chest, and with the destruction of the building, all the air inside the balloon had been released, and I could finally breathe.

EPILOGUE
ALEX

A scream startled me awake. I kicked the covers off, ending up tangled in the sheets as I threw myself off the bed.

"Wren?!" I launched myself down the stairs, taking them two at a time, still hearing the shrieking.

Then a dog barked. I headed up the hall to the kitchen, stopping at the door.

Wren was playing with King and Queen. She ran down the hill, holding a large ball over her head. King jumped, trying to get to it. She chucked it as hard as she could into the water. King shot off the dock to go after it. Queen stopped at the edge of the dock and barked at it.

"Come on, boy!" Wren called, and like the good boy he was, King managed to swim out, get ahold of the handle and bring it back to the grass. I watched as he dropped the ball, keeping his head low and shaking the water off.

She laughed again, and took off running to avoid the overspray, and King chased after her.

She was laughing, not screaming. I put my hands on the ledge of the window, dropping my head between my shoulders, trying to calm myself.

My fear was my own issue that I was working on getting through. My worst nightmare had happened, and she'd survived.

She always survived.

Even the girl she was as a child was a survivor. She would always survive, and I had always just wanted to help her live. I wanted to give her a life she always deserved. I didn't need to protect her.

Once I had gathered myself, I pushed open the back door. The storm door squeaked and Wren looked my way.

She was barefoot, dressed in some black sweats, a cropped shirt, and a cardigan over it.

"Good morning." I grinned at her.

Wren wrapped her arms around my neck and kissed me. I leaned up against the door frame, slipping my hands under her cardigan and pulling her tight to me.

"Good morning yourself." She beamed. "You ready for today?"

"Of course." I nuzzled her neck, enjoying her warmth on me. Today would be a busy day, and moments alone would be scarce.

"Excuse me?" Riley walked down the hall, already popping my little bubble, a black clothing bag in her arms. "It's bad luck to see the bride on her wedding day."

I scoffed, pulling Wren tighter to me. "Red, if you really thought you were going to get me to sleep in the guest room last night, you are delusional."

"Don't come crying to me when you have bad luck for the next seven years."

She laid the bag over the back of a chair.

"That's breaking a mirror." I rolled my eyes at her. I liked Riley, she made Wren happy, and that was all that mattered to me.

"I'm pretty sure all the bad things happened to us," Wren said, looking between Riley and I. She shrugged. "It can't get any worse."

I stared down at her before I picked up her hand and brought it to the wooden door. "You knock on wood right now."

"Hah! See! You are superstitious!" Riley shouted.

Wren started to laugh and slipped out of my arms, hooking an arm through Riley's. "Alright, you two, I have a wedding to get ready for, and you do too."

I stood at the end of the dock, looking out onto the lake. The sun was setting. casting an orange hue over everything. The trees around us, dressed in their fall colors, looked like they were on fire.

Soft music played on the outdoor speakers that had been set up for the occasion. I could still hear nature's music, frogs and wildlife singing the last of their songs before it got too cold for them.

I could hear the click of Foster's camera as she took photos for us for the occasion.

Wren wanted a wedding. So, she got a wedding.

She hadn't been too happy with my forging her signature. It was the first time I had taken her choice away from her. There was no excuse in the world that could justify it.

I offered to sign divorce papers, and to my relief she didn't want that either.

She wanted a wedding at our home, so all our friends got together to help us set up and plan it.

"You ready, man?" Troy asked as he, Gavin, and Mario joined me out at the end of the dock, taking their spots.

"I've been ready."

Mario had gotten an officiant's license online as soon as Wren asked him to be the one to marry us. Ezekiel and Nikolas took it upon themselves to get me fitted for a suit. It was all black, with the green cufflinks.

The music grew louder, and we all turned. Riley came down the aisle first. She wore a forest green dress with a small burgundy bouquet in her hands. Once she was in place, the music changed, and Wren stepped out of the house.

She followed the stone path to the dock.

Her dress was a two-toned long sleeve. The top was black lace that gradually flared out to a white skirt, the bottom looking like it had been dipped in black ink. Her hair was down in her natural curls. A larger burgundy bouquet in a teardrop shape was in front of her.

My heart swelled seeing her. Her smile was radiant.

She walked down the aisle and passed her flowers off to Riley before she took my hands.

Mario started in on the vows. We promised to have and to hold but left out the death do us part. We weren't speaking of death today.

WREN

The crisp air in late September sent a chill down my spine. It was in the early morning and dew clung to everything. I pulled my long coat tighter around my body as Alex pulled out the basket.

"Are you sure this is okay?" Alex asked as King and Queen jumped out and he closed the back end of my SUV.

I turned to him, cocking an eyebrow.

"If someone comes up to us and says it's not okay, what are you going to do? Pack our things up and go?"

Fire ignited in his eyes at the prospect. The once gentle and kind boy I knew made his appearance every so often, but the man with the fire in his eyes was the most prevalent.

"No," he firmly said.

"That's what I thought." I turned and headed up the gravel path, the pups ahead of us.

Alex's hand came around my arm, tugging it free from my coat and claiming it for himself. I looked up to him and smiled softly. He brought my hand up and kissed my wedding ring.

"I lost six years of being able to hold your hand, don't you dare keep them to yourself."

"You are so clingy," I teased him, wrinkling my nose.

Alex stepped in front of me, bent down, and hauled me over his shoulder with one arm.

"Alex!"

"I'll show you clingy. I'll start carrying you in my arms everywhere we go," he threatened while smacking my ass.

"Ow, Alex you're—"

I was gently placed on the ground, the basket on the ground. Alex's eyes were wide as he knelt in front of me, running his hands over my body. "Where do you hurt? Is it your ribs? Your head? Sweetheart, I'm so—"

A sly smile curled at my lips.

"Oh fuck," he breathed, bowing his head. He pulled me close so his head brushed against my stomach. "I think I just died a thousand deaths."

I giggled and brushed my hand down the back of his neck. "Serves you right."

He stood, and I could still see the concern in his eyes, his hand brushed down my cheek, pushing a loose lock of hair behind my ear. I leaned into his touch, feeling a little guilty.

"I'm fine," I said softly. "See?" I took in a deep breath, my shoulders lifting as I held it. "No pain."

Seeming satisfied, Alex gathered the basket and put his arm around me, guiding me to our destination. He laid the blanket on the grass in front of his parents' headstone. King whined and nuzzled my leg, so I pulled a ball out of my coat pocket and tossed it across the cemetery. He and Queen launched themselves after it.

I brushed the top of the headstone off with a cloth I'd brought. I wiped the dust off the shiny marble surface pulled some of the weeds that had gone without maintenance since the last time I was here at the beginning of summer. I tossed them to the side. I felt Alex's eyes on me as I went about my routine, gathering the dead flowers out of the vase, placing them to the side, and arranging the new ones.

I knelt down on the blanket and pulled out the arrangement of food I had packed for us. Fresh fruit, some rolls we picked up from Tony's with the blackberry cinnamon honey butter I'd made to go with them. I looked everything over, satisfied with my placements.

Alex lay across the blanket. I moved to sit in front of him, using him as a backrest. I handed him an orange slice, taking one of my own. We sat there eating in amicable silence for a while. I was happy to be here in front of his parents, married. He wearing his father's band now, and I his mother's.

"I never knew your middle name was your dad's first name."

"Really? I thought you did. James was a family name, I guess. All the boys were named that from what I understand." He paused. "Wait, how *did* you find out about my middle name?"

I grinned. "It was that one day Gloria overheard you swear. She hollered your full name. I thought it had a nice ring to it, so I started using it." I nudged him with my shoulder. "Alexander James Harper."

He shook his head, laughing. "I swear, I can still hear her yelling my name in my sleep. I knew I was in trouble if she said my full name." He picked up a cheese stick I'd brought with us. As soon as he started peeling the wrapper apart, Queen and King were there. He broke two pieces off and gave it to them.

"Hey, what's your middle name?"

I shrugged my shoulders. "I don't have one."

"Really? Why not?"

"I don't know. I just never had one. Lynn was never close to her parents, so I don't think there was ever a family name to pass down. Dad picked my name, so I guess they just didn't give me a middle name." I slouched down farther, using the dip in Alex's side as a head rest. "I remember wishing I had one before Dad passed."

"Don't girls normally take their mom's names as their middle names?"

I scrunched my face up in disgust. "Wren Lynn? Ew. That sounds awful." Plus, I didn't want the weight of carrying my mother's name around. I didn't need another anchor to hold me down.

"What was your dad's name?"

That brought a smile to my lips. "Emerson." I thought back to my dad's curly black hair and his bright green eyes.

Alex was quiet for a moment, before he said. "Wren Emerson Harper." At those words, I looked at him. A soft smile on his lips. "I like the sound of that."

"Me too."

ACKNOWLEDGMENTS

First, a thank you to my husband. One random day he looked at me and said, "You know you can write your book, right?" It had always been my dream to become an author and he's known since we met back in high school. Thank you for pushing and supporting me since the beginning.

I love you. Forever and always.

Thank you to my sister who is my best friend and sounding board. I know I annoy you. Love me anyways.

My author bestie, Ivy Darling. Thank you for existing and all your help. You helped me shape these characters and pushed me to keep going. I am so happy to have found you.

To my alpha readers, Chelsey and Haley, thank you for loving these characters as much as I do.

My beta readers, Mickie, Katy, Medeea, Brittni, Kristen, Jordan and Tess. Thank you for taking your time to read my words and help me clean things up. You are all amazing and I appreciate every single one of you.

Thank you to my editor, Hannah, who polished this story into the beautiful gem that it is. It was an absolute pleasure working with you and I can't wait to work with you again.

To Lanii, Hannah, Justine, Mrs. G, Nyk and Allison. My OG crew. For always showing up. I love you all.

To H.D. Carlton, for telling me to not give my story ideas away and write them myself. I needed to hear that, at exactly that moment. Thank you.

To my Mama. Best thing you ever gave me was my love of

reading and my sister. I know I don't say it enough, but I love you. Thank you.

And to everyone who finds me after this has already been published and is in your hands. I'm glad you are here. Thank you for reading.

ABOUT THE AUTHOR

Author Dae Graves was born and raised in Idaho, where she lives with husband, her high school sweetheart.

As far back as she can remember she always wanted to be an author.

She works her day job and writes in her spare time.

You can catch her up reading past midnight.

Follow Dae on her socials to keep up to date on her new projects.

You can also visit her website at
www.daegraves.com